Lusitania Lost

by
Leonard Carpenter

Cover Design: Georgiana Goodwin
Layout & Design: Roberto Núñez

For permission requests, please contact the publisher at:
Mango Publishing Group
2850 Douglas Road, 3rd Floor
Coral Gables, FL 33134 USA
info@mango.bz

For special orders, quantity sales, course adoptions and corporate sales, please email the publisher at sales@mango.bz. For trade and wholesale sales, please contact Ingram Publisher Services at customer.service@ingramcontent.com or +1.800.509.4887.

Lusitania Lost: A Novel

Library of Congress Cataloging-in-Publication number: LCCN 2017952095.
ISBN: (paperback) 978-1-63353-655-5, (ebook) 978-1-63353-656-2
BISAC category code:
FIC027260 FICTION / Romance / Action & Adventure
FIC027200 FICTION / Romance / Historical / 20th Century

Printed in the United States of America

Table of Contents

Chapter 1
May Day 1915_____10

Chapter 2
Good Hunting_____18

Chapter 3
Setting Sail_____22

Chapter 4
Neutrals_____30

Chapter 5
Troubled Waters_____34

Chapter 6
Code Breakers_____42

Chapter 7
Saloon Class_____47

Chapter 8
Out of the Blue_____59

Chapter 9
Marconi Waves_____64

Chapter 10
Dark Seas_____67

Chapter 11
The Hunted_____76

Chapter 12
Outward Bound_____79

Chapter 13
Gallipoli_____87

Chapter 14
Deck Games_____91

Chapter 15
Stowaways_____102

Chapter 16
War News_____107

Chapter 17
Central Powers_____113

Chapter 18
Roll Call_____117

Chapter 19
Bridge_____122

Chapter 20
Dark Rooms_____128

Chapter 21
Spies_____132

Chapter 22
Cruiser Rules_____140

Chapter 23
Unrequited_____145

Chapter 24
Camouflage_____149

Chapter 25
Openings_____153

Chapter 26
The Plot_____177

Chapter 27
Buddies_____184

Chapter 28
Saboteurs_____187

Chapter 29
Lace Curtains_____191

Chapter 30
War Zone_____194

Chapter 31
Kaiser William_____201

Chapter 32
Hunter_____205

Chapter 33
Landfall_____212

Chapter 34
Fog of War_____214

Chapter 35
Envoy_____227

Chapter 36
Evasion_____235

Chapter 37
Deck Watch_____239

Chapter 38
Bearings_____244

Chapter 39
Flight_____247

Chapter 40
Attack_____256

Chapter 41
Looking Ahead_____262

Chapter 42
Stricken_____266

Chapter 43
Crisis_____270

Chapter 44
Abandoned_____274

Chapter 45
Holocaust_____278

Chapter 46
Rescue_____288

Chapter 47
Mutiny_____293

Chapter 48
Boats Away_____296

Chapter 49
Chaos_____299

Chapter 50
Survivors_____312

Glossary of Characters and Devices_____317

Bibliography_____332

To Cheryl, in loving memory

"In spite of all its horror, we must regard the sinking of the Lusitania as an event most important and favorable to the Allies."

Winston Churchill, *News of the World*

CUNARD

EUROPE VIA LIVERPOOL
LUSITANIA

Fastest and Largest Steamer
now in Atlantic Service Sails
SATURDAY, MAY 1, 10 A. M.
Transylvania, Fri., May 7, 5 P.M.
Orduna, - - Tues., May 18, 10 A.M.
Tuscania, - - Fri., May 21, 5 P.M.
LUSITANIA, Sat., May 29, 10 A.M.
Transylvania, Fri., June 4, 5 P.M.

Gibraltar—Genoa—Naples—Piraeus
S.S. Carpathia, Thur., May 13, Noon

ROUND THE WORLD TOURS
Through bookings to all principal Ports
of the World.
Company's Office, 21-24 State St., N. Y.

NOTICE!

TRAVELLERS intending to
embark on the Atlantic voyage
are reminded that a state of
war exists between Germany
and her allies and Great Britain
and her allies; that the zone of
war includes the waters adjacent to the British Isles; that,
in accordance with formal notice given by the Imperial German Government, vessels flying
the flag of Great Britain, or of
any of her allies, are liable to
destruction in those waters and
that travellers sailing in the
war zone on ships of Great
Britain or her allies do so at
their own risk.

IMPERIAL GERMAN EMBASSY

WASHINGTON, D. C., APRIL 22, 1915.

Chapter 1

May Day 1915

Alma saw him coming a long way off, shoving his way through the crowd on Pier 54. She knew him, and the realization froze her with dread. It was Knucks, the killer.

Edging back into her group of nurse friends on the pier, she couldn't take her eyes off the tall, hawk-nosed man. Of all Big Jim's hooligans, Knucks was the worst. He certainly wasn't there to admire the big luxury liner taking passengers at Chelsea Piers. Every New Yorker knew the *Lusitania*, even with the name on her bow painted over for secrecy in the Great War. She was still the fastest steamer on the Atlantic, and the most famous once again, ever since *Titanic* went down.

The hoarse blast of the steam whistle as the big ship called for departure brought Alma out of her momentary trance. The ruffian Knucks hadn't seen her yet but kept coming, past the celebrities pulling up in their sleek motorcars and the reporters rushing to greet them. His ungainly height made him easy to spot as he pushed through the throng of passengers bound for Europe with their suitcases and steamer trunks.

Alma knew he wasn't there just to warn her off, or to invite her back into the loving arms of Big Jim Hogan. It would be a snatch, as the hoodlums liked to call it. At gunpoint, if need be—unless Jim had given Knucks the okay to shoot her down right here on the dock, as punishment for running out on him. Or maybe knock her out with his brass knuckles and throw her into the Hudson—yes, Knucks would be just the one for that.

But was he working alone? Alma felt suddenly conspicuous in her white shoulder cape, with the blonde hair that wouldn't stay put under her nurse's cap. She ducked in to hide among her four female companions, all of them dressed in last-minute *chic* variations of nursing garb.

"What is it, Alma?" Florence's pert face peered up from the shade of the enormous straw hat she'd insisted on bringing, even though it would never fit into a bandbox. "What's the matter? Do you see someone you don't like?"

"It's Knucks—no, don't look around—the long-necked palooka who's too big for his suit!" Alma turned aside, raising a white-gloved hand to conceal her face as the big man passed along the dock. "He's one of Hogan's gangsters."

"Where is he?" Demanded Hildegard, their chief nurse. "I'll give him a talking-to!" The elder woman, who wore a dark-trimmed cape and a bronze Red Cross pin on her cap, wheeled her matronly figure around.

"No, Miss Hildegard," Alma pleaded, "don't even look! Let's just make it aboard without him seeing me." She kept out of sight behind her companions as the hoodlum moved off down the pier.

"Don't worry, Alma," Florence said from under her oversized hat. "We'll soon be away from here. Won't we, Hazel?"

"Yes we will," Flo's look-alike sister replied from beneath her equally extravagant flowered *chapeau*. "Far from New York and all its gangster troubles."

"And off to Europe, with its war and Kaiser and Hun troubles," the fifth nurse Winnie added defiantly.

"I'd rather face an artillery barrage and a cavalry charge than Big Jim right now," Alma said, keeping her voice low to avoid drawing attention. "Whatever happens, I don't want to go back."

"Never you mind, girls," the chief nurse declared. "Once our ship has sailed, Boss Jim Hogan and all his thugs can't turn it around!"

Her words drew Alma's attention at last to the imposing sight before them. It was the Lusitania's hull of sea-stained black, crowned by sunlit gray decks. From here it looked like a fairy castle, steep and impregnable, so it seemed to her. Its long row of lifeboats took the place of battlements, and the tall smokestacks rose like towers. From the four evenly spaced gray funnels, smoke floated out over the river as the great ship built up steam. A tall mast on the foredeck, which faced in toward Manhattan's fast-growing skyline, flew the British Union Jack above the red and gold pennant of Cunard Steamship Lines. Both flags fluttered in a light morning breeze that failed to reach the hurrying, overheated passengers on the dock.

Knucks had passed out of sight down the pier. So, even though their berths lay astern in Second Class, Hildegard led the nurses straight to the First Class gangplank. The line of well-dressed passengers took them smoothly along the ramp with very little waiting, up to the ornate vestibule on the ship's Shelter Deck. Luckily for them, the crew in First Class seemed to be short-handed, with no ticket checking being done by the few blue-jacketed stewards. There was also no offer of help with their luggage.

Once out on the covered deck promenade, they carried their bags up to the less crowded Boat Deck, open to the sky. Then, to be inconspicuous, they climbed farther upstairs to the very top of the ship. The five of them headed astern past funnels and skylights on the nearly empty Marconi Deck, where the wireless antennas and stays crisscrossed overhead.

"Just look at the view from up here," Florence said, stopping by the rail. But no sooner had the others set their bags down to rest, than a redhead holding an oversized camera appeared from behind a haystack-sized ventilator and snapped their picture.

Winnie challenged the intruder. "Young man, what do you think you're doing?"

"Give me that camera plate immediately," Hildegard demanded, moving out in front of Alma and the rest.

"Now, ladies," the cameraman said, "I'm with the press. You wouldn't want to stand in the way of the news, would you?" Removing the glass slide from his camera, the fast-talking youth shoved it into a bag at his hip and just as smoothly reloaded a fresh one. "Tell your friends they can see your May Day portrait in tomorrow morning's New York *Inquisitor*."

"Definitely not," Alma said, stepping out from the others. "There'll be no pictures of me, at least. I've got to insist that you destroy the one you just took."

"Oops, sorry, too late," the redhead said, edging back for another shot. "It's already mixed in with my morning batch."

Winnie appealed to him in a kind, big-sisterly tone. "Here now, what would your name be?"

"They call me Flash," he told her with an impish smile. "No need for my flash pan today, though, with looks that shine out like yours. You'll probably make the Sunday rotogravure section."

"Indeed, young fellow!" Hildegard icily came to the bemused Winifred's rescue. "We find that kind of talk most impertinent."

"Excuse me, ladies. Is there anything I can do?"

The man who appeared before them was dressed in a brown suit and matching bowtie, in contrast to Flash's shirtsleeves and suspenders. Above his pomaded black hair he tipped his hat–a brown bowler, more businesslike than the flat straw skimmers worn by most of the male travelers. His manner was serious, his gaze resting impartially on each of the women, until he addressed Alma at the front.

"I'm Matthew Vane, reporter for the *Daily Inquisitor*. This is my photographer, Lars Jansen–though he likes to be called Flash," he added as the redhead winced. "It's certainly a pleasure to meet you ladies." He glanced up at Hildegard's Red Cross hatpin. "Nurses, are you bound for the war?"

"Mr. Vane," the chief nurse scolded, "whatever our business may be, we definitely aren't here to give a press interview. Your assistant snapped a camera slide of my companions and hid it away in that bag of his."

"Certainly, Ma'am," the reporter said. "I apologize. His job is to capture anything that seems newsworthy, or that might appeal to our readers. But I can see to it that the photo won't be printed, since you insist. If you'd prefer a posed group shot...." With a hint of humor in his eyes, he beckoned to Jansen.

"Most certainly not!" Hildegard rebuked him. "We have to hurry along and check into our accommodations."

"Well, then, let me assist you." Stooping, Vane snatched up the large traveling bag belonging to the head nurse, along with a satchel and hatbox. "Flash, let's help these ladies with their luggage. Just sling your camera for now." Starting astern, he said, "We're passengers on the ship too, so we may as well get acquainted. This is my last day of reporting here in New York."

Hazel asked, "Oh, really, Mr. Vane?"

The young nurses closed in quickly on the men, heading off any further protests by Hildegard.

"Are you going to be a war correspondent?"

"Which side will you be on?"

"Call me Matt, Ladies. I'll be in London for a while, then to Paris and the war front. We may get to Berlin later, by way of a neutral country."

As they moved chattering along the top deck from funnel to funnel, Hildegard followed with Alma, watchful but seemingly resigned to the intrusion. Matt Vane, lacking any formal introduction, asked where the women were from.

"I come from Concord, New Hampshire, where I took Red Cross training," Alma's brunette friend said. "I'm Winnie, short for Winifred, but don't call me that! I'd rather go under an alias, like your friend Flash."

The redhead beamed his approval as she went on.

"Florence, here, and Hazel are from Albany upstate." Winnie indicated the two petite black-haired girls. "They're sisters, as you can see."

"So, is it just the nurse uniforms, or are you two twins?" Matt asked, looking at them over his burdens.

"People always ask us that," Hazel said demurely.

"Yes, but we don't tell them," Florence added with a mischievous look.

The silent Alma, watchful at the center of the group, remained un-introduced by the others since she was supposed to be in hiding. She began to feel even more conspicuous because of this, and finally found something to say. "Shouldn't these chimneys be red?" she asked no one in particular. "They are in all the *Lusitania* postcards I've seen."

Matt turned to her. "The funnels were painted gray just after England declared war." Stopping beside one and setting down his bags, he took out a penknife and scratched at the painted steel. "See, there's red-orange paint underneath," he said. "The color change has to do with the ship being under command of the British Royal Navy."

"Does that mean we're on a warship?" Hazel asked.

"Is it a dreadnought?" Florence eagerly chimed in.

"No, technically just a cruiser. Both the *Lusitania* and her sister ship *Mauretania* are." Matt picked up the bags. "But no guns yet, not so far as I can tell at least. *Maury* was converted to a troopship, and *Lusi* has been kept in passenger service, but modified to carry extra cargo."

"Why *Maury* and not *Lusi*?" Florence asked. "I guess they don't draft girls," she concluded, to laughs from the others.

"But how can the enemy tell them apart?" her sister asked. "If they're really twins, I mean?"

"*Mauretania* is repainted in Royal Navy dazzle colors," Matt explained. "She's camouflaged all over to blend in with the sea mists."

"So, the enemy can't see her at all?" Florence said wonderingly.

"We should have some of that paint." Hazel said. "We could put it on Alma, to help her hide."

Alma felt herself blush at this, but Mr. Vane politely seemed not to notice.

Amid the suppressed giggles, Flash announced, "I saw the *Mauretania* last year up in Montreal. I photographed her loading Canadian troops for the front. She was gray all over, with guns on the fore and aft decks."

"Mr. Vane," Hildegard interrupted, "what do you think about this U-boat scare?" Her grandmotherly gaze was solemn, with a glance to her young charges. "It's overrated, wouldn't you say?"

"They were posting German submarine warnings all over the dock," Hazel chimed in. "And street peddlers are selling black-bordered funeral pictures of our ship."

"Yes," Flo added with concern. "'Lusitania's Final Voyage,' the heading said. But you must know all about that, as a reporter."

"I wouldn't pay any attention to it," Hildegard reassured her. "Would you, Mr. Vane?"

Still bundling their luggage along, Matthew Vane paused. Alma saw him hesitate as he looked around at the expectant faces of the young women, all of them volunteers for the greatest war the world had yet known. Finally he said, "I wouldn't worry too much about it, ladies."

"That's right," Winnie chimed in. "Lusitania's still the fastest ship on the ocean. I'd like to see one of those sub tubs try and catch us!"

"Anyway," Florence added, "we're in the Royal Navy now." She gave them all a snappy military salute.

Alma, still worried more about mobsters than any war, stayed separate from the rest. As they approached the stern companionway, she peeked down over the rail and saw something dead-ahead.

"Stop here," she called to the others in an urgent, hushed voice. "We have to go down those stairs, over there on the port side."

"That's starboard," Matthew Vane corrected her. "Port is this side—your left, if you're facing forward with the ship. But why?"

Alma just shook her head.

Over her stubborn silence, Winnie said, "There's someone here she's trying to avoid."

Alma shot her a pained look, reluctant to share her troubles with the daily papers.

"Well, it's not a customs official, I hope," Matt said, making a show of carefully setting down the nurses' boxes and bags. "We're not carrying war contraband, are we?"

Hazel explained, "It's someone who's after Alma." She looked sheepish, as if she might have said too much.

"Is it, now?" Matt said, moving toward the port rail. "Which one?"

"The tall, gawky one with the beak," Alma finally said in distaste. "He was talking to that steward and gave him something."

"That's Knucks!" Flash informed them, already turning back from the rail.

"Right," Matt said after a quick look over the side. "Born Elmer Steegle—he's Hogan's man." He zeroed in on Alma with a newsman's intensity. "What's he got to do with you? Do you know something about his operation? If you're on the outs with that bunch, I can see why you booked yourself on a fast ship out of town."

At her reproachful look, Matt added, "Just kidding...Alma, is it? Don't worry, it shouldn't be hard to dodge them until this boat sails. Should I go down and distract him?"

"Mr. Vane," Nurse Hildegard intervened, "you and your assistant have helped us quite enough." She reclaimed her bags. "Thank you, we'll go and find our staterooms, alone!"

"Ladies, it's been my pleasure. Miss Alma..." He gave her a special, respectful nod. "If you need anything else, just call on us. We're in Suite 34, forward." He nodded toward the First Class section.

But then, as the women hurried on with their bags, he turned instead to the port companionway, motioning Flash to follow.

* * *

Reaching the bottom of the stairs, Matt edged over toward the rail to draw attention away from the open passage that led across to the starboard side. He knew Knucks was serious trouble, an ex-pug and leg-breaker, probably armed with more than just the brass knuckles that were his trademark. But even so, he should be housebroken enough to respect the power of the press, as Matt had seen in his past efforts

16

to interview Big Jim. Knucks was still chatting with the Second Class steward; then his watchful eye caught the two men moving toward him.

"Hiya, Vane," the hoodlum said loudly, silencing the crewman. "What's up? You over here coverin' *Lusi's* last voyage, like all yer reporter pals down on the dock?" He looked a little warily from Matt to the cameraman, as if worried that Flash would take his picture.

"I don't know about that," Matt said. "If I thought this ship was going down, I wouldn't have booked passage on her."

"Oh yeah, dat's right, yer headed for bigger stuff, a war reporter. Bigger wars den here." Knucks turned away from the ship steward, who made his escape. "I better wish you a bone voyage."

"Thanks, Knucks. Is that why you came, to see someone off and tell them *bon voyage*? Did you deliver a goodbye wreath?"

"Nah, just takin' care o' some business. What about yer little stooge dere?" he asked, changing the subject. "He goin' wit' you?"

Flash answered, "Sure thing, Knucks. Don't you know, war photography is the coming thing?" Beaming proudly at the big thug, he stayed a little way back for camera work.

Matt prodded, "And what business does your boss Jim Hogan have here, aboard a British liner? Has he got a piece of the illegal traffic in war *materiel*?"

"So what's this, a third degree? You bein' the grand inquisitor again, from the *Daily Inquisitor*?" Snorting a laugh at the stale joke, Knucks moved in on Matt. "There ain't no traffic here, no business, no nothin'. Specially none o' yours!" He advanced a step but seemed to be held in check, more by the threat of Flash's camera than anything else.

"Okay, Knucks, cool off," Matt said with equanimity, having seen his nurse friends disappear astern via the starboard stairs. "I'm just doing my job on my very last day in port. Tell Big Jim so long for me." He reached up and patted the big goon on the shoulder.

"Yeah, I'll tell 'im," Knucks said, wrenching away. "He'll send you a goodbye wreath, all right, to yer funeral!"

Chapter 2

Good Hunting

Herr Kapitan-Leutnant Walther Schwieger surveyed his boat, the *U-20*, in the submarine dock at Emden. The first dawn light shining from Wilhelmshaven in the east etched the slender vessel's conning tower and deck gun against the glassy harbor. Briskly in the morning chill, Schwieger's men were busy loading the *Unterseeboot* with arms and provisions for a two-week cruise.

Schwieger watched as a bronze torpedo, twice as long as a man and heavy as ten, was hoisted down through the sub's forward hatch. His crew of thirty men and several dachshunds—whose matriarch Maria they'd captured from a Portuguese merchant—would be crammed in with crew, supplies, and eight of those explosive projectiles primed to destroy shipping in the Atlantic sea lanes.

Arming, refueling and provisioning was always a struggle. It was more physically taxing than the hunt itself, which mainly required patience. Like their captain, the crew would be looking forward to setting out to sea so that they could finally get some rest.

Schwieger turned from the dock into the officers' shack. He'd better refuel himself with coffee—or what passed for it in these war-rationed times, with Germany smothered by the *verdammt* British blockade.

Inside the tiny hut he bumped into Otto, another submariner accustomed to jostling in close quarters. "*Guten Morgen, Kapitan Hersing*," Schwieger said, reaching for the warm pot. "How is your *U-21*?"

"Excellent, Walther. You're away soon for England in *U-20*?"

"Within the hour, I hope. Bauer has ordered me off to Liverpool, to sink troopships, so he says. Big things are afoot. Wegener will be going too, in *U-27*, and more boats to follow."

"Ha, Bernie Wegener, that schemer!" Otto Hersing snorted. "You heard what happened on his latest run to Liverpool, just last month?" He obviously didn't care if it was an old story, and told it anyway. "Bernd lay in wait there for three days, hoping to bag the *RMS Lusitania*! He let two other steamers go by, he was so greedy to get the big score! But he came back empty-handed, with no kills except for a few fishing trawlers. *Ach*, poor Wegener!"

"Well, *Kapitan*," Schwieger said, "he was only trying to beat your record." Walther addressed Otto with respect, knowing that he was more than just a big-mouth. He was the first U-boat captain to sink a British warship and escape alive with his boat, only last September at the start of the war. "You just downed those ships in Liverpool Bay, right under the Englanders' noses...how long ago was it?"

"Back in January, in the Happy Times!" Hersing laughed heartily. "In those days, we didn't even waste torpedoes on cargo ships. I just surfaced, fired a shot across their bows, and forced the crews to abandon ship. Then I sank the merchant tubs with scuttling charges, or hurried them along with my deck gun."

"Ah but, *Kapitan*," Schwieger ventured, "what if you caught the *Lusitania*? Would you still expect to board her under those old-fashioned cruiser rules?"

Hersing squinted at him, then laughed. "Ha-ha, Walther, you jest! The *Lusi* and *Maury*, all these big steamers, are too fast. They'll breeze right past you and risk a torpedo–not that just one fish, or even two, is certain to stop a ship of that size." He shook his head sadly. "And now, with this devil Churchill ordering his merchant ships to speed up and ram our boats on the surface, it's hard to take a decent lead position so as to threaten them properly." Then he paused, regarding Schwieger. "Why do you ask? Did Bauer give you some special instruction on this?"

Schwieger shrugged. "*Herr Kapitan*, you know that if *Fregattenkapitan* Bauer had given me any special orders, I could not reveal them. But we've both heard his line–no restrictions at all on submarine attacks."

"Ah, yes," Otto declared. "And I agree. Conditions for us commerce raiders are hard enough, and always changing. We captains must have total freedom to protect our boats and crews. There are the new British Q-ships, armed decoy merchant liners. And the mines, the nets, and sub-hunting trawlers. *Ach*, if only those landsmen in Berlin knew what we face!" He shook his shaven head under his officer's cap, his mustached upper lip in a pout. "But the glory is still there for the taking, and the chance to win this war for our homeland. I would not trade this U-boat command for anything!"

"Nor I, *Herr Kapitan*," Schwieger agreed out of patriotic duty. He then returned to his former question. "And so, given full discretion, you would sink the *Lusitania*? From below, with a spread of torpedoes? No mercy?"

"My friend," Otto assured him, "I would not hesitate an eyeblink. You and I know what those big ships carry, the war supplies and troops! It would be a mighty blow against England, and a proud distinction for any captain in this service."

"And what about the women and children?" Schwieger asked. "And with Americans almost certainly on board, too?"

"Why, if any of them didn't escape, that would make a big noise in the press and teach them all a lesson–England and her reckless allies, and the so-called neutral America! Another great victory for Germany." He laughed and clapped Schwieger on the shoulder. "You'd better hurry along on your cruise, Walther, or I might catch her first!"

Schwieger checked his pocket watch. "You're right, I must go. Good hunting, Otto."

"Good hunting," his friend replied. As Walther passed through the door, Hersing further saluted him, clicking his heels together in the Prussian style and barking out the current fashionable motto: "God punish England!"

"*Gott strafe England*," Schwieger answered in kind, returning to the dock.

Aboard *U-20* he found the loading practically complete. But the stowage still had to be checked. Schwieger was ultimately responsible for cramming every loose item into the tightly packed sub. He ordered the diesel engines started up for surface cruising, and to keep the batteries charged for a dive.

The crew was all present, and all seemed sober...torpedo officer Weisbach, Rikowski the radioman, Lanz the pilot, little Dachsie and her pups, and all the engineers and deck gunners. The only new one to keep an eye on was young Voegele, a draftee and an Alsatian by birth. He was a native of one of the long-contested German districts along the French border, the Alsace-Lorraine, that this war was partly being fought over. As such, his loyalty to *Der Kaiser* was subject to question. But the lad seemed to be a decent electrician. Once he was out under the sea, his life would depend on diligent service and cooperation, just as much as everyone else's did.

In the late morning sunlight, standing up top and waving *auf Wiedersehen* from the conning tower and the gun deck, the crew cast off and cruised into the already-rising western breeze. Once clear of the harbor bar, Schwieger went to his bunk and immediately slept, wanting to rest while he could with *U-20* still in friendly waters.

After all the exertion of getting to sea, his sleep was deep. By the time he rose, the pilot Lanz told him they were entering the war zone. Well east of England, still surface cruising. It was already Saturday the First... May Day, 1915.

Chapter 3

Setting Sail

In their cabin on E-deck, Alma and the other nurses stowed their belongings in the Lusitania's ample drawers and closets. Having gotten past the hoodlum on the promenade, they felt they could relax. Their four-berth cabin was tastefully appointed, each mahogany bunk hung with flower-patterned drapes for privacy. The room had a sink, and the lavatory was only a short distance away down the passage. Their space was cramped by the addition of a foldaway cot; but with no larger cabin available in the overbooked Second Class, Alma found this preferable to sharing a two-bed cabin in steerage with some stranger.

Alma Brady—that was the name she must think of herself by, now and perhaps forever. She felt relief mixed with sadness as she put away her luggage. She had only these few belongings left, and most of them came with memories that were far from pleasant. Apart from this and her new friends in the stateroom, every shred of her old life had fallen away—the boarding school, the music, all of the art and refinements. Those months spent with Jim Hogan had been a mistake, a dream that turned into a nightmare. In escaping from it, all of her past hopes were gone, poisoned by Jim's unguessable hostility over what she had done.

Now she was forced into the timeworn role of the wronged woman, cruelly deceived, her virtue tarnished—but she had to play out the melodrama in secret, hiding from Hogan's mob. There was no one to forgive her sins, and it didn't help that she'd been orphaned three years ago, at seventeen. Thank goodness for the United Nursing Service League and the busy weeks of training at the charity hospital, where Hildegard kindly hid her out. And thank God for this war, too—dreadful as it was, it could be a new start.

As evident from Knucks's vigilance on the docks, the heat wasn't off. And so, for the future, this was it. Family name, friends, social expectations and cherished truths all were gone, along with the whole world she'd been bred to. Instead she must discover what beliefs and values held constant from one side of the Atlantic to the other, from peace to war, from the penthouse all the way down to the gutter, or the trenches.

This real world seemed a pretty dismal place. For now, the best she could do was listen to her new friends' light-hearted chatter.

"What a delightful stateroom," Florence was bubbling over. "Just look at the bedspreads. There's Cunard's symbol embroidered on all of them, a British lion gripping the world. How darling! This is going to be such a jolly cruise after all!"

"And what about the men?" Hazel mused aloud. "What did you think of that dashing reporter, Mr. Vane?"

"Handsome!" Florence rolled her eyes dreamily.

"But Flash, the red-haired one, is cuter," Winnie said. "A little young for my taste."

"Young but willing," Florence added in a worldly tone.

"Now girls, you beware," Miss Hildegard scolded them. "Reporters are men of the street, to be avoided. They claim to be interested in our work, but if I know them, they'll end up trying to take advantage."

"Well, I should certainly hope so," Winnie declared, winking and being intentionally scandalous.

"It seems that U-boats aren't the only danger on this voyage," Hazel sagely added.

The elder woman harrumphed while emptying her satchel and clothes-press. As she stepped outside to dispose of some fruit peels, Winnie whispered, "Frankly, I don't think Miss Hildegard has a thing to worry about."

"Why not?" Hazel asked.

Florence piped up, "You mean, because no man is going to torpedo her?"

Even Alma had to laugh at that, and she couldn't quite stop in time. When the head nurse returned, it was to a muffled storm of giggles. She took it in with a stern look but didn't scold them. Alma thought she must secretly be pleased at her crew's good morale.

"Well, that's it," Winnie announced a few minutes later. "I'm all unpacked. What to do next? Shall we go topside and wave goodbye?"

"Oh yes, we have to!" Hazel cried, putting an arm around her sister. "Our parents said they'd be waiting on the pier to see us off."

"If they made it in time," Flo said. "I suppose we must go."

Alma would have much preferred to keep out of sight below decks, but none of the others seemed inclined to stay behind with her. Hildegard obviously felt it necessary to chaperone the group, probably to keep any of them, and Alma in particular, from falling prey to males or jumping ship. So all together they gaily dressed one another in what finery was available. After decking out their nurses' garb with the best hats, jackets, shoes and gloves from their luggage, they set forth to conquer the ship.

The corridor was busy, and as they climbed toward the open decks, the bustle of passengers in the stairwells increased. The gong ordering all visitors ashore had sounded some minutes ago, so they could safely assume Knucks was out of the way.

Even so, to avoid being seen close to their room before sailing, Hildegard led them forward again toward the First Class section, which was not closed off as yet or noticeably restricted. The traffic on the way was brisk and somewhat confused at departure, with bosun's whistles shrilling and tugboats hooting. Deep throbbings in the deck underfoot told them the ship was coming to life.

They emerged onto the Shelter Deck on the port side, facing the pier. Where the crosswise passage opened onto the promenade, a crewman was handing out miniature American flags. They each took one, eager to be part of the brilliant sailing spectacle. Alma, though, used hers as a fan to hide behind while discreetly watching for danger.

The rail of the promenade astern was jammed with passengers, so the nurses began to edge their way forward. Before long, an elegantly accented male voice sounded at their side.

"Good day, lovely ladies. Might I offer you assistance?"

The speaker was a plump, mustached man, his accent sounding Northern European. He addressed himself to Hildegard, gallantly raising his low-cut sable top hat. For once, the chief nurse didn't lead her flock right past; she paused, with a less disapproving look than usual. They all took in the man's fur-lined green frock coat over striped trousers, matching green spats, and elegant silver-topped cane. Here, Alma thought, was a man of means.

"Surely you want a place at the rail," the foreigner said, speaking exclusively to Hildegard. Turning away from her to some cigar-smoking loungers nearby, he tapped the deck sharply with his cane tip. "Gentlemen, make way, please," he declared. "These ladies need to see, and be seen," he added to the men, who tipped their hats appreciatively. Falling back, they let the nurses take their place along the waist-high barrier.

The European lingering next to Hildegard introduced himself. "Madam, I am Dirk Kroger, fur merchant of the Netherlands." After an elegant bow, he produced a calling card from his vest pocket.

"Pleased to meet you, Mr. Kroger," Hildegard said. Accepting the card and sliding it into her velvet drawstring purse, she fell into polite conversation with him.

"Oh, look, there they are!" Hazel suddenly cried out. "Mama, Daddy, goodbye!"

She leaned from the rail and waved, fluttering her little American flag. Her sister did the same—though, amid the waving crowd on the dock, it was hard to pick out the two they recognized, and harder still to tell if anyone below noticed them, in all the flapping and fluttering of gloved hands, pennants, and fashionably oversized bonnets spread out along the ship's seven hundred feet of hull.

From the long Cunard transit shed on the pier, summer-skimmer straw hats waved in the air and cameras glinted and flashed right opposite the nurses' place at the rail. Against the rising sea breeze, some of the ladies were already tying down their hats with the yards of pale chiffon fabric they had wreathed about their heads.

"How splendid," Winnie said. "It's all so bright and cheery!"

"Yes," Hazel sighed. "If there's any such thing as a festive goodbye, this is it."

"Parting is such a sweet sorrow," Florence quoted, wiping a tear from her eye.

They saw much last-minute activity, the gangplanks re-lowered and people hurrying on and off the ship. Perhaps it had to do with the U-boat warning, and with passengers changing their minds. The young ladies watched in serene wonder...all except Alma, who felt it necessary to look over her shoulder for enemies. One face gave her a start of recognition, but surprisingly, she found it a pleasant sensation.

* * *

Matthew Vane made his way along the crowded deck, scouting for news. The ship's departure spectacle was too lush to ignore. He planned to keep busy on this voyage, even though there was no chance of wiring copy back to New York, much less sending any photos before the *Lusitania* docked in Liverpool in a week. Still, if things worked out as he hoped, this would be no idle pleasure cruise.

Cunard Steamship Lines didn't seem to make any provision for journalists at sea, least of all in wartime. Very likely they didn't want their celebrity guests being hounded by reporters. And now there were military secrets for them to keep, plenty of those.

But there must be a way in, or so Matt figured. No luck so far in getting a look at the passenger list. But if he could find the crewman who'd stood at the head of the First Class gangplank, he'd learn something.

Then he saw a striking face. This one he would've gone after even if she hadn't been familiar.

"Alma, hello!" Smiling assuredly as he edged through the crowd, he saw her look of wary alertness turn to relief...and was there deeper interest in those snazzy blue eyes?

"Hello again—Matt, isn't it? How nice to see you! But no pictures, please," she added to Flash, as the redhead showed up at Matt's side.

Florence spotted the men and pivoted under her large straw *chapeau*. "Why, Mr. Vane, back so soon?"

"Hello, Flo, whadda ya know?" As the girl giggled, Matt tipped his bowler hat to all the young nurses. He took a place behind Florence and Alma, even as Flash moved in between Winnie and Hazel.

"I'm glad you're not missing all of this," Matt told Alma confidentially, glancing around to indicate the leave-taking spectacle around them. "Being up here shows real spunk. Even Big Jim can't keep you down."

"Thanks for handling Knucks," she said. "I saw you cornering him. Did he say much?"

"Nah, he wasn't gonna spill anything to me. Knucks and I've locked horns before, and his boss Hogan doesn't like me any better. But it doesn't matter now, Flash swears he saw him leaving the ship."

"You didn't see anyone else...?"

"None of Hogan's crew, no," Matt reassured her. "But you might keep an eye on that steward. Knucks could have slipped him a few bucks to make trouble. I can try to find out—"

His words were drowned out by the sudden rumbling bass of the ship's steam horn announcing final departure. In the stillness that followed, they could hear a brass band strike up a tune from the bow—*It's a Long Way to Tipperary*, the British–Irish marching ditty.

As the cables were cast off, they felt the slightest lift underfoot. Then a sputter of small engines rose as tugboats began to muscle *Lusitania* away from the dock.

The moment brought most everyone to a brief silence, followed by a sea-swell of cheering from the ship's decks and the dockside. Over that same interval, a space of water opened out between hull and pier, as if their mutual cheers were driving the ship on its way.

"Hurray, we're off!" Florence cried out with the others, tears still gleaming on her sweet young face.

The crowd's enthusiasm had something brave and carefree about it, echoing the Lusitania's past departures when the great ship hadn't been heading off to a terrible war overseas. Regardless of modern-day reality, everyone seemed to join in the *bon voyage* spirit.

Then, gradually, the docks and loved ones receded and became something remote, just part of the scenery. The cheering along the rail subsided, and faint currents could be seen among the land-dwellers ashore as they turned to go home.

The huge vessel backed out into the Hudson and swung downstream, aided by valiant little tugboats snubbing at her bow and vigorously tooting their whistles. The passengers were left with a broad view of Chelsea Piers and the lower Manhattan skyline. The day was bright at noontime. A fresh breeze carried away the black smoke from the boilers as river currents hurried them along. Then came the full throbbing of the steam turbines below decks, the pulse-beat of their journey.

"There's the Woolworth Tower," Hazel said, pointing to the tallest building jutting up from the city spires passing before them. "The five-and-ten-cent store empire! Just think of how many nickels and dimes it took to make that."

"Yes, and there's the Singer building," Winnie called back, pointing. "Easy to remember—it looks just like a big sewing machine needle, doesn't it?"

"Singer's used to be the tallest in the world," Alma said to Matt, "before Woolworth's came along."

"You'd know that all right, if you're a New York girl," Matt said approvingly. "But see that one there, the big double one that's almost finished? That's the Equitable Assurance Company. It's going to be the biggest building in the world—not the tallest but the largest, 45 acres of floor space."

"Just like this ship, the *Lusitania*," Florence said. "Biggest in the world when she was made."

"One of the two biggest, you mean," Hazel put in. "Along with her sister ship the *Mauretania*," she added, sticking up for sisterhood.

"Largest, fastest and most luxurious," Alma sighed. "I remember the celebrations with fireworks, and the aeroplanes flying over when the *Lusitania* first came to New York."

Matt saw that, now that Alma was safely at sea, she seemed to be enjoying the conversation. "Right," he agreed. "And *Lusi* stayed number one for years, didn't she, until the *Titanic* came along...a shame about that." Hoping to impress her, Matt saw his remark fall flat as Alma turned abruptly aside.

"Yes, and then *Titanic* sank right away," Florence volunteered. "On her maiden voyage, with all those people drowned."

"The Germans have launched bigger steamers since, the *Imperator* and *Vaterland*," Matt added, trying to liven up the conversation. But Alma kept her gaze averted, not seeming cheerful anymore.

Hazel was lamenting, "Yes, but all those really huge liners have been converted to warships in disguise. Now they're shooting and sinking each other, like the *Cap Trafalgar* last year. Or kept interned in port."

"Oh yes, isn't it just awful?" Florence said.

Matt let his little group fall silent. Conversations, it seemed, could run into rocks and icebergs, just like ships.

But Flash still happily chattered with Winnie as the engines and tides swept them rapidly to sea.

"Look, there's the Statue of Liberty," the photographer said. "Seems like she's waving goodbye." He raised his camera for a picture.

Leaning out and looking forward, the others could see the giant effigy facing out to sea, until it was obscured by the ship's turning bow.

Matt decided to get back into the conversation. "Who's that fellow talking to your head nurse?"

"Oh, he's a Dutch trader who helped us find this spot," Hazel said. "He seems to be partial to Miss Hildegard."

"Dutch, eh?" Matt said, taking in the man's dapper appearance. "I'll have to try and make his acquaintance. Holland is another neutral country. They could help out a foreign journalist."

"Can anyone really be neutral in this war?" Winnie asked. "I know America is supposed to be. But the Dutch are probably just praying the Germans won't attack them, the way they did poor Belgium."

"Is that why you became a nurse, to stop Germany?" In his reporter's way, Matt answered her question with a question.

Winnie replied tartly, "Last I heard, the British Expeditionary Force wasn't taking women. Nursing is the next best thing."

"Anyway, someone has to do something," Hazel put in. "There's so much suffering over there! What could be more useful?"

"Yes," her sister added. "So many nice young men could lose their eyesight, or a limb, without good nursing. Or even die! We can do so much good."

"As long as the lousy Huns don't try to rape us, the way they did Brussels," Winnie said sharply.

"A nurse is a close as you can get to being an angel," Hazel declared. "That's what our father said, after reading about Clara Barton in the Franco-Prussian war."

"An angel? Yes, I suppose so." Getting his chance at the interview he'd wanted, and seeing the young women's innocence, Matt hesitated. "I'm sure there are ways to get closer. Plenty of ways to become one," he added, echoing some of Winnie's bitterness—until at last, his reporter's instincts took hold.

"But please, ladies, tell me more about yourselves...."

Chapter 4

Neutrals

US Secretary of State William Jennings Bryan was admitted to the Oval Office at 1:45 p.m. The President's private secretary, Joe Tumulty, nodded the elder statesman through without any small talk. This was in keeping with the brisk, businesslike air of Woodrow Wilson's Democratic administration, so Bryan took no offense.

Even so, he went in feeling slightly awkward, like a tardy student carrying a note from his mother up to the teacher's desk. Even after two years in office, he was never quite sure where he stood. Bryan was in the cabinet by agreement, having stepped back from his own presidential candidacy out of respect for Wilson's talents and similar beliefs. He certainly wasn't one of the President's closest friends, the tycoons and Eastern highbrows from Wilson's days as chief of Princeton University. Bryan sensed that, by many of those and even by his fellow cabinet members, he was regarded as a hayseed with his farm- and Bible-based Populist views.

Still, having just returned from a railroad tour of the Western states, Bryan felt fit and ready for vigorous engagement. His reputation as a stump orator, the true voice of America's rustic heartland, had never served him better. Rather than being tired from his journey, Bryan the Great Commoner, felt energized by his contact with the throngs who'd applauded his inspirational words across this vast continent, all the way to California and back.

Now the earnest, businesslike atmosphere of the White House steadied him. There was no call for expansive flights of rhetoric here.

President Wilson sat at his writing desk in shirtsleeves. "Good afternoon, Bill," he said, glancing up without bothering to rise.

"Hello, Mr. President. It's good to be back."

"Back? Oh yes, from your speaking tour out West. Please, have a seat." The President looked distinguished and professorial even without a coat. His handsome face and pleasant, dignified manner gave him the perfect presidential profile. "Your trip went well, I hear."

Bryan wondered if Wilson had even noticed his absence. "Yes, it was most inspiring. But now I've returned to the hornet's nest, with this European nightmare going on! I'm pleased to say that, among the ordinary rank and file of Americans, the spirit of neutrality remains strong, with plenty of support for your administration and our efforts to secure peace."

"Well, I'm glad to hear it. There's constant pressure to take sides, particularly from our British friends with their claims of German atrocities. These naval incidents don't make it any easier."

"I can imagine," Bryan said. "I heard about this latest *Gulflight* torpedoing. Two Americans drowned, and one dead of a heart attack...a tragedy. But it's hardly a *casus belli* worth taking the whole nation to war over. And here is something even more dangerous." Relieved to get so soon to the point of his visit, Bryan reached to his vest pocket. "Have you seen this German warning about passenger ships in the war zone? It's printed right next to this morning's *Lusitania* sailing schedule in a dozen of our papers."

Wilson's right sleeve was held taut by a ladies' purple-stitched garter at the elbow, to keep his white cuff clear of the drying ink on his letters. He loosened it as he reached for the clipping. After scanning it he nodded to Bryan.

"Yes, Bill, this was read to me by courier. I've been told by the German embassy that it's official, the wording approved by their High Command."

"But not necessarily by the Kaiser or their Prime Minister Bethmann-Hollweg? I've found that he's a moderate on this matter of sea warfare."

The President took a breath and handed back the clipping. "Well, that's an old story, Bill. We know there are cross-purposes high up in the German government. But Wilhelm might easily have approved this. His speeches are fiery enough."

Wilson gave the emperor's name the proper German pronunciation, with a "V" sound for the "W" in Wilhelm.

After a moment's silence, Bryan pressed him, "Well then, Mr. President, I must ask, how we are going to reply to this new threat?"

"I understand, Bill. It is provocative. How would you suggest that we respond?"

It was just like Wilson the Professor to question his student, rather than rendering an opinion. Bryan seized the opportunity.

"Another warning should be issued, by us—if not to the Central Powers, then to our own citizens who may think they can travel with impunity under a foreign flag in wartime."

The President laid down his pen beside the inkwell. "I already have issued a stern warning to Berlin, strict accountability for any attacks that harm our ships or citizens. In your absence, it was drafted by your Assistant Secretary, Robert Lansing."

"Yes, Mr. President. But earlier, before the *Gulflight*, we did nothing about the *Falaba* sinking, and the press furor about that was bad enough."

President Wilson sighed. "One American lost to heart failure, on a British vessel trying to flee at first, and then allowed by the U-boat to lower lifeboats and abandon ship. You see, Bill, if I reacted strongly to the smallest tragedy that can occur in war, I'd be drawn into the fighting in a matter of months. I knew that you as a strict pacifist would agree."

"Indeed, as a good Christian I do," Bryan said whole-heartedly. "And I know you are too. But we must do more, in an even-handed way. Warn our citizens as well as the Germans. And warn the Western allies too, or forbid them outright to carry American passengers."

"Perhaps. But what I say as President is vastly significant, don't you see? Americans might take it as a sign of weakness. Businessmen will hate any restriction on trade—and our friends across the pond, as they say, could use that to pressure us further."

"I have to say you're being too sensitive to Britain, Mr. President," Bryan said, risking bluntness. "That's not neutrality. It can only get us in deeper over the long run. And today the *Lusitania* is setting sail once again with Americans on board."

"Well, Bill, the British do set an example." Wilson spoke in a judicious tone. "They abide by a legal standard that I can justify to our voters. King George's bunch may not always play by the rules, but at least they avoid getting caught."

"Yes, they're good at it," Bryan said. "Meanwhile, they invite neutral trade to Europe, but use the Royal Navy to divert all of it into their own ports. They also carry on arms traffic hiding behind false flags and passenger bookings, possibly with the aim of luring Americans into harm's way."

"There's truth in that," Wilson agreed. "But how are we to respond to this printed warning, which reads like a challenge? The *Lusitania* is a British vessel and would never obey an American order to return to port. And the Admiralty, or even King George himself, would ignore such a demand in time of war." The President shook his head hopelessly and went on, "For this crossing, our American nationals will just have to trust the Royal Navy to protect them from the Prussians with all their new toys, aeroplanes, Zeppelins and U-boats."

"Never a comfortable prospect," Bryan agreed. "And the Brits must know that if a big ship gets sunk, with more American losses—pardon my language, Mr. President, but there'll be Hell to pay."

Chapter 5

Troubled Waters

The nurses were having a pleasant time on deck with their male devotees. By mutual if unspoken consent, they lingered at the rail long after most other passengers had gone below. As New York harbor deepened into the blue Atlantic, the Lusitania's sharp bow cut the waves so cleanly that none of the party even thought of seasickness.

Winnie in particular felt carefree and a bit flirtatious, and she knew that her lighthearted banter showed it. Whether it was the attentiveness of the reporters—especially this charming boy Flash, who'd taken such a shine to her—or just leaving old North America behind and venturing out into the wide-open vistas of a broader world, she found it liberating.

Not that her home was a bad place. Concord, New Hampshire combined the advantages of city and small-town life. But it was a bit too small-townish for her. The staid Puritan values, complacent morality, all that neighborliness and prudish gossip, made Winifred Dexter impatient for something more real. As for the town's name—well, there wasn't much Concord in the world lately, so she gathered. Discord, to the contrary, was the order of the day, complete with war and its profiteers, marauding Huns and poor suffering refugees.

Winnie couldn't just ignore the larger reality, this new menace. Instead she felt she had to understand and deal with it. If that meant going over there and becoming part of the great tragedy, to try and change things, so be it.

For now she could enjoy her newfound freedom. The spring day felt so fresh, with a westerly breeze gently urging them along, that there was no need to shelter down below on the Shelter Deck.

"There's Liberty again, still waving," Flash said to her, beaming his boyish smile. He tugged softly at her arm as the ship's stern cleared the now-miniature statue.

"Goodbye to Liberty!" Winnie called out, waving back. To Flash she added in a whisper, "And hello, United Nursing Service League!" By rolling her eyes back over her shoulder, she indicated Hildegard. The head nurse was still engaged in conversation with her new European acquaintance, the dapper Dutch merchant.

Flash laughed in sympathy. "I know what you mean. My boss is along too. But look."

Placing careful, respectful hands on Winnie's shoulders, the young news hound adjusted her position to face forward with the ship. "Here comes the Royal Navy, already keeping its eye on us."

A warship was closing with their course. Now Flash readied his camera, stepping up on a cable mount to take a picture. The ship was the first of three vessels whose approach was pinpointed by smoke plumes off the port bow. The two-stacker in the lead flew a large, stately Union Jack from its masthead. But the pattern on its hull was a crazed array of stripes, checks and angles in blue and gray tones, like the most modern cubist paintings.

Winnie looked on in surprise. "What *is* that paint job?"

"It's called dazzle paint," Flash explained, stepping down from his perch. "It's wartime camouflage."

He lowered his voice as if to keep from frightening the other nurses, who were deep in conversation with Matt.

"In fog or battle smoke, those bright, sharp angles hide where the ship begins and ends. It's supposed to make it tough to target guns or torpedoes at her."

"Again, why not give the *Lusitania* some camouflage?" Winnie said, matching his muted tone. "What ship is it, I wonder? I can't see any name on the prow."

"Actually, it's a passenger liner like ours." He leaned close to her, propping an arm against the rail. "The *Caronia*, if I'm not mistaken. Converted to a cruiser last August, when the war broke out."

"You mean, it's Cunard Line's *Caronia*, from our very same shipping company?" Winnie resolutely kept the topic on business, though very much aware of her male companion's nearness. "They ought to rename her the *Zebra*, with that paint. Is she going to be our escort?"

"No, I doubt it," Flash said. "Not this far from the war zone. She's probably just patrolling New York harbor."

"Why? To guard it from submarines?" Suddenly reminded of the danger, Winnie scanned the water around them for periscopes.

"No, just to keep the German ships from leaving."

"What German ships?" Winnie felt scandalized at the idea. "Do we let German warships in our ports?"

"Not warships, no. And the German merchants almost never show up anymore, with the British blockading the continent." Leaning in close, Flash set out to explain. "There are some German liners that we just sailed past, docked right back there in Hoboken. They're interned by the US government because they could be converted to cruisers just like this British one here. Technically, all of them now are warships under command of the German High Seas Fleet. If they ever do get up steam and try to leave, these armed Royal Navy ships are ready to sink or capture them."

"We'd let the British do that, in our waters?" Winnie asked. She didn't want to argue with Flash, but she didn't see the justice of it. "Not that the lousy Boches don't deserve it," she added as an afterthought.

"Well, the Royal Navy stays just outside our three-mile limit. So we can't stop them, not unless we want to fight. This is open sea."

Florence, who had been listening in, piped up with a protest, "That doesn't seem fair. Does America have any British or French ships interned?"

"No, I don't think so." Flash sighed and turned to her. "What happened is this. The *Caronia* was a passenger liner in New York last August. She received a coded message that war was about to be declared, and she left port before anyone else knew of it. She made it home to England to have her guns fitted, get the fancy paint job and all that. Now she's back as a Royal Navy ship blockading New York harbor. The German liners didn't get away from port in time, so they're stuck."

"But they let the *Lusitania* come and go," Winnie said a bit mischievously.

"Yes, they do!" Florence's small stylish heel stamped the deck. "We're standing right on a British liner that could just as easily be made into a cruiser, too...couldn't it? Her sister ship was, wasn't it? That's definitely not fair."

"Yes, but...technically, she's still a passenger ship." Flash took a long breath. "It's all about the rules of engagement."

He obviously found it hard to explain naval doctrine, even at close quarters and with such charming debaters. But he went on.

"The real story is that our ship, the *Lusi*, burns too much coal—twenty-some trainloads of it, just for a one-way trip to England. She's too expensive for this kind of patrol duty. So they enlarged her cargo hold instead and returned her to passenger and freight service."

"Well, fine. But doesn't the *Mauretania* burn just as much coal?" Winnie turned to him as she delivered her next salvo. "Lusitania's a cruiser too, and she's just as big and fast, or even faster. I thought speed was a good thing for navy ships."

"Yes but with no armor above or below the waterline, she can't stand up in a fight."

"Neither can the *Mauretania*, then!"

"Sorry, Win, you'll have to ask the Captain about that one. You've got me stumped." Flash gave up with a shrug. "Look, they've lowered a boat while we've been talking."

He moved aside and snapped another picture, catching the crew of jolly white-clad British tars on the job. Toiling at the oars in the ocean swells, they didn't look quite so jolly.

"Feels like we reversed our engines to meet them," he added. "We've stopped. I wonder what's up."

Steadying themselves against the rail as the two ships slowed and wallowed together in the ocean swells, they watched the launch row up and exchange mailbags with Lusitania's foredeck.

Their own Captain Turner, a squat seamanlike figure in his blue coat and white hat, came out on the portside wing of the command bridge to wave. He hailed across through a speaking trumpet to the *Caronia*, but his words couldn't be heard astern, and no sailors came aboard or left their ship. It was all a mystery.

"Just exchanging mail, I guess," Flash said. "*RMS Lusitania* stands for Royal Mail Ship."

"How interesting," Winnie said with a yawn. Standing close to Flash, but not too close, she took care to observe her own rules of engagement.

* * *

After the mail transfer, with *Lusitania* picking up speed and Long Island dwindling away to port, the party broke up. They'd missed lunch;

but since their departure had been so late, Hazel thought something might still be had in the second-class dining salon.

Hildegard's new friend, Mr. Kroger from Holland, shoved off soon after the British blockader did. Now, seeming suddenly to regret having left her girls to the mercy of the *Daily Inquisitor* staff, the chief nurse led them away below deck.

At their departure, Matthew Vane felt almost relieved. Alma, the main focus of his interest, had wholly withdrawn from their chat, and the younger nurses' eager questions and gossip had for once overloaded his reporter's patient ears.

"What a bunch of babes," Flash remarked to him as they headed forward. "Even the old one is still in circulation."

"You don't seem to be having a tough time taking your pick," Vane said.

"Nah," his assistant confessed. "That Winnie is a peach. The girl has a head on her shoulders—and what shoulders, so nice and soft! Seven days to England should be fairly interesting."

Matt said, "I've got to get the blonde, Alma, alone. She could be a useful source." He knew there was more to it, but then, he'd never seen any real need for detachment in his job. On the contrary, passion for the news was a better guide. "Those two young sisters, now, it's a shame to think of sending them off anywhere near the front. Imagine what they might run into over there! And your friend too, Winifred, is it? I hope she's as tough as she sounds. But that Alma—she doesn't say much, but she's been around the block. I know she'll have a story or two for me from her time with Hogan. Purely professional interest, of course," he added, smiling inwardly.

"Yeah, sure!" Flash said as he headed off to find the First Class eatery.

Matt returned to their cabin, or rather, their suite. He'd had to start a war of his own to get a First Class booking from the *Daily Inquisitor*. It cost him as well, but he needed the space for his photographer and to secure his own gear and papers. He set about unpacking, arranging their belongings between the two rooms, and making sure all the manuscripts, passports, letters of introduction and banknotes were locked away.

His so-called Saloon Class accommodations were all that Cunard promised, lavish as anything else on the Atlantic. Matt paid only passing attention to the decor—the creamy-looking paneled ceilings laid out in gilded ovals and rectangles, the mahogany furniture and silk hangings over doors and portholes. The rooms had been designed to attract wealthy passengers in an era of what his writer friend Thorstein Veblen had famously called "conspicuous consumption." *RMS Lusitania* marked the high point of a quite literally Gilded Age.

The decorative feature that Matt valued most was their private bathroom. But the bedroom too, when sealed off with wartime blackout curtains over the windows, promised to be serviceable as a darkroom.

As he finished tidying, a sharp knock came at the outer door. Matt opened it, expecting to see a uniformed steward. Instead there stood a large, mustached man in a tan tweed suit. The gray homburg hat in his hand was shiny in places with long use.

"Excuse me, Soor, are you the ticketed occupant—Mr. Vane, is it? Might I come in?" The man's northern Brit accent was thick and none too cultivated.

Matt stood fast in the doorway. "And who might you be?"

"Detective-Inspector William J. Pierpoint, Soor, on detachment from the Liverpool Police." The big man touched his hat brim with one finger. "You should know this ship is British territory. I've been assigned to keep an eye on things during the voyage."

Matt grinned and moved back to let the man in. "Ship's detective, huh? Well, I guess with all the war doings, you must be busier than ever." He extended his hand as Pierpoint stepped over the raised doorsill. "I'm Matt Vane, reporter for the New York *Inquisitor*. My job used to include the police beat. Can I call you Bill?"

"Pierpoint will do." The handshake was beefy, powerful but careless. "Mr. Vane, I'm told that you've been taking pictures around the ship, and my job is to enforce security." Still wearing his hat, Pierpoint looked around the parlor. "Might I see your camera?"

"What?" Matt stalled him, thinking fast. "Nope, sorry, my assistant has it with him. He's off somewhere just now. What's the matter, has there been a complaint?"

Pierpoint waved a large hand dismissively. "We'll be sailing into a war zone, and there may be vessels or installations that are secret. I'll have to ask you to keep any photography strictly to passenger areas, interiors and so forth."

"Well, sure," Matt said. "Always glad to oblige. Anything else?"

Pierpoint took his time while moving about the cabin, which was too roomy for Matt to block off with his body. The ship had a slight roll, and the cop used it to amble around the place like a sailor. By casually shoving the inner door wide, he managed a look into the bedroom. He finally paused at a sideboard where Matt had set out the morning news.

"*The Daily Inquisitor*," Pierpoint observed, picking it up. "That's a Socialist paper, isn't it? I see here they've announced today's May Day rally in New York's Central Park. Too bad you missed it. Are you a socialist agitator, Mr. Vane?"

"I just report the news," Matt said carefully. "It's best to avoid any political bias."

"Oh, aye. We have our Social Democrats in London, and a few out on the Liverpool docks." Pierpoint squared on Matt. "They stir things up, talking against the war, pushing for strikes and the like. Just a lot of German sympathizers if you ask me." He pronounced the nationality *Joor-man*.

"No sympathies here, old chap." Keeping his irritation in check, Matt managed a shrug.

"What about these Bolsheviks who're making trouble for our Russian allies and the Czar? Are you in league with them?"

Matt felt himself turning red, though not necessarily Communist red. "I'm a neutral...an American, remember, the kind that Cunard Lines likes to have as passengers."

At this jab to his employer, Pierpoint looked almost offended. "There are a good many Joor-man sympathizers in America, I know that. And plenty of them are active Joor-man agents as well."

"Yes, and a lot of just plain Germans too," Matt said. "The agents, I might add, are all trying to stop my country's massive support for your country's war effort. But without much success, so far." Matt resolved to be patient with this stubborn British Bobbie. "Tell me, really, what's the problem? Sit down if you want." He waved toward a plush, green-patterned Louis-the-Something settee, but the big copper remained standing on the carpeted deck.

Matt went on, "I know the Germans have been claiming there are guns mounted on the *Lusitania*, but frankly I haven't seen or heard of any—sounds like baloney to me. What is it that's going on, spy stuff?"

Pierpoint reddened a little and looked exasperated, but he finally spilled. "Just after leaving port we caught three stowaways, all Germans, hiding out in a kitchen pantry aft. They had a camera, the newest sort with a film roll inside, and had already taken some pictures. Until we get the film developed in port, who knows what they were after?"

This last question had a ring of untruth, but Matt said nothing.

"Do you know anything about it?" the detective pressed him with a challenging look.

"No, I don't even speak German. But if it's photo developing you need..." Matt added, smelling a story.

"Too late, I'm afraid," Pierpoint said with an almost regretful tone. "We handed off the camera and film to the blockade ship *Caronia* to send back to New York."

"Nobody went over with them," Matt recalled. "So the stows must still be on board? What's their story?"

"They're in the brig. They'll be interrogated in Liverpool. They're not saying much, not even in German." Pierpoint removed his Homburg and scratched his pomaded scalp. "But you know, there could be other agents on board that we didn't catch."

Matt was considering. "You mean to say, if they got the picture they wanted out to the press, or to the German embassy, it could be used to justify some kind of attack on this ship?"

"That's why I want you to be careful with that camera of yours," Pierpoint said. "You'd best turn it over to me for safekeeping."

"But there are no guns aboard, aren't there?" Matt evaded. "No troops, and no contraband cargo, I'm sure," he innocently added. "So what could be the problem?"

"Just you have a care, Mr. Vane, Soor." Pierpoint donned his hat and turned to leave. "Keep your eyes and ears open for the good of this ship, and keep me informed. How do you Yanks say it? ...we're all in the same boo-at."

He glanced back from the door. "And don't forget, I'll be keeping an eye on you."

Chapter 6

Code Breakers

Admiral Reginald "Blinker" Hall was late getting across to the Old Building at the Admiralty in London. Many of his days ran late; as Director of Naval Intelligence in wartime, he was expected at every port of call. But he controlled the demands on his time, striding the dark-paneled ancient corridors without undue haste. It was wise to keep irregular hours now and again, just to take your minions by surprise—and maybe your enemies, too. He felt confident that Room 40 would be fully active, even this late on a Saturday afternoon.

As a very recent recruit to this intelligence role, appointed by First Sea Lord Churchill at the outbreak of hostilities last August, he was yet no rank beginner. His father had held the same post in decades past. Reggie was literally bred to this spy game, long before he'd earned his Admiralty rating as a skilled sea captain.

Now, commanding a desk instead of a battlecruiser, he felt confident shaking up and modernizing his Papa's musty organization. Starting out by ordering the intercept and reading of all Continental mail and cables, seizing all cargo shipments to enemy powers, and using spies to tap into the diplomatic dispatches of enemies, allies, and neutrals alike, including the United States, he had vastly expanded his agency's reach. His network of agents and code breakers were driven as much by the confident, slightly sinister force of his personality as by their loyalty to the British Crown. Through his shrewdly narrowed gaze, which caused his fellow officers to nickname him Blinker, he saw his job as being to confuse and outwit the enemy, whether it was the treasonous Sinn Fein Irish rebels or the German–Austro-Hungarian Alliance of the Central Powers.

Yet here in Room 40, he hid his newest and most effective weapon.

And sure enough, when he opened the tall antique door he found a dozen shirt-sleeved "translators" bending over codebooks. More young men and women carried parsed messages from desk to cluttered desk. It was a thriving cottage industry, all of it due to the German radio-telegraph codes that had been providentially captured from enemy ships, retrieved off floating bodies, or dredged up in trawlers' nets from the sea-bottom during the early months of the war. Or so at least the stories went around the Admiralty. But Blinker Hall knew that Churchill and his crew could be quite inventive when it came to protecting old-fashioned espionage sources, particularly their agents inside the German High Seas Fleet.

Scanning the room with his acute gaze, Hall saw, seated at the central desk in the rear, Sir Alfred himself in one of his unmistakable mauve dress shirts. The glaring pink color supplied an odd relief to the dark brown of old wood and flat white of papers, cuffs, and pale flesh untouched by sun in this drippy, foggy London spring. One would think there'd be more suntans among captains of the Admiralty, but not so in a paper war. Pasty-white seemed to be the *de rigueur* fashion this season.

Well, Alfred Ewing could afford to defy convention in his shirts, at least. Although his operation was a secret one, he was known to insiders as the mad Scottish genius who had assembled a roomful of mathematicians and linguists to streamline the code-breaking process. As an academician and math wizard himself, lately an Oxford don, the Room 40 chief was lax about saluting. But he welcomed Blinker over with a wave of his hand.

"Working late, I see, Alf." Approaching Ewing's command post, Hall saw that it was papered-over with dispatches, many with cover sheets marked Strict Secret and For Your Eyes Only.

"Yes, Blinker, hello," Sir Alfred said, arranging security folders on his desk. "You're running a bit late yourself."

"Better late than not at all. Are you worried about getting out to a party tonight?" Hall spoke with reference to the screaming polka-dot bowtie that topped off the shirt garish enough to make anyone blink.

"If time permits," Ewing replied, "I'll go out on the town. But I can't say for sure whether or when. Traffic right now is heavy, both by wire and over the aether."

"The U-boaters are still proud of their new Marconi sets, I see." There was no private place to talk, but the bustle of Room 40—clicking telegraphs, thudding of vacuum tubes, and the endless shuffling of pages—tended to mask conversation.

"Oh, yes. They test their wireless faithfully at the start of each patrol, and report back their positions each hour while in range of Germany." Ewing pointed up to his large wall map of Western Europe. It had a bright red semicircle drawn from the North Sea down to the Bay of Biscay, broadly girdling England and Ireland—the German-declared Naval War Zone blockading Britain. "They're chatty as ever, and our radio triangulation is quite good enough to confirm the locations. No false reports as yet."

"I see." Blinker said. "They've taken the bait, then?"

"So it appears, sir. Last week, as you'll recall, they assigned four U-boats to the Irish Channel, and just yesterday three more sailed, presumably with the same orders to sink our troopships."

Behind his poker face, Hall did mental calculations. The supposed troopships didn't exist; they were mere planted rumors, full of phantom doughboys headed for a northern invasion of Germany that would never take place—unlike the real troop carriers steaming for the Gallipoli campaign against Turkey, down in the Mediterranean.

"So, Reggie, judging from these intercepts, our ruse is successful. The Huns are more worried about defending the Baltic Sea than attacking us on their western front. They think we've men and ships to spare. And whether we do or not, they'll hopefully hold back their punches in Europe."

"And Gallipoli, which seems to be turning into a bloody cock-up."

Blinker held back, as was his prerogative. An intelligence operation could have multiple aims–to reduce enemy pressure on the main line of trenches running through France, and perhaps also distract from Churchill's blow at the "soft underbelly of Europe," as he put it, the Gallipoli naval landing. Hall felt his blink-rate accelerating with wrath as he thought of the young Sea Lord's impudent, overly ambitious scheme.

"Let's just pray he can pull it out of the bleeding fire," Hall said at last. Or not, he added to himself, if that will put an end to his schoolboy meddling.

"We can hope and pray," Ewing said. "As I hear it, the army lads, our Irish and the Anzacs alike, are having a devil of a time there in the Dardanelles, worse than the Navy did navigating the sea mines. The Turk's belly hasn't proven so soft after all." As he spoke, he tidied the papers on his desk, sorting them into neat piles. "And meanwhile, of course, we face the same plague of commerce raiders here in home waters."

"A damned nuisance, I know, ever since the Huns declared unrestricted naval warfare," Hall said. "But we seem to be getting things in hand."

"April wasn't really so bad." Ewing produced a report in a tan cover which read Absolute Secret. "Eleven ships lost, as compared to eighteen in March. You'll see it all here." He handed over the folio. "We can quite reliably tell which U-boats are out, and where they're headed, before they're outside wireless range of home, or after they head back in and brag about their kills. The rest will still be up to the coast watchers and channel patrols."

And just as well, Blinker told himself. The coast guards and common sailors, even the fish trawler hands, knew their roles and would act for the common good. That was the great thing about Britain, and the reason why they would eventually win this war. As a sea captain, and now as spy chief charged with maintaining the broadest empire the world had yet known, Admiral Hall saw it clearly. England was a seagoing nation, relying on shipping for its food and defense, its wealth and employment. A ship depends on obedience by its crew, and on the absolute authority of its captain and officers. Without instant submission to a single will, the ship cannot survive long; elsewise everyone may perish, along with the vessel itself.

This theme ran through English government, as Blinker saw it, and through the very fabric of society. British subjects understood it and valued their places in the inflexible order. The basis was class–an aristocratic few, acting in enlightened cooperation, had to submit to the will of a single monarch, and in turn control the masses. Without this unity there would be chaos, and the ship of state would founder. In other earlier monarchies, the Church had been the main support of the kingship, with its hierarchy of God, angels, saints, men and beasts. Yet religious faith could falter, but this natural order of captain and crew, elite officer-caste and commoners, was impossible to deny, at least for an island kingdom surrounded on all sides by seas and rivals. Privileged Britons like himself and Ewing, acting by authority of the King—in a common understanding dictated by shared class, from their schools and social clubs and cabinet departments—could steer the land through any tempest of war, or of peacetime competition.

These were the views Hall had come to believe in, and that were held by some few others, so he thought. But now they were the inner convictions of a spymaster, profound secrets—like so many other secrets, never to be written down or even discussed. The captain of a vessel at sea did not need to share his plans with any lesser officer or deckhand.

"An arrogant lot, these U-boat *Kapitans*," Ewing was saying. "And competitive to boot. Just as pushy as their Kaiser, or even more so."

"Yes, well, they have their new underwater weapon that was barely tried out before." Hall was glad to be back on conversational ground. "Now it's beastly effective."

"It challenges the old rules of naval combat and any notion of international law." Ewing added, waxing professorial.

"Well, that's the downside for the Huns, don't you see?" Hall replied. "The idea of destroying merchant ships and passengers without warning—without even taking the ship as a prize, or its cargo—it's wasteful and barbaric, as if...."

"As if aircraft were to come and drop bombs on a city at random," Ewing supplied. "As the German Zeppelin balloons so recently did on Yarmouth. Such a shame! I suppose the old, chivalrous days of warfare are past."

"Yes, well, the time-honored Cruiser Rules are out the window—or out the porthole, so to speak. But it may still work to our advantage," Blinker confidently added. "You can always trust these bloody-minded Huns to push things a bit too far."

Chapter 7

Saloon Class

As was the custom in First Class—which Cunard quaintly called Saloon Class—Matthew Vane dressed for dinner. On this first night at sea, he thought it important to fit in. The voyage, so he'd resolved, would be no vacation from news reporting. On the contrary, this transatlantic run offered a rare chance to cross social lines and pick up useful news and gossip.

His black tuxedo afforded no space for a notebook. Only the smallest pencil stub and a folded sheet of paper, necessary for jotting down names, cabin numbers and a key word or two, would fit unobtrusively into the inner pocket. He adjusted his black bowtie and turned from the vanity mirror to brave Flash's wolf-whistle.

"Not bad," the photographer said, "but be sure to carry smelling salts. All the ladies will swoon."

"Should we find you a dinner jacket?" Matt parried. "For Saloon Class, you'll have to do better than that old coat. Though it might do OK in a Bowery-type saloon back home."

Flash shrugged. "I'll just make the rounds," he said, and winked. "I think Second Cabin society is more my speed."

That meant he'd be chasing nurses. No great loss, Matt thought, since having him around snapping pictures on the first night out might seem *gauche* and put the newsworthies on their guard. "If you're not taking the camera with you, hide it well," Matt said as he left. "It's wanted by the authorities."

From their suite on Main Deck E, Matt went up one flight of stairs to the dining palace on D. Their stateroom lay toward the rear of First Class, in a favored area amidships where the vessel's noise and motion were least noticeable. So it was a smooth walk, like strolling down Broadway, along the carpeted passage to the Grand Dining Saloon's double doors.

Matt's tuxedo, combined with a four-bit tip to the steward at the entry, earned him a seat on the main floor of the luxurious room. On entering the vast gallery, he was glad he hadn't been diverted up to the mezzanine, with fewer chances to mingle in among the smart set.

The place was posh as they come, more elaborately gilded and paneled than his deluxe suite. At the center of the ship, a double ring of white pillars held up first the gilt-railed circular balcony, and above that a filigreed dome stolen straight out of the Palace of Versailles. Matt saw no skylights or portholes, just electric lamps hung all round the ceilings. Mirrors set at strategic places in the walls gave the room an illusion of endless size. The flooring was pale wood parquet, and the swivel armchairs anchored to it were upholstered in rose velvet. White embroidered tablecloths draped long tables, displaying place settings all aglitter with silver and crystal.

The table he was conducted to had several guests already seated, and they glanced up politely at the new arrival. Matt took his place opposite a matronly woman in a black evening gown, with a double strand of pearls across her bosom. Her black hair was done up in a massive coiffure which bobbed in welcome as he came up. The one unique touch to her *ensemble* was a small pair of *pince-nez* glasses perched on the stately bridge of her nose.

"Hello," she said. "I'm Mary Plamondon, and this is my husband Charles. We're from Chicago. Are you American?"

"Yes, originally from Philadelphia," Matt said. "I'm Matthew Vane, now a reporter with the *Daily Inquisitor* in New York."

Before settling into his chair, he reached across the table and shook hands, first with the husband and then the wife. The man was stout and balding, dressed in a black dinner jacket and bowtie identical to Matt's.

"Oh, Charles, he's a reporter traveling to Europe! Are you going to cover the war, Mr. Vane?"

"Yes, I expect to," Matt said, shaking out his napkin.

"How exciting! We think it's so important, the war effort. Don't we, Charles?" She nudged her husband, who nodded with an agreeable grunt but didn't seem called upon to elaborate.

His wife went on with the introductions: next to Matt was Mr. Bowring, a British gentleman in shipping, and across from him an American named Gauntlett.

"But oh, a foreign correspondent," Mary Plamondon said. "There must be so many interesting stories to be told! Is this your first time abroad? Our own trip isn't quite so romantic. My dear Charles here manufactures brewery equipment, and he wants to sound out the Europeans to buy our products. Just the Allies, of course."

"Beer brewing, is it?" Bowring asked on Matt's right.

"Yes, definitely," Charles Plamondon answered, finally moved to speak. "I'm interested in closing a deal with the Guinness concern in Dublin. They make a fine stout, but they'll need our high-capacity vats and cookers if they want to expand their output."

"We've done all our business until now in the States," Mary added, shaking her head, "but if this Temperance Movement has its way, who knows what the future holds?"

"Yes. It's a shame," her husband said. "A little beer never hurt anybody, not like the hard spirits that some people can't handle. But if this Prohibition thing passes, it'll likely be just that, a flat ban." He shook his head sadly. "These fanatics are sure to throw out the baby with the bath."

"But the Europeans aren't going to fall for anything like that," Mary added brightly. "Least of all the Irish."

"What about the Germans and Austrians?" Matt asked, a little mischievously. "They're the biggest beer-drinkers of all. Wouldn't you want them using your products?"

"Are you kidding?" Plamondon laughed. "Those German industrialists have been our biggest competitors in America, with their boilers that do double duty for beer and sauerkraut! This war can help us with European business by cutting out the German and Austrian competition, even if our US market goes bust."

"But enough about our troubles," Mary put in quickly. "There are some newsworthy people right here at our table. Mr. Bowring, there next to you, has a lot of ships at risk in this war."

Matt turned to the tuxedoed man, who sat waiting good-naturedly. "Charles Bowring, of Bowring Shipowners?" he asked. "I recognize the name from covering the New York docks. You're right in the middle of it all."

"Quite so, old man," Bowring said. "Business has expanded quite a lot, but so has the risk. We lost two vessels in April, one commandeered by a German surface raider, and one to a floating mine."

"How awful," Mary gasped. "Were any lives lost?"

"No, fortunately not," Bowring replied. "But the crew of the captured ship was interned by Germany; I'm going now to see about getting them out. The shipping business takes me back and forth quite regularly to England, so I always take the fastest, safest liner, good old *Lusitania*."

"How interesting! So you see, Mr. Vane," Mary added, "you can write a news story about that! And Mr. Gauntlett, here, wants to make submarines in Rhode Island! Fred, maybe some press coverage would help you promote your venture."

Matt looked to the man with mutton-chop whiskers across the table. "Submersibles, is it?"

"Well, yes, at least partly," Gauntlett said. "I'm with Newport News shipyards, and I'm going to see about having the British license their designs for US manufacture. We could turn them out quicker, and every bit as well-built. It could help the Brits overcome this U-boat menace."

"Subs fighting subs, you mean?" Matt asked, itching for his pencil and paper but afraid to pull them out. "The problem is, finding them while underwater. Is there some new gadget for that?"

Gauntlett looked reticent. "Well, if there were, it would be highly secret just now. Not something for the daily news. But they have made progress with underwater listening devices."

Their talk was becoming more and more interesting to Matt when it was interrupted by the arrival of a new diner, a mustached and somewhat frail-looking Englishman. He was escorted to the table by a white-clad waiter.

"All right, steward, if I must," he was irritably telling the man. "This spot right here will do quite nicely...Madame, if you don't mind."

Slipping into the vacant seat next to Mary, he gave no further heed to the crewman and suddenly became charming.

"Sorry for the fuss," he told those already seated. "I thought I had another table reserved, but it was filled up. With these fixed seats, there's no making allowances." He thumped on the arm of his swivel chair.

"You probably didn't tip the bloke enough," Bowring said, "and now you're stuck with us business travelers, the lowly *hoi polloi*. Tough luck, old chap!"

The remark brought laughs around the table, but it flustered their new arrival.

"No, no, terribly sorry, I didn't mean anything of the sort." He smiled winningly. "I'm Ollie Bernard out of London, but fresh from Boston. On the lam from the States, you might say."

Rising again, he offered his handshake all around. "I've made this voyage a dozen times, but never before on the *Lusitania*."

"Oliver Bernard," Mary echoed with interest. "Haven't I heard that name associated with show business?"

"None too prominently, I'm delighted to say." The Englishman gave them a wry, self-deprecating smile. "I've worked as a production designer, it's true...hidden safely away backstage, on several highly notable Broadway flops and farces. And then, weary of the Great White Way, I decided to take my curse to the Boston theatre scene..."

As the fragile-looking *émigré* was getting started, Matt was distracted by an urgent hand on his shoulder—that of Flash, who, under the baleful gaze of the steward, had eased down into the last vacant seat beside him. The photographer was still in his street wear, and Matt guessed he hadn't come to dine.

"If you could help me out with Alma..." the redheaded youth whispered in his ear. "She's scared and thinks she's being tailed. The nurses are in a tizzy."

"Well, why aren't you there with them?" Matt asked, turning aside from the group. While feigning irritation, he was actually relieved by the interruption. As they spoke, he took out his pencil stub and jotted down the names and occupations of the dinner guests he'd met, to save them for interviews later.

"We don't think Alma should be linked with the other nurses, not at the back part of the ship," Flash was murmuring in his ear. "That steward or crewman that Knucks paid off, he may get wind that she's aboard, and where she's booked. He could tip off Hogan's mob contacts to be waiting for her in port. So they had her dress up in disguise, and I snuck her away forward."

"Where, to our cabin?" Matt rolled his eyes in mock amazement. "What is it you adventurers need from me?"

"She hasn't had much of anything to eat today, and she shouldn't have to rely on scraps sneaked in for her." Flash gazed around the splendor of the Grand Saloon. "This could be the best place for her, if you'll bring her in as a guest."

"Oh, really? Hide her in plain sight, you mean, like a purloined letter? Couldn't we just order room service?" Matt sighed, seeing that he'd have to handle this in person.

Rising from his seat, he told the hovering steward, "My assistant here needs me. Can you save our places?"

He slipped him another two bits, and the man nodded. Their seatmates were all caught up in Ollie Bernard's stage banter, so Matt said nothing more and followed Flash out. He was surprised by this sudden turn of events—gravely interested to see the cause, but afraid it might all be getting out of hand.

In all things practical, Matt trusted his young protégé. Flash was a product of the New York streets, a clever assistant and dedicated hustler. Even dealing with the criminal element and the rough-and-tumble side of city politics, his red-haired antennae were generally keen, with instincts, in some ways, sounder than Matt's. But where lovely and lively women were concerned, what young man could you ever trust? And trusting Alma...that would be an experiment, especially under the acute lens of shipboard society.

As for the problem of class, Matt saw it as workable. From the lore of the Atlantic ferry trade, he understood that First Class passengers were often allowed freedom of the ship and the courtesy of entertaining guests of lesser class bookings, usually female—even though they might occasionally turn out to be gambling cheats, sneak thieves or confidence tricksters. Matt didn't expect this of Alma, in spite of her shady past. But the close personal scrutiny of Detective Pierpoint could make things touchy.

On the other hand, crossing class barriers was evidently going to be easier now with the severe wartime crew shortage. And if extra fees, fare upgrades or a bribe were required, Matt could pay it out of his own funds. It might even be reimbursed later by his employer, depending on the news value of the arrangement.

The two reporters went to their stateroom without saying much. In the corridor and on the great spiral staircase, they passed some late, hurrying diners and a few strolling couples. When they reached the door of the suite, Flash knocked three times, then unlocked it and eased it open.

Stepping inside, Matt was stopped dead by what he saw. A lovely stranger stood before him, slender in a black evening gown. Her abundant raven hair was bound up in an artful cluster, with a few black ringlets dangling against her pale cheeks and delicate neck. She fit perfectly in the gilded stateroom—from her coiffure, to the stylish choker glittering silver at her throat, down to her ankles hemmed in the elegant gown's foamy lace. Even the shoes, low-heeled with delicate black bows— all of the suite's high-priced King Louis decor was just a gaudy frame to her Art Nouveau portrait.

It was Alma, Matt slowly realized, and not wearing a wig...she had evidently dyed her hair a deep black.

"Flash told me to put on the best things I had," the woman explained, almost too demurely unaware of the effect she created. "I hope this passes for First Class."

"And then some," Flash murmured under his breath.

Matt finally trusted himself to speak. "If they're looking for a blonde on the run, they won't have much luck."

Just then, Winnie appeared from the back room. Wearing a dark flowered dress beneath a fur-trimmed coat, with her plentiful auburn hair unchanged, she seemed informal but definitely not nursy—as fresh-looking as a Gibson Girl advertising poster.

"Oh—you, too," Matt said, still recovering from the first pleasant shock.

"Don't worry about us,' Flash put in. "We already ate." Confidently he took Winnie's arm. "We'll just have a quick turn on deck."

"Well then, Alma." At a loss for more words, Matt held out his arm. "Why don't we head back to the dining saloon?"

Not looking the least surprised, she took his arm.

They left the suite a little before the other two, to be inconspicuous... avoiding Flash who, with his red hair, was conspicuous in everything he did. When the couple arrived at the grand stairway, the elevator was waiting, so they rode up one floor through the center of the spiral, trying to look perfectly at ease in their gilded cage. The lift attendant seemed impressed, either by Alma's high style or by Matt's nickel tip.

In the passage there was time for talk. "Who're you supposed to be?" Matt asked.

"I can be your typist, Alma Brady." Seeing his interested look, she added, "Yes, I can type. But don't get any ideas."

"Do you really want to be known by the same name, here forward?" Matt asked. "That could be easy to trace."

"No need to worry," she said, slightly breathless as they hurried along. "Big Jim, Knucks, and all the others know me as Maisie Thornton, a singer. Alma's the name my ticket's under."

"But don't you think Hogan checked you out, enough at least to know your real name? He's good at that."

"Maisie Thornton is my real name. Or it was," she added grimly.

"Maisie...is that May, or Mary?"

"It was short for Mairead," Alma confessed. After spelling the name out at his insistence, she added, "Way too Irish." Then she fell silent to take in the spectacle as they entered the Grand Saloon. Looking about, her eyes glittered with more than the reflection of gilt and crystal.

For another two bits, the steward guided them back to the same two chairs, still vacant. The first course on the bill of fare was ready to be served: *Creme de Champignons*, mushroom soup from a silver tureen. New travelers had filled in most of the nearby seats, but all paused appreciatively in their dining as Matt seated his companion.

"This is Miss Brady, my private secretary," he declared. In the hushed aftermath, he realized that a breath of scandal would be impossible to avoid. But then, if it scared them away from any direct questioning, so much the better.

"Sorry to be late," Alma announced as the waiters spread napkins on the newcomers' laps and ladled soup into their bowls. "But I would have been sorrier to miss this," she added, turning to her plate.

Hungry as she was, Matt saw that she knew how to sup...the spoon held between thumb and fingers, dipped away from the body and delicately raised, the soup drawn in silently from the near edge between her lips. Lovely pert lips, Matt couldn't help but notice. He saw other eyes checking her comportment as well as her looks. She would pass muster, he decided.

The rest still sat attentive under the picaresque spell of Oliver Bernard. Once Ollie set down his soup spoon, he immediately started in namedropping.

"There's Kessler over there. New Yorkers call him the Champagne King." He nodded toward the vintner at a distant table, with his trademark black beard. "He'll probably be throwing a fancy party or two this trip. Not that I'll be in on it. I'm just small-fry."

Wanting to make Alma feel included, Matt muttered aside to her, "Do you know Kessler? He's a drink promoter who's flooded Broadway with his new champagne brand, White Seal, for a French bottling company. With his lavish parties, chartering steam yachts and uncorking dozens of cases at a time, he's a match for any thousand or so temperance crusaders."

Dabbing at her lips with a napkin as Matt spoke, and then sipping delicately from her own champagne fife, Alma merely smiled back at him.

"But, Ollie," Mary Plamondon was gaily asking, "you do know the big names on Broadway, don't you? Like Sarah Bernhardt?"

"Never met the Divine Sarah," Bernard said. "But the actress Rita Jolivet is here. Josephine Brandell too, I know both. And the playwright Justus Miles Forman, and Charles Klein, who doubles as an actor."

Still scanning the tables, he added, "There may be others. Charles Frohman, the producer, is one of the biggest. I don't see him, but he's on board. He has to go over to London each year to get the pick of the season's plays for New York production."

"He's quite a personality. Didn't he launch *Peter Pan* stateside?"

"Yes, and he may be secretly married to the actress we all know, who did the part. He's quite a wit. On the dock before sailing, someone asked him, 'Aren't you afraid of U-boats?' and he said, 'No. In my business I'm only afraid of the IOUs.'"

The quip brought a flutter of laughter around the table.

Their self-appointed hostess Mary followed up, "What about Isadora Duncan? I just read about her leaving for a European dance tour. Is she aboard?"

Bernard shook his head. "No, she and her troupe sailed earlier today on the *New York*. They were set to depart about the same time we did, but under an American flag, the dirty cowards! That may be why

Frohman's with us. He doesn't always adore the biggest stars, unless he made them himself."

Mary obviously enjoyed the gossip. "And what about you, Mr. Bernard?" she pressed him. "Why are you sailing for England? Not really running from your flops, as you said...?"

Ollie laughed awkwardly. "In point of fact, I mean to enlist. I'd like to see something of this war business before it's all done."

Suddenly he seemed almost self-conscious. "I've tried to sign up twice before, in Canada, and once Over There." He pointed ahead of them toward Europe. "But recruitment is in an awful muddle, and my being deaf in one ear doesn't help." He laughed again. "I don't see why—if they send me close enough to the cannons, I imagine I'll end up deaf in both ears."

His joke fell flat, whether due to the gravity of the subject or to his obvious sincerity. Charles Plamondon said, "Good luck, old man, I hope it works out for you,"

"Well, thanks," Bernard shot back, "Or perhaps my good luck will run out, and they'll finally take me!"

Still onstage, he scanned the room for a distraction. "Oh, look! Here comes Hubbard, just the man to liven things up." He swiveled his chair and waved a hand. "Elbert, here's a seat! Come and dine with the Olympians!"

The man who veered toward them was a quaint, familiar character, but impressive even so. His dignified, square-featured face was framed by a wide-brimmed black hat, which he defiantly wore in the formal company, and by long gray Pilgrim locks cut in bangs. For the mandatory bowtie, he substituted a flamboyantly knotted artist's foulard in the wide collar of his shirt, and his long black coat was no dinner jacket.

"Pleased to meet you gents," he said to the diners. "Ladies," he added, with special bows to Mary and Alma.

"This is Elbert Hubbard, the sage American philosopher you all know." Ollie said. "Elbert, where's Alice?"

"She's below, seasick," Hubbard said, removing his hat with a flourish and taking his seat. "Don't worry, it's nothing that a day or two of fresh air won't cure."

As the second course, a buttered fillet of sole, was served, Mary said, "Mr. Hubbard, I've heard so much about you and read so many of your writings! What takes you to Europe? Are you spreading your message of self-reliance?"

Between bites of bread, while still spooning up soup in a casual rustic style, Hubbard replied, "It's true, they could certainly use it. A little American spunk and know-how could work wonders over there. You've seen it, haven't you, Oliver, the difference in spirit?" he asked of Bernard. "Why, I imagine if we sent over Teddy Roosevelt with his Rough Riders, they'd clean up those Germans in a couple of days."

"So you and your Roycrofters are siding against Germany?" Ollie asked.

"Why, yes. Haven't you seen my article on *Der Kaiser* Wilhelm? I titled it, 'Who Lifted the Lid Off Hell?'" He glanced sternly up and down the table to see if anyone objected to his strong language. "Without Kaiser Willie, of course, there might be a hope of world peace and true socialism. But those arrogant Prussians need to be put out of the way first. I plan on doing some writing to help the process along."

"Well, I don't think anyone here would disagree with you, Mr. Hubbard," Mary said, looking around. "Mr. Vane here is going over to be a war correspondent. Aren't you?" she asked, turning to Matt. "Would you put all the blame on the Central Powers?"

Finding himself on the spot for the first time, Matt set down his fork. "Well, there could be larger forces at work, economic ones," he said. "And I'm not sure this war is a step toward world socialism, not by any means. A year ago a writer friend of mine, Jack London, went over to London—the city he's named for—and wrote a book, *The People of the Abyss*. You know, Jack is famous for getting out there and living what he writes, whether it's South Seas pirates or the Yukon gold rush. So he spent a month or two with the English unemployed—hordes of them, trudging the length and breadth of London, going from soup lines to relief missions, sleeping out in parks, unable to find work. Not bums, but honest workers kicked out by the economic system."

Matt looked around, seeing that his audience was caught up.

"And the same thing was going on in Berlin and other European capitals, job shortages or a labor surplus, whatever you want to call it. These people were agitating for socialism, putting on the pressure, and the word was getting out.

"But now there's war. Suddenly all those men are fully employed... in the army, or filling in for the others who've gone to the front. A lot of them will never come back...and the socialist agitation has all but died out." Matt shrugged. "Labor surplus solved. The End."

After his speech, there was silence at the table. Matt saw Alma glance up at him with a bemused look. The rest seemed unsure how to respond, until Hubbard spoke up.

"Come on, now, Vane...Matthew, is it? Are you really suggesting that the British ruling class would drum up a war just to get rid of their indigents, as cannon fodder? Or that the Prussian officer class would do likewise? Well, maybe them. The bosses and rulers get blamed for a lot nowadays, but that's going pretty far."

"I can't say who," Matt replied. "It's as I said, economic forces. A lot of people on both sides stand to gain by this war."

"I could believe it of the Germans," Ollie said. "They started it by invading Belgium, after all."

"After the Austrians went into Serbia," Mary added. "They're just as bad, aren't they?"

Hubbard announced, "It doesn't really matter how it started. I'll tell you how it will end. When the Americans get involved, with real fighting spirit, true physical fitness and Yankee ingenuity, we'll wrap it up in no time. There won't be any stalemate in the trenches once the Yanks are in!"

"Well, Mr. Hubbard," Mary said, "I think we're still a long way from that."

"Last time I checked," Matt added good-naturedly, "America was neutral."

"That could change anytime," Hubbard declared. "Even by the end of this voyage."

As their meal progressed to a potted ham dish, sirloin of beef with potatoes and vegetables, and small delicate sausages, the conversation continued. Alma didn't volunteer anything, concentrating instead on her food. And Matt couldn't question her in the company of these new acquaintances, however well-meaning they might be. As the desserts arrived–Mexican cake, petits fours, and Bavarian chocolate–he barely ate anything, anxious to get her alone.

Chapter 8

Out of the Blue

Morning was clear on the Western Front. It was a fresh spring day under bright blue sky, a freshness that made Bernhard queasy with fear. No fog and no rain meant the French artillery and spotters would have a clear field of operation. Even worse, the scent of French meadowlands wafting eastward on the dawn air might inspire his own Prussian commanders to order new assaults—more lives squandered, for what? To enlarge Germany by at best a few hundred paces of blasted, treeless hell?

Before him stretched *Niemands Land*, the place for no man, a pitted chaos of mud and barbed wire sown with mines and unexploded shells, and well-fertilized with the blood and bodies of men. The stench of death in the moldering, flooded shell-holes was carried to him intermittently on the cool morning breeze. The other men in the trench, strangers all, were equally afraid, even as breakfast bread and *kaffee* and salt pork were handed out down the line. They ate in silence, oppressed by the clear blue sky. No one sat near him, since their line had been thinned by casualties and transfers out. He was alone in this bend of the great trench, but did not dare desert his post to be with others.

It hadn't been like this in those first exuberant days of the war, or so Bernhard remembered it. He thought of the cheering townsfolk at the rail depot back home, the oompah-ing brass bands and the flowers stuck by flaxen-haired maidens into the young men's gun barrels. Like a dream to him now was the long overnight train ride, and then the brisk march into Belgium, along straight roads with seldom even the sound of a gunshot. A triumphant beginning, but it all stopped suddenly when they reached the fortresses around Liège and Namur.

That brought weeks of anxious waiting, listening to the rolling thunder of the three-hundred millimeter siege cannons and the howl of the really huge Big Bertha gun as the forts were reduced. Then at last came the forced marches down country lanes, following the thump of smaller howitzers, which finally led him here to this long, open grave called a trench line.

How strange it all seemed, thinking back. His first certainty of war had come when they drafted his beloved Putzi from the farm. Returning from the fields, he saw her trooping away down the road at the head of a line of livestock. She was a fine horse, a dappled bay, his favorite to ride. But like every mule and ox in Germany, she had a registry number in the event of wartime mobilization. Early the next morning the telegram arrived–after all his reserve training, Bernhard too had been called up and was to report in town that same afternoon.

He was willing, and his parents and sisters helped him pack. Everyone had said the war was coming. The foreign encirclement, depriving Germany of warm-water ports, had to be broken. A strong young nation like the newly formed Germany, if they were to have any standing in the modern age, needed trade and colonies. To be continually met by foreign obstacles and insults, and held down by legions of inferiors, was insufferable. Every German knew that, given the chance, they could regain all the stolen territories and more than equal France and Britain's global empires. And they had set out to do so. But who would have thought such a noble crusade would stumble to a halt here, in a muddy field in Flanders?

Well, Bernhard was ready to fight. But he prayed that, if he was to be wounded in an assault, it would come late in the day, with some hope of rescue by night. Those who fell and lay in no-man's-land in the early hours–whether just hurt and playing dead, crying out for help or moaning in delirium–faced a daylong ordeal in the sun without treatment for their wounds. With no relief possible, they lay at risk of being pierced again by random shellfire, or shot by tortured listeners merely to silence their cries.

Worst of all was the jagged wire, where men, even if unwounded, were caught without food or water in steel barbs for days. Though exposed to enemy fire, sometimes they were left alive as bait to lure out would-be rescuers to their deaths.

In the assaults, leading men were detailed to throw themselves onto the concertina wire, to flatten the coils for their comrades to advance over. Bernhard had never yet been one of those. When trapped, if the attack was successful and gained ground, they could be cut loose and saved. If not, they might be trampled by the retreating troops or pulverized by shellfire.

This morning, as it happened, it was the French who decided to attack. With weather reports from the British Isles far to westward, they may have known this clear spell was coming and made secret preparations. At breakfast, while crouching in the muddy trench and trying to keep his feet dry on the slimy boards, Bernhard heard the thunder of the enemy cannon as the first shells came whistling in. He felt the mud quiver as the explosive rounds struck, and he dove into a revetment to cower from the flying dirt and whining shrapnel.

The bombardment lasted forever, an eternity of cringing, praying, and bracing his whole body against the direct hit that never came. When it ended, there began the terror of the assault. A shrill whistle shrieked in Bernhard's dulled hearing, and he squirmed up the parapet to defend his post.

Here they came, through smoke and vapor lingering from the shellfire. The French *poilus* trudged forward in their ridged helmets and long coats. Bayonets gleamed on their rifles as they charged into the morning sun; it was those blades Bernhard dreaded, more than the few bullets that whizzed overhead or spurted mud from the parapet. He had been trained to thrust his own bayonet, twist it and then, if the blade stuck in bone, fire his rifle to dislodge it. But the one time Bernhard used his bayonet, he'd jerked the blade smoothly out of the downed, writhing man and stumbled onward in his attack. He didn't have the heart to twist the knife. He never knew what became of his French adversary, whether the *poilu* lived or died. But that victorious charge had won Bernhard this little place in hell.

Before the bayonets came near, the defending machine guns in his line opened up. Chattering, hammering from side to side with industrial efficiency, they swiftly and blessedly mowed down the lines of attackers that materialized out of the smoke. The unevenly spaced figures strode forward through the sunlit haze...then danced, spun, capered and fell to earth as the bullets stitched them. A Spandau Ballet, their death-dance was called, named after the Berlin suburb where the automatic guns were made. By the grace of the Spandaus, the gleaming blade-tips stayed far away; the *poilus* never got close to the German trenches. Bernhard discharged his own Mauser rifle twice in their direction, with no clear target. Then the morning onslaught was over.

Now would come the worst horror, the counterattack. To follow up on this glorious success, to exploit the enemy's weakness, to take new land for Germany and finally break through the immobile trench lines... all of these illusions would lure his commanders to waste more lives. It did not matter, could not matter that they had just killed hundreds of French. It would take only a few more behind their machine guns and barbed wire to hold those enemy trenches.

Where was his Putzi right now, he wondered wildly. Was she dead in some field, bloating in the sun like the cavalry horses he had seen? More likely pulling ammunition carts for the endless bombardments. Or maybe between the legs of some lucky courier, carrying orders to and from generals far behind the lines. How he would love to leap on her back right now and gallop her out of here, right back to his farm!

Bernhard huddled head-down, not risking a look over the parapet, still waiting for the attack whistle. Would there be artillery first, to soften up the mud and warn the French? It didn't matter, since shelling never silenced the machine guns for long. Soon enough would come his turn for a death-dance in the teeth of the French Maxims.

But then a new sound intervened. It was a grating, throbbing noise that came along the trench line, rapidly drawing near. Bernhard rolled aside and saw it approaching, fifty meters above, a biplane with red and yellow Belgian markings on the bottom wing. No machine guns fired, but there was a flurry in the German trenches beneath. A babble of shouts and cries grew louder as the engine pounded overhead. Then he saw it...a fine spray of glinting sparks spilling out of canisters fixed between the landing wheels.

Bernhard writhed for cover, squirming in the mud, but there was no overhang, no protection from this new menace. Filthy water splattered up near him, and a lancing pain pierced the back of his left knee. He heard himself shriek in agony and bent to feel the wound, but the flexing of his body intensified the pain and so he lay, paralyzed and sobbing as the enemy aeroplane droned onward.

He'd heard of this terror, and now it had found him. Flechettes, metal darts dumped from Allied aircraft that could pierce straight through huddled troops on the ground. Here in the bottom of his trench he'd been struck from the skies. He would lose his leg, the racking pain told him. No other way to avoid lethal infection in these filthy mudholes,

Bernhard lay sobbing, involuntarily heaving with waves of agony from his knee. As the medics finally came and dragged him onto a stretcher, he knew that the tears on his face were not from mere pain, but tears of joy and thankfulness as well. He wouldn't be in any more assaults, or test any Frenchman's bayonet point. He wouldn't lie wounded all day, raving in the sun, or be blown apart by artillery. The pain he felt wasn't fatal, so long as gangrene didn't set in. What he had now was more precious than any medal or victory. With a clean amputation, it meant a million-*reichsmark* wound that would take him out of Hell and send him home.

Chapter 9

Marconi Waves

In the wireless room at the center of Lusitania's top deck, night hung heavy. The steady throb of the ship's engines was broken occasionally by faint, nervous pulses of Morse code coming in over a speaker. Second Telegraphist Dave McCormick sat at a table in the tiny radio shack. His senior Cunard officer, Chief Telegraphist Bob Leith, wore headphones as he turned the dial of the large gleaming Marconi set, scanning the airwaves for signals.

McCormick listened for coded traffic on the main channel, meanwhile leafing through the morning's *New York Herald* newspaper. He waited patiently to relieve his superior at the end of his shift, still getting used to the routine of the job, six hours on duty and six off, day in and day out.

When McCormick came to the page that listed the ship sailing times, he held the paper up to the light to make out the small, black-bordered warning from the Imperial German Embassy: "Vessels flying the flag of Great Britain, or of any of her allies, are liable to destruction...." To McCormick, the dull menace of the words contrasted strangely just then with the stray notes of dance music that wafted up through the ship's ventilators, or else from the blacked-out skylights of the Grand Saloon.

"Traffic is slow," the senior telegraphist remarked as he spun his dial.

Dave took this as an OK to speak. He'd found that idle talk to keep the wireless operator awake during the last weary hour of a shift was an unwritten part of the job. "Seems slow for wartime," he said, laying down his newspaper.

"Aye, bloomin' slow," Leith repeated, stifling a yawn. "Just a quick burst of code now and then, like a chicken scratchin'. Most everyone keepin' radio silence." The chief ruffled his hatless hair under the headphones.

"We might as well be down below, dancing with the ladies," Dave remarked, trying to liven things up as louder strains of music thrummed from below. "Better than wireless dots and dashes."

"Well, don't sell us short," Leith said. "Just remember, this very Marconi wireless set was visited and blessed by its inventor, the great Guglielmo himself, on our last Atlantic crossing in March. That was when he was heading back home to Italy from New York, before you came aboard."

"Well then, if it's so great," McCormick joked, "why doesn't it play music? It's bigger than a church pipe organ."

"You'll be surprised sometime, Davie m'boy," Bob Leith said, taking his cue. "Someday a bloke will talk at you right out of this box. The Yanks are tryin' out voice transmission more and more now; they call it radio-telephone. It's goin' to be weather reports, sport games and music, not in any code. A few years back, they transmitted Enrico Caruso from the New York Metropolitan Opera. I wasn't on shift to hear it, though."

"And how about band music?" Dave suggested. "We'll all be dancing to that box someday, won't we, here aboard Lusty *Lusi*?"

Shoving himself up from the table, he tried a few foxtrot steps, cutting a suave figure in his blue jacket and white trousers.

"Not too much skylarkin' about, now," his superior good-naturedly chided. "And on your watch, don't even think about leavin' this room. You'll have to stay on the alert. Captain Turner keeps late hours, and he might just drop by durin' your first solo shift under his command."

"Hardly a problem, with traffic so slow." McCormick said, resuming his seat. "Not like back at dockside this morning, with all those cables coming in. Even for Alf Vanderbilt himself, the Yank tycoon."

"Aye," Leith mumbled, yawning. "It was wires from the newspapers beggin' for interviews first. And then later those batty, anonymous warnings, likely from reporters tryin' to stir up news or start a panic. *Lusi's* last voyage—make the ship stop dead in port, they would! A good thing the captain put a lid on it. Sealed all those anonymous cables... nothin' in them anyway, except scare talk."

"Aye," McCormick said. "And did you see, Captain Turner held a press conference right down on the pier, with Alf Vanderbilt and Frohman and all the reporters. He told them everything was fine, and both of the Yankees backed him up."

"Yes, I heard. And not a minute too soon, either...Cunard could 'a lost half her customers. No sense scarin' all the passengers and having a jinxed voyage. Or stoppin' the ship in port for days on end."

Leith gave up the banter, yawned, and looked at the illuminated clock. "Well, ten minutes to shift change. Are you ready for your first night's solo duty?"

"Yes, sure," McCormick said. "You can knock off right now if you like."

"No, thanks, I'll stay till midnight," Leith said, not surprising to McCormick. Among Marconi men, especially on shipboard, it was a point of honor to hold out to the bitter end of a watch.

"It should stay blighty slow," Leith said. "Just ring down to the cabin if you need me."

"OK," McCormick said. "But not likely. Cunard's wireless station won't even be on the air for hours yet, right?"

"Aye, at daybreak in bloomin' England, about 0400 hours ship's time. But there's the Admiralty; you never know about them. They can broadcast day or night. That's where our real orders come from, not from Cunard. In wartime it's the Royal Navy that'll likely be warnin' us about raiders, tellin' us where to go and how to get there."

"Right, but all that will be in navy code, won't it? We'll never even know what they said. I'll have to ring up the quarterdeck and have a deck hand carry it to the captain, for him to decode in his cabin."

"Aye, and that's the way it always worked on board the *Caronia* too," Leith said. "But then, it's not likely they'll be sending us any orders tonight. We're not in the war zone, and they don't make a U-boat yet that will cruise this far from the Channel. We shan't be hearing from them just now."

"No, not unless they order us back to New York," McCormick mused. "Atlantic too bloody dangerous–it wouldn't surprise me, these days."

"Quite right, that could happen. So keep alert," Leith said.

He put his officer's cap on his head in place of the headphones. "Well, I guess I'll be turnin' in."

"Aye, sir. Good evening to you, and sleep tight."

Chapter 10

Dark Seas

After the supper dishes and tablecloths were cleared away, the Grand Saloon was prepared for dancing. As tables and chairs were unbolted from the deck, the ship's band set up on the mezzanine and began tuning. Alma went off to powder her nose, and Matt, having agreed to meet her at the saloon entry, headed below to fetch an overcoat from the stateroom.

He wanted to get her alone and speak freely, away from friends, table acquaintances and other interruptions. But it had to be in public, enough so that his news source wouldn't feel threatened or mistake his intent. Accordingly, he'd invited her to take an evening stroll on deck, and she'd accepted.

He would have to tread carefully. The danger wasn't just from Big Jim's goons, but from any unknown female in Alma's position. It was from his own feelings and reactions, too. As a worldly male, he wasn't ready to become a patsy to some sorry frail with a sob story. Being alone with her could be risky, just as much as being seen in her company.

If Hogan really was after her, it could be for some secret she knew. Or else he might believe she'd stolen something from him—a risky proposition, knowing Jim. If it was a case of romantic obsession, that could prove more dangerous to any man caught in the middle.

And how far was Hogan willing to go? It was a safe bet he wouldn't just forget her. He had that vengeful, possessive streak that seemed so prevalent in New York ward politics. Or was that kind of ruthlessness, perhaps, the defining trait of all leaders?

Returning to the ballroom and listening to the band play a maudlin refrain of *Sweet Adeline,* he felt a thrill as the equally sweet-looking Alma appeared at last. She still fit in splendidly, tall and shapely against the slow press of dancers. Moving with short quick steps measured by her frilly hemline, she suddenly seemed irresistible.

* * *

When taking leave of Matt, Alma parted cordially from Mary Plamondon as well. She fled, lest the gregarious woman should go along to the powder room and pump her for information. On her own, she then had time to reflect. Dinner in the Grand Saloon had been marvelous, the society convivial, the meal courses delightful. But once it was over, she felt weary from her masquerade.

After escaping New York and having to hide out from the prying steward, she'd been unable to rest that afternoon in the cabin. It had taken much coaxing by the others to disguise herself for First Class, and it was going to take a lot more nerve to impose on near-strangers for shelter and food during this voyage.

In spite of all Flash's assurances, how would Matt Vane react? Would he even be there waiting for her, Alma wondered, or might he neglect to come back at all? Did she have a right to expect anything of him on such short acquaintance? And just how far would his gallantry go? Could he be trusted?

Now, more than anything, she dreaded being left alone and vulnerable to strangers, especially strange men...to their conniving looks and unwelcome advances. Was Matthew Vane really any different?

So far, Matt seemed dependable and straightforward. He was no drinker, at least; she'd seen him leave his one glass of wine unfinished at dinner. And as yet he hadn't been forward with her, merely considerate.

But then he must, as a reporter, believe that she had something of value to him, likely in the form of information. To get it, how far would he go? And if she did yield to him, what then? If he managed to ferret out her whole story, would he still have any regard for her? Would he abuse her and try to take advantage? Or would he put things into print without considering her safety, which could be even worse?

The First Class women's lavatory was suitably splendid, with its gold-plated fixtures and marble wash basins sculptured as seashells. Here was real luxury, though it wasn't really hers. The ship's electric lighting was strong and pitiless. But even so, and in spite of the sleep she'd lost, she came off looking fairly well in the mirror. This new formula hair dye, she decided, had altered her appearance markedly enough to hide behind.

Her looks still gave her considerable sway over men, so it seemed. But it was a risky power, she now understood—one that could enrich its holder, or imprison her like a gold bar in a vault. This fickle thing called beauty could also lash back and destroy her, as it had almost done in the jungle of the New York underworld.

Was she finally safe, even here in First Class? If she worried too much about being recognized, she could always pretend to be seasick and keep to her cabin. If, that is, she had a cabin. She faced uncertain times and had better have her wits about her.

Alma restored herself in the women's room until she felt the gray-haired female attendant begin to notice her. Then she departed, unable even to leave a tip.

There was Matt by the door as promised, watching the dancers with his overcoat folded on a chair. He cut a fine figure in his tux, not stooped over or sucking on a cigarette like most reporters she'd seen. As she drew, near their eyes met and he smiled in his confident way.

Just then the tempo changed as the orchestra struck up the *Blue Danube* waltz. Matt stepped forward with a gallant gesture, and she must have looked as if she accepted, because an instant later his arm was about her waist and they were launched out across the floor.

It was alarming at first, but captivating too, because he could dance well and his encircling arm was assured. Her dress limited her steps, but he seemed to allow for it. His male strength, the scent of his aftershave and firmness of his limbs brought back feelings that thrilled and unsettled her. Without the odors of drink and tobacco, with the stately energy of the music and the extra lift of the ship's gently rolling dance floor, she found that she could still bear a man's nearness and enjoy it.

Even so, drawing attention to herself like this certainly hadn't been her intent. So when the waltz ended—with a quick, spirited embrace from Matt—she turned and fled the dance floor.

* * *

A short while later Matt walked Alma arm-in-arm along the Boat Deck, which lay open to a sky of piercing stars.

"So, Alma, why is Hogan after you?" In the wake of his impulsiveness in the Grand Ballroom, and before natural urges tempted him any further, Matt thought they'd better get down to business.

The varnished deck planking was lit by puddles of yellow electric lamplight, spaced at intervals before the doors and windows inboard. Evidently there was no U-boat threat here, and no blackout. Ocean air flowed over them, chill and damp, but Matt wore his tux, and Alma his overcoat that reached down to her ankles. He took the outside, so with the gentle outward slope of the deck plus her inch or so of heel, they were almost equal in height. Except for occasional late strollers and a couple or two hugging the rail, they were alone.

"Why is Jim after me? He wants me back." Alma's sparse answer to Matt's question made him understand that it might be a long walk.

"But really, why?" he asked. "I mean, aside from your obvious appeal." She'd left herself open for that crack.

Alma still didn't hurry to reply. "Well, Jim likes his things, you know. He likes his cigars and his yellow Stutz Bearcat. And he likes me...or he used to."

"The feeling wasn't mutual, I take it."

Again, no hurry to respond. The setting was romantic, and the night's chill drove them together, but he could tell that her thoughts were far away. "Jim can be very nice. A lot of people just love him and spend their time singing his praises. He's been kind to his voters, to widows, orphans, job-seekers..."

"Yes, I know the story," Matt said. "Jim's one heck of a nice guy. He's especially nice to people who don't cross him." He felt her presence close, the pressure of her arm on his, restrained but firm. "What I'm wondering is, how does somebody get on the wrong side of a nice, decent fellow like Jim?"

Another light pool passed before her voice murmured again. "Nice guys like Jim, they're very giving." Her tone was level, cautious. "They have a lot of friends. Sometimes they like to share the things they like, with friends that they especially like."

Matt felt his stomach flip, as if a little sea wave had tilted the planks of the solid deck beneath them. Had she been passed around the gang? He doubted it, but it must have been tough on her holding out. He had to tread carefully, his steps barely hesitating. "Old Jim's quite a generous fellow," he came out with at last.

"Oh, yes. A real prince...I mean the Borgia kind." Alma's pace had also grown uneven, and for just a moment her arm bore in unsteadily on his, heavier and warmer.

But in a few steps Matt was back on track, his reporter's meter ticking relentlessly. "When a person is as giving and generous as all that, you'd like to repay him. What would someone do, I wonder, to reward a terrific fellow like Jim Hogan?"

Alma too was back in stride. "Oh, maybe just tell the world. Have a record of all the great things he's done, and make sure everybody knows about them."

Matt couldn't quite believe his ears. His feelings were in a jumble—professional zeal, compassion, attraction, and now this. "What a great idea," he said. "But Jim would never go for that, would he—him being such a modest type." Growing suddenly tired of the back-and-forth, he pressed her.

"Seriously, Alma, a lot of people could benefit from that kind of information, whatever form it's in. The other side of political patronage is obstruction, graft and waste. Reform can open up opportunities for the little guy..."

"Why, Mr. Vane, are you a muckraker?" Alma suddenly seemed amused. "You sounded like one downstairs at dinner. But I'm surprised at you! I thought all big-city reporters were supposed to be cynical and hard-boiled."

Matt was glad it was dark. He felt like she had him blushing. "The cynicism's a part of it, yes," he said. "But the other side is seeing the stacked deck, the hopelessness, and how different things could be." He knew how futile his sudden idealism must sound. "The street reporter sees the corruption at the top and the confusion at the bottom. But the best ones see how they can change all that. Lincoln Steffens...now, there's a writer who can set you straight, rake all the muck aside and build something solid. Frank Norris does likewise, I know, I've worked with him, and Ida Tarbell. Sinclair, too...I met Upton Sinclair on a trip to Chicago. If my work could accomplish one-tenth of what *The Jungle* did, I'd die happy."

"And you mentioned Jack London, who's in the magazines," Alma said. "Big Jim doesn't think much of newspapers. I heard him say once, 'Reporters are just prostitutes, they write what they're paid to write.'

Pardon my coarse language," she added, "but I guess you've been around. And Jim certainly has."

From her overly apologetic tone, Matt imagined she might now be blushing; but he valued her frankness. He answered dryly, "Then I guess I'm not one of his favorites. My editor gives me a long leash...Jim didn't ever mention me by name?"

"He did complain once about the *Inquisitor* being a Socialist rag. It was after they did an article about something called the Transit Gang, I think. What was it, crime on the subways?"

Matt laughed. "No, corruption in laying out the new streetcar lines, so as to favor insider land speculators." He smiled, a warm glow spreading inside. "He knows my work, then."

"So you're not on the take?" Alma asked. "You don't even take orders?"

Matt shrugged. "Just my city editor's story assignments...the ones I don't come up with myself. And he loves getting the goods on crooked bosses. We try to stick up for the common people."

"How do you rate traveling Saloon Class, then, with the elite? Does your paper think that much of you?"

"I must admit, I have some money of my own," Matt said. "Or had it. Not a lot, just a backstop. I had to press for this assignment, the front-line war reporting, and pick up some of the travel costs myself. So I thought, why not see the view from the top? If Flash and I are going to Hell, we're going First Class!"

They paused then, having arrived at the front end of the promenade where it crossed from port to starboard under the captain's bridge. Ahead their view looked out over the ship's bow, across flat ocean shining silvery in the moonlight. The breeze here was chill and penetrating, making the two of them stand close together for warmth. The white-fringed cloud bank dead ahead made a dark fleecy cushion that seemed to pillow the full, rising moon.

"How lovely," Alma breathed, taken out of their discussion for a moment. For once, she seemed content just to stand there just holding his arm.

Matt said nothing, not caring to voice his own thoughts. To him, the moonlit cloud ahead looked faintly ominous. It wasn't really the smoke of cannonades and cities burning in far-off Europe, but it could have been.

"So," he said as they resumed walking, "What would Hogan do if he caught you?" A rough question, but he hoped it might get at the precise nature of Alma's offense. "Is there really any danger, do you think? Even now, when we're out at sea?"

"Well," she confessed with a faint nervous laugh, "I was worried about going overboard. I saw some stokers on our deck–huge, sooty men–and I was actually scared for a moment that they'd take me below and throw me into a furnace. It's silly, I know, maybe. But when our ship arrives in England, one of Jim's mob contacts is sure to be waiting for us, to turn me around and send me back. They're good at that kind of thing. They can slip you a Mickey Finn, put you out for days, shanghai you and sell you into white slavery if they like. I've heard of it happening before."

"Serious stuff," Matt said. "So it's not going to be just a tongue-lashing, or getting back whatever he thinks you owe him?"

"No, more than that." She stopped there without taking his bait.

"Have you tried running away before?" And too, he watched her face closely for a reply to the unasked question, implicit as he piled on the pressure: When all this is over, will you end up going back to him?

"No, never before, and never again. Really, it didn't start out as something bad," she confessed. "But I was naïve. My parents kept a townhouse on the East Side. They were in society. They spent most of their time traveling in Europe, until they died three years ago."

"Oh, I'm sorry to hear it. What was it, a train wreck?"

"No, they went down on the *Titanic*."

Another emotional dip in the smooth deck; Matt had to steer carefully in these waters. "How awful for you," he said at length, cradling her arm more gingerly in his. "And surprising to me, if they were traveling First Class." He found himself trying to keep things on a factual level. "It was mainly the lower-class passengers who lost their lives, wasn't it, due to the shortage of lifeboats?"

"From what I was told, my mother made it into a lifeboat, but it overturned. My father jumped overboard to save her, and they both were lost."

"A tragedy, just part of the greater tragedy," Matt said. "How hard did it hit you?"

"A shock, mostly," Alma said. "And a huge comedown, the end of everything. But to everyone else, a romantic story," she added with a note of bitterness. "They were loyal to each other, if not to me, their forgotten daughter. I didn't really know them all that well."

Matt digested this. "But did it bring hardship? They must have been financially well-off."

"Not so well-off as we thought, apparently." Alma shrugged as if uncaring. "Before long it was the end of finishing school for me, and no Music Institute for my singing. I was switched over to a cheap boarding school."

"No other family?" he asked. "No inheritance?"

"There's a small trust, but Father's attorney controls it. He's an old family friend, very attentive and concerned with me. Too much so, really." She kept her face averted. "I don't like going there to beg him for money."

"Sounds rotten," Matt said at length. "I imagine Hogan could've straightened that out for you."

"Well, once I was under his wing, there wasn't any need," Alma said. "I met Jim at a charity ball. He heard me sing and took a kind, fatherly interest in me. Later he promised to marry, but I ended up moving in under his roof first. How I regret that...except that now, I feel lucky not to be bound to him by marriage." She sighed. "And then of course, he didn't want me performing or studying in public. I was only supposed to be his songbird in a gilded cage."

"Can I get you to sing for me, I wonder?"

"No, it would draw too much attention—" Surprised, she looked up at him. "Oh, you mean, sing as a stool pigeon. I don't know, I'll have to think about it. Along with surviving."

"I've been thinking," Matt said, finally deciding to take the plunge, "I can offer you our stateroom to lay low here in First Class if you don't feel safe astern. Whether you tell me any more or not. It's up to you."

While being magnanimous, he suddenly doubted whether she'd be willing to repeat the mistake she'd just escaped from. "Don't worry, Flash and I can sleep in the outer room," he added, thinking she must have heard that before.

"Maybe," Alma said matter-of-factly, as if she'd expected his offer. "Thank you for the thought, but I'll have to ask Hildegard. She and the girls have been so kind, I wouldn't want to cause any trouble for them."

"How did you meet them?"

"Through Nurse Krauss, Hildegard was at a war charity concert special event. Jim wouldn't let me sing there, but she gave the talk and I managed to get her alone. A few days later I was able to slip away and join them, with only the one suitcase and a small bag. They kept me hidden during a whole month of nurse's training. So there's still hope that Jim doesn't know I'm on board with them. We'd better be getting back," she added.

Arriving amidships in First Class, they headed down. On opening his stateroom door, Matt found Flash and Winnie in the parlor, sitting a discreet distance apart on the sofa.

"Hello, you two," Matt said, striding in. "Say, you both should know, I've just made Alma an offer—"

"Don't worry, it's all fixed," the photographer cut him off, grinning. "I gave them the proposition you and I discussed. The nurses have seen that steward nosing around, and they don't think it's safe. Alma can stay here with us if she wants to, but there's a catch." He turned to his smiling seatmate and winked. "Winnie has to come along with her, as her chaperone."

"That's right," Winnie said brightly. "So don't get fresh, you two!" She waved a reproachful gloved finger up at the late arrivals. "I brought along everything we'll need, including both of your bags, Alma. The others will keep our bunk downs in Second Class looking slept-in."

"Splendid," Alma said. "Thank you, Flash, and Matt! I'll rest much better knowing we're all safe."

"So it's done, then," Matt said. He felt unnerved by the rush of events, for once taken by surprise. But it was a good feeling, if slightly intoxicating.

Flash squeezed Winnie's arm in his, to her answering smile. "Sounds like everyone gets what they want."

Chapter 11

The Hunted

"Alarm! Prepare to dive!"

The command, barked from atop the conning tower, caused a disciplined scramble on the exposed deck of the U-boat. The gunners sprang to their weapon in the drifting North Sea mists, capping and securing the long barrel. Picking up their ammunition boxes, they raced back astern around either side of the low tower and ducked down the hatchway. The stern lookout had already vanished below, but *Kapitan-Leutnant* Schwieger watched the two gunners descend and saw the hatch secured before slinging his binoculars and sliding down his own ladder inside the tower.

Once below, he slammed shut the hatch and levered it tight, then clanged the bell to signal that the hull was sealed.

Instantly, Lanz rang the shrill *Klaxon*. The raucous noise sent the crew running and jostling to their dive stations, most of them racing forward to weight down the nose of the slim craft.

"Was ist?" Schwieger heard crewmen ask the lookouts. "What is it this time? Prize or peril?"

They knew better than to disturb *Herr Kapitan* at his periscope. With seawater hissing into the dive tanks, as the daylight through the two portholes dimmed to a frothy-gray, and then a deep sea green, Schwieger wrestled the scope around in the direction of the threat: six British destroyers advancing in a search line—now, there was a menace to contend with. These new small warships, driven by high-speed turbines, could travel at thirty-five knots to head off or overtake any vessel—faster than the twenty-five knot maximum speed of the largest warships and ocean liners, and more than double his own boat's best surface speed of sixteen knots. Armed with torpedoes and depth bombs as well as medium guns, they were the deadliest of all to submarines.

Schwieger hoped the searchers hadn't noticed his *U-20* yet, and wouldn't spot it during the nervous moments it took to dive. He watched the nearest destroyer in his attack periscope, then swung the heavy apparatus to glimpse two others before the lens submerged. There was no evident change in their course, so very likely the mists had concealed the low profile of his *Unterseeboot*.

He wouldn't dare raise the scope back to the surface anytime soon, much less launch a torpedo. He wasn't particularly afraid of the enemy's explosive depth charges, which hadn't proven effective so far in the war. But if the English knew that he was in the vicinity, they could spread out and wait for his air and battery power to run low. Then if he tried to surface they would ram him, or just scuttle his fragile craft with shellfire. And without mercy—these Englanders weren't known to accept surrender or take any prisoners from U-boats.

Now the crew sat silent as they settled toward the sea bottom. Listening, they heard the heavy thrashing of a pair of steam-driven propellers overhead, with others churning nearby. The noises reached a peak, then subsided. Strange; it was almost as if the British had known they would be here.

Soon afterward came the slight thump and shock as their own keel grounded in North Sea sand. With electric motors stilled, they listened, hoping—but the churning of the destroyer engines did not cease; it merely changed pitch and frequency. The enemy ships were turning, ending their patrol perhaps, or searching for a known target. There was no telling how long they would hunt the sea lanes off this heavily trafficked promontory, the easternmost tip of Scotland.

What brought his U-boat so far north, halfway to the Arctic Circle, was caution and the harsh necessity of war. In the early months of the blockade, it had been easy to set a course due west from Germany, then dip south around England into the rich hunting grounds of the eastern Atlantic. But of late, with the English Channel heavily mined, chained off with anti-submarine nets, and patrolled by sub-hunting trawlers, the risks were too great. It was necessary to detour farther north, through chillier waters around the desolate tip of the British archipelago.

And now, with anti-submarine warfare heating up the Irish Channel too, Schwieger had half a mind to circumnavigate Ireland as well and pass down the Atlantic side of that island. He wasn't sure that

Fregattenkapitan Bauer back in Emden would entirely approve of the detour. But then, his commander always championed the absolute freedom of U-boat captains to make independent choices.

Schwieger knew he'd better come up with something. The previous day and night had brought them nothing except a load of fish purchased from a passing German trawler. It had all been easy surface cruising, except while sneaking past the approaches to the port of Edinburgh. They had sighted one small steamer there, but the weather was too rough to plot a proper attack.

So now began this tiresome skulking underwater. When the destroyers' engine noises gradually faded, Schwieger ordered his officers to raise *U-20* off the bottom and cruise due north at ten meters depth, going at a mere six knots to nurse his batteries. The rest of the crew he advised to go to sleep and save air. He and his pilot would stay awake and steer the boat through the subsea dangers ahead, past Moray Firth and the Orkney Isles, which guarded the menacing British naval anchorage at Scapa Flow. His mission, after all, was to find and sink troop transports– or, failing that, to choke off Britain's vital sea commerce by destroying merchant traffic.

Near the day's end, Schwieger raised his periscope and saw nothing—no targets, no warships. A good thing, with his batteries almost discharged and air depleted.

Surfacing, he went topside and scanned the horizon from the tower. Against the sun's dying light, he was able to confirm their landfall in the desolate Orkneys. Now it was time to run on the surface and recharge batteries on diesel power, westward and then south, toward the rich hunting grounds along the Atlantic approaches to England.

With the crew wakeful, and without risk of being overheard on the open ocean, he entertained the ship over the loudspeakers by playing one of his favorite gramophone recordings, *Die Meistersinger, The Master Singers of Nuremberg*, by the national favorite composer Richard Wagner. The music's vaulting crescendos and plunging descents, reminiscent of the wildly romantic landscape of the Alps, might help to relieve the strain of this long and arduous hunt. And they were particularly well-suited to the heights and depths of submersible voyaging.

Chapter 12

Outward Bound

Steaming into the first sunrise of the voyage, the *Lusitania* didn't take long to awaken. Crew and passengers soon began to venture outside in the bright morning, to find the early sun warm and the trailing breeze mild. The great ship lay on the blue-gray sea like a compass needle pointing steadily east, with the smoke from her funnels rising and dissipating in the dawn sky.

Flash, after a quick shave with his new Gillette safety razor in the public lavatory, tried to capture the sea scene in a photograph. Still aglow from the evening hours that he'd spent with his brand new sweetheart Winnie, he felt invigorated and restless. Even so he'd been in no hurry to disturb his sleeping cabinmates, but had taken his camera out on a walk instead.

Flash understood about shipboard romances, being himself the product of one. His father and mother, on their respective immigrant journeys from Sweden and Norway, had met in steerage on the White Star Line's *Germanic* steamship some two dozen years ago. Fleeing the hardships of the Old World, they'd been full of hope and, evidently, passion for the new one. While they both claimed to have pledged their love on Ellis Island, during the long wait for resident status, Flash had reason to suspect that their union had come earlier on shipboard. But with discreet Scandinavian vagueness about arrival and anniversary dates, they'd always managed to turn aside his guesses.

To young Lars as a newsman, their broken English made it frustratingly easy for them to dodge his questions and pretend uncertainty. But even so he was grateful. Since English was his parents' one common language, he himself had learned only American speech as a boy. In an age when being One Hundred Percent American was in fashion, he wasn't burdened in life with a heavy foreign accent and old-world beliefs. His first name Lars was an impediment, but he'd been able to shake that off. And without his "pure" Brooklyn-ese, he might not have been able to land such a plum job as news reporter and photographer–and now, a war reporter.

The current object of his affection, Winnie, was an all-American girl too, a real plum. He didn't have to ponder as yet whether their flirtation would lead to love and marriage. Unlike his parents, he and she were outbound from America. They met on the verge of travel and adventures that would certainly separate them in the very near future. For the duration of this war, it seemed to him, there could be no thought of settling down.

In view of this, Flash had no intention of bringing a nice girl to ruin. But then, Winnie was a modern like himself, a city kid with a nurse's knowledge and a matter-of-fact outlook. Keeping her sweet smile always in mind, he was interested in seeing how far it could go–maybe a week, maybe forever. For now, with her snugly asleep, he could warm himself on the sun-bright deck, take in the blue sky and sea, and feel alive.

When he returned to their cabin, the others were already rising. Matt on his settee, bachelor-like, was folding and smoothing his blankets for concealment in the Louis-the-Sixteenth lowboy. Accordingly Flash tidied his sleeping place on the lounge. The two women could be heard bustling about and murmuring in the bedchamber, and soon they opened their door to allow their hosts access to the private bathroom.

"Well, the men are up," Winnie's cheery voice greeted them. "Oh, and see how tidy! They make such good housekeepers! All we need now is breakfast."

By mutual agreement, Flash traded his First Class meal ticket for Alma's in Second. That way she would avoid going astern and possibly being recognized by anyone in the pay of Knucks and Hogan. Flash could dine with the other young ladies–but when he and Winnie left the cabin, they agreed to go separately. He felt that his red hair made him too memorable as an associate of Matt's. Besides going his own way, he wore a visor cap to partly conceal his carrot-top.

Flash found the Second Cabin dining hall to be a two-level, slightly less spacious version of the Saloon Class eatery he'd seen last night. The room's cutaway mezzanine was circled by the same white Greek columns, but lacking the rich gilded trim. The décor was white paint set off by green-patterned carpeting and swivel-chair upholstery, behind white tablecloths without the lace. Flash didn't much miss the mirrors, rose-tinted wall panels, or the hovering paintings of semi-nudes lining the central dome in First Class. His own four nymphs seemed to him just as beautiful and far more animated.

As Winnie joined her nurse friends in the dining lounge, Flash kept apart and let them reunite. Taking a seat at the next row of tables alongside some neatly-dressed male passengers, he gave the men his nickname and joined in their casual talk.

"A war correspondent, eh?" said one lanky mustached bloke, a Canadian and proud of it. "Well, keep your eyes peeled for me in the trenches. I'm headed off to Brixton for Army officer's academy. I hear the training period has been shortened before they send you off to the front, so it may not take long."

"You don't seem too worried about it."

"What, the front lines? Hell, no! The sooner the better, I say, to thump these arrogant Krauts and teach them a lesson. I'll see you out there. What about you gents?" he asked the men across the table. "You joining up?"

"No thanks, no front lines, the shorelines is good enough for me!" The speaker, seated to Flash's left, was a short fellow in a motorman's cap. "I'm a steamfitter, so I'll go where the money's good. Right now that's Liverpool an' the shipyards. Better pay than Biloxi, where I'm from."

"Well, at least you're behind the war effort. And you?" The Canadian dubiously eyed a skinny Irishman across the table on Flash's right.

The man gave him back an elfin wink and said, "Nay, I'll not be a-seein' you at the front, sorry to say. I'm only off to County Cork for the summer, to visit me dear ol' mum. And your English lords won't be a-draftin' o' me neither, 'cause I'm a Yank now." He patted his tweed suit's breast pocket. "I have here me papers as a full-fledged citizen of the US an' A."

The Canadian eyed him. "Made it good in the States, did you?" he asked skeptically.

"Good enough," the man winked. "Boston's the place. And dare I say that on the River Charles docks, lumpin' cargo, I've done as much to support your war as any man here. Though I don't much care which side the stuff goes to," he added pertly.

"Hmmph." The Canadian, visibly provoked by the Irishman's attitude, muttered aside to the others, "Just listen to this little Mick, was his mother a Hun?" He sneered. "Nah, he's just one of Sir Roger Casement's Sinn Fein traitors, trying to throw in with Germany."

The Irishman shrugged it off, speaking to no one in particular. "These second-hand English Canooks are surely true to their empire. But it matters little to me, since I'm no longer a subject of His Royal Majesty." Finishing his breakfast, he rose from his seat and departed, to a farewell snort from his adversary.

Once the threat of fisticuffs had receded, Flash followed the table talk with half an ear. His nurses, meanwhile, were having a jolly time, issuing frequent shrills of laughter even under Hildegard's stern eye. He couldn't help glancing their way, as did the other admiring males at his table. Watching Winnie's lighthearted manner with her friends, alternately gay and demure, knew he'd found something special.

"And what about you, Red?" the pushy Canadian was asking him over breakfast. "Any chance you'll catch the bug and enlist?"

Flash smiled. "Not likely, as a war reporter, not on either side. The news business makes me too cynical for that. But I can do a lot to inform people, and maybe even shorten this war. There's a growing fashion, some call it photo-journalism, of combining words with live, action pictures that don't lie. They make cameras now, collapsible and light, that record dozens of photo negatives on a roll of celluloid film. It all fits into a tiny canister instead of bulky glass plates. The Germans and Austrians are ahead of us right now in camera design. But pictures can be sent by wire too nowadays, using the telephotograph. And motion pictures...did you notice, there was a movie crew on the dock yesterday, using special naphtha lights for close-up shots. They recorded our departure from the top of the Cunard shed. The trend is to photograph actual news events as they happen, and I plan to get in on the ground floor."

His enthusiasm suitably awed and silenced the Canadian. The others soon turned to discussing the vibration of the ship at cruising speed, which could not only be felt through the fixed dining table, but seen in concentric rings inside their teacups. Flash knew this was limited to the Second Class quarters astern over the propellers, but he couldn't share his knowledge, lest he be accused of slumming. After finishing his ample breakfast, he rose to follow his nurses out.

The deck bridge forward was unguarded, so they contrived to meet again amidships, well out of sight of Second Class. Flash and Winnie had independently agreed on a protocol, in diplomatic parlance a *double entente*: if they passed each other in mixed company and wished to get together alone, each would go and wait for several minutes at the same spot on the opposite side of the ship, port or starboard, for a rendezvous.

But this morning all five of them, Flash, Winnie, Hildegard and the two sisters, felt safe going forward to the sunny starboard rail of the Boat Deck, just past the Verandah Café. The promenade there was less crowded, frequented only by the best class of stroller.

"Well, Winnie," Hazel was innocently saying to her friend as Flash arrived, "you and Alma are getting along in the world. Just one day at sea, and you've already made it up to First Class!"

Winnie gave her a wan look, with a worldly glance to the others. "Yes, it's true," she confessed, affecting boredom. "It's all just a race to see who can finish up the voyage in the Captain's cabin. Alma's already setting her cap for First Mate."

"Now, girls, don't you tease," Hildegard warned as she caught up with the group.

"No indeed, Hazel," Florence chimed in, scolding her sister. "You watch that kind of talk! Our Alma isn't some cheap baggage who runs off with men!" She looked around indignantly, then suddenly appeared flustered. "And neither are you, Winnie," she added, blushing and hardly daring to look up at Flash.

"Well, how is it up in First, anyway?" Hazel continued, examining the well-dressed people on the upper promenade. "Is everything up here gold-plated?"

"Well, I haven't gotten to see the Grand Saloon yet," Winnie said. "The stateroom is darling, two rooms really, with lots of paint and decoration. And no double beds," she added with a prim look at Flo. "The parlor has couches that serve very nicely as berths, single ones. Don't they, my dear?" she inquired playfully of Flash.

"Fairly comfortable," he agreed, laughing. "But you have to curl up to fit, and if the ship rocks too much, it could dump you out on deck."

"Even so," Winnie went on grandly, "the lamps and curtains are adorable, and the plumbing is simply divine. Maybe sometime we can sneak you girls in for a look."

"Oh, that would be delightful," Florence said, perking up.

"Let us please save the visit for the last day of the voyage," Hildegard declared. "We don't want to call any unwanted attention to Alma, and spoil the whole trip for everyone."

"No—or have that nosy steward hanging around anymore," Hazel said.

"We'll wait until we're almost there, safe in English waters," Florence agreed.

"Well, all right," Winnie said. "But I'd hardly call it safe, when there'll be German U-boats lurking all around. Not to mention floating mines, aeroplanes and Zeppelins coming after us." She huffed in disgust. "We could all be sunk to the bottom, and if we do make it over to the Continent, we're just as likely to be caught and raped by Huns."

"Winifred Crocker, what a thing to say!" Nurse Hildegard waxed indignant. "The United Nursing Service League is better organized than that," she haughtily added. "Besides, we shan't be anywhere near the front, not if we're assigned to a convalescent center or a refugee hospital."

"Well, what does that matter?" Winnie challenged back. "The Huns raped all of Belgium, didn't they? That's a whole country, even if it was just a little one—burning cities, poisoning wells, putting babies on bayonets!"

"Now, Winnie, don't exaggerate and frighten the others," Hildegard admonished. "And don't you give in to this war hysteria. The Austrians and Germans aren't savages, after all."

"Well, it was the Kaiser who first named them Huns, not me," Winnie said. "They do terrible things wherever they go."

Flash felt obliged to step in. "Some of those war atrocity stories are overblown," he said. "The babies on bayonets thing, nobody's ever photographed that. And raping a whole country, that's just propaganda."

"Well, what about sinking passenger ships? I've seen pictures of that! And machine-gunning the survivors in the water, and in lifeboats? Isn't that real?"

"Wasn't that after the ship tried to ram the sub?" Flash was facing Winnie, leaning on the rail and trying to be easy-going, not wanting to start another tedious fight. "Bad things happen in war. Are you really that down on the Germans?"

"Why do you think I signed up as a nurse?" Winnie said. "I don't suppose they'll give me a gun, so it seemed like the next best thing."

"Well, sure," Florence put in. "It may be years before America gets into the war, and meanwhile we've got to do something to save civilization."

"I'll definitely grab a gun if one of those Huns comes after me," Hazel added defiantly.

"I see," Flash said, amused by their ferocity. "You ladies certainly have a lot of spunk."

"May I remind you girls," Hildegard declared, "that our nursing service is over there to help people, not shoot them! America hasn't taken sides in this war, and neither have we. You very likely could be called upon to treat the wounded from both sides." She cast her chin upward in a noble pose. "Mercy is our watchword."

"Yes, sure, I'll treat them," Hazel said. "But do I have to treat them nice?"

The others laughed at this, and the skirmishing seemed to be over. As milder and more ladylike banter resumed, Flash drew Winnie aside.

"Say, Win, I have an idea, and it sounds like you'd be up for it. Why don't I do an article, an interview with you and the other nurses? But focusing on you, I mean."

"Am I that newsworthy, Flash?" Winnie's look at him was forgiving, even teasing. All she needed was a parasol to twirl over her shoulder.

"Well, yes, a typical American girl—and the whole nursing mission, this voyage, facing danger to help others—the readers eat that stuff up. I'm talking about a feature story, maybe for next Sunday, if I can get it to a wire in England soon enough. With a few good pictures, we'll have it made." Stepping back in the bright sunlight, he raised his camera and snapped her profile.

"I thought Matt was the reporter," she said. "Will he mind getting scooped?"

"I can write too, and the photography leaves me lots of time. I've got to break into reporting eventually." Changing camera slides, he lined up another shot. "Anyway, Matt was interested in this story when we first met, obviously. But now he's onto bigger things."

"Alma's secrets, you mean, and getting the goods on Boss Hogan."
Her voice became hushed and discreet. "But what about Alma? Won't a
story like this endanger her?"

"Nah, we don't have to mention her at all," Flash said, shooting his
picture. "And it won't be printed until sometime after we reach port.
Nothing much is going out from the ship's Marconi because of radio
silence. We'll have to cable the story and photos from Europe."

After reloading the camera and slinging it over his shoulder, he took
a pencil and notebook from his jacket pocket. "Now, then..."

"Since you put it that way," Winnie said, "where do you want to start?
I was born in Concord, New Hampshire, in 1895..."

Chapter 13

Gallipoli

Reggie preferred the nights to the days here in Turkey. The invasion beachhead looked almost lovely by night, a cluster of bright electric lamps stretching below his post, instead of just a mass of dugouts on a hill. Down the brushy slopes on the night breeze wafted the scents of wild coriander and thyme—fragrant Mediterranean herbs trying their best to sweeten the foulness of war.

True, the night sky would intermittently be lit by gun-muzzle flashes and shell bursts, garish fireworks blazing in silence, until their thudding reports echoed back across the darkness of Anzac Cove. Australia–New Zealand Army Corps, that was, the awkward English initials given to an ancient, foreign strip of water. The shells would hit mainly ashore, but at night you could hardly see the effects, the rubble and dust and tumbling bodies as men dove or were blasted to earth.

"How goes it, Reg? Is Johnny Turk coming down tonight?"

"Not so far, Willie. Nothing moving out there yet."

The nights were cool on the coast, so you didn't feel the thirst. You could go a long time between sips, making your water ration last, and the Tommies could wrestle up fresh barrels along with ammo and biscuit and bully beef. You could move supplies up in the dark, or go to the tank to refill your canteen, without being so worried about snipers.

"I don't know why we're just sittin' here," Willie the Aussie newcomer said. "We should push inland to Constantinople."

"Onward and upward, eh?"

Upward, indeed. You couldn't see the impressive landscape at night, the tall, rugged coastal ridges. There was no joy in scenery anyway, knowing that every hill and ridgetop was controlled by the Mustafas, and that sooner or later you'd be ordered to go up and capture a crest, very likely getting yourself killed in the bargain.

"You Pommies have it easy," the Aussie said. "Barely here a week, and already you're dug in, set. No initiative."

"So, you think it was easy digging these earthworks?"

"Well, you won't need 'em much longer, now that enough Anzacs have landed. We'll be movin' you in off the beach just as soon as the order comes."

"Could happen," Reggie said. "Maybe tonight."

It could indeed, he knew. The only trouble with the nights here in Turkey was that most of the infantry assaults, British and Turkish alike, came at night.

* * *

Word came up the line later that evening. Attack at midnight, relying on surprise, without any naval bombardment. Straight up the hill, and swarm the trenches before Johnny Turk could wake up.

"Trench warfare, they're calling it," Willie muttered to Reg, pulling out his hip flask and taking a swig for courage. "Here at Anzac, we don't have trenches, just ledges."

He waved his flask at the camp below, crowded with new men filing into place. "These goat trails, cut into the hillside with a few cubby-holes dug in...but don't dig too deep, or it's your grave, ain' it? Crikey, I can't wait to see the last of this place. Here, let's have a drink to it!"

Reggie took a pull from the flask. Having dug some of the trench lines in far-off Belgium and fought in them too, he had to agree. When they pulled him out through France, and he gladly boarded the big four-stacker troopship in Calais harbor, he never would have believed it could be taking him anyplace worse than Flanders.

"And the no-man's-land," Willie was saying. "Here it's bad, because you don't charge across it. You *climb* it, up these jolly hillsides steeper than attic stairs."

Reg handed the flask back, also delivering solemn counsel. "For every foot ahead, you've got to clamber a foot up, and dodge machine gun sprays, bombs and rocks rolling down, not to mention your own fallen mates." He passed the flask back. "Stay low if you can."

"Right enough," Willie said, taking his final nip. "Now we just wait for orders from godly General Godley."

* * *

The attack went off on time, except for some New Zealanders who were delayed getting into position, lucky blokes as it turned out. The whispered command passed down the line, and the troops heaved themselves up the embankment to clamber along the slope.

Rifle butts scraped on rock, boots crunched gravel, and it wasn't long before the machine guns woke up. Over shouts from the Turkish trenches and scattered rifle fire, the German Spandaus hammered here too, stitching industrial death into the ragged Allied lines.

Reggie pushed on ahead as his mates fell on either side. In the darkness lit by staccato gun flashes, Willie was nowhere to be seen. Reg ran alone, stumbling and staggering upward, his lungs burning with effort after a dozen steps. The Turkish trench was close, so close; already Reg was past the deadly arc of the machine gun. Falling on one knee, he felt a bullet pluck at the shoulder of his coat, shock but no pain, and he fired his rifle at dim figures ahead.

Then he was up, lurching into someone in the dark. The heavy stink of Turkish tobacco told him it was an enemy. He shoved the man back, leveled his rifle waist-high, and jabbed savagely with the bayonet fixed to the end. The man groaned and fell at the edge of the trench, pulling the rifle barrel downward.

Another enemy shape rushed down out of the dark, the wide-mustached face lit by gun flashes. Reggie wrenched free his Enfield, but the second Turk fired first, striking him in the hip. As he toppled into a chasm of pain, the man lashed out with his rifle butt, knocking Reg back downslope. He rolled, tumbled, and sank into the blackness of night.

* * *

Weeks later, the days and nights were measured only by sun yellowing the olive drab canvas of the hospital tent. Hot summer gusts and occasional sea breezes blew through the field hospital on Lemnos, out in the Aegean. The staging island was safely removed from the battle, so far away that only an occasional thundering of naval bombardments could be heard. Life, likewise, was quiet and far off, the time's passage clouded by pain, morphine, and laudanum to bring sleep.

The staff was mostly Aussies and Canadians. The male orderlies and female nurses were patient and understanding with the few Brits in their midst. One Saturday morning, three of the men came in and rolled Reg, over his protests, onto a stretcher.

"What is it, another surgery?" he mumbled vaguely, flinching from the fear of the pain even though it was dulled by narcotics.

"The surgery you need is in England," the lead nurse told him with a smile. "We saved your leg, but if you want to use it, it will take better than we can provide. You're being invalided out, now that transport has arrived." She patted his cheek in gentle farewell as the stretcher-bearers carried him out into blazing daylight.

"What ship is it?" he asked, shading his eyes. "I heard a whistle out in the bay last night." Cocking his head up and craning his neck, he could see a vast gray shape anchored in the harbor before them, the four tall stacks getting up steam. "Looks like the same one I came over on from England."

"Why, it's the *Mauretania*, mate," one of the medics told him. "She'll have you home in no time. A regular luxury liner, she is."

"Aye," the other stretcher bearer agreed. "And the fastest ship on the ocean, speedier now than her sister *Lusitania* ever was."

Chapter 14

Deck Games

Matt had resolved to be patient with Alma. Keeping company with her was pleasant, certainly, and she was easy enough to get along with. There'd been none of the moodiness or scheming he might expect from someone with her past. But there was also a feeling of unfinished business, and it was more than just his reporter's instincts at work. He sensed that her secrets and past fears were obstacles that held her back from him as a person, and from any close relation they might have. Whether it was mere secrecy or outright deception, he had yet to learn... if, indeed, she knew the difference.

On the other hand he allowed that, after what she'd been through, it must take him time to win her trust. And all the more so her intimacy. Could a seven-day sea voyage possibly be enough?

For strolling, Alma said she favored the forward areas of First Class where she felt less likely to be recognized. The two of them didn't join in the deck entertainments that were held there, such as the three-legged race and the egg toss. But they did, in their roles as professional journalist and secretary, watch from a discreet distance.

With her new dark tresses, she seemed at ease in public. She even ignored the admiring second looks from passers-by, which Matt knew were inevitable. Her seemingly unlimited wardrobe included a tailored brown waist jacket and a slightly daring mid-calf skirt—worn with plaid knee socks to protect her pretty legs from intrusive ocean breezes, or so he speculated. But the prevailing winds blew from home, out of the west, so the effect of Lusitania's eastward progress was to cancel most of their force and make the spring days mild and pleasant.

"Have you seen the ship's pool?" he asked, idling with her by the port rail.

"A swimming pool?" Alma marveled. "Where, below decks?"

"No," Matt laughed, "it's a betting pool in the Grand Saloon. Every morning, you can write down the distance you think the ship will travel that day and place your dollar bet. Next day, the most accurate guess wins the pot."

"Hmm, in miles or knots?" Alma asked.

'Nautical miles," Matt said. "Knots are a measure of speed, not distance."

"Well, a knot is just over a mile an hour," she said. "So, at top speed, twenty-four hours times twenty-five knots would be, let's see, six hundred miles."

Matt nodded, genuinely impressed. "More than land miles, too. A nautical mile is over six thousand feet instead of 5,280—at least ten percent farther," he calculated.

"Oh, is it?" Alma asked, meeting his challenge. "But then, I guess you'd have to allow for that, too."

She pointed astern and upward, toward the smoking funnels that rose behind them.

"Are we at full power, do you mean?" he asked, following her gaze to the smoke plumes. "That looks like quite a head of coal to me."

"Yes, but don't you see," she insisted, "none of it's coming out of the rear stack. Nothing at all, so far on this voyage. In news photos of the ship, I've always seen all four chimneys smoking."

Matt looked again and saw that it was true. The mingled smoke and steam that billowed from the funnels was driven along with the ship by the westerly breeze in three blackish-gray columns braiding skyward. The fourth funnel by itself gave off only the faintest wisp of vapor.

"By damn," he said, puzzled. "I'll have to ask the crew about that. Maybe they're cleaning the boilers or something."

He turned back to Alma. "I've got to hand it to you, that's pretty darned observant."

"It's not like the *Titanic*," she explained patiently. "The fourth stack there was just a dummy, a ventilator. I read about all of that after the sinking."

"Oh, was it?" Matt sobered, remembering her tragic family story. This special knowledge of hers seemed to confirm it.

"Well, it's hard to see how we're making full speed on three boilers." he said at last, leaning back against the rail. But then he saw Alma glancing over her shoulder. "What is it?"

"Behind me, but don't stare...the man we met at departure." She rolled her eyes back to indicate a stout, mustached fellow. He was approaching among the passengers scattered in deck chairs and along the rail. "It's the Dutchman who was talking to Miss Hildegard. He might recognize me. Should we let him see us here?"

"Well, if he's in First Class, he'll run into us at meals," Matt said. "You've changed your look, and we have a cover story. Here's our chance to try it out."

"Do you think he'll suspect anything?" she asked, edging slightly away from Matt along the rail.

"We'll soon find out." He winked. "I'll keep him busy. You can take off if you want, and wait for me on deck. I won't be long."

Straightening up from his slouch against the rail, Matt stepped forward and held out his hand as the man's steps angled toward the couple. "Good day, sir, I'm Matthew Vane. We met yesterday, but we weren't introduced."

"Mr. Vane." The man took Matt's hand in his elegant gray-gloved one. "I am Dirk Kroger of Holland. You are American, yes?" At Matt's assent, he added, "I've been on a trading visit to your country, buying some of the finest furs from your Great Lakes and Canada." He touched his top hat, stylishly low-cut for travel, made of brushed sable.

"New York, of course, is still the great trading center," he added with a smile aside to the lady, "ever since it was founded by my Dutch ancestors three centuries ago."

"You can call me Matt. I'm pleased to meet you, Mr. Kroger." Matt spoke to reclaim the man's attention, which was wandering to Alma.

"Thank you, Matt," the Dutchman told him cordially. "Call me Dirk if you like, in your informal American fashion." He glanced pointedly again to the woman by the rail.

"Dirk, this is my secretary, Miss Brady." Matt said, indicating Alma. "She was just leaving, I'm sorry to say."

"Miss Brady." Kroger tipped his hat, making a small bow.

His urbane smile didn't hint whether he recognized her, though Matt guessed it would have been hard for an alert gentleman not to.

"Good day." Barely nodding to the Dutchman, Alma turned and headed away forward.

Kroger looked after her, still smiling. "A lovely lady, but I regret that she has changed her hair since yesterday." He turned his gaze on Matt. "At home, too many of our pretty tow-headed Dutch girls want to look like the raven-haired songstresses of Paris."

"Anything for fashion," Matt said, dismissing the matter with a shrug. "I'm a reporter for a New York paper, so I'm always on the track of interesting people. Will you be able to get back home to Holland from England, do you think?"

"Yes, I expect so. Traffic from Britain to the Netherlands has just opened up again. A terrible thing, this war. Will you cover the fighting in France?"

"I hope to, yes," Matt said. "I might even travel to Germany and report from their side. Would it be possible to go through Holland, do you think, Dirk?"

"I don't see why not, though you might be the first. It would help you give the news fairly. I salute you as a fellow neutral." Kroger shook his head in concern. "I must say, some of your press coverage in America seems biased toward England."

Matt smiled tolerantly. "With the language difference, and all the traffic between America and Britain—this ship, for instance—" he waved at the deck around them— "it's hard for an English-speaker to be impartial. But American opinion is still very much divided."

"And this American opinion, as you call it...is that the thoughts of ordinary Americans, or is it the cleverly worded preaching of a few opinion leaders, with various goals in mind?"

"Well, Lippmann and Mencken, my writer colleagues, would have something to say about that. They'd probably argue along those same lines. But I'd still say that Americans, if they have access to all sides of a story, can form their own opinions."

"I hope you are correct in that, Matt."

They talked on for some minutes, a little light morning sparring. When he'd finished, having jotted down Kroger's cabin number and his business address in the Netherlands, Matt went off in search of his secretary.

* * *

Alma had crossed through a passage to the sunny starboard promenade where morning games were in progress. She didn't want to confine herself to the stateroom just yet on this bright day. And she knew that the first place for Matt to seek her should be, under what had become protocol for the nurses and their male protectors, the side of the ship directly opposite.

In any event, rather than hiding away, she felt safer being seen and accepted here in the First Class *milieu*. As much as she feared exposure, a part of her dreaded solitude even more. Matt had already gone a long way toward restoring the pride and confidence she felt in male company. And now her need for his protection was growing into something more, small rhapsodies of girlish urgings and yearnings that she'd left so far behind she'd almost forgotten them. Would there come a time when these feelings again drove her to risk everything?

As she emerged onto the deck promenade, a race was underway. Six women were running and stooping to pick up potatoes, which they placed in baskets carried under their arms. The spuds were laid out at regular intervals along painted on deck, which ended at a finish line attended by a Cunard officer with a whistle.

As Alma watched, a spry young woman in a long cloth coat bent to scoop up her last potato. With a final dash she reached the finish line, her shoes clattering on deck along with those of the other racers. When the last contestant crossed over, a whistle was blown to scattered applause. The deck officer recorded the winner's name and handed her a small prize. Smiling, the woman scanned the dispersing crowd, looking for some face but not finding it. She then wandered alone to the rail near Alma.

Alma felt attracted to the pleasant-looking girl, perhaps because she seemed slightly out-of-place in First Class. Her brown Oxford shoes, brown coat and hair pinned up in a simple bun were ordinary—not dowdy, but *déclassé* for the setting. Yet her manner, as she shaded her eyes to look out over the bright sea, was simple and youthful. On an impulse Alma said to her, "Congratulations! You race very well."

The woman met Alma's smile with a frank look. "The game wasn't so different from working on the farm, really, back in Manitoba. We grew no end of potatoes there." She glanced up and down the promenade. "My... Robert, my husband, wasn't here to see me win. He was called away when

I'd already joined up for the race. But I have the proof right here, to give him when he's free." From her coat pocket she took the silver *Lusitania* medallion with a blue ribbon that read: "First Prize Ladies Potato Race."

"Very nice, Mrs....Matthews," Alma said, reading the name inked on the ribbon. "My name is Alma," she added.

"Mine's Annie," The Canadian farm girl put away her medal and pressed Alma's extended hand. "Annie Matthews," she added somewhat needlessly, glancing over her shoulder for the one she missed.

"Is your husband an officer, then?" Alma asked.

"Oh no, not on the ship," Annie said, looking a bit flustered. "He's not one of the crew, I mean. He was just called off on business with some friends of ours, below."

"Why are you two going to Europe?" Alma felt herself moved by sympathy and curiosity to ask. Evidently, too, she was picking up some of Matt's questioning habits. "Is he planning to enlist?"

"Yes, that's it exactly," Annie answered in a rush. "Well, not exactly, not really," she added. "It's just that—" She stopped in confusion, a blush spreading over her fair features.

Alma felt sorry for the simple farm girl. "Oh dear, I didn't mean to pry," she said, moving close and touching the young woman's shoulder to put her at ease. "I was just making conversation."

"No, it's all right. It's just that..." she blushed more deeply, and then blurted out her confession in a whisper. "Robert and I aren't really married–not yet, anyway. But we will be soon, in England, before he joins his regiment." Clinging close to Alma's sleeve, she spoke in an urgent murmur. "He's really very kind and attentive, but he owes his first duty to God and King and Country, of course. I'll stay over there and see him when I can."

To Alma's relief, the girl stopped speaking before any tears poured forth. "Oh, my dear," she said, putting her arm around both of Annie's sturdy shoulders. "It must be sad for you. So many of us are in the same... situation." She stopped then, not wanting to be too confiding.

"Well," Annie said bravely, "it all will work out just fine. It'll be so much better once we're married."

"Oh yes," Alma said, giving Annie a final pat on the back. "It will be just wonderful, I know."

As the two disengaged, a brisk male figure strode up and took possession of Annie. "Well my darling, your games are over, I see." Tall, short-haired and hatless, he looked around, his gaze seeming to pass right over Alma's head.

"Oh yes, Robert," Annie breathlessly said, turning to give him a hug. "I won the race, in First Place...Alma here is my witness," she added, beaming in pride at her new friend.

"You did? Very good, then. We'd best be on our way." Turning ramrod-straight on his heel, he led bride-to-be off as she chattered happily, showing him the medal she'd won.

Alma was left alone to muse about the strange, confessional meeting she'd just had. She debated going back to the cabin, but it wasn't long before Matt found her there on deck. As he breezed up, she took his arm and fell into stride with him.

"I'm glad you remembered our system," she said.

"Flash's system, you mean," Matt answered. "He's a resourceful lad. I could use more of his techniques. Who was that couple you were talking to?"

"Oh, that was Annie from Manitoba. Her boyfriend came and got her. They're not really married, but don't tell."

"He looks military," Matt said.

"Yes, well, he is, or soon will be. They're going to tie the knot in England. Or so she was telling me, while he was off on some kind of business below, with some friends."

"Hmm, suspicious," Matt said. "Makes me wonder if the *Lusitania* really is serving as a troopship, as the Germans claim."

"Fine, just what we need, troops to protect us," Alma said with a shiver. "What about Mr. Kroger? Did he ask about me?"

"No," Matt said. "But he recognized you and noticed your hair. He didn't press me about it." With a confiding glance he added, "These Continentals tend to be broad-minded about male-female relations."

She didn't react to his implication. "He's for real, then?"

"Well, he's European. But his accent sounds *Hochdeutsch* to me, more High German than Nether-landish. And if I'm not mistaken, that's a dueling scar on his cheek."

"So he's really a German," she mused, "like so many of our 'Pennsylvania Dutch' back home? I can't say I blame him for hiding it, if he wants to do business in England or the States."

"I think he's military, too. At Prussian officer's schools, they wear special fencing masks with cutaway cheeks, to give each other what they call a beauty mark. Then they rub salt in the wound to make it really pretty."

"You think he's a German spy, then?" Alma asked, amazed.

"It wouldn't surprise me," Matt said. "Being a Dutch fur trader sounds to me like a good cover story for getting all over the world and meeting every sort of person."

"Strange to say, that sounds like a relief," Alma decided. "He's not so likely to be after me, then."

Matt laughed. "Maybe we all should be relieved. With a German spy on board, the U-boats may not try so hard to sink us." Abruptly he changed the subject. "Have you decided what to do about Jim Hogan?"

Alma suddenly felt on her guard again. "Other than just disappear, you mean?"

"Well, there's a fair chance of that, in this war. But you'll still be looking over your shoulder."

She could see him preparing his sales pitch, putting on his reporter's face.

"The question is," he said, "do you want to hit him back?"

"Try to ruin Hogan, you mean?" Oddly, she didn't feel particularly frightened by the idea. "And then not worry about the consequences?" she added, almost as an afterthought.

"Sounds to me like it wouldn't make much difference," Matt said with evident frankness. "At least, if you hurt him enough, he may not want you back anymore."

His keeping up the pressure like this made her think with a perverse touch of pride that he really was good at his job.

"What is it he wants from you anyway, exactly?" Matt was saying. "Do you know for sure? It's more than just revenge, isn't it? And not just ownership of you personally?"

"You're right," she finally had to admit. "There's something I took. He wants it back, or maybe just wants it destroyed."

"It's information, then?" Matt's voice managed to sound casual, or at least not too terribly greedy.

"Yes, maybe...I'm not sure," Alma admitted. "I'll show it to you when we're alone later." She gripped his arm. "You could make it public...but not too public." She clung to him, not caring if her closeness made her seem desperate.

* * *

On the Boat Deck, standing well astern near the Verandah cafe, Winnie huddled with Flash over a cherry phosphate. The small tables of the Saloon Class diner were open to the air like a Paris café, but sitting there would have been less private. She wouldn't have minded it, but he preferred to stand in the lee of a lifeboat a little way off.

Winnie enjoyed sharing her personal history with the intrepid young reporter. "Concord is the state capital, you know. Miss Hildegard came there on her speaking tour. My parents were so impressed that they gave a hundred dollars to her United Nursing Service League. But I don't think they ever expected to donate their daughter to the cause."

The intimate press interview was great fun. Flash even took notes, jotting down names and dates. But when a commotion of shrill piping and stamping feet broke out nearby, Winnie stopped suddenly.

"They're manning the lifeboats," she said, gazing astern.

Flash turned to look at the small group of stewards and crewmen assembled by the rail. "It must be a drill."

"Let's hope so," she said, watching how perfunctorily they gathered around a single rowboat. With much grunting and scuffling, they pulled the heavy canvas cover off the craft and laid it aside, then turned in a ragged line to salute their officer.

As the two watched, the pipes shrilled again. The crewmen began climbing one-by-one into the boat as it rocked on its wooden cradles. "Aren't they going to practice lowering it?" Winnie wondered aloud.

"If they did, they'd need more men on the ropes," Flash said. "And maybe five times that many more to haul it back up again."

He pointed up at the block-and-tackle moorings of the heavy boat right next to them. "Those tackles are set up to lower boats, not necessarily raise them. Especially not with a load of passengers aboard."

Another whistle sounded, and the men in the boat held their oars vertical while seated, sitting upright as if at attention.

"Anyway," Flash added, "They can't lower any boats into the water while we're moving. The hulls would drag behind or swamp in the bow wake."

"Well, if there's danger, at least the crew knows how to save themselves," Winnie said, laughing. "What a relief–will they have boat drills for the passengers, too, I wonder?"

"I don't know," Flash said. "They may not want to frighten us."

"They're doing a fine job of frightening me already."

As they watched the boat being covered up again, another passenger standing near them caught Winnie's attention. He appeared to be dressed in Highland fashion, not in a kilt but short breeks buckled at the knees, a wool jacket and a tam-o'-shanter cap. Under his arm, instead of bagpipes, he held a life vest. It was of the ship's standard type, trademarked as Boddy Belts, that were stored in racks around the decks and in all the staterooms.

"I wouldn't worry about putting that on," Winnie reassured the man. "It's only a drill, after all."

The young Scotsman smiled back. "I know, but judging from that sorry performance, we'd all best learn to use these—if only for jumping into the sea before we crawl into the boats."

He slipped the jacket on over his head. "See here, it's not as easy as it looks. If you put it on like a coat, you've got it upside-down and you'll end up floating that way. My name's Holbourn, by the way, Ian Holbourn from the bonny isle of Foula, off the Scottish mainland." He extended his hand. "So you see, I know my way around boats."

The couple shook hands with the slight figure, smiling at his appearance in the bulky jacket on top of his other regalia.

"I'm Winnie, and this is Flash. We're from America."

"Well, I think the crew should give lessons in how to use these...what are you Americans calling them, Mae Wests?"

"You bet," Flash said, "ever since Mae introduced the Shimmy last year on Broadway." For his enthusiasm, he received a mock-jealous pout from Winnie.

"Well, these life belt instructions are far too easy to miss," Holbourn said. He pointed to an illustrated placard on the wall nearby. "See here, the main part goes over and the straps go under."

He turned to one of the blue-clad officers leaving the just-completed boat drill. "Excuse me, this is the correct way, isn't it?"

"Looks fine to me, sir," the man said.

"Really, you should offer lessons in putting these on, and make sure that everyone attends and learns how. It's not as simple as it looks."

"I wouldn't worry, sir," the crewman said politely. "In one hundred years at sea, Cunard's never lost a passenger, sir."

"Well, I doubt that the submarines were quite so formidable a hundred years ago," Holbourn replied. "There really ought to be lessons for these. Tell me, to get approval for my suggestion, whom should I speak to?"

"Why, the captain, sir," the crewman said respectfully. "He'd have to approve any scheme like that."

"Right enough," Holbourn said. "Then I'll be having a chat with Captain Turner." He turned to his newfound friends. "How about you two, are you with me?"

Chapter 15

Stowaways

Steward Smyte carried his tray of warm suppers below, riding the service elevator down to E Deck. The food smelled good...sausages with fried potatoes, green beans, and even a small helping of plum duff for dessert. Along with it came a big pot of steaming tea. It was ample fare for prisoners, and for non-paying German ones at that. They could hardly complain about their treatment aboard the *Lusitania*. A sight better than he himself, Jeremy Smyte, had gotten last year while in German custody.

Their temporary brig was in Third Class. Steerage, it once would have been called, though it was far from the creaking, leaky rudder gear of the old sailing-ship days. This improvised lockup lay well forward under the bridge, in easy reach of the Captain and deck crew. Though, like as not, they never visited down here.

Third Class was sorely under-booked in this direction, with so very few homesick emigrants traveling back nowadays to visit a war zone. The ship was losing money, the older hands said, even with a large share of the lower-paying cabins knocked out recently to expand the forward cargo hold. The increased transport was for war shipments, of course... but no one would discuss that.

The guard on duty at the brig was Clive, another lowly steward. No surprise, with so many of the deckhands and officers drawn off to the Royal Navy and the merchant fleet. Jeremy greeted him in a playful Cockney accent as he drew near. "'Ey, Guv'nor, 'ow goes it?"

"Oh, Smyte, is it?" Clive straightened on his stool against the corridor wall. "Bringing supper, are we?" Standing up from his stool as Smyte approached, he lifted the lid off one of the plates, peeked in and sniffed it. "Not a bad supper, for rats."

"How are they behaving?" Jeremy asked. "Is it safe to open the door?"

"Oh, one of them's a bit 'round the bend," Clive said, reaching into his pocket for the key. "But I imagine the two of us old tars can handle any three sneaking German spies."

As he brought out the key with his right hand, his other hand patted the steel marlinespike that sagged out of his left pants pocket.

"You swabs in there!" he announced loudly. "Are you ready for mess call?" He put an eye to the peephole that had been cut in the door. "Stand well back, if you are...aye now, and sit! Down on your bunks, the three of you!"

His commands were greeted with murmurs in German, including one shrill, plaintive voice that rang through the bulkhead. But after a moment the big steward grunted in satisfaction, applied his key to the lock, and pushed open the door. Leading the way in, he announced, "Here comes your vittles. Stay put, now."

Maneuvering his tray through the entry, Jeremy saw three pale faces fixed on him. He set out the plates, cups, and spoons, all the utensils the prisoners were allowed, and poured the tea for them. Then he backed out through the door, with Clive following and locking it after.

"A pity the blokes don't speak English," Jeremy said.

"Oh, they're probably good enough at it, but won't admit to it," Clive said. "No matter, the ship's German interpreter couldn't get anything out of them anyway." He eyed Jeremy. "So, will you be off now?"

Jeremy shrugged. "I'm to wait here for the crockery and return it. Nothing much else to do meanwhile." He kept his tone casual. "I imagine you'd fancy a break from watch duty?"

"That I most certainly would," Clive said heartily. "I could go for a wash-up and a change, and then maybe a few of those fried bangers for me-own self. Thanks, Matey!" He started off up the corridor.

"Should I have the key?" Jeremy called after him.

"Not on your life, mate! I'm charged with it, and I'll keep it safe." He left, also taking along in his pocket the steel knout. "I won't be any time at all."

*　*　*

At the end of the Third Class corridor, Dirk Kroger kept out of sight. The yellow electric dimness allowed him to look around the corner of the passage unobserved, while the metal walls carried the two stewards' voices to his ears. He had no wish to be seen, since it could be awkward explaining his presence in this unpopulated section of the ship.

When the watchman finally turned and left, he walked forward to join Steward Smyte.

"There you are," Smyte murmured to him, glancing warily up and down the corridor. "I have no key, but you can talk to them through the peephole."

"That is fine," Kroger said. "It isn't time yet to get them out." Walking to the door, he swung up the cover plate. "Meissner!" he barked in brisk German fashion. "Is Gerhardt Meissner here?"

"*Sie kennen meinen Namen,*" came the reply.

"Yes, I know all your names," Kroger sternly answered. "You will know me as Farber. I am an agent of *Kaiserliches Marines Befehl*, German Naval Intelligence. The code word for this operation is *Reichstadt.* Do you agree?"

"*Jawohl, Herr Farber,*" the man inside the door said in guarded German. He moved close in an effort to peer through the spyhole, which Kroger quickly blocked with one hand. "*Reichstadt Immer,*" the prisoner said, giving the countersign.

A second anxious voice broke through in German. "Are you here to release us?"

"*Nein,*" Kroger said. "That would do no good, since we are all on this ship under the eyes of the enemy. Step back from the door, if you please. My presence here is secret, and you must say nothing of it to the crew, or even to your fellow prisoners, any more than is necessary. Is that understood?"

"*Ja, Mein Herr,*" Meissner said. "How can we be of service, sir?"

"I am here to deliver a message of assurance, that your situation is known, and it will not be forgotten. When the time comes, you will be released, and you may be called upon to assist us in other ways. Now, tell me, has your mission aboard this ship been successful?"

"In part, sir. We did obtain photographs of the starboard gun emplacement on B deck, amidships. No guns in sight, but the gun rings were there. Recently installed for six-inchers, as we were told. Heinz and Erich raised the wooden deck planks, and I took several photographs. However, our camera and film were taken from us by the *Anglischer* Pierpoint."

"You did not manage to pass any exposed film off the ship?"

"No, sir. We were pursued and had to hide. We hid in a pantry and were locked in." The man, Meissner, was clearly ashamed to give the report.

"No guns," Kroger said, "but did you see any evidence of their recent presence? Shell casings, or anything of the sort?"

"No, sir. The gun rings were newly painted and hadn't been greased."

"What about the cargo? Did you see any evidence of illegal war materiel?"

"No, sir, we did not inspect the cargo section."

"Very good," Kroger said, meaning the phrase in a formal sense only. "Is all well with you, then?" he inquired. "Do you stand ready for further orders when the time comes?"

"Sir," Gerhardt said, "there is a serious concern. We are all worried, and one of our men is especially troubled, because of the position we find ourselves in."

"Being captives, you mean?" Kroger asked. "Do not fear, steps are being taken."

"In particular, sir, it is the situation of being held on a ship that may have been targeted by our own High Seas Fleet for attack. We came aboard to aid our country, and were willing to face capture and imprisonment..."

"Imprisonment, yes, and death," Kroger put in. "Are you not aware that spies are shot in time of war?"

"Indeed, sir, that was always a possibility. But we came on board to obtain photographic proof that would, in effect, justify the Lusitania's sinking. And now, if that should occur—as it very likely will—we find ourselves penned up below decks, disregarded under lock and key, with no claim to sympathy from the enemy crew. It preys on the mind, sir, for all of us, but especially Heinz, who is a family man. He has become very frightened."

From the background inside the lockup, presumably on hearing his name mentioned, an inmate raised his voice plaintively. "*Nein, nein, ich muss nicht sinken nach Davi Jones. Hilfe uns, bitte...*"

The whimpering threatened to go on and on, and Kroger barked as harshly as he could through the small peephole. "You, there, you speak utter nonsense! Get hold of yourself! Do you think that our navy would send this ship to Davy Jones' locker, with me on it? It's all part of a plan, so just sit tight and wait for orders. If I wanted to sink this ship or cripple it in mid-ocean, I could do so at will. For now, you are safest right here. Stop whining, and remember your duty to the Fatherland!"

"Yes, sir," Meissner answered for the whiner, suitably cowed by the German's unmistakable tone of authority.

"Come closer," Kroger said, screening the spyhole once again with his hand but bringing his mustached lips near the aperture. Into Meissner's obedient ear, he murmured: "The coward will probably continue to complain. That is not a problem; it will deceive the British. I leave it to you to tell your men what they need to hear. But if he seems in danger of revealing my presence on board, that is a different matter. In that case, I expect you to keep the fool silent. By any means necessary...is that understood?"

"*Jawohl, Herr Farber. Ich verstehe.*" The humble voice on the other side of the door had no choice but to promise compliance.

"Very well, you understand. Finish your meal." With a snap, Kroger closed the peephole cover.

* * *

Steward Smyte followed the one-sided briefing with his limited German, not needing to hear the prisoners' answers. When Kroger used his tone of command, Smyte felt a perverse British pride. He would never, after all, be one of these strutting Prussian tin-soldiers. He might take the Germans' money and do odd jobs for them, but he was independent. They hadn't managed to break him down in their jail, for the petty offense of throwing some drunken sailor into the Kiel Canal. Instead, they'd offered Jeremy Smyte a profitable business engagement, and he would take it and work for whomever he wished—Germany, American gangsters, even the British Crown if the money was right.

Speaking of which, the Dutch-German spy had unrolled a pound note from his money clip and was pressing it into Smyte's hand. "I will leave now," Kroger said, "before your shipmate returns. I know I can trust you to keep silent about this visit. Check for my messages at the usual place. There will be generous rewards for your services to come." So saying, he turned his back on Jeremy and retreated down the dim hallway.

Chapter 16

War News

When the ladies required the stateroom to themselves, Matthew Vane knew of places to go. The First Class reading room on the Boat Deck was the best-stocked library on the Atlantic. Its plush chairs sat grouped informally under painted glass skylights showing the Four Seasons, depicted as aerial nudes after the manner of Boucher...a quiet place to write letters home and catch up on recent, if not up-to-the-minute, journals.

But for Matt this morning, the library was a place to brood. He expected his new friend Alma to reveal all her secrets to him anytime now. But...what then? Until he knew what she had on Jim Hogan— and what he had on her— it was all but useless to wonder how a reporter might deal with it. Best to think of other things.

Today, posted on the board just inside the library door, was the *Cunard Daily Bulletin*. The broadsheet was intended to keep passengers updated on world events, aided by the miracle of Marconi telegraphic news transmission. The main headline read, "Steady Allied Gains at the Front," and the accompanying story painted a decidedly rosy picture. To Matt's way of thinking, all the paper's war-related articles reflected a similar pro-Allies slant. There was bland, breezy coverage of England's Gallipoli invasion in Turkey, which Matt had seen described elsewhere as a bloody stalemate worse than France, if smaller. And in this nautical journal he found no mention of sunken ships, mines or U-boats.

"Things must have taken a turn for the better since we left home," a voice at his elbow said. "That is, if you believe Cunard's news-hounds." Matt turned to find the naval architect, Fred Gauntlett, standing behind him.

"Maybe they don't want the passengers getting frightened," Matt answered good-naturedly. "And then, say, ganging up to turn the ship around."

"Well," Gauntlett said with a wink that barely ruffled his mutton-chop whiskers, "I just hope things don't get too nice and peachy before I've had a chance at signing a production contract with the Brits."

"Not much danger of peace breaking out, I suppose," Matt said, feeling resigned. "I'm certain to get my crack at war reporting, too. Say, Fred," he added, "I'll understand it if you can't talk openly about weapon secrets—or trade secrets, for that matter." He did his best to sound innocently curious. "But just for the sake of my background knowledge, off the record, I'm interested in this new aspect of submarine warfare." Smiling, he tried to hold the man's suddenly restless gaze.

"For example, what could England want with more submarines, with the entire German navy and merchant fleet pretty effectively bottled up in port—no port-wine pun intended there—and her partner Austria-Hungary almost landlocked to begin with? Except for their Austrian U-boats, of course—what's left for an Allied sub to sink?"

Gauntlett looked reluctant, as if torn between the military requirement for secrecy and the more basic American instinct to promote his product.

"Well," he offered at last, "there's always a danger the German High Seas Fleet could break out into the North Atlantic. They'd try to challenge the Royal Navy's supremacy, or else scatter far and wide to do even worse damage to Allied shipping. In that kind of sea combat, submarines would be vital. And they can do even more damage by slipping undetected into ports or naval bases and sinking enemy ships at anchor."

"Yes, the sneak attack— but then, the Central Powers are constantly trying that as well. Aren't there adequate defenses, nets and mines and patrol boats, to keep it from happening?"

"Well, it's a very active part of the war," Gauntlett said, still cautious, "even though not much reported on. Submarine reconnaissance, sub-hunting, mine-laying and detecting—it started with armed fishing trawlers, and now we have Churchill's Q-ships, the armed merchants and Mystery Ships, whether they're real or just talked-up for propaganda purposes. The author Rudyard Kipling has done a whole series of stories about it, called the *Fringes of the Fleet*. It's good propaganda to enlist young sailors, but that's about all you'll find on the topic, stateside at least. This war's still new and changing, with plenty of room for fresh ideas, just ripe for American know-how."

"What new ideas?" Matt prompted, eager to keep up the flow.

"Oh, lots. Take a look at this." Gauntlett led him across the room and handed him a book from one of the shelves that lined the walls. It was a bound volume of London's *Strand Magazine*. Matt took it and sank into an armchair, pleased to see the other man take an empty seat opposite him. Opening to a page that had been bookmarked, he saw a fiction story by H. G. Wells entitled "The Land Ironclads." The illustration showed strange wheeled battlewagons advancing on foot soldiers, firing cannons at them and mowing them down under steel tire treads.

"See, there...and that issue's a few years old. But we could certainly use something like that now, to break the deadlock in the trenches. It's the harsh necessities of war that bring out new technology."

"Necessity's the mother of invention," Matt said, setting the book down. "So what's next? Submarines that crawl out onto the land?"

"Well, maybe." Fred laughed. "I'll make a note of that one. In the long run, in war, a new idea can save lives as well as take them, whether you see it as being offensive or defensive."

"What's this, Freddy?" a third voice abruptly put in. "Are you still pushing your Rube Goldberg schemes?"

The British shipowner Charles Bowring had arrived, evidently to join Gauntlett. He came up and saluted Matt as well, settling into a nearby seat.

"Watch out for this fellow," he told Matt. "Some of his ideas are a bit over the edge."

"Not really," Gauntlett said, looking mildly annoyed but also challenged. "Just consider, if a big merchant vessel like the *Lusitania* sights a U-boat, or is attacked by one—if it, or a whole convoy of ships, were protected by a defensive submarine, one that could ram the attacker at any depth, say, or tag it with an explosive mine—why then, that U-boat would have no choice but to run. With a threat like that deployed under the sea, it wouldn't dare hang around. Maybe not even long enough to launch a torpedo."

He turned to Matt. "U-boats are very fragile, you know, with their thin metal skins under heavy pressure. In time, the threat of such a defense could scare them out of the shipping lanes entirely."

Matt couldn't stay out of this controversy. "Still," he said, "that leaves the problem of finding the U-boat underwater. How are you going to chase it through dark, cloudy seas?"

"Well, I hear there's some work being done with hydrophones." Gauntlett sighed, frowning. "But yes, that's the shame of it all. If not for that one detail, we might be onto something really big."

Matt tried asking about the hydrophones but got no reply. It surprised him how easily Fred seemed to abandon his pet idea. From his sudden change of mood, one might almost suspect that he had a solution in mind, but felt obliged to keep his methods secret. Had he been just toying with his questioners all along?

At that moment, two more men entered the library and came directly over. Both were puffing on cigars, and the air around them was immediately filled with pungent smoke.

"I see we have our foursome for cards," Gauntlett remarked. "Sorry, Vane, but I'm afraid you're the odd man out." Nevertheless he introduced the new arrivals.

"Matt Vane, this is Isaac Lehmann, the big cheese around here in war supplies and munitions, and here's Frederick Stark Pearson, Consulting Engineer. I'm sure that you, as a reporter, have heard of them."

Matt had indeed heard of both men and was quick to engage them while he could. "Fred Gauntlett here was just laying out some ideas on military strategy," he said, keeping it open-ended. "Sounds like more wonders are still ahead."

"Well, if you're contemplating naval affairs," the engineer Pearson said with a wink, "the coming thing is petroleum. The English will be needing more of it soon to drive their fast destroyers, and the new fast battlecruisers with the heavier guns."

"What's wrong with coal?" Matt asked. "We're running on it now, and Lusitania's the biggest, fastest liner on the pond." He politely waved a hand to decline the cigar that Pearson offered him.

"Not fastest at the moment," Lehmann said. "Because of wartime coal costs, and the shortage of crews to shovel it in, we're running on three-fourths of this ship's boiler rooms."

"That's it," Pearson said. "Oil is easier to load aboard on land or sea, and it requires less manpower and crew space. If this vessel were converted to oil, it would have a longer cruising range, like a battleship, and far more cargo or ammo capacity, instead of a few hundred coalers to feed, house, and pay."

"Oil practically pumps itself," Gauntlett pointed out. "It just gushes right out of the ground, and it flows by gravity."

"And it's lighter," Pearson added. "Oil floats, coal sinks. Why, this very ship, on her last voyage to England, sailed with a load of oil pumped into her double hull space, with no one the wiser except her captain and a few of the crew. But don't worry, there's none on this trip," he added with a wink to the others. "I think they were afraid a torpedo might set it on fire."

Matt was good at hiding his surprise. "Well, I know we're building oil-burning ships in America, both merchant and navy ships," he said. "Haven't the British started yet?"

"No need. Steamships can be adapted from coal to oil. This one could easily be, and probably will someday. The problem is, supply...their problem, not ours," Pearson said. "The British Islanders have plenty of coal, but no petroleum to speak of. If they want to float their Royal Navy on oil, their vast fleet that makes them lords of a worldwide empire—they'll have to come to us, their former colony, or else find another reliable source overseas for their petrol."

"It's not safe enough for them to rely on the international markets, I suppose," Matt said tentatively.

"Oh, no indeed, not for the long run," Pearson said. "Markets change and prices are volatile. Pipelines can break or be shut off."

Lehmann leaned forward confidingly. "The inside word, my boy, is Persia. The British Crown has influence in the Middle East, with all their troops in Afghanistan, and this fellow Lawrence of Arabia stirring up desert tribes on the Arabian Peninsula. There's oil there, plenty of it, under the deserts and right around the ancient city of Baghdad, and our British friends have their eye on it. In a month or so from now, they're planning a conference to pinpoint an oil supply, and that's likely to be their target."

"Is that so?" Matt asked, wishing that he dared to take out his notebook.

"Sounds right, young man," Pearson added. "If you want to do some real war reporting, go and visit Mesopotamia, the place they're now calling Iraq. Things'll be heating up there soon."

"Well, there you go, Vane," Bowring the shipper said. "My insider friends here have given you your inside scoop." He reached in his pocket and drew out a deck of cards. "But now, if you'll excuse us, I believe it's time for some bridge."

"Yes indeed, that's our game," Lehmann agreed. "Just so long as it's contract bridge," he added with a wink.

Chapter 17

Central Powers

"*Danke schoen, mein Herr.*" The coachman nodded respectfully, taking the banknote handed over his shoulder. The passenger steadied himself in his seat, and the open carriage clattered to a halt on the cobblestones of old Berlin. The horses whickered as they reined up in front of *Bendlerstrasse 14*, the Naval Ministry.

A government automobile would perhaps have been more fashionable, the lone rider knew. But he personally didn't mind the jolting informality of a short trip from the government complex in the *Kaiser Wilhelmstrasse*. A coach trot around the *Tiergarten* and along the river wasn't too old-fashioned, not even for the Chancellor of all the Reich, and not even in a time of war.

Bethmann-Hollweg didn't wait for his cabbie to dismount. Opening the door, he stepped out unaided and waved a hand to dismiss the carriage.

Undoubtedly the man recognized the tall, distinguished Prussian with his Van Dyke beard and trim officer's uniform. Bethmann-Hollweg habitually dressed in military costume, like most imperial German officials including *Der Kaiser* himself.

The Chancellor paused to inspect the grand façade before him. The peak-roofed portico of the Naval Ministry jutted forth like a great ship's prow along the riverfront. Already the giant building was famous as the Bendlerblock. The structure's size and newness signaled not only the importance of the *Kaiserliche Marine*, but also the growing power of the agency's new master, Tirpitz. Now that Bismarck and Von Bulow were gone, dismissed by a fickle emperor, Admiral Tirpitz was seen as *Der Kaiser's* oldest and most trusted confidant...though how he could be more cherished than Bethmann-Hollweg himself was a puzzle. Had it not been the ever-loyal Chancellor who, in boyhood, offered Kaiser Wilhelm his own shoulder to steady the rifle that killed the one-handed emperor's very first stag?

Striding through the front entry, Hollweg breezed past guards and receptionists toward the inner quarters where the Admiral lived and worked. He had pre-arranged the visit by telephone, and not even Tirpitz would dare to make him wait for long. The two of them were old acquaintances, old adversaries.

At the broad desk of the Admiral's secretary, a busy naval adjutant, Hollweg didn't need to announce himself. He didn't bother taking a seat, but remained standing. He was inspecting a model of the fleet's newest battlecruiser when Tirpitz emerged to greet him.

"*Willkommen, Herr Reichskanzler,*" his host said. "I'm very sorry to have kept you waiting," he added, in a way the Chancellor could not help but find patronizing.

The admiral advanced to clasp Hollweg's hand. To add formality to the meeting, he clicked his heels together and curtly bowed, making his long, and gray, two-forked beard brush against his blue navy lapels.

"*Guten Tag, Herr Admiral.*" Hollweg responded in kind, maintaining the formal tone. As a patient negotiator, he was willing tolerate this jumped-up naval officer's show of importance. Had he not always done so in the past?

"Many thanks for coming. I would have been glad to go and see you at the *Reichskanzlerei*, if not for the harsh maritime demands of this war."

There it was again, the arrogance of a wartime military leader over a peacetime official. "I understand, Admiral."

"Come. If you don't mind, let us walk outside in the courtyard." Tirpitz led the way toward his office's exterior door, which stood open on a tree-lined quadrangle. "To what do I owe the honor of this visit?"

"To the same thing as my last visit, I fear," the chancellor said. "I must ask again that our navy's actions against neutral commerce vessels be more...restrained. I refer to this recent sinking of an American ship, the *Gulflight*, on May the first. With three of the neutral vessel's crew members killed, our foreign office is facing renewed protests from abroad."

Tirpitz sighed. "I, too, feared as much when I read the press account. But come, Theobald—" his sudden switch to a first-name basis signaled, perhaps, that they had passed beyond earshot of the office staff. "This neutral ship, the *Gulflight*, was an oil tanker carrying vital fuel to our enemies. The crew was allowed to escape, but two of them panicked, jumped overboard and drowned. Then after being rescued, the tanker's captain also died of a heart attack. I don't see how Germany can be blamed for that unfortunate chain of events in wartime."

"The ship was torpedoed without warning, against naval law," Hollweg said. "They call us criminals, pirates."

"So says the English press, as ever," Tirpitz countered. "But my U-boat captain let his boat be seen first as a very obvious warning. He stayed on the surface a good three minutes before submerging, but the American ship did not stop or turn around." The admiral paused in the sparse shade of one of the small new courtyard trees. "The very same newspaper account acknowledges that this supposedly neutral American tanker was also being shadowed by a British warship. What are my captains to do?"

"They are to do what you tell them, Alfred," the chancellor said. "Can you not control your subordinates?"

Tirpitz sighed. "A ship is not a land brigade, Theo. A captain at sea bears, first of all, the responsibility for his vessel and the lives of his crew. He must make instant decisions as conditions dictate. I cannot approve or countermand those decisions, even by the miracle of Marconi wireless." Pacing again under the linden trees, the Admiral smiled. "A vessel's captain has more freedom of choice than do I, or you...or even our dear friend the *Kaiser*, with all his ships and officers."

"Yes, but these ships are more than just playthings in *Der Kaiser's* bathtub," Hollweg snorted. "These are real vessels with real lives on board. Innocent lives, some of them, and when they perish, we hear about it. God help us if a great passenger liner is sunk, with important Americans on board. Should that happen, Britain will have a strong new ally in her war against us."

"Britain already has such an ally, but in secret," Tirpitz retorted. "Her former American colony supports her with food, supplies, fuel, and all manner of weaponry and ammunition. My concern is to stop that traffic. If we do not, all is lost."

"All is lost..." Hollweg repeated. "That, as I recall, is what you cried out when our great enemy Britain first entered this war." He scanned the admiral's bearded face for any sign of embarrassment. "Hardly an expression of confidence in our German armed forces."

"All of us make ill-considered statements at times, *Herr Kanzler*," Tirpitz parried, "...such as when you told the British ambassador that our attack in the west was illegal, and that Belgian neutrality was a mere scrap of paper." He stopped again in his pacing and turned to Hollweg. "What I saw then, old friend, when Britain entered the war, is that they are above all a naval power. With control of the seas, they have Germany blockaded. We must in turn blockade them from the battle front, using these miraculous new weapons, the U-boat and torpedo, or all will indeed be lost." The old Admiral smiled at the Chancellor in a direct appeal. "I know navies, and I know these tools, Theo. Years ago I helped perfect the torpedo as a weapon for our *Reichsmarine*."

"As did your opposite number in Britain, their Admiral Fisher, for his Royal Navy in the early days," Hollweg pointed out.

"Yes, he saw the future, as I did," Tirpitz matter-of-factly said. "That is why he is now Britain's Sea Lord, and I am Germany's Secretary of the Navy."

"Secretary *of State* for the Navy, you mean," Hollweg reminded him. "With your increase in authority, to equal mine or the army's, there comes a broader responsibility. Your decisions now affect diplomacy and foreign affairs, not just *Der Kaiser's* battlecruisers and other pet projects." He turned to face the admiral directly. "In that capacity, I ask you: Can it help Germany if every nation in the world turns against us?"

Tirpitz frowned at last. "The only thing that can help Germany now is to choke off the enemy's commerce, before they strangle our homeland. In that, the U-boats are vital. Any restriction on submarine warfare threatens our survival as a nation."

Chapter 18

Roll Call

When Matt finally was about to get Alma alone below decks, he found himself behaving with propriety that was exaggerated, if not awkward. To his request for a couple of hours to themselves, his cabin-mates agreed with sly, knowing permissiveness.

Not wanting to give out any hint of Alma's secrets, he explained, "It's just to be uninterrupted while we get some things done."

"Oh yes," Winnie blandly agreed with him. "I'm sure you too will get quite a lot done."

Flash added helpfully, "As long as you take care not to interrupt each other. Winnie and I have a problem with that sometimes, when we're interviewing."

"So it's purely business then, you understand," Matt held out heroically. He dared a glance at Alma, who seemed amused.

"Why, of course it's business," Winnie said as she pinned on her hat. "Very important business at that."

"Now," Flash said, "if you'll excuse us—" He opened the door, checking for spies as was their custom. "Winnie and I will go and find someplace private."

"Yes," she finished, waiting a decent interval before following him out. "Flash and I have personal business to attend to."

With the door finally shut and locked after them, Matt turned to find Alma demurely at ease.

"Well, those two make quite a pair," he said. "They should take up vaudeville."

"Or maybe burlesque," Alma said lightly. "Though I've never really seen it. Big Jim would take the boys out to the burley-Q now and then, but he wouldn't let me go, much less sing there." She stood poised against the roll of the cabin, waiting calmly. Her cotton dress, flower-printed and tied at the waist, wouldn't have stood up to the chilly sea gusts on deck.

"A burlesque house hardly would have been a showcase for your vocal talents," Matt said. "Those places are pretty raunchy."

"I can guess," she said bitterly, "from having to fight off his drunken friends when they got back."

"Big Jim didn't mind his friends bothering you?" Matt asked.

"Usually Jim didn't come back till next morning," she said.

So much for the charms of intimacy, being alone with Alma. Just as well, Matt thought. "So you split on him," he said. "But you didn't go empty-handed."

"No, I packed up all I could of the clothes he gave me—I had the cabbie help carry it down, and I took his— I don't know what you'd call it. He always kept it in a satchel." She turned toward the bedroom, and he followed.

At the bottom of the narrow closet, she bent and unbuckled her large suitcase. Reaching inside, she drew out a carpet bag with leather straps and handles. She gave it to Matt and sat down on a bed, as he seated himself beside her.

"You took this because...?" he asked, loosening the straps.

"Well, it was important to Jim, and I just wanted something to defend against him with, in case he came looking for me." She sighed. "And to get even."

"Did you want him to come after you?" From the satchel, he lifted out a leather-bound account book and set it on the bed.

"I...don't know. I was confused then. I certainly don't want him after me now."

"Well, the issue may not be so personal, after all. He could be looking for this." From the bottom of the bag, Matt dredged up handfuls of greenbacks, twenties and fifties, and held them up for her inspection.

Alma's jaw dropped. "My heavens, I didn't know that was in there—I never even looked inside, I swear it!"

"The bag's lined with cash." Matt took out several bundles of money and laid them on the embroidered Cunard coverlet.

By their count, there was about six thousand dollars.

"You're pretty good at getting even," Matt remarked. "But would Big Jim, flush as he is, chase you halfway round the world for this? We can assume he didn't report any theft to the police, because of what's in here."

Letting the cash lie in neat stacks, he turned his attention to the ledger. As he opened it, Alma moved across to peer over his shoulder.

Each lined page of the book contained one or more last names, some with initials. Underneath were grids of number entries—most likely whole dollars, in tens or hundreds—arranged in columns by month. Some entries were in pencil, others in red or black ink. A few lines had cryptic labels such as "Station 26" or "Market Village."

"Who else writes in this?" Matt asked, noticing different slants to the entries.

"Besides Hogan, you mean? There's a bald-headed little man who brings it to him."

"Hintermann, the lawyer," Matt said, and she nodded confirmation. "See here, these are family names. Say, are you really sure you should be hiding out in First Class? You might feel safer at the other end of the boat. There are some powerful clans here—Van de Vere, Felton, Bass. I don't see anyone yet that's actually on board. But they're all connected, and they wouldn't be too happy to know we have them in this hoodlum's black book. They'd want it overboard...and maybe us, too."

"What is it, a gambling book?" Alma asked. "Are those racetracks?"

"Bigger than that," Vane said. "They could be transit lines that have to be redrawn to benefit somebody's real estate holdings." He turned a page. "It looks like what we have here is Hogan's muster list, the record of all the payoffs he makes and receives in his borough for graft, vice, and favors, some of them to city leaders. A lot are regular as clockwork. See, here's 32 dollars, month after month, to Atterly—a crooked cop maybe, or a building inspector? And here's $70 a week coming in from Dawkins; I think he runs a tavern with a casino in the back. It could be protection money." He riffled through the pages, which were more than half full. "There's room in here for a whole criminal dynasty. I'll have to spend time with it to follow the threads. And it would take legwork back home to nail down details. But I could put some kind of article together based on this, and then send it back to my friends who'd love to take Hogan's empire apart, brick by brick."

"But if it's published by you, they'll guess where we are and that we're together."

As she said it, Matt felt her anxiety, the soft arm clinging to his. "That's true," he said. I'd have to write under another name and hand it off to others, since I'm going to the war front."

He turned to her, seeing that she looked a little wide-eyed at what she'd stolen. "Don't worry about it now; there's no hurry. The money isn't much good on shipboard, and nothing is going out by wireless. If you decide to make it public, I'll help. If you want to hang onto this..." he patted the ledger, "...Flash might even be able to photograph the pages. Through my contacts in New York, you could mail back the book and the money to Jim in a nice little package."

"What you said..." Alma spoke uncertainly. "Could there really be friends, cronies here in First Class, who'd be looking for me, and who would get word back to Jim? Can he reach that high?"

"No, no, it was just a bad joke." Feeling protective, Matt patted her shoulder. "I'd say we only need to worry about anyone that Knucks may have talked to." He tried a smile. "It's still tough being on the run, isn't it?"

She broke down then, not in sobs but with tears flooding into her deep blue eyes. She let him hold and comfort her as best he could. As he broke off their embrace there was a moment's hesitation, but Alma excused herself and went into the lavatory to wash away her sorrow.

From within the room, after some minutes of freshening up, he heard her singing to herself. Her voice sounded pure and innocent through the paneled door, but with a performer's *timbre* behind it. Real talent there... it was a familiar tune, a love song, a bit melancholy. He'd heard it on a gramophone somewhere but couldn't place it.

All I have left behind
Is just a memory,
A feeling long gone,
Like some half-forgotten melody.
What lies ahead,
A search for something true—
All I have left
Is you.

Later, seated next to Matt on the divan, she confessed, "It's been a different world ever since my parents died. Jim charmed me at first, and all my hopes came back; but then I saw that it was far worse than I ever dreamed. I don't think I could have been happy, even if I'd become what he promised—a respectable wife in a well-to-do household, with sweet children—knowing what was underneath it all. Better to be a nurse in a far-off country, helping poor soldiers and refugees. Even if my life should end there."

Chapter 19

Bridge

Captain Turner stood in his chart room on the command bridge, pondering the Lusitania's course. On the table before him was a map of the North Atlantic seaway. Above it, a window looked directly out over the ship's arrow-pointed bow.

Ahead of them spread the flat, blue-on-blue horizon, blank as the map, and featureless as the view in any other direction. What good is a map, Turner wondered, if it doesn't show what lies beneath the surface?

It had been a fair voyage, though too eventful at the start. Far too much so, with all this stir about U-boat warnings, telegrams, press reporters, and the delay for last-minute transfer of passengers, crew and cargo from another ship. And then came a further delay, a personal embarrassment when his own niece Mercedes, now a New Yorker performing on the Broadway stage, had overstayed her onboard visit with him. He'd had to order the gangplank re-lowered to let her off the ship. Doubtless some of the onlookers had believed her to be his pretty young doxy.

And then of course, the German spies. But that matter had been handled quietly and expeditiously. Now those three were interned below, safe on their way to a full interrogation in England, which lay somewhere beyond the cloudless eastern horizon.

Just outside his inner window ran the glassed-in officers' bridge, centering on the steersman's wheelhouse to the right. Before him in line, as if saluting, stood the bright brass engine telegraphs with their crank handles, speed-setting dials, and chimes for alerting engineers and other key officers. Telephones and electric indicator lights were mounted close by to command and monitor the rest of the ship. And from each end of the control room, covered walkways extended sideways, bridging the vessel's entire width of eighty-seven feet and overhanging the outermost rails. From those vantage points, an officer could look aft along either side of the ship, from the rows of covered lifeboats right down to the waterline. He could also see, signal, or telephone the equally wide docking bridge some six hundred feet astern, just short of the vessel's overall length of seven hundred eighty-seven feet.

Captain Turner's officers, standing forward watch on the military-style bridge, shared his broad view, with three-fourths of the world laid out before them. But they could not easily peer into his sanctum, the room with charts and weather maps where the course was set, and where ultimate responsibility for his ship lay...not unless he invited them in, to be instructed or made privy to some of his innermost thoughts.

Now one of those, his new Junior Third Officer What's-his-name, was tapping at the door, sticking in his white-hatted head and saluting.

"Sir, a deputation of passengers is waiting to see you. I believe you were told of it earlier."

"Yes, yes...is it this Scotsman, then?"

"Aye, sir, with another man and a lady. There has been some disagreement among the passengers, I'm told."

"Has there, now?" Captain Turner sighed, having long since lost track of the fine difference between boredom and impatience. "I'll see them in my day cabin. If you would kindly have them wait there, Mr....Bissett, is it?" Waiting might settle them down a bit.

"Bestic, sir. Aye aye, sir." The mate's head vanished as Turner watched in approval. A new young officer, this Bissett, but straight out of the old sailing ships, like himself. That gave Turner hope for him.

Captain Turner hated dealing with passengers—the bloody monkeys, as he'd been known to call them in a vexed moment. He much preferred letting his Staff Captain Anderson, the suave fashion-plate, distract them. Better to tell them as little as possible. But this Holbourn, a stubborn Scottish lord, couldn't seem to be put off. Sometimes the customers insisted on going all the way to the top, and Cunard Lines had to keep them happy. They weren't under full naval discipline, not quite yet.

Turner's recent predecessor aboard the *Lusitania*, Captain Dow, would have been more ready to deal with pushy passengers. He was a suave, sociable fellow who liked to hobnob with landlubbers, the elite travel set, simpering womenfolk and even their pesty children. "Fairweather Dow" needed no staff captain to cater to them.

The former Captain Dow also put the passengers' concerns first, above his own command—as when, during a torpedo scare a month ago, he'd hoisted an American flag to the mainmast for the final dash into Liverpool harbor, to confuse a lurking sub. His posing as a neutral ship had raised international protest from Americans and Germans alike, but old Fairweather didn't care. He'd resigned his captaincy, so great was his dread of U-boats and of losing a ship full of passengers...along with the knowledge that such brazen false-flag tricks couldn't be repeated forever.

Captain Turner, when asked by Cunard to return to his old post, hadn't hesitated a moment. *Lusitania* had always been a successful command for him. He'd polished his reputation by setting new speed records and tightening up the Atlantic Ferry run. Nowadays, as to enemy action, he didn't worry much. He had faith in this big vessel's speed and durability, in the protection to be afforded by the Royal Navy, and most of all in his own seamanship. Any captain who wanted to serve during this war, merchant or military, would have to get used to dodging U-boats, as Turner had already done successfully aboard Cunard's *Transylvania*. If Dow didn't have the stomach for it, he certainly did.

After waiting a decent interval, he went down the adjoining stair to his day cabin. It was a good-sized room with divans and a locked desk, formal if not quite Spartan. At his order, the former captain's more lavish furnishings had been removed.

As Turner entered, there stood the young Scotsman in his Highland cap, breeches and knee-socks, a compact-built fellow like Turner himself with a serious look. Seated by him were two others, a red-haired Yankee youth and a lovely young lady resembling the captain's own niece, a brunette with a saucy American look about her.

Turner judged that it might not be too trying an interview, since they didn't appear stuffy and pompous, or wide-eyed with awe. But these Scots could be a handful.

"Good day to you," the Captain greeted them, walking up to the leader. "I heard that you wanted to see me—Mr. Holbourn, is it?"

"Ian Bernard Stoughton Holbourn, Laird of the Isle of Foula in Scotland. We're away up in the Shetlands, sir, in case your voyages haven't taken you so far north." The young lord took the captain's hand, shaking it a bit too energetically for Turner's liking. "I'm just returning home from an American lecture tour on classical Scottish literature."

"Pleased," the captain said, escaping from the handshake. A backwoods nobleman, yet traveling Second Class at the wartime fifty-dollar rate, according to the passenger list. A typical thrifty Scot, Turner told himself as the fellow spoke on.

"These are my friends, Miss Winifred Dexter of Concord, New Hampshire, and Lars Jansen of New York, a reporter."

"Call me Flash." The redhead reached out to shake hands, evidently abashed at the use of his given name.

"Oh yes," The captain said, shaking his hand minimally. "I heard there was a press photographer on board." He was relieved not to see a camera pointed at him. "And you, ma'am?" He turned his gaze more congenially to the young lady.

"Call me Winnie," she said, putting out her gloved hand. "I'm a nurse, just a trainee really, traveling to the front."

"Good for you, Miss," he told her, allowing himself a smile as he pressed her delicate fingers. "That shows spirit. Now, what can I do for you?"

"I'll get right to the point, Captain," Holbourn said. Reaching to the chair behind him, he took up a life jacket that he must have brought in.

"There seem to be plenty of life belts, and I've seen crewmen showing people how to put them on." He held up the bulky fiber-filled vest before his host. "But half of the time, the passengers try to don them upside-down. If it's done wrong, it won't save your life—it will positively drown you, if you're unlucky enough to go into the water."

Turner was quick to respond. "These are Boddy's Patented Jackets, the Cunard standard. I've seen them used with good results. Instructions for putting them on are posted everywhere, on all the decks and in the cabins. There shouldn't be any difficulty."

"Yes, Captain, I agree there shouldn't," Holbourn respectfully said. "But then, most people pay the written instructions no heed. In emergencies there's always a scramble, and some of these passengers may not follow any directions that haven't been practiced in advance. In this state of war, it could cost lives."

"It's true, Captain," the one called Flash added. "I've even seen some of the crew start to put them on the wrong way, while they're trying to show us how."

Captain Turner felt himself growing impatient. There were deficiencies with his hastily assembled crew; he knew that only too well. But it wouldn't do share them with this lot.

"I'm told there's some disagreement among the passengers about this," he said coldly.

"Yes, sir," Holbourn admitted. "I was pointing out the problem to some of the officers, and showing people how to wear them properly. Several of the male passengers approached me and said I was frightening the women."

"Yes, precisely," Captain Turner said, deciding to use this argument. "If people become too frightened and any small thing happens, it could cause a panic, which might have far worse consequences than a delay in putting on belts. Such talk can lead to no end of trouble."

"But Captain," the girl Winifred spoke up indignantly, "isn't it better to frighten us a little if it keeps us alive? Women aren't children, to be sheltered from the truth!"

"Why no, of course not, madam," the captain said, putting on a comforting face to answer this new challenge. "But these passengers, men and women alike, can't walk around in a constant state of alert. That's my job, and the crew's. Why spoil everyone else's voyage?"

"Worse than a German torpedo would spoil it, you mean?" Flash blurted out. The red-haired Yank evidently saw the effect of his remark in Turner's face and coloration, for he added, "Captain, sir," several seconds too late.

While Turner recovered from this impertinence, the Scot was on him again. "Sir, these men who don't want to know, they're the real alarmists. I call them the Ostrich Club. They try to hide from danger by burying their heads in the sand and not seeing it. But if the instruction came from you, Captain, they would respect it. Why not have mandatory life belt lessons to make sure everyone learns the proper way? Then at least, if some of them want to be blind, it's their own fault, and others will be there to show them when the time comes."

"Yes, Captain, he's right," the Yankee maiden chimed in. "And the lifeboat drills are a joke too, if you'll pardon my saying so. Instead of just climbing in and saluting, they should swing out the boats for the practice, and lower them, if only partway. Then we'd know what to expect in an emergency."

126

"Hmmph. Should they, now?" Having heard enough, Captain Turner did not intend to describe to them the kind of chaos that could result from unlimbering lifeboats in open sea, with a rolling swell, under full steam. And far worse too if he were to stop the ship for a drill.

"Well," he declared, "you have some very interesting ideas, I must say. But as to their practicality, I'll have to consult with my second officer, Mr. Hefford. He'll know more about crew availability and scheduling. I'll have a word with him about it, so you needn't trouble yourselves any further. Now, thank you for bringing your concerns to my attention. I'm glad that you're going to be prepared, all three of you, in the unlikely event of anything happening."

As ever, the captain's authority worked. His full uniform, firm step, and tone of command overrode any further objections as he strode forward and ushered his visitors out the door.

Chapter 20

Dark Rooms

Will you have another glass of White Seal?" Matt asked, pouring at the sideboard in the stateroom. "Nice of Kessler to supply us with a free bottle."

He turned to Alma where she sat on the sofa, and felt a pleasant sense of vertigo as he looked down on her elegant beauty from his swaying height.

"Just a half glass, please," she said, passing him her goblet. "We'd better save some for our friends, if they ever come out of there."

The two waited alone in the parlor while the other couple used the bedroom. Flash was showing Winnie how to develop photo slides, and they had sealed the space under the closed door against light with a rolled towel. Muffled wisecracks and giggles filtered from within; otherwise they were cut off.

"Or else," Matt said, "we could kill the whole bottle ourselves, and they'd never know." He handed Alma her glass and sank down beside her. He found her especially lovely in the close-fitting deep red gown she'd worn to dinner, with the ruffled hem that flared around her delicate ankles, over mid-heeled black pumps.

"Oh, I think they'd know just from looking at us," Alma said.

"We'd be rolling more than this ship," Matt added.

"So much for being chaperoned," Alma said. "We can get drunk and do anything we want." Leaning close she stole a kiss, a firm peck on his lips.

"Anything?" He pulled her to him in a close embrace, her fragrance engulfing him, the tidy weight of her body falling against his chest.

After a long, wine-sweet kiss, she relaxed in his arms, and it was Matt's turn to break off for air. He didn't want to push too far, too fast. Letting Alma rest on the sofa with eyes half-closed, he forced himself to rise, light-headed. He walked across the cabin almost reeling, whether from *champagne* or *amour* or the Lusitania's surging progress over the waves. When he came to the bedroom door, he steadied himself and rapped on it. "How are you two doing in there? Almost finished?"

"Don't open that door," Flash's good-natured voice came through. "You might expose something!"

"No, don't rush us," Winnie called out in equally high spirits. "We're just fine in here. Things are developing very nicely."

Matt looked back at Alma, who was also laughing. Steadying himself against the roll of the ship, he returned to the sofa and into her welcoming arms.

After another interlude, she stretched luxuriantly and smoothed her evening gown, then ran the fingers of one hand through his rumpled hair. "This is really too much, Mr. Vane. A first-class dinner with dancing, and now champagne and romance. You know just how to treat a lady."

"I hope it meets your highest expectations," Matt said, stroking the dark tresses that lay against her lily-pale neck.

Alma laughed. "You're better at it than Jim ever was," she said. "I keep waiting for the cigars and cards to come out."

At that moment the bedroom latch turned, and the door pulled slowly open. "All right, you two, here we come," Flash announced. A discreet moment later his carrot-topped head appeared in the doorway. "Photo operations are complete, and the lights can come back on." He entered with Winnie close behind him. Each of them held up a pair of print papers, still damp, which they laid out on the coffee table.

"Good work," Matt said, inspecting them. "And you prepared fresh slides?" he asked, to Flash's nod.

"This one of the ship is lovely," Alma said. "Oh, and Winnie, what a stunning portrait of you! I wish I dared to have Flash make one of me."

"When you're ready, just say the word," Flash said. "I could shoot a special one for Matt," he added with a wink.

In due time they filed back into the bedroom to look at the other prints hanging over the sink: deck scenes, photos of the crowds at launch, the British blockaders, and a feral-looking candid shot of Knucks stalking aft.

"That's from before we left port, right?" Alma asked with a shiver.

"Yes," Flash reassured her. "Haven't seen hide or hair of him since."

The four of them cleaned up and removed the photo gear, then returned to the parlor to finish the wine. Matt and Alma clung close on the divan as the group gaily talked, while Winnie occupied Flash's lap in one of the armchairs.

* * *

Alone later, getting ready for bed in their reclaimed *boudoir*, Winnie asked Alma. "How is it with Matt? Have you two gone far?"

"Oh, no," Alma said innocently. "Matt's been very gallant. He's one heck of a kisser, though," she added, slithering into her nightgown. "Ready, willing, and able. What about Flash...he's not too pushy?"

"Oh, plenty playful, I like that in a fellow." Winnie leaned away from the mirror, then shut her eyes dreamily. "He's all man, though. I could feel it." She turned to Alma. "Would you...would you give yourself to Matt?"

Alma caught her breath and then sighed, wondering what to tell her younger friend. "Why, yes, I suppose I could." Thinking: he's as good a man as I've ever known...not married, it seems sure. And he knows my secrets. What else is there to hold out for?

At the realization, a thrill passed through her. "I guess it's just a matter of time for me and Matt," she said aloud.

"There isn't a lot of time left," Winnie observed, switching off the electric lamp and groping her way to bed. No light came from under the men's door.

"You're right," Alma had to agree, easing beneath her own blankets. "The *Lusitania* travels fast."

"Yes, and it's wartime," Winnie said in the dark. After a long moment she added, "I think I could be with Flash."

"Oh," Alma breathed. "But wouldn't you worry?"

"What about?" Winnie asked. "It's not as if a nurse doesn't know birth control. We both took Hildegard's classes and read Margaret Sanger's book."

Alma said nothing. She lay there for some time, dreaming awake. She imagined Matt's firm body, his thrillingly prickly jaw line, his bay-rum-and-tobacco man-smell—not from smoking, she was sure, but from being among smokers, in the places he went. Her thoughts flickered off the ship, to the past and future, the strange, nighted continents lying before and behind them. But her wistful mind recoiled from all that. She stirred restlessly in bed, and she heard Winnie still wakeful in hers.

At last she pivoted in her sheets, swung her feet over the side, and sat up. "Shall I go?" she asked softly.

"Yes, do," Winnie's reply came back faintly. She added with a brave effort at humor, "You might just tell Flash I want a word with him."

Standing up, Alma went to the door. She opened it quietly, expecting to hear deep breathing or sleepy murmurs of surprise.

But in the faint light coming under the passage door, she found the blankets still folded, untouched on the sofa and cot. The men were gone.

Chapter 21

Spies

The pair of idlers ambled down the third-class corridor as if they belonged there. They wore drab, nondescript clothing and rubber-soled work shoes. If anything betrayed Matt as being the more posh of the two, he supposed it would have been his recent haircut, which he'd taken pains to rumple. Flash, who was burdened with his leather shoulder bag, wore a close-fitting wool watch cap that made him look like a deckhand.

"It covers you up nicely," Matt told him. "Where'd you get it?"

"From a talented young lady we know," his friend discreetly answered. "She knitted it for me on our deck walks. I didn't tell her what it was for, just that photography takes you to chilly, breezy places. But she must have guessed I need it to disguise my hair, like our other mutual friend."

As usual, Matt was impressed by his helper's resourcefulness. "Well, if we're spotted, keep on wearing it, at least till you're back in First Class. If they chase us, three things: split up and let me be the decoy. Hide the camera bag where we agreed. And head for the Third Class Saloon if you can—that's the only place where men gather at this hour who're not overly friendly to authorities. If they're still after you in First, change your appearance and act stuffy. These coats can go overboard, if need be."

"I wouldn't worry too much," Flash said. "It should be easy to get through at the watch change, I've cased it...the evening watchman always has to go and fetch his replacement."

"Maybe," Matt said, thinking ahead. "But there could be more guards inside, especially if they're shipping contraband. Be on the lookout for Pierpoint, the ship's cop."

Passing between rows of Third Class cabin doors, close-set due to the small size of the rooms but seemingly unoccupied, they stopped where the passage turned toward the center of the ship. A stairwell on their right led upward, but no steps sounded on the metal stairs. Flash peeked around the corner and then made way for Matt to look.

Ten yards away, under an electric light at the ship's midpoint, a crewman slouched on a stool before a closed door leading forward. The two men pulled back and assumed a pose of idle conversation, in case anyone happened along. Loitering was hard work this far forward, with the pitch and roll of the ship more noticeable.

"That's new." Matt nodded at the freshly painted bulkhead that blocked the passage before them. "When the war came, I'm told, they cut into Third Class to enlarge the cargo space."

He glanced at the empty corridor behind them. "Even so, they're having trouble filling up steerage on the eastbound run."

Flash peeked around the corner, checking his pocket watch at intervals and occasionally letting Matt look. They saw the guard waiting at his post, obviously bored and growing impatient. Finally, at the faint chiming of a midnight bell, he strode off toward the port side of the ship and up the far stairwell.

"Go," Matt said.

The two went around the bend, not hiding their hurry. At the entryway, Flash took a slender steel pick from the outside pocket of his satchel and went to work on the lock. It was no mere door but a stoutly made, water-sealed hatchway, most likely put there for safe access to the cargo hold in bad weather. A small glass peephole in the top half was blocked from the far side.

Matt watched until he heard the snap of the latch and then helped Flash raise the lever that drew out the floor and ceiling bolts. Together they pushed the panel open on a dim, silent interior.

"It's an easy lock," the young burglar remarked, after they'd crossed the sill and levered the hatch shut behind them. "This side doesn't need a key," he pointed out. "But I think I can make one for you, if we want to get back in."

"Great, but let's see how we get out first. We'd do better to find a different, unguarded route, instead of waiting for the six a.m. watch change."

The room they'd entered was a storehouse lit by an electric bulb in the ceiling. A small watchman's booth was set up in the vestibule before the door, its table and seat fortunately vacant. Reaching into his shoulder bag, Flash took out a battery lamp and used its beam to brighten the dimness.

The room was crowded with crates and barrels small enough to be shifted by one or two men. Most of the cargo here was tied down to brackets in the deck by ropes and netting, to secure it against the ship's roll. From what they could see without disturbing things, it was all labeled as crockery, canned and bottled foodstuffs, linens and patent medicine. One box was stenciled "Vermont Maple Syrup," and the next, "Soothe-All for the Cough."

"Fragile goods for special handling," Matt said. "Not passenger baggage—that's in separate holds fore and aft for quick unloading, along with the transatlantic mail. I don't think we'll see much to interest us here. But have your camera ready."

Taking the lantern from Flash, he led the way forward through the maze of small crates. The feeling of creeping through the storehouse was that of being a thief, although what they were looking for he wouldn't want to steal.

The next door, unsecured, led not to a room or passage but to an open stair landing. A section of E deck had been cut away to provide cargo space of double height, twenty feet or so, stretching forward into darkness. The pair of bulbs hanging from the ceiling didn't light this main hold's farthest recesses. And they didn't show the floor, tightly packed as it was with oversized crates and bundles. There was another watch station here on the landing, again unoccupied. Thanks to the Great War for causing a crew shortage, Matt thought.

"I see ambulances over there," Flash murmured, shading his eyes against the electric light. He pointed to a pair of white automobiles lashed down on planks laid atop other cargo crates. "Is that what you'd call war *materiel*?"

"No, not medical goods...military stores or ammunition, maybe. Guns would be the clincher. But we'll shoot pictures of them anyway." Matt shrugged at the sight of the white-painted fenders and headlamps. "Careful from here on, in case any crew can look in on us."

The two descended silently on their rubber soles. On leaving the stairs they had to climb over the close-packed cargo. As they went, they examined what was under them, which was generally labeled in stencil on top of the crate or bale. Of course, there was no telling what might have been mislabeled to deceive the customs inspectors in New York or Liverpool.

There were sounds here in the dimness, even this far from the engine throb: the faint metallic slap of waves against the ship's bows, for they were now at or below the waterline, and the creaking of wooden crates as the ship rolled. Most of the goods weren't tied down, but set or wedged together in the hold, with some timber braces added to prevent the cargo from shifting in rough weather.

The smells here were also muted—seawater and damp wood overall, but with an occasional waft of spices, sour vinegar from pickle kegs or the musty smell of fur bales. There was a faint scent of gasoline or lubricants...could it be gun oil, Matt wondered?

Some bulk cargo was lashed to pallets. He had to flick on his lamp to read stencils and manifests tacked to the boxes, which could not always be checked by sight or smell. Still, he jotted down items in his notebook while Flash held the lamp. With a pry bar produced from his colleague's camera-and-burglar bag, Matt was able to peer into a few cases and verify the contents...leather goods, cheap tableware and salt-packed beef tongues. The loosened lids could easily be pressed back down again or pounded shut, using the same nail holes.

Finding little out of the ordinary, Matt grew impatient and moved them along faster. They climbed around the ambulances, looking in only to see that the interior of each was empty. He didn't consider them illegal, since they were well-meaning donations to alleviate the sufferings of war. Their intended drivers might even be among the passengers, and he made a note to try and find out as he hastily checked the cargo.

Looping back along the starboard side of the hold, they found crated motorcycles, barrels of live oysters, and then a large pile of boxes and kegs stamped with numbers prefixed by RA, which Matt thought could mean Royal Arsenal. As he pried up the lid of one shallow crate and peeled back the rubber sheeting, Flash gripped his shoulder.

The photographer pointed silently to the silvery dust that was packed inside, and tapped on the stenciled lid which read, "Handle with Care."

"Why, what is it?" Matt whispered.

"Aluminum dust, highly flammable...it's what I sometimes use for flash powder," he whispered back. "It's also added to high explosives like Amerol, so I'm told. It goes off better than gunpowder, but quiet, pfft, bright white for the pictures. And don't get it wet." He eyed the gray-painted hull plating nearby, which was damp with condensation or seepage. "That's when it really gets unstable." He pointed to a red stencil on the box which read, "Keep Dry."

"We'll leave it, then." Matt carefully replaced the liner and lid and tapped the nails back in place with his pry bar. "I doubt if it's for taking flash pictures." The case was one of a dozen or so of similar size and labeling.

Nearby, another consignment looked official but was labeled only by bracketed numbers. The foot-high crates were small enough for two men to lift, so they dragged one out of the close-packed pile and pried it open.

Seeing the contents, Matt turned abruptly to Flash and whispered, "OK, set up."

The case contained artillery shells, four of them, each as big around as Matt's forearm. He touched the steel shells in the wood bracings, with plugged holes in the round nose. That was for fuse detonators to be fitted at the battle front. He couldn't tell if the shells were filled with explosives or shrapnel, and he didn't particularly want to find out. They definitely were packed with high-explosive propellant charges inside their brass cartridge casings, each with its own detonator set in the base. He carefully pulled out two and stood them up in the box, set against dozens of identical boxes, and he propped up the numbered lid so it could be read.

Meanwhile, Flash set his camera tripod to aim the shot. It was too dark for a timed exposure, so the photographer filled his flash tray from a flask of the same silvery powder they'd seen in the nearby crates.

Matt stood well back. As the electric spark ignited the pan, its bright flare lit the room, followed by a billow of white smoke, and Flash had his picture.

No sense now hiding from watchmen. They shot quick photos of the aluminum cargo crates, the ambulances and the motorcycles in their wood frames, uniformly painted a flat military tan. They also found scores of smaller cases marked W for Winchester, containing rifle bullets dumped in by the thousands. Flash took the picture of Matt's hands sifting through the bright brass cartridges.

The next photos they took were of two enormous packing cases occupying the large central well. The names painted on the sides seemed to indicate agricultural or storage gear of some kind—the smaller oblong one read "Hopper" and the largest one, "Tank," but with no destination or origin label.

Matt climbed up onto the monster crate for a peek, but levering up the wooden access panel would be a two-man job.

"I wonder what kind of tank it is," Flash said as he aimed the camera. "Water, or maybe fuel oil? Do you think it might be full?"

"It could be beer," Matt half-joked, thumping on the side for an echo. "There's a distillery outfitter on board, headed for the Guinness brewery in Dublin. The hopper could be made to feed in the grain and hops. Or they could be for military use."

As Flash was setting up the shot, Matt dangled his legs over the side to be in the picture and provide scale. He watched his assistant drag his tripod back to get the huge box into focus.

Then suddenly, just as the flash went off, something happened. Matt heard a shout of surprise and found himself momentarily blinded by the intense glare from the pan. He had to edge his way over in the blazing darkness to a corner of the big crate and drop down to join his friend, who was quickly folding the tripod and packing up.

"Did you see that man?" Flash asked, hurriedly zipping his bag shut.

"No, I could hardly see at all," Matt said, rubbing his eyes. "I heard someone yell—was it a guard?"

"A man in dark clothes—he came around the side of the box, so I snapped him," Flash said, shouldering the strap of his bag. "I probably blinded him too. He took off, maybe to get help."

The photographer strode forward and looked around the corner. "No sign of him now."

"Time to scat," Matt said. "Not the way we came—we'd have to get past the guard, and they could be ready for us. Better look for the panic exit."

They hurried astern through the dim hold, past the stairs they'd descended to the aft bulkhead. There another stairway led them down... to the Lower Orlop Deck, Matt figured, very near the ship's keel and the ocean depths. At the bottom, by their battery light, they saw a heavy door leading forward deep beneath the hold. This one read in damp yellowed lettering: "Powder Magazine—Keep Out."

It was double-padlocked, and they had no desire to break in. But just up the stairway heading aft, a stout escape hatch was operated by a hand wheel. Matt had known it must be there, but not exactly where. Spinning the wheel to open it, they pushed their way through and then tightened it shut again behind them.

The passage on the other side was literally pitch-dark. By their lantern light, they saw that it was glossy-black with coal dust: a screened catwalk, leading left and right above the jumbled black sea of a transverse coal bunker. With the voyage half over, the coal was mostly gone, and both ways appeared to be open. But rather than split up yet, they chose the port side. At its far corner a broad, dark ventilation shaft led straight upward, with steel ladder-cleats set into the bulkhead wall.

With no way to point the lamp, the climb had to be made in darkness. The rungs proved slick with briny moisture, hard to cling to, and the roll of the great ship seemed to worsen as they climbed higher. Slipping once from the rungs, Matt found himself dangling in space one-handed, until Flash guided his flailing foot back onto the ladder. Pausing then to shine the battery lamp around, the two saw no alternative but to climb the whole way, seven stories to the deck, with the hope of finding escape at the top.

The ventilators were not broad, open cowls as on the *Mauretania* and other big liners, but squat round stacks with heavy hinged lids canting open or shut. No glow of light from the night sky filtered down. Still, arriving at the top of the shaft, Matt found that the hinged cap wasn't chained or painted tight. Its widest part at the front offered a narrow egress onto the foredeck. Peering out the narrow aperture, he saw no sign of pursuit and heard no alarms. It was deepest night, four in the morning by his pocket watch, with the moon sinking far astern.

"You go first," he said, edging aside on the ladder for Flash. "Try to keep out of sight, and I'll be right behind. If they're about to catch you, drop the bag and run for it. I'll pick it up and go to the starboard side. One of us should be able to get the camera through, along with all of those plates."

"If they catch us, act drunk," Flash suggested. Taking a hip flask from his shoulder bag, he washed out his mouth and passed it over to Matt. Smoothly then, he eased out through the crack and was up on deck, slouching aft along the rail.

Matt waited a few moments, swigged shallowly from the flask and sprinkled some on his sleeve for good measure.

Then he followed, squeezing out through the crevice and heading for the moon-shadow of the tall white superstructure. He saw no watchers on the wide bridge, and only one figure moved inside the bright-lit pilot house. No shouts sounded out, no whistles and no running feet. Tossing his coal-stained jacket overboard and staying a dozen yards behind, he followed Flash back to the stateroom.

Chapter 22

Cruiser Rules

The *Earl of Lathom* creaked and leaned in a fresh breeze that rippled the sunny blue sea. The antique schooner was broad-reaching southward in westerly airs, making its way around the Old Head of Kinsale. Off to port the rocky headland loomed, a dark cliff topped by ancient castle ruins, but from which a new white-painted lighthouse rose. Beyond the headland lay the open ocean south of Ireland.

"Aye, an' it be a ravishin' day in these fair waters, now the fog is lifted." Rory McCray on the timber deck spoke grandly to his mate in the wheelhouse. He felt expansive in this easy sailing after clawing out of Bantry Bay by dawnlight, and then a choppy Atlantic run around the west tip of Ireland. With this breeze, there was no longer need of a smoky diesel engine to keep them underway. It felt it downright restful, after a night of loading eggs and chickens in tiny, foggy Bantry harbor.

"Ravishin' day, aye," Mate McGonagill replied, keeping a restless eye on the horizon.

"The wind freshens. And we need not fear runnin' aground on yonder rockpile," Rory added with a nod toward the castle. "We could be makin' a straight run into England this day."

"Sure, an' that we could," the Mate agreed. "But there may be other dangers beside fog and rocks. Remember, there's a war on."

"The war, aye," Rory said. "But it all seems so far away, does it not, on such a splendid morn as this?" From his place near the wooden schooner's wheel, he took a deep breath of heathery land fragrance. "It's glad I am that I ain't lookin' out upon all this from the bridge of a warship."

"It's glad I am they ain't seein' us neither," McGonagill answered, keeping up his watch.

"And what would they be wantin' from the likes of us, pray tell?" Rory rambled on. "We carry no guns, powder, pikes or bayonets, an' no battle troopers seethin' for the kill. None but the fruits of Kerry and Killarney are aboard, innocent country eggs and butter for the market. A few harmless potatoes and carrots...and the eggs' mothers, too." He took one hand from the wheel and waved it at the overflow cargo lashed on deck, the chickens in their crates, clucking and ruffling their feathers in the morning sun. "No war contraband here."

"True enough, and they can be well assured of that," McGonagill said. "Assumin' they don't shoot first and ask questions after."

"Well, I'm not goin' to worry about it," Rory declared, "not on such a day as this. I reckon we've cleared Kinsale now, so our course is to be set due east."

"I reckon," the Mate said with a glance down at the compass card in the binnacle. He raised his speaking trumpet. "Hands ready to adjust sail!" he called forward to the other idlers on deck.

The men barely stirred at his order. Slow to react—no, worse than slow. They were staring dumbfounded off ahead and to starboard. One of them, Seamus O'Donnell, pointed to where something was coming up out of the water

"Slacken sail," McGonagill called at once through the speaking trumpet. "Ahoy, you spalpeens, hop to it! Loose the main sheet!"

Going astern himself, he untied the mizzen sheet of the two-master and let the rear sail flap free in the wind. As the mains'l flew out to leeward, the schooner rapidly lost way and began to wallow, rocking in the mild swell.

Off their starboard quarter, a wedge-shaped bow cut through the sea's surface, spraying foam. Behind it a blunt turret had emerged, a tower topped with vents and pipes. Now suddenly the whole craft rose up onto the surface, its scuppers streaming white foam. Even as it leveled, it slowed to a halt alongside the *Earl of Lathom*, a mere hundred meters off the old ship's bow. Judging from the emblem on the side of the tower, a broad-bladed Maltese Cross on a circular field of red, the craft was German.

"*Begorrah*, 'tis a sea monster!" young Gavin of Limerick cried out, having run from the rail and taken shelter behind the crates of chickens.

"Nay, 'tis a soob—a soobmarine," said Brian of Ballinskelligs, the more savvy in naval affairs. "An undersea boo-at. They proobly just want some fresh booter an' eggs from oos."

"Maybe 'tis the patriot Roger Casement returning home," Seamus said. "I hear that over in Germany, he's raised up an army of Irish war prisoners to invade the homeland and cast out the British for sure."

As the motley, barefoot crew stood gaping in awe, hatches were flung open in the top of the strange craft and uniformed men swarmed out onto the narrow deck. Two went to the main cannon on the foredeck and cranked it around toward the *Earl*. A captain and mate stood in the conning tower, and slender black-clad crewmen filed out along the narrow stern with rifles and pistols at the ready.

The captain raised his bullhorn and announced in the King's English, harshly accented:

"In the name of the *Kaiserliche Marine von Deutschland*, the Imperial Navy of Germany, I claim your ship and cargo as a legitimate prize of war. All shipping of any kind, foreign or neutral, is subject to seizure in the war zone. You will leave your ship and surrender your papers without delay, and without interfering with my crew in any way. If you act swiftly and do not resist, you will be allowed to go unharmed."

To drive home the point, the sub's deck gun fired a shot across the *Earl of Lathom's* bow. It screamed through the air overhead and raised a plume of water a thousand yards to port. Simultaneously, the U-boat's men cocked their rifles and raised them to their shoulders. The response of the schooner's crew, without any further orders from their own officer, was to scramble for the ship's launch amidships, roll it upright, and ready the tackle to sway it over the side.

"Now, that seems hardly fair, does it to you?" Rory McCray said, keeping his place by the wheel. "Can't you inform them that we carry no contraband?"

Mate McGonagill deferred to Captain Hardy, who had just come up from below. His first look of consternation at feeling his ship go dead in the water had, upon seeing the U-boat and hearing the gunfire, transformed to wide-eyed recognition.

His response to the wheelman's question was a helpless shrug. "Do as they say, boys," he said to the pair. He then turned and called out to his crew, quite unnecessarily, "Abandon ship!"

As he hurried below to salvage money and personal effects, the others manhandled the launch to the rail and hoisted it over. As it struck the water, a prize crew from the sub was just rowing up in an inflatable boat to take possession. Seven leather-clad Germans swarmed nimbly aboard like pirates into the waist of the ship. They carried weapons and metal canisters, with what looked like detonators and coils of fuse.

Pushing past the Irishmen they headed below, unreeling slow-match fuse as they went. Evidently they did not intend to sail the *Earl of Lathom* back to Germany.

"Should we loose the chickens?" Young Gavin called, standing beside the crated birds, which squawked and fluttered in the excitement. "Looks like they're going to blow us up."

"Don't be an idiot, lad," Rory called from the rail, where he stood ready to climb down into the launch. "Those poor creet-ers cannot flap or swim ashore from here. Nor can you! Come and join us, and we'll be away."

As Captain Hardy came last into the boat with his logbook, and the crew shoved off using their oars, Germans were already emerging from below carrying tubs of butter, cheeses and egg baskets. Rowing briskly away, the Irish crew watched the marauders snatch up pairs of chickens by the neck and carry them off to their rubber boat. In moments the captors had shoved off as well.

"By Mary and Joseph, there she goes!" Mate McGonagill called out. "They've sunk her."

As the inflatable craft was rowed to the sub, twin fountains of water erupted from either side of the schooner, the scuttling charges having detonated. The wooden *Earl* began to list, its loose sails thrashing in the stiffening breeze.

"'Tis a sorry thing to do," Rory remarked. "And all for a paltry few hen-fruit we would have given them for nothin'!" He felt truly glum at the loss of the old ship...how was he now to find another seaman's berth outside of the Royal Navy?

He rowed with the others toward the emerald hills visible over his shoulder, just past the cliffs and the lighthouse. Then with a start he heard the U-boat's deck gun open fire again.

But it was not at the survivors, praise be to the Almighty. It pounded away at the listing hulk, sending chickens flapping in the blue as it hastened the watery demise of the old *Earl of Lathom.*

Chapter 23

Unrequited

Alma heard the two men return to their stateroom in the hour before dawn. After making sure that they were well, she couldn't trust herself to speak to Matt. She didn't dare to focus her thoughts on him too pointedly. While trying to behave as normal, she remained silent and found herself avoiding his gaze.

After all, she still felt indebted to him,—dependent as ever, hiding from one man's ownership by the grace of another. Robbing Peter to pay Paul, it now bitterly seemed to her. Yet it would be unwise to lash out at Matt with her injured feelings. And unfair too, since he owed her nothing. All that she really ought to feel was relief, a profound thankfulness at avoiding the same dreadful mistake she'd almost made...again.

Winnie seemed to sense her deep disturbance. In their early hours alone, while the weary men snored in the parlor and they tried to catch up on their own ruined sleep, the younger woman offered counsel.

"I wouldn't be so upset about it, Alma. After all, they came back all right."

"Yes, in the wee hours of the morning, smelling of gin." Alma had to restrain her voice to keep it from veering into a sob.

"They said that was just a ruse."

"Men are full of ruses." She turned her back on Winnie to discreetly blink aside a tear.

"Well, even if it wasn't quite true," Winnie said, "they were trying to spare our feelings."

Alma refused to answer further. Whether the men had been night-catting about, merely drinking or, as the coal smudges on their clothes and camera bag seemed to prove, creeping though some secret part of the ship, the fact remained: they were not dependable.

Having been through everything she had with Jim—the late nights, the liquor, the foul companions and murky underworld doings, and the ultimate cruelty—she needed some stability in her life. She had thought she'd found it in Matt, with his calm air, his confident and reassuring focus on her, and what seemed like his sensitivity. But if she was going to be put second to this other life of his, could she risk that? Was she just another news assignment, to be abandoned at night, and left defenseless, without even knowing!

What if he never came back! Or if his exploits dragged her into the spotlight, a ship's inquiry or even a spy drama? Was he himself a German spy, could she really say for sure? Or perhaps one of those anarchists who'd blown up Wall Street?

Even if his intentions were of the purest, she shuddered to think of the consequences—not so much for her as for Matt himself! How could she ever imagine being emotionally tied to such a man? If he behaved this way here, on a genteel pleasure cruise, what would he be like in the trenches?

Did he have the slightest chance of surviving his war assignment? And his young henchman Flash, leading him further into danger...Alma had seen plenty like him in Big Jim's criminal outfit.

* * *

As the day resumed, Matt sensed the change in her. At lunch they kept up appearances, conversing with Chuck and Mary Plamondon and some of the usual set; but as he waited for his Lamb Pot Pie to cool, he wholly failed to get her to look up from her Lobster Mayonnaise.

Later, returning from the Grand Saloon, he tried to engage her.

"My dear, are you feeling quite well?" It came out in his best British manner, doubtless picked up from their dining companions, that had become a joke between them.

"Fine, thanks," she minimally replied without looking at him.

"Oh, good," he said, still trying to engage her. "But I should apologize for keeping you up last night—you and Winnie both, and worrying you, needlessly."

The last word came out by itself. He knew it was a mistake, and she was quick to seize on it.

"I'd hardly say it was needless, since anything could have happened." At least she now shot him a brief glare.

146

"But Alma, nothing did! See here," he added to her as they came up to their door. "The room isn't cordoned off by ship's police."

Ignoring their protocol of sneaking about, he gallantly opened the door and followed her in. Once inside he pleaded, trying to corner her. "I'm sorry, Alma, really,"

Still seemingly unconcerned, she remarked, "You could at least have told us you were leaving the cabin, the two of you."

"We didn't think you'd even notice," Matt sighed, trying out petulance. "We were back well before dawn, as you know."

"And that makes us safer? You didn't worry about leaving two women unprotected?"

"We were protecting you, by not telling you," Matt explained in weary patience. "This news reporting business has an unsavory side to it, especially the muckraking part. We thought it best you knew nothing at all, in case there was some kind of alarm or questions asked later."

She clearly wasn't buying it. "You mean, if they came chasing after you and wanted to throw us all in the brig?"

She had remained standing, ready for a fight. No chance for him to sink down next to her and ply her with his masculine charms.

Now she continued, "We thought you must have sneaked off somewhere, taking pictures you weren't supposed to. The camera bag was the first thing we looked for."

From her fighting stance, she now seemed to draw back into simple appeal. "You could have taken me, or the two of us with you…did you even think of that? Where did you go, anyway?"

Matt took a breath, feeling the need to be stubborn. "Alma, the same reasons for secrecy I mentioned just now still apply. You'll be better off not knowing anything."

"Oh, really, just an ignorant female?" His remark had obviously stung. "Well, I can guess where you two were…looking for guns, or hidden troops, or poison gas bombs stowed aboard this ship! It's fine being protected, but not from the truth!"

"It's strictly business, dear, to be kept confidential between me and my employer. You weren't even supposed to know."

Seeing her lips tighten, Matt hid his exasperation and tried to retrench his position. "What made you come looking for us so late, anyway? Was there something you needed?"

A hurt look flashed in her eye. He'd obviously hit a nerve. But then came a knock at the door, followed by Winnie's brisk entry, with Flash trailing in after her a few moments later.

The young investigator rapidly sized up the situation. He heartily announced, "Well, gang, I hate to interrupt, but fun and games are over! Time to develop some pictures."

* * *

Then the two women were alone, barred from the darkened bedroom where the men worked in private. Alma gave her friend a final summary of her woes.

"He'll always be that way, searching out trouble and putting his job first. He's drawn to danger for the thrill of it, and he's never going to change. So you see," she resolutely finished, "I just can't feel safe with him."

"Oh, Alma, that's so sad!"

"Yes, life is sad," she said, refusing to dab at her moist eyes. "Well, what about you? Would you still take Flash into your bed?"

"In a minute," Winnie proclaimed, bright-eyed in her girlish bravado. "Just try me."

Chapter 24

Camouflage

Steward Jeremy Smyte moved down the corridor with watchful pride. He was the authority here, he told himself—he had the run of the whole ship, didn't he? And this stern section in particular, the second-class cabins, set off in their three-story island behind the mainmast, were his domain, his little England. Here he ruled and kept close watch on his subjects.

Still, he didn't want to appear nosy. Certain persons shouldn't suspect that they were being spied on. Else they might find grounds for complaint, and make things difficult. He had to be discreet. But if challenged, he would be firm in his authority.

The nurses were out, some of them anyway. The tall old battleaxe and the two snippy sisters...he'd seen them on the promenade just minutes ago. But according to the roster, there should be two more. It was a four-bed cabin, and his tally told him that a folding cot for a fifth occupant had been delivered. He'd seen them all together that first day out. And who could miss them, the fair-haired lass and the flirty-eyed brunette, along with the other three, all showing themselves off so brazenly at departure. That tall blonde was the one, he was certain of it. Knucks had been willing to pay real money for her.

But since then she'd managed to disappear, she and her dark-haired sidekick. Where'd they gone, overboard? Not without a fuss, that was sure. And there'd been no opportunity to jump ship. They were stowed away somewhere out of sight, weren't they? After a couple of days at sea, most of the *mal de mer* sufferers below decks had gotten over it. And those who didn't were more of a nuisance than the regular passengers, always asking for service in their cabins, and for slop-ups when they couldn't hold it in.

Well, now was the time to find out, wasn't it? Jeremy rapped firmly on their door, and after a moment announced, "Cabin service, coming in!"

There was no answer, and no stirring from within.

"Comin' inside." A few more sharp raps and he applied his passkey to the lock. Slowly pushing open the door, he found the room empty.

Too empty. There in the middle was the unfolded cot, artfully mussed but not truly slept-in. Three of the four bunks were disordered too, in true slovenly American style; but the fourth was barely touched. And the luggage...stored on the closet shelves, and floor, and under the bunks. No five Yankee maidens, Smyte told himself, ever traveled with so few trunks, satchels, cases and bandboxes. At least two of the five were gone, bag and baggage. Their toothbrushes were still there on the sink, perhaps, but little else of the lasses remained. Even the trash basket wasn't overflowing as he would have expected.

Hmm, the trash. Kneeling and inspecting it item-by-item, he came to something at the very bottom, a small bottle with square corners. "L'Oreal—Safe Hair Dye Company of France—US Patent 1909," so the label read in English. An export product, well on its way back now to the home continent. The color wasn't indicated on the label, but from the unused bottle dregs it was obviously *noir*, jet black.

That suggested much. Who in the nurses' little group, then, would be using black hair dye? The old biddy? No, Jeremy had seen her just lately, under an iron-gray bun resembling a war helmet. The raven-haired young sisters, then? Or the lush brunette, not likely. It was the blonde, most certainly, to disguise her pale hair that flew like a distress flag in the Atlantic breezes. The slippery sly one, who seemed to be entered on the passenger list as Alma Brady, but whom the gangster Knucks had described to him as a faithless little hustler named Maisie Thornton.

So she'd changed her appearance as well as her name, and fled to another cabin...another part of the ship, then, but where? To First Class, very likely, with some accommodating gentleman. Or, perhaps, to one of the unused third-class bunks tucked even farther away forward? And was she alone, or had her nursey friend, the brown-haired Winifred, gone with her? What kind of con might the two little vamps be pulling off...or were they merely hiding from justice?

There were many sly tricks used by card-sharpers and floozies, the sea dregs who frequented ships on the Atlantic run, to dodge suspicion and evade authority. Jeremy had already heard the tales at the stewards' mess table. But this pair was seemingly new at the trade, and should be easy to detect.

True, as a newcomer himself, Smyte had no great trust or influence among the crew. But given the watchful eyes of the serving staff and their love of gossip, he felt confident of being able to find his quarry, even on a ship as vast as the *Lusitania*.

And then, once he found her...well, there'd be a reward, of course, on handing her over at the far end of the voyage. But before that...a young woman of loose morals, and very likely flush from her last caper... no telling what further rewards she might offer for silence, or for his promised complicity in her schemes. A good spy could play both sides of the trenches; he was learning that. No need to stick blindly to principle— or, as the Yanks would say, go down with a sinking ship.

Ah well, his search was complete for now, with a new clue to work on. That left him just enough time for his noon engagement. Carefully replacing everything as he'd found it—the luggage and the dresser drawers, even the trash—he exited and headed deeper below decks.

The Trimmers' Mess lay for'ard of Second Class, but still well astern. Its electric-lit cavern, buried under the passenger quarters, throbbed with the sound of the engines beneath and was faintly redolent of their oily smell. But its long dining tables lay mercifully far from the heat of the boilers and stokeholds where its customers, the Black Gang of coal stokers and trimmers, worked their long hours. Fare-payers never saw this place, and Steward Smyte had to move carefully to keep his white uniform un-smudged by coal dust from its dusky denizens.

One figure stood out in the mess line as being taller and gawkier than the rest. As the troglodyte turned from the steaming kettles to find Jeremy waiting, his eyes and teeth glared with frightening whiteness out of his coal-blackened face. It was a good thing the mess tray brimming with slops and crusts occupied both of his grimy hands, or the filthy giant might have seized hold of his visitor and shaken him.

"Hello, Knucks," the steward meekly said.

"Smyte, there you are!" the scarecrow yelled with no concern for secrecy. "It's about time, you lousy skunk!"

"All right, chap, keep it calm," Jeremy nervously said, staying well back from the apparition.

"Calm, eh?" Knucks veered from Smyte toward a table. "I've been stuck down here for days humping a coal shovel, with never a word from you!" His growl was made worse by a stoker's customary hoarseness.

"Sign on with the crew, Jim said, they'll be needing men!" His towering wrath didn't keep him from plunging into a chair and eating, but he continued his rant with a mouth full of beans and noodles.

"Take a job, be un...un-conspicuous...and here I am, shut away as a lousy stoker, piloting a wheelbarrow and steering a shovel. It's worse than the Big House!"

Knucks was no stoker, Jeremy knew. That was a skilled job, throwing in the coal onto the grate, smoothing it and then raking out the ash, all carefully timed to the burning of the fuel and the roll of the ship. The big hoodlum was just a raw trimmer, shifting coal out of the side bunkers and putting it in reach of the real stokers. But Smyte didn't trouble to correct him on this fine point.

"So, what's the scoop?" Knucks demanded, greedily stoking his own boilers. "Is she on board, or ain't she? Have you got a line yet on the stuff we want?"

"I daresay she is on board," Smyte said. "I know I saw her that first day. She's not where she's supposed to be, but I've an idea where I might look—"

"Spill it, you Limey scum!" Knucks said, spraying food. He reached across the table to grab Smyte's collar, and the steward had to lean back on his bench to avoid the sooty, greasy paw. The other coal-scuttlers alongside paid them no mind amid the hunger and clamor of the dining hall.

"All right, all right," Jeremy said, regaining his balance against the ship's roll. "She's changed her hair. I saw a bottle of black hair dye in her room...what used to be her room. I think she's hiding out in First Class."

"Hiding out, eh? Well you find her," Knucks grated at him. "And get what we want, or else I'll have to."

Leaning forward, he lowered his gravelly voice so that only Smyte could hear the grinding whisper. "I want you in on it. If I end up having to do it on my own, it's the both of you who'll be goin' overboard."

Chapter 25

Openings

After a dreary supper in the Grand Saloon, having to explain to
the other diners that his secretary felt indisposed, Matt returned to his
stateroom. As his next adventure on this Continental junket, he needed
to dress formally for the mid-voyage party on B deck. He found that,
with a little touching up—a sleek black cummerbund, a carnation from
the ship's florist, and an added dash of hair pomade—he could go in his
dinner jacket. He would look presentable, whatever the state of affairs
with his escort.

Matt learned with relief that Alma would be going. He'd accepted
the invitation for them both, but that was before her glum preoccupied
spell and their ensuing argument. Still, he wasn't sure until he found her
primping and grooming in the bedroom.

As ever, she required more serious wardrobe enhancements, whether
for disguise or to blend in with the ritzy Broadway set in the impresario
Charles Frohman's suite. In light of her recent moodiness, Matt had
thought she might decide to stay in the cabin and avoid the risk of
exposure. But now she seemed more intent than ever on going.

As Alma renewed her lipstick, the bedroom door stood open. Matt
discreetly glimpsed her transformation in the mirror—in her new evening
gown, a marvel of black Chantilly lace, black satin and black glass beads.
Much had changed between them since his unannounced absence the
previous night. She was still civil to him, even patient, but what had
become of their romantic spark? Perhaps it was only the element of trust
that was gone.

Well, he still had his job to perform and whole new worlds
to conquer. To think of them becoming lovers had probably been
unrealistic, anyway. Or at least unwise, in the uncertainties of wartime—

and a needless risk in view of the chancy business prospect they were engaged in, his planned journalistic exposé.

But they could still try to get along, rather than spoil the evening—or the whole voyage—any worse than it had already been spoiled.

"Everything all right, then?" he asked through the doorway in this damnable clipped English manner that seemed to come over him now, whenever he addressed her.

"I think so," she answered into the mirror, just as sparsely. And then, after a pause, she dug deeper: "As long as you can tell me that what you did last night, when you were gone...it had nothing to do with me and my troubles. Big Jim, the muster list or the money, nothing like that."

"No, not at all," he assured her, surprised by the question. "Those are serious matters that we can work on together. I wouldn't make a move on that without your okay."

Feeling a little of the old closeness, he dared to appraise her as she turned from the mirror. "Looks like you've been spending some of Jim's ill-gotten gains."

He spoke in reference to her new silver choker studded with tiny gems. It circled her throat neatly, set off by her darkened hair and the splendid black gown.

"Just a trifle from the gift shop," she said. "Diamonds being a girl's best friend, after all." She unboxed a new pair of accessories, long black gloves, and began drawing them onto her bare arms up to the elbow. "If that canvas money bag should disappear, I won't have lost it all." She posed before the mirror, oblivious to his gaze.

"An investment, you mean." He averted his eyes from the taunting vision in the *boudoir*, now so painfully remote. "And a wise one, I'd say." He adjusted his bowtie in his own tiny mirror. "You don't feel bad about spending Jim's money?"

"If he ever finds me, he can have it all back. This, too," she added, touching the jewels at her neck, "as long as it means I've seen the last of him."

Matt decided to make a bid for her goodwill. "If it ever comes to real, imminent danger, I hope I can be of help to you."

"Well, I hope I'll never be needing it."

Feeling the rebuff, he couldn't help but try one last time. "Say, Alma, you never did tell me, what made you look for us so early in the

154

morning...or was it Winnie who got up? We thought sure you'd turned in for the night."

She stayed serene, avoiding his gaze and taking up her black knitted wrap from the sofa. "Just a restless night at sea," she said. "As I recall, there was a lot of rolling and tossing going on."

She turned, waiting calmly for him to open the door as he puzzled over her remark.

Out on deck as agreed, they met up with Winnie and Flash. The assistant cut a trim figure in his tux, though his bright red smudge of hair could never really look formal. To balance it, the carnation he wore was stunning pink. Winnie, with Alma's help, had augmented her wardrobe with her friend's cleverly altered pink gown. Shortened with draped pleats below the knees, it looked *très vogue*. It should certainly pass in a light-hearted gathering of the Broadway theater set...even under the white nurse jacket that she'd improvised as a wrap.

"What a delightful couple," Alma said brightly. "Just look, the all-American boy and the girl in uniform!"

"This way to the Regal Suites," Matt said, sizing up the scene as he led them forward. "But remember, don't be too dazzled by the toffs and entertainers, or too muddled by strong drink. For me it's a news beat. I need all of you as my eyes and ears, so stay alert."

The event was already spilling out of Frohman's rooms onto the covered Promenade Deck. Small groups of elegant dressers huddled together in the shadows, and waiters circled with trays of drink and canapés. The light was masked by canvas blackout curtains rigged outside the promenade, billowing gently in the night breeze. From within the glowing rooms issued the strains of a live band making a very credible effort at ragtime. In all, it was a magnetic scene that might have graced an Upper East Side penthouse, or one of New York's finer restaurants.

The Cunard steward who'd been posted to intercept party crashers let them pass with barely a nod. The four moved onward into the radiance that poured forth from the open doors and casement windows of the grand suite.

The first to greet them was their first-night dinner companion, the designer and gadabout Oliver Bernard. Just emerging from the crowded rooms, he was obviously a bit ahead of them on the gaiety and drink.

"Well, if it isn't our own war correspondent, Mr. Vane...Matt, is it? You're wise to come; you'll find plenty of warfare going on here between these Broadway folk."

"Good to know, Ollie," Matt said, shaking hands. "It's a fine thing to be needed."

Releasing Matt's hand, Bernard turned to the others.

"Ah, Miss Alma, the intrepid secretary, looking delightful as usual!" He didn't shake her black-gloved hand, but snatched it up and pressed it to his thinly mustached lips, while she looked on amused.

"And here's Flash—without his camera, I see," Ollie said, briefly clasping the young reporter's hand.

Then he seized Winnie's white-gloved hand and kissed it. "But who is this lovely young nurse?"

"Miss Winifred Dexter, from Concord," she said, withdrawing her hand from his fond clutch. "Winnie to you, Ollie."

"Well, Nurse Winnie," he said, winking, "it's still a bit early for your services. But don't worry, the patients should be lining up by ten or so."

He turned to the others. "Here, come on in, all of you! I just stepped out for some air, but it's almost as crowded outside." He led them back through the bright doorway.

"This is one of the ship's two Regal Suites," Ollie said. Acting as tour guide, he pointed out the high mahogany ceilings and carved moldings in the spacious rooms. "The other suite belongs to Alf Vanderbilt, but he's here with us tonight."

He nodded toward the tall, handsome tycoon across the parlor, who was speaking to a petite, delicately featured woman in loose-cut chenille. Amid the cheerful hubbub, it was possible to make out that the pair conversed in French.

"I recognize her, too!" Winnie said. "That's Rita Jolivet, the actress. She's been in the entertainment pages." She turned excitedly to her escort. "Flash, I'll bet you'd love to have your camera here!"

Ollie said, "Rita's returning from her American tour, headed for her London opening."

He nodded his head in the direction of a tall, stately young woman talking to a thick-set older gentleman. "You've probably seen Josephine Brandell in the playbills too—or in the press, if your paper covers the

Great White Way. She's with our host, Charles Frohman. Come on over and I'll introduce you."

Matt and the others followed Oliver, who strode fearlessly up to the Broadway producer. Frohman, a jovial froggy-faced man, finished speaking to the actress and pivoted on his cane. "Hello, Ollie," he said. "I meant to greet you earlier but was called off to duty...and a very pleasant duty at that. Have you met Miss Brandell, the star of plays and operas on both sides of the Atlantic? I can't claim to have discovered her, since she was already starring in *Come Over Here* when I first met her in London. Josephine, this is Oliver Bernard, a top-notch set designer fresh from his latest stint in Boston."

"Fresh is the word, I think." The smiling actress gave Ollie her hand to kiss, and Frohman hurried him along by saying, "I see you've rounded up some of my guests. Is this fellow the journalist you were telling me about?"

"Yes," Ollie said, bobbing up for air. "Mr. Matthew Vane of the *Daily Inquisitor*. And this is Miss Alma Brady, his secretary and traveling companion," he added as the producer shook hands perfunctorily from the anchor of his cane. "Here is his photographer—we call him Flash—and Miss Winifred Dexter of Concord, New Hampshire."

"Oh, Mr. Frohman," Winnie gushed. "I've seen some of your plays. *Peter Pan* was wonderful!"

"Call me C.F.," Frohman said. "Yes, it was a dandy. Maybe we'll find another one like it on this trip to London. But I doubt it—successes like that come along once in a lifetime."

"Mr. Vane," Josephine Brandell said as she clasped Matt's hand, "I'm told you're a war correspondent, so perhaps you can help me. I'm concerned about this German warning that was printed, and that we're heading into a war zone. When I try to discuss it, everyone says it's only a bluff. They treat me as if I'm nothing but a silly little girl." She flashed a reproachful glance at Frohman and turned back to Matt. "Do you think this threat is just a hollow bluff?"

Matt considered carefully. "Well," he said at last, "my newspaper wasn't given the advertisement, so I didn't have a chance to check it out. But it did come from the German Foreign Office."

His lovely questioner had let her hand remain in his as they spoke, and he held it gently. "In a poker game, you never know if it's a bluff until some other player calls it. In this game the stakes are high." He glanced around them to indicate the whole spacious room and its glittering guests. "But I'd say, someone in very high places has decided to call the German bluff. I'd like to know just who, but the cards may tell." Finishing, he returned Josephine's earnest gaze.

"Thank you," the actress said after a moment, squeezing his hand warmly and releasing it. "Thank you for taking me seriously."

"Well, now, Jo, don't be too hard on C.F. and the rest of us," Ollie put in to lighten the moment. "Frohman here doesn't take anybody seriously. A reporter on the dock asked C.F. if he was afraid of the U-boats, and he said, No, in his business, he's only afraid of the I.O.U's."

"Well, really," Winnie gaily said, "if he was frightened of submarines, he could have taken passage on a neutral American ship. I heard that Isadora Duncan and her dance troupe were just setting out for England on the *SS New York*, along with a lot of other show business people, the same Saturday we sailed. Didn't you want to cross with them, Mr. Frohman?"

The producer turned to her with a pained but patient look. "As I told Jerry—my good friend Jerome Kern, the composer, who is supposed to be here with us—when I consider some of the great stars I've had to deal with, mere submarines make me smile."

As the flutter of laughter subsided, Ollie asked, "What about you, Nurse Winnie? Since you're on board, I take it you're not afraid of the Germans and their torpedoes?"

"I wouldn't do them the honor of changing ships," Winnie declared with an indignant toss of her head. "Anyway, I'm headed straight for the war front...as we all are, all four of us and my other nurse friends...so it wouldn't have occurred to me to pick the safest way. If I wanted safety so badly, I'd be staying home!"

"Well, if you're going across to serve as a nurse," Frohman said, taking up his role as host, "I know just the person you should talk to. Madame Marie de Page, the Belgian envoy, is here at our little *soirée*. She's been lecturing in the USA and raising money for the Red Cross relief effort...a wonderful speaker, very passionate."

He gazed around the suite, leaning on his cane. "So, gentlemen, have your wallets ready. Ollie, you'd recognize her, wouldn't you?"

"Oh yes, C.F. I just saw her in the other room."

"Very sorry, Miss Winnie," Frohman added. "I'd introduce you to her myself, but I have to stay put and take care of my wife." He held up his bronze-headed cane to show them. "Here she is. We've been inseparable ever since I fell head-over-heels in 1912, down my front porch steps."

"Don't worry, you poor dear," Winnie said, patting the elder man's hand. "We'll go by ourselves and find Madame de Page. I so wanted to hear her speak back home!"

Matt thanked their host, and Alma spoke up, finally breaking her discreet silence. "Yes, thank you, Mr. Frohman," she told him. "It's been wonderful meeting you. And you too, Miss Brandell."

Ollie again led them off through the fashionable crowd into the suite's private dining room, paneled in rich dark teak and lit by a gilded chandelier. As a reporter, Matt felt satisfied just to tag along and let this glib Broadway insider do his work for him.

Two stately ladies stood talking near the punchbowl, and as the little company approached, the smaller, darker-haired one turned to acknowledge their presence.

"Madame de Page, isn't it?" Ollie saluted her, leading the way. "Charlie Frohman sends us over. I'm Oliver Bernard, a play writer and designer, heading back to England to enlist. I'm very pleased to make your acquaintance."

Accepting the Belgian woman's hand, he kissed it elegantly and then introduced the others, one by one. "My American friends here also want very much to meet you."

"Oh, and one of you at least is a nurse!" the Belgian said. "How delightful, that so many Americans have such a great concern for the sorrows of the world."

"Yes, I guess it's true," Winnie said. "There are, uh, four of us on board from the United Nursing Service League. Our headmistress is Hildegard Krauss."

"Oh yes, I know the name. Tell her and your other friends that I would love to meet them all. You've heard about my appeal, as special envoy from my country?"

"Yes, ma'am," Winnie said. "My parents sent in a donation, but I was dying to see you when you were lecturing in the States. It's just terrible what those brutish Huns have done to poor little Belgium."

"Thank you...but of course, there is suffering on both sides. If you come to Brussels, I would like to show you our clinic."

Reaching into her tiny handbag, she gave Winnie a calling card. "My husband, Antoine, is Surgeon General of the Belgian Army. And we have a British nurse there, Edith Cavell, who is doing marvelous things," she added with a glance to Oliver.

"Oh, I read about Nurse Cavell too," Winnie said eagerly, slipping the card into her jacket pocket. "We don't know yet where we'll be stationed, but I'd love to come."

The taller woman standing beside the envoy came forward and shook Winnie's hand. "Hello, I'm Lady Margaret Mackworth. It's fine to see women stepping forth and taking a role internationally. You Americans have been leaders in some ways, but we in England are trying to do our part."

Ollie was first to react. "Lady Mackworth, the famous suffragette! Most delighted..."

He reached forward, but the aristocrat swiftly drew back her hand rather than have it kissed.

"Most honored to meet you, Milady," Ollie ended with an *impromptu* bow. "May I ask if your husband Sir Humphrey is with us on this voyage?"

"No," the lady said with dignity. "I am traveling with my father, who has been looking after his coal interests in America. We were advised by friends at the Waldorf to consider taking a neutral ship," she added, "but David didn't particularly care to change flags. I personally believe... like you, Miss Dexter...that women shouldn't shrink from danger in these times. If we are to win acceptance," she declared, flashing affirmative glances to the other women, "we must be bold."

"I, too, believe that women should be accepted in the world of men," Madame de Page said. "But we also have our special strength, which is nurturing and caring for the weak. That is one way, besides bravery, that we can make our influence felt."

"But Marie, my dear," Lady Margaret protested, "if you are saying, 'The hand that rocks the cradle rules the world,' I must disagree with you."

"No, Margaret, I only mean that there is some further skill and sensitivity that we can bring to the struggle...."

With that, the two women were back in their earnest conversation, and the others soon moved on. Ollie observed with relish, "Apparently Lady Mackworth is quite decent to talk to, when she's not stuffing firebombs into letterboxes."

"Oh, I heard about that," Winnie said. "To burn up the mail in England, as a protest to win women the vote! Is she really the one?" she added with a speculative look in her eye. "And she was released after only five days?"

"Yes, after staging a hunger strike in the jail."

"Now, Win, don't be picking up too many foreign ideas." Flash placed a protective arm around his sweetheart. "I don't want to have to print your brand new biography piece on the crime pages."

Both reporters in the party had been fairly silent during the introductions, testing the waters, watching and listening. But the levity of the group, and the champagne dispensed from trays by roving waiters, were having an effect. Now the four agreed to split up and mingle separately. Flash was content to stick with Winnie, and Alma with Ollie. After a moment's uncertainty, Matt decided to trust them and struck out on his own.

He soon recognized a face from the news wire, standing bearded and distinguished under a dark blue sea captain's hat. It was Commander J. Foster Stackhouse, the British polar explorer who'd been lecturing in America to raise money for an Antarctic expedition. Matt joined him in conversation with two others, including Staff Captain Anderson, white-clad in his immaculate Cunard uniform. The fourth man in their group was diminutive and Continental-looking, with a glossy black bowler topping off his dinner suit. He turned out to be an American, the novelist and playwright Justus Miles Forman.

"Do you think we'll be seeing Captain Turner at this affair?" Matt asked after introducing himself.

"The *real* captain, you mean?" Captain Anderson good-naturedly said. "No, he keeps himself busy with petty details like running the ship. But he leaves these important social functions to me."

"I don't blame him for laying low," Stackhouse said. "With the war on, and with all these worries about enemy action, it must be hard dealing with passengers' fears–not like the old days, when all we thought about was racing across the Atlantic and winning the Blue Riband prize for best speed."

"And with the speed came all this luxury, don't forget." Captain Anderson nodded at the splendor around them. "The Germans and Anglo-Americans have always tried to best each another in grandeur and comfort."

Matt asked, "Who holds the Blue Riband now, by the way, Captain? I suppose the *Titanic* would have, but did she ever officially make the list?"

"No," the staff captain said. "She was White Star Lines' one effort to beat Cunard, but she tripped coming out of the gate. The record holder is, or was, our sister ship *Mauretania*...at least until the war came, and she was drafted into the Royal Navy. Before that it was *Lusitania*, and before her, the *Deutschland* and *Kaiser Wilhelm der Grosse*...oh, and *Kronprinz Wilhelm* too, in 1909."

"Another war draftee," the writer Forman observed. "His ships are on the front lines, even if *Der Kaiser* himself isn't. How many British merchant ships did the *Crown Prince Willie* catch and scuttle, anyway, steaming around the Atlantic as an armed commerce raider? We were reading about two or three a month going down for a while there."

"Fourteen," Captain Anderson said, "until she was interned last month in Chesapeake Bay. But our *Lusi* here—" he thumped his heel against the polished parquet deck beneath them—"she could do much better than that if she were just given the chance." He winked at Matt to show that his wistful tone was in jest.

The remark caused Matt to reflect. Here he was with the international set, the globetrotters. These three men were all influential, all newsworthy. Yet could any of them affect destiny, war, or even the course of this ship? They spoke like bettors at a horse race, but who were the fixers? Where were the decisions really made, the clashes and alliances? Was it by great financiers, the Morgans, Rockefellers and Rothschilds? Or was it in some circle even higher?

"The shipbuilding contest," Justus Miles Forman was saying, "was about more than luxury and speed. While the ocean liners raced, British and German shipyards have been working overtime to build heavier-armed battleships, dreadnoughts, the new submarine-destroyers too, and now battlecruisers. This fight has been a long time in the making."

"It was the *Kaiser's* love of big ships that did it," Anderson said.

"And his healthy German appetite for colonies and warm-water ports," Commander Stackhouse added.

"Why, yes," Forman mischievously put in, "colliding with jolly old England's divine right to control the seven seas and her manifest destiny to rule a global empire."

In spite of his small size, the writer's Continental manner and self-assured speech gave him an air of equality to the two distinguished, uniformed sea-captains. His pert black bowler seemed more than a match for their glossy visored uniform caps.

Turning to the novelist, Matt said, "You wrote a play that dealt with the issue of war neutrality...*The Hyphen*, wasn't it called? Charlie Frohman produced it on Broadway."

"Yes," the author said. "An utter failure, alas! It dealt with divided loyalties and the dilemma of the hyphenated Americans...German-Americans, Irish-Americans, the ones who aren't quite accepted. Unfortunately, the just-plain-Americans didn't pay much attention."

Captain Stackhouse asked, "Do you carry around a hyphen of your own?"

"Far too many, I'm afraid," Miles admitted with a smile. "After crossing over so often on your fine ship, I love France, I love England, I even love Germany. I simply adore Denmark and Belgium, Spain and Austria, all the cozy little corners of Europe. I love America too, my homeland. So I've signed on to be a foreign correspondent, to warn my Yankee kinsmen, our naïve, native innocents abroad, about the perils of our modern world. But I dread seeing what this war has done to Europe."

"Do you have an assignment to cover the front?" Matt asked.

"Yes, from the *New York Times*. Exclusive, of course, but I do share stories."

"We'll be brothers-in-arms, then, Miles." Matt slapped the smaller man on the back, taking care to do it lightly. "I'm going over for the *Daily Inquisitor*."

"Sounds to me like you two will be competitors," Stackhouse said. "Isn't that the way it's supposed to work, vying to get all the news in print?"

"Well then, Commander," Matt responded, "how about a scoop for us both? Are the plans final yet for your seven-year Antarctic voyage? Or is the war going to postpone it? Has your ship the *Discovery* been drafted by the Royal Navy?"

"No, not as yet," Stackhouse said. "This war has definitely raised difficulties, though. It was the main reason for my fundraising trip to your country, with money so scarce in Europe. And my crew has suffered sad casualties...losing our chief surveyor Lord Congleton, late of the Grenadier Guards, was a dreadful blow.

"But we'll find someone to fill his berth, and our other volunteers may soon be released from military duty for this vital mission.

"It's quite an undertaking," the visionary seafarer went on, "and not merely a voyage of Antarctic exploration. Most of our time will be spent charting sea routes and maritime hazards off South America and in the South Pacific, as well as studying land forms and native peoples. We can leave our anthropologists on some of those remote islands for months at a time, and then return to pick them up, along with their findings. And our round-the-world trip will take us into the Atlantic, to finally chart the Azores and other sea zones, even to the site of the *Titanic* sinking."

"Really, Commander?" Captain Anderson asked, while Matt scribbled busily in the notebook he'd produced from his cummerbund. "Is it true that you believe the *Titanic* may have struck a rock in mid-Atlantic?"

"Not a rock, no," Stackhouse explained, "but an iceberg grounded upon a rock. An undersea mountain, perhaps." He stroked his gray beard and nodded significantly. "If such a recurrent hazard to navigation exists, rest assured that we'll find and chart it."

* * *

While the men mingled, Alma found herself in one of the groups in the dining room. Here she was without Matt or her close friends, but in lively company. And in Ollie's ebullient and somewhat drunken presence, she didn't feel like the target of strange men. Yet there was plenty of distraction. The Roycrofter commune leader Elbert Hubbard, invited or not, had appeared in his full Quaker regalia and been accepted, floppy hat and all, among the fashionable set.

"I still say we should join up and end this thing right away," Hubbard was saying of the European War. "Teddy and his Rough Riders could thump those goose-stepping Krauts in a week. The Brits and Franks can use a kick in the pants too, a good example of Yankee know-how."

"Do you really think the Americans would wish to join a war?" the French actress Rita Jolivet asked. "President Wilson and your Secretary of State, M'sieur William Jennings Bryan, are peace advocates. They have kept America out of the war."

"Bryan's just an old sissy," Hubbard said, "and Wilson's a college professor. Do you know what the problem is with college professors? They all have two hands—" he held up his big craftsman's paws—"so they're always saying, 'on the one hand this, but on the other hand, that.' They can never decide." After waiting out the flurry of laughs, he added, "As for the American people, they know what to do better than any politician."

Oliver Bernard said, "Moving a great country like America to war, though...that will take time, and a lot of production."

"What, you mean war production?" Hubbard asked. "America's output of armaments and provisions can more than match any European country."

"I don't doubt that," the stage designer said. "You're already producing plenty for the Allies. But I mean theatrical productions, grand openings! Big, lavish affairs, with songs and dance numbers that sway the public and get them marching." The scrawny Englishman raised his arms half-drunkenly. "Pretty girls with guns, in brief costumes, dancing on the deck of a battleship! That will get your young men charged up to enlist! If you want to have a war, especially in a democracy like yours, you've got to first get the public behind it...get some war spirit going, strike up the band!" His ending bow drew applause from the onlookers.

Only momentarily upstaged, Hubbard replied, "Nonsense! America is ready to fight right now. If you want to know more about it, read my essay on *Der Kaiser*." He drew a handful of booklets from his wide-lapelled coat and handed some out. "Here, listen to this." He read from one: "If you will examine the present war situation carefully, you will find it stamped and stenciled, 'Made in Germany.'" He closed the book. "The war is theirs. America's job is to help end it."

"Well, Elbert, if it takes you some time, don't worry," Ollie blandly assured him. "This war is firmly established, and it isn't going anywhere. It'll still be there when you Yanks finally arrive."

Drawn in by the commotion, Flash and Winnie rejoined the group. Alma, who as yet had spoken little, edged over to them to discuss something that had been bothering her.

"I'm trying to watch and listen, and not be conspicuous," she said. "But there's a man here who's been looking at me. I don't know if he thinks he recognizes me, but I can't place him. Don't look now, he's right over there."

She indicated a slight, distinguished man in a Van Dyke beard.

After a leisurely survey, Flash laughed softly. "No worries about him, I'd say. That's the Irish art connoisseur, Hugh Lane, who's been in the papers lately. He's been in the States buying back old Rembrandt and Rubens masterpieces to take home, cheap...it seems they're too highbrow or racy for our provincial American tastes. He's probably just enjoying the scenery," he added with a wink to the ladies.

"Oh, Sir Hugh Lane!" Winnie gasped, suddenly excited. "Alma, my dear, haven't you read about him?" She moved closer to speak in her friend's ear, the champagne sweet on her breath.

"To help support the Red Cross, he's offered to pay ten thousand pounds for a painting to be done by the famous American artist, John Singer Sargent. It's to be a portrait, a female, but he hasn't yet chosen the right woman to pose for it." She self-consciously reset her nurse cap on her head.

"Alma," she went on, "he's probably considering you! You should go over and talk to him. See there, he's looking our way again!"

"Oh no, that's not what I need right now!" Alma turned her back on the keen-eyed Irishman. "I'm supposed to be in hiding, remember? What if Jim should see a painting of me? He'd probably buy it for top dollar and then shoot it full of holes!" She shivered. "What am I even doing at a party? Let's get out of this room."

"Nonsense," Winnie said with a wink to Flash. "All you need is a little more to drink...here," she added, grabbing two flutes of champagne from the tray of a passing waiter.

The three of them edged away from Ollie and Elbert, who were still playing off one another like expert vaudevillians. They found Matt in the parlor of the lavish suite. He was standing by Frohman, who had settled into a plush chair to give his cane a rest. As they approached, their host smiled up at them.

"Well, my young friends, are you enjoying our little *salon*?"

"Yes indeed, C.F.," Flash answered. "I'd say it's every bit as good as one of your stage shows."

"Well, I wish I could circulate more freely and enjoy it. But my better half here is a harsh mistress." Frohman spoke with a rueful smile, tapping his stick on the polished hardwood floor.

Matt said, "Our kind host was just telling me about a problem he has. He's short a singer."

"Oh my, you didn't volunteer our Alma here, did you?" Winnie blurted out with an air of mischievous and slightly tipsy innocence. "She won't like that one bit...being so talented, but shy." She covered her mouth as if realizing she'd spoken out of turn. "Sorry," she murmured aside to Alma's urgent look. "Too much bubbly, I think."

"I didn't suggest anything," Matt said to Alma, obviously anxious to cover himself. "Anyway," he added, "it shouldn't be hard to find talent in this Broadway bunch."

"Actually," Frohman said, "it's a little touchy dealing with these stars. When they're together socially, they'd rather stand back and kibitz somebody else. Are you saying this lovely lady of yours can sing? Do you read music, my dear?"

"I'm not saying it," Matt hastily said as Alma felt herself blushing. She was suddenly light-headed, too, from this sudden attention. Or was it the drink?

"Well, I can tell she has a voice, even from the very little she's said tonight." Frohman turned back to Alma. "I'm sorry, my dear, it shouldn't have been a problem to begin with. My friend Jerry Kern—you know, the young Broadway songwriter—is supposed to be here with us. He was going to sing and perform at the piano for this party, so I brought the set of sheet music to his latest hit and gave it to the band." He reached into the chair beside him and drew out a music folio.

"But Jerry didn't make it...he sent me a radio telegram apologizing. It said he'd overslept and missed the boat, after staying out all night at a party singing and playing. So far, I haven't been able to line up a replacement."

"Coming from you, C.F.," Flash said, "it ought to be a command performance for any of these actors."

"Well, yes...but the stars," Frohman lamented, "the temperamental stars..."

Alma spoke up in desperation, looking around the room. "What about Josephine Brandell, the opera singer? If they're afraid of being compared to anyone, it's her."

"I tried." Frohman shook his head sadly. "She's saving her voice, she said. She may be too worried about the war, or a bit seasick. She's gone back to her cabin." He pressed Alma. "If I could just prevail on you to look at this...?" He held out the printed song sheet.

"I'm not really that good, and my voice isn't in condition," Alma protested, sipping champagne to moisten her throat.

"Methinks the lady protest-eth too much," Flash mischievously said. "I've heard her belt one out when she thought nobody was around. She's dynamite."

"You can practice in the spare bedroom if you like," Frohman urged her. "It's Jerry's best tune so far, really something special. *They Didn't Believe Me*, it's called." He thrust the folio into Alma's hand. "I put him to work polishing up some of my British import musicals, and he's transformed them. This song's more free-form and dramatic than the usual show stuff. A male part, written as a duet, so you'll have to tinker with the lyrics."

"I've heard it performed. It's lovely." Alma's reluctance as she looked over the music was shot through by a sudden yearning, fueled too by that last sip of champagne. "I do feel that I owe you something for showing us all such a wonderful time. If you really think..."

And so it was arranged. Winnie hurried Alma off to the bedroom to practice, the two of them clasping hands in excitement.

* * *

Matt carried Frohman's copies of sheet music over to the bandleader and the piano player. He felt a thrill of stage fright himself for Alma, worrying less for fear of exposure than for how the experience might affect her after her recent distemper. But then, you had to take chances in this life. He hoped the alcohol might smooth over the risks and expectations, both for Alma and her cosmopolitan audience.

He rejoined Flash to watch and wait. Around them flowed the chatter and glitter of the social scene—a last, carefree remnant of the peacetime world they were so rapidly leaving behind. Or so it seemed to his reporter's eye, only slightly sentimental after two drinks.

When it came time and the giddy, slightly tipsy girls returned, Charles Frohman stood up. He tapped his cane sharply against the underside of a table, waiting for the local hubbub to subside. Alma stood by, flushed and alert.

"Ladies and gentlemen," the impresario said, "May I introduce to all of you an unknown but talented performer, Miss Alma Brady. Tonight she's consented to sing for us one of Jerome Kern's latest hits from Broadway. He sends deep regrets that he can't be here to accompany her, but I hope you'll be kind to our guest and show her your appreciation." Amid the polite round of clapping, he signaled to the orchestra.

The band struck up a gentle introduction, and Alma stepped to the front with the poise of a trained singer.

"Don't know how it happened, quite. Must have been the summer night..."

She sang simply and beautifully with almost no hesitation, holding the sheet music before her. The partygoers remained silent, and only faint chatter came in from the other rooms. The atmosphere was one of subdued appraisal of this brash newcomer.

"Your lips, your eyes, your curly hair, are in class beyond compare..."

"Your girl's a natural," Flash murmured in Matt's ear. The youth kept his arm snug around Winnie, who beamed with pride.

About the room, murmured remarks and conversation resumed, signaling acceptance and perhaps relief. But when the song's already familiar refrain swelled forth, with Alma's voice following, it brought a newly attentive hush.

"And when I told them how wonderful you are..."

The small band's music rose heroically, and the singer's voice soared above it like a bird caught in a sudden tempest, arching over wind-driven trees to find a perch.

"They wouldn't believe me, they'll never believe me, that from this great big world you've chosen me."

She sang through the first verse and the second with growing confidence. As she finished, the applause from the cultivated crowd was genuine and spontaneous.

A success, no denying it! Alma looked radiant, her wide-eyed gaze roving the room and lingering on Matt—or so it seemed to him as he vigorously applauded.

Then someone shouted for an encore. Instead, the singer fled the limelight into the arms of Charles Frohman, who gave her a congratulatory hug and a peck on the cheek.

"What a joy to catch them on the brink of success," he remarked to Matt as he handed her over. "Before they become great stars."

Matt was all congratulation, bolstering her as well-wishers came by. But after her triumph, Alma couldn't stay long at the party. There were too many interested stares, too many questions. At her earnest entreaty, Matt found their coats and swept her away. He told Flash and Winnie to stay at Frohman's as long as they liked—advice that the younger couple received with a mutual wink, as the other two headed out on a moonlight walk.

As they went, Alma clung close. It gave Matt reason to believe that the Atlantic's restless tides had shifted once again, this time in his favor. Well apart from the rest, he took Alma into his arms and experienced something he hadn't known from her as yet—earnest, eager passion in her kiss.

The two lingered in the deepest shadows of the promenade. Drawn together in a tight embrace, they said very little before returning to their stateroom.

The most penetrating stare that followed them was from one of the ship's stewards standing party-watch to starboard—a compact, sandy-haired man who nodded in quiet satisfaction.

* * *

Black satin gleamed and diamonds glittered. Seen against Alma's soft, pale skin, her red lips and raven locks overwhelmed Matt's senses. As their faces brushed, her warm nearness was a medley of pleasure and fascination. The drawing room's single dim lamp set off the beauty of her upturned face.

Those black-gloved hands fumbled at her tight diamond choker and flung it aside, offering up her smooth neck for him to kiss. Still the satin evening gown was in the way. She arched her back against the lounge and let him reach behind. Loosening the clasp, he peeled the garment down her ivory shoulders.

Her chest against his face was creamy silk. He grazed across it gently, hoping his few hours of stubble wouldn't prickle too harshly. He heard her breath sighing and could feel her heart race.

Writhing with his help, she drew her elbows clear of the tight dress to force it down from her pale, pink-tipped breasts. Watching them quiver free, Matt felt a velvet hand on the back of his neck. Alma's other gloved hand clutched one breast in an erotic confection of white, pink and velvety black which she crammed up against his lips. He tasted one sweet bud, then the other in its turn.

His dinner jacket slid to the floor as they strove together. She clutched at him, groping with soft black fingertips to tug away his bowtie, cummerbund and shirtfront. He took charge, lifting her waist and undoing the last clasps of her gown. But the costly garment clung to the fullness of her hips. Not to tear it, she twisted artfully. Lifting her arms, she let him draw it up over her head, and in an instant wriggled free.

The silk chemise that remained was as nothing. He brushed it aside, only to pause at the wealth of beauty, nature and art before him—her slender limbs, shapely body, the lush curvature of hips and soft blonde nest of her lap. All were framed by the wicked black of dyed hair, elbow-length gloves, knee-high stockings and patent leather pumps. Before this delirious vision he reeled against a heady surging of alcohol, fevered blood, and the sea tides shifting underfoot.

* * *

Alma's head swam, her breath coming in ragged gasps. She wasn't weak but energized—eager and impatient for more of these delicious sensations, the pleasant shocks of closeness and intimacy. She wanted these moments not to end but go on, more intensely and urgently.

The warmth of Matt's enfolding and the breathless crush of his embrace thrilled her. The tickle of his lips on her ear and the gentle rasp of his breathing wiped out all other sensations. She clutched to feel his reality, kissed to goad him into more passion, and squirmed to make their bodies touch everywhere possible. Each limb, each cell, each hair of her was alive and found a mate in him. This energy—this love—she'd never known it before and didn't want it to end.

He had paused to come up for air. She gazed at him, feeling breathless with excitement, and even more with wonder at her own abandon. All the fear, frustration and doubt of recent years seemed to find a marvelous, sensuous release in Matt. Standing before her only half-clothed, he was more of a man than she'd yet seen. His hungry gaze, tousled head and strong, eager hands didn't frighten or repel her. He seemed ready at any moment to topple onto her—and that bulge in his trousers must soon become painful. She was ready. And yet, fighting through the mists of intoxication and lust, she knew what she had to do.

He'd stopped. Had she been too forward, too brazen? In his present state it obviously didn't matter. She must take the chance.

"Matt, darling, I have to get up." Kicking off her shoes she arose, thrillingly aware of her nakedness and how the chemise barely slid to mask it. Matt swayed into her, his hands questing; but she slipped past him with a quick embrace and a kiss to his neck. He remained gentle, his body firm, his breath no more scented with alcohol than her own. He deserved her. Hadn't he earned her?

Passing through the bedroom into the washroom, she found her metal case with the diaphragm. It was new. Her old one she'd thrown away, never intending to need it again. But Hildegard had said she must have one, like all of the girls, as part of a nurse's readiness.

After relieving herself, she inserted it—trying not to think of past encounters with Jim, the whiskey breath and tobacco stink of his rutting bulk, in the pitch darkness that she'd always insisted on. And those vile attempts by the others, awful!

Here tonight already was more pleasure, more promise, more heaven with Matt. At what lay ahead, what could yet happen, a hot shiver of excitement coursed through her, sweeping away the past.

One more thing from her bag, a secret weapon she'd never meant to use, but saved: a filmy chiffon robe, all but transparent, ruffled at neck, wrists and knee. She laid aside the long black gloves, stockings and chemise. Having brought her to this promise of love, they'd served their purpose.

Still she must take care, or even be ready to resist. Passion and intoxication must not rule over good sense. Could it be true, as she'd read, that six in ten American wives suffered from a vile disease, gonorrhea? And countless more hapless mothers and babes, syphilis?

She had to be sure. Being a nurse should count for something.

When a woman sheds her clothes, she sheds her shame. Where had she heard that? As Alma moved to the lavatory door, the ship's mild rolling caused soft chiffon to brush against her thighs, nipples and intimate parts, making her nudity more thrilling.

Matt sat on the bed in his briefs. At first she thought he was playing a musical instrument. But then she realized he was inflating something—a condom! Alma had learned that even the new rubber sheaths had defects. He was testing it to be sure it would protect him, and her, too, not just against disease but pregnancy.

In a passion of relief and thankfulness, she moved close. Kneeling down, she assisted him. Her nurse training was a help and she handled him with tenderness. His caution and responsibility were the greatest gifts that she could imagine.

Then in a mad surge of affection, she risked everything—and knew in a terrible moment of certainty, she'd lost him forever.

Yet love prevailed. Again he crushed her in his embrace, this time flesh to flesh, tongue to tongue, without barrier or restraint. His kiss ravished her rudely, alarmingly. If Boss Jim had tried this, their mouths would have been full of blood. But she gave in and gave back, trading intimacy for intimacy, invasion for intrusion. Again she felt possessed by the need to possess him, every fiber of her body throbbing in tune with his. Her lips, legs, arms clutched to draw him in, until finally they were joined.

The presence of his maleness inside her was a dynamo, a piston pumping electricity through her core. Her desperation matched his as their hot, moist friction became a searing fusion. She strove fiercely, building to heights of sensation she'd never known.

* * *

Before waiting resignedly outside the lavatory, Matt had gathered up their loose clothing from the drawing room and laid it on the far bed. To it he added his trousers, but retained his briefs. This Saloon Class heating was superb, driving out the sea's chill.

The champagne had worn off, and there was no more. Just as well; he still might need his wits.

Hopefully their romantic enchantment would resume. She'd surprised him with her extreme ardor in the drawing room. He thought of other women he'd seen, but not known, the hard women of the street, the wild ones and later, broken and wilted ones, fallen to sickness or addiction. She wasn't one of those, she couldn't be. He didn't know what

Jim and his crew might have done to her, but there was still a strength here, and joyous innocence.

Was she safe for him? To be certain, he took a condom from his supply and tested it.

The washroom door swung open, its electric light dazzling. Through it came a vision, all of Alma's charms outlined by the glow and revealed in filmy gauze. Barefoot she stood before him, wearing only her loose translucent robe and a loving smile.

By the bedroom light he saw that she'd renewed her lipstick—a softer pink, that she now moistened with dainty pink tongue-tip. Moving close, she bent forward over him on the bed. Her loose breasts swayed in chiffon, and her thighs brushed tantalizingly against his knees.

"I want to see all of you," she said, undoing the button of his shorts. Deftly but not expertly she tugged them down, a delightful feeling, and whisked them off his legs.

He fumbled with the condom, trying to drag it onto his maleness, which was now almost as slack as the thin rubber.

"Here," she murmured, "let me help." Carefully with red-nailed fingertips, she re-rolled the sheath and leaned forward to apply it. By then, under her caressing touch, it slipped on more firmly.

With a sudden impulsive movement she bent down over him, pressed her lips against his cloaked penis, and kissed it.

Shocked, he looked down at her pink lip-prints on the back of the sagging sheath. He'd heard of this, a whore's trick! That lovely face—how could he ever have guessed her base desires?

Gazing at her, he saw uncertainty, concern and—innocence. On a savage impulse of his own he lunged forward, seized her shoulders and returned her kiss forcefully, with deeply probing tongue.

It was her turn to stiffen in surprise. Still, she surrendered her soft mouth to his invasion. His perverse urge overcame hers, and became mutual as he drew her up, twisted and bore her backward onto the bed. He could feel that his manhood was no longer in retreat.

Lips, tongue, breasts, the magic funnel of her waist and spreading glory of hips, thighs, derrière—every part of her belonged to him. His fingers probed her soft wetness, eliciting gasps of pleasure as her red-nailed fingers plucked at his hardness. Relenting, he eased her backward and placed a firm pillow behind her neck, before pinning her with his entire weight. His swollen shaft soon found its place, to be dragged deeper by her eager clutching fingertips.

* * *

The dizzy lift of the party and its aftermath had faded into sleep, replaced by sensations even more pleasing, comforting and intoxicating. Alma felt no regrets, though she knew she'd done a complete turnabout, throwing aside all her resolutions of the previous day. She'd challenged herself, and won—but what had caused it? Even in the warm haze of contentment, she had to wonder.

Why, it was Matt, of course, this fine man who'd been so giving and forgiving, who'd aided and supported her. He'd shared so sincerely in her success, the evening's musical novelty before the Broadway elite— just a fleeting moment, perhaps, but the dream of her girlhood. For that to be followed by this...marvel, the miracle of sexual completion! And somehow too a healing, a shaking off of everything that went before.

It was the evening itself, too, the social blossoming and the inspired company, a turning point that had to be memorialized and made part of one's deepest being.

But even more, in a way, it was the ship. Sweet *Lusitania*, this wonderful gathering-place and transition-point, that brought so many different people together from so many lands, to create within its splendid realms true magic and excitement—and love! Alma could see why her parents had been so devoted to this kind of adventure. Now it was hers.

"You don't think it's wrong, what we've done?" she asked Matt as he stirred sleepily beside her.

"How could it be wrong? It's the only possible thing, the one true thing."

"Yes, you're right, it is. But will we remember that by daylight? Can you possibly still respect me in the morning?"

"In the morning, if it ever comes—I hope it never does—but yes, I'll respect you! I've learned to respect you tremendously, in so many ways— as a gentle nurse and divine singer. A *very* private secretary, and the greatest lover since Cleopatra—"

"Quiet, you."

"Anyway, why worry about the future? We're headed into—who knows what? How can we control it? The best we can do is to survive this madness, and try to end it. We only have right now, my love—and perhaps, just perhaps, a future."

"Yes, but for now—"

"I am a bit worried about when the others finally come back," he said. "Can we stay here together, do you think?"

"We can stay."

"Winnie won't mind?"

"No, she won't mind. Flash won't mind it either, I can promise you."

"I don't suppose he will. Mmm, shipboard romance, there's nothing like it."

"That's enough, you!"

Chapter 26

The Plot

The Map Room at the Admiralty House in Whitehall was hushed in expectancy. Sea Lord Jackie Fisher, fresh from his daily church attendance at Westminster Abbey, sat waiting by the broad chart table. He sensed that his sullen presence caused the room's usual bustle to be muted. But he didn't care. The Sea Lord's mood this morning was dark, and he made no effort to conceal it by polite chatter.

This war was going badly for England, both on land and sea. Now Fisher, as much as anyone, stood to be held accountable. The Admiralty, whose decisions loomed large in both areas, appeared to be in turmoil over it. It seemed crystal-clear to the old seafarer that the weather must change, and soon.

His Lordship Jackie, as they all knew, had fought his way up "through the hawsehole" to his high position, starting out at the rank of novice seaman in an old square-rigged sailing ship. Now at the peak of naval power, as his reward for talent and persistence, he found himself under the thumb of an over-ambitious Public School boy who'd never even been to sea. Shades of *HMS Pinafore*; the comic opera was less funny now. He'd never expected to be the butt of the joke.

True, the young Lord Winston had been pleasant enough to work with at the start. Churchill and Fisher were both reformers, both with visions of the future to impose on the crusty, centuries-old naval establishment. They had begun as a team, but now Churchill was clearly more intent on his own visions of glory than on the slow, patient task of shepherding a navy. He had pushed forward this grand wager of a Turkish invasion, drawing Fisher and others reluctantly along, and now that it was failing, someone would have to pay. With the trenches dug deep in Europe and an undersea blockade bleeding England dry, the young firebrand was casting about for some other schoolboy exploit to break the deadlock and win acclaim. Between the demands of war and overweening personal ambition, tensions had been growing that must soon lead to a fracture. All sensed it.

The staff worked on silently, avoiding the gold-braided curmudgeon brooding in his armchair and awaiting the young firebrand. They spoke in whispers as they shuffled their papers and updated the charts.

The focus of their labors was the Plot, a large map covering one twenty-foot-tall wall of the broad room. On it, ruled over with a grid of latitudes and longitudes, were the outlines of Europe, England, Ireland, the Atlantic and all of the adjacent seas, bordered by Africa and the Americas. The known positions of significant merchant vessels and warships, be they friend, enemy or neutral, were pinned onto the map as color-coded disks of various size, all marked with arrowheads to indicate the vessel's last known direction. Each disk was large enough to cover the approximate area of open sea that a ship's lookout could survey from the height of its crow's nest. In that way, search patterns could be easily set up for all ships—or at least those visible on the surface, not the submersibles.

Inversely, as Jackie knew, the size of each disk also showed the area of sea from which a ship of that height could be sighted—though not necessarily figuring in the smoke-plume, which could make a large ship an even easier target to spot, depending on weather conditions.

Now, from sightings and orders passed along by other departments, including the secret wireless intercepts of Room 40, the staff was busy updating ship positions on the Plot in preparation for the regular morning briefing. From his seat, Admiral Fisher watched the unfolding situation with a gloomy sense of foreboding.

The door opened...to Rear Admiral Henry Oliver, the Admiralty's Intelligence Officer. Fisher barely acknowledged him with a nod, leaving it to the lesser commander to start a conversation.

"Morning, Jackie," Oliver said as he took a seat across the table. "I'm sure you know that, in Churchill's absence, I am to be Deputy First Lord in addition to my regular duties. If you have any suggestions or special requirements for the Admiralty—"

"Splendid, just peachy!" Fisher interrupted him, not troubling with excessive courtesy. "You're behind and overworked already, as am I, so now your responsibilities and mine are to be doubled, while Winston takes off to Paris to court the Italians."

"Yes, and doubtless pay a visit to his French Mistress as well." Oliver's gossip was delivered *sotto voce* with a wry smile. "Now that things are looking glum here in the Navy, our friend spends his time courting Field Marshall John French over there on the land battlefront. Word is, he's thinking of becoming a doughboy."

Well now, this was truly outrageous. After digesting it a moment, Fisher had to speak out. "While he's off on a jolly, Admiral, instead of taking on new tasks, you'd do well to attend to the job you've already got."

Oliver finally took offense at this. "Now, Jackie, I'm sorry to hear that you feel behind par and overworked, but I wouldn't describe my own operation in quite the same way—"

"Is that so, Admiral?" Fisher retorted. "Then why is it that reports from Ewing's code room take from twelve to twenty hours to reach me, or any others who can do anything about them? Ewing with his bright fellows isn't the bottleneck. So it must be your in-box, where they sit for half the day waiting for you to censor and water them down."

Oliver flushed and glanced around, obviously nervous about the open discussion. "Really, Jackie," he began, "the demands of secrecy—"

"Secrecy? If you ask me, there's too much of it around here, secrecy from the people who count! I'd do better to ask our First Lord's mistress than wait for the facts from you." Fisher's eyes rolled as he shot a look around the room, challenging anyone to raise an eyebrow. "Could it be that there's a secret reason behind all this secrecy? I sometimes wonder."

"Jackie, excuse me," the chastened Oliver murmured in reply, "but you really should know that, when the wags here talk loosely about Churchill's French mistress, they are merely referring to Marshall French—"

The door opened then, cutting off all talk. Through the open half of the double panels came a man's backside, attired in pinstripe trousers and tailcoat, backing in as if the new arrival were chatting and bidding farewell to someone outside the room. Then he closed the door, still facing away as if fussing with the lock. He finally turned to greet those inside, giving a polite tip of his black top hat as he removed it. It was

Winston Churchill, First Lord of the Admiralty, coming down from his residence upstairs.

"Greetings, chaps," he said, setting his black top hat and cane on the broad tabletop. "Jackie, hello. I hope all is well on this morning of my departure. We soon shall find out, I trust."

Sea Lord Fisher found himself a bit subdued at the appearance of young Churchill, whom he had usually considered a friend. But his bitter spirits rallied him to speak up. "It's a wonder to me that you can depart at all in these difficult times. Isn't your presence needed more urgently here?"

"Now, Jackie," Churchill said tolerantly, "if Italy can be brought into the war on our side— " he paused—"it will greatly hasten our victory," he finished with a smile.

"Victory, eh!" Fisher gained strength from his indignation. "See here, Winston, all of Italy will mean less than Gallipoli and Turkey would have, if our navy remains powerless in the teeth of a U-boat blockade. As always, the fate of England rises or falls on the sea tides."

"Now, Gentlemen, if I may have your attention..." The three of them turned to face Sir Reginald "Blinker" Hall, Director of Naval Intelligence, who had entered from an inner office. Quick to rescue the situation, he took his place before the Plot with a long pointer in hand.

"I'm to deliver today's briefing on the naval situation, before our chief heads away to the Continent to deal with the land war. First off, Jackie, you're quite right, there is rather an unprecedented flurry of U-boat activity just now. It's all to be expected, I assure you, and nothing much to worry about...merely a side-effect of troopship rumors that our division had put forth as a cover for the Turkish landings."

"More Gallipoli nonsense," Fisher grumbled. "That fiasco just gets costlier and costlier. I wonder how many careers it will cost," he muttered with a glance at Churchill.

"Well," Blinker continued, unruffled except for a flurry of eye-blinks, "we can expect the sinking of some additional merchants. The *U-30*, that we have identified from radio intercepts, is running home northward after a cruise off Dartmouth."

His pointer indicated a red marker east of England and north of Ireland—a square one, not circular like the ship tokens.

"Here we see other U-boats on patrol...*U-35, U-36, U-41, et cetera...*"
He waved the pointer to indicate a scatter of red squares around Britain.
"This one, the *U-20*, is arriving from Emden, headed for the Liverpool
Channel." He pointed to a red chip off the southwest corner of Ireland.

"*U-20* just scuttled a small freighter, the *Earl of Lathom*, near
Fastnet Light. Here you see we have a cruiser, *Juno*, on station nearby."
The pointer dropped to a large blue circle slightly southward. "But she is
old, the pre-dreadnought design, very vulnerable to torpedo attack."

"Then what in God's name," Admiral Fisher demanded, "is she
doing defending the main Atlantic sea route? Isn't she a sister to those
unfortunates, the *Aboukir, Hogue,* and *Cressy*, that we lost to one U-boat
in the space of an hour? Are we forming up another Live-Bait Squadron
for the Huns to scuttle?"

At his use of the term "live bait," Jackie saw Churchill scowl. The
triple sinking last fall, with great loss of life, was something the First
Lord had been blamed for—perhaps unfairly, since he had ordered ship
reassignments that should have prevented it. But ever since then, the
notion of one vulnerable vessel being targeted to lure other rescuing
ships to their doom was a sore point in the navy.

"*Juno* is from our South Irish fleet," Oliver said. "She's under the
command of Admiral Coke in Queenstown."

"Coke's Gilbert-and-Sullivan Navy," Fisher observed with a snort. "A
ruddy travesty, I've heard tell of it."

"The *Juno* is Admiral Coke's flagship, sir," Hall explained,
blinking furiously.

Churchill joined the outcry. "Then what is she doing there alone?
Make it quick, man!"

"She is on escort duty, awaiting rendezvous with the *Lusitania*
inbound." Blinker's pointer moved westward to the largest target in
the Atlantic, a huge white disk whose direction arrow pointed south
of Fastnet.

"Well, she must be recalled, then," Churchill said with decision.
"Send her back to port at the first opportunity."

"Which one?" Blinker asked. "*Juno* or *Lusitania*?"

"Why, *Juno*, of course," Churchill said. "The *Lusitania* hasn't enough
coal to return to New York, surely. And her passengers would be furious
at any delay."

"Quite right," Fisher seconded. "*Juno* cannot match speeds with *Lusitania* anyway, and would only slow her down."

"What shall we do for an escort, then?" Oliver asked.

"Two or three fast destroyers would make a perfect escort," Fisher said. "*Juno* is worse than useless. A U-boat, freshly armed from Germany, would sink three old *Junos* first and serve us up the *Lusitania* for dessert. Anyway, this *U-20* will reach Liverpool far ahead of our passenger liner, even at submerged speed, and will probably spend all of her torpedoes along the way on lesser targets. Unless she's gunning for *Lusi*, that is, lying in wait and saving torpedoes."

"Well, in any case, destroyers are in short supply," Churchill declared. "I fear an escort is quite out of the question."

"But what is this here?" Abruptly rising and going to a stepladder, Admiral Oliver reached up to the map and pulled down a stack of four coin-sized gray disks at Milford Haven, the southwestern port of Wales. "These are submarine-destroyers, are they not?" he asked, descending. "Indeed yes, just a few hours away, the *Lion*, *Linnet*, *Lucifer*, and *Laverock*," he read from the disks. "I'd think they would make short work of any U-boat. Or at least, give it a good fright."

"They're reassigned elsewhere," Churchill said shortly. "In point of fact, they may already have left the Irish Channel."

"Well," Oliver observed, setting the disks down on the table, "an escort, any escort, could at least give the *Lusitania* time to escape at speed."

"You're proposing, what, to sacrifice a Royal Navy cruiser and its crew for a passenger liner?" Fisher demanded. "We're in the business of war, man, not peace."

"In the past," Oliver pointed out, "we've escorted or diverted passenger liners carrying valuable military goods."

Lord Fisher rose to his feet. "I don't even care how valuable her cargo might be. We can't go trading ship for ship, warship for civilian!" The old admiral found himself genuinely outraged for the first time that morning.

"The *Lusitania* is a Royal Navy ship too, under our command," Oliver reminded the rest. "Can we at least notify Captain Turner that his escort will be withdrawn? Otherwise he might delay in waiting for the rendezvous."

"The more fool he, if he does," Fisher snapped. "As far as we know, *Juno* could have been sunk already. And a warning message, with Germans listening posts decoding...why, man, that could bring the U-boats circling like hounds to a hunt!"

"So it's resolved," First Lord Churchill decreed from his place at the table. "I'm afraid that *Lusitania* will have to take her chances, just like any other merchant. No destroyers can be spared now, certainly not any cruisers. And I do not expect this order to be countermanded in my absence."

Watching the young lord's confident, decisive manner in the impossible situation, Fisher was struck by an inspiration. "Oh-ho, I see what's afoot here," he burst out abruptly. "Winston, you dog! You were saying a while back that neutral shipping should be encouraged, especially American merchants...how did you put it? Oh, yes: 'If one of them gets into trouble, so much the better.' Well, this can be the playing-out of your scheme. Except this time it's a British ship that's in play, under our command, not an American one...with a thousand or more English men, women and children aboard, as well as our gullible Yankee cousins. You think it's worth it to get the Yanks into the war?"

He glanced around the other officers in the room, but barely gave them serious consideration. "Well, so be it, Winnie. Under your tender mercies, I pray for all their souls."

"Nonsense, Jackie," Churchill said. "You're just making up scandalous rumors as usual—no harm done, so long as they're confined to this room. I'm only doing what's necessary to preserve England's fleet-in-being, a harsh necessity in these times. We face difficult choices, now more than ever. But in any case, I must be off to Italy and the front lines in France. Farewell."

Jackie saw the young lord make an exit, marveling at his nerve. Well, Churchill likely was on his way out anyway, due to this Turkey foul-up, and his own youthful restlessness. Might as well hang for a horse as for a sheep, eh?

And yet a passenger tragedy, or one large enough to massively stir sentiments abroad, might by way of atonement require more heads to roll—even possibly his own resignation?

Well, why not? Maybe it was time.

Chapter 27

Buddies

Trevor felt lucky the rain had stopped for the moment. The cold, fickle drizzle had threatened to flood his small trench. And the bombardment, too–the rain of steel death and TNT concussions having retreated, or at least marched away to another part of the wasteland.

He was lucky indeed to get his morning ration, a sodden biscuit and a tin of bully beef tossed from an adjoining foxhole in a greasy paper, with a twist of tobacco bundled in for his pipe.

Lucky, yes, to have survived the final month of winter in this hellhole—to have made it from knife-hard frozen mud to soft, yielding, reeking mud.

And lucky, most of all, to have a buddy.

"Breakfast time, my friend," he said to the one below. "Wish I could split it with you, but all I can spare is a few crumbs." He began working on the tin with his trench knife...a difficult task with numb, chilled hands. But it was still a familiar, purposeful activity that promised a reward. All he lacked was a third hand to wave away the flies. A pity that his buddy was otherwise occupied.

"We've done it, friend. We've lived to see the spring." These wretched flies were a sure sign of spring. They swarmed around his face and the half-cut can in a dizzy haze, an aerial frenzy of buzzing greed. When he reached into his trenchcoat pocket to take out the bun, they immediately covered the greasy bread, in a seething mosaic of beautiful blue-green bodies and shiny lace wings. He had to practically scrape the blighters off with one cupped hand to wolf down a mouthful. When done, he put away the biscuit and brushed the crumbs, with their pursuant flies, onto the body beneath him.

"There you are, friend. A token of thanks for keeping me out of the mud."

The corpse, all but buried, was a Boche, he felt sure from the gray patches of coat still visible. An imposition to squat on a fellow, true, and one that might be taken as a sign of disrespect. He was the enemy, after all—but even so, a faithful buddy. Without someone, anyone, to stand on, you would sink right in and stick. By night you could be frozen into the mud, with no way to move unless some patrol risked their lives to chip and pry you out. The mud clung and crept, sapping your strength and making you heavy and damp. One could find himself rotten with trench foot, too, like most blokes out here—but for the blessing of a stout friend.

Now something new was coming...a mist, drifting down the trench line on the morning breeze. This wind, like most, brought only the smell of death from more unburied bodies—unburied because, early in the deployment, they had retrieved and respectfully interred the fallen, friend and foe alike, for sanitation and out of simple human decency. But then the shelling came and unburied them, resurrecting each one horribly and blowing some apart in the process. They would then re-bury the pieces. But again when the smoke cleared, the bodies would be unburied again in tinier fragments, so what was the point? Death permeated land and air, with the flies and stench, and the only thing that would cover it was tobacco smoke, a good pipe-bowl of the precious stuff. That killed death itself, the smells of it at least.

Or else, as sometimes happened, a fresh gust wafted in fragrance from the spring pastures just a few hundred meters away, a warm blast redolent of trees and flowers. Almost worse, that, a reminder of the living world one might not survive to see again.

But this breeze was neither stench nor spring. The mist had a greenish tinge as it moved toward Trevor and his friend across the blasted ruin of landscape. The air that bore it had a tang, a sharp antiseptic scent that made the eyes water.

Then Trevor noticed something: the flies, the maddening swarms that filled his vision, were dissipating—no, dying, he could see as the little bodies dropped to the mud bank in front of him. They lay there twitching, quivering their tiny legs in the air.

The mist was over him now, a rolling green curtain, and he flinched in agony. His eyes burned and watered, and when the tears streamed down his cheeks, they burned too. As he tried to draw breath his lungs were instantly afire, spasming in his chest. He pulled a filthy handkerchief from his pocket and covered his nose and mouth, without reducing the pain. So this was it, gas warfare, the rumor that had spread down the line in recent days.

Then troopers appeared through the mist, monsters in his blurred blinking vision, with bulging eyes and canister-shaped snouts jutting forth. The most recognizable things about them as he struggled to breathe were the points sticking straight up from their heads, the German *pickelhaube* spiked helmets.

One of them turned its snouted gaze on him, its weapon raised high. Choking on poisonous air, he groped for his rifle and tried to aim it; but the bright bayonet came lancing down. Remorseless it stabbed home in a wave of cleansing pain, and Trevor's vision exploded into whiteness. As consciousness faded, he felt himself sliding down to join his buddy in the bottom of the hole.

Chapter 28

Saboteurs

The two men met along the starboard Shelter Deck. Matt slowed his pace on recognizing the other, as did Dirk Kroger heading straight for him. The *ersatz* Dutchman was, after all, the one that he and Flash had identified, in their photograph taken deep in the hold the other night. Matt wondered if he wanted his picture back.

Now, though watchful, the spy seemed unwilling to turn away and avoid this chance encounter. Matt glanced around at the other passengers taking the promenade, or else lingering at the rail in the late afternoon sun. It wasn't too lonely here, he decided; not dangerously so if they didn't stay past dark. This stretch of covered deck might be perfect after all for a safe, private meeting. Here they were out of sight of the bridge and beyond anyone's earshot, but well within view of the nearest idlers.

"*Guten Tag, Herr Kroger.*"

"Hello, Matt."

The two halted, facing one another but reluctant even to shake hands. After a moment, by unspoken agreement, they stepped aside to the rail to converse as innocent friends. The roll of the ship and the slight outward cant of the deck made it inconvenient to loiter anywhere else on the promenade.

"Pleasant enough afternoon," Matthew Vane said. He braced an elbow on the wood-topped rail, rather than leaning out over it and turning his head aside.

"Yes, it is restful," Dirk Kroger said, similarly placing himself against the rail. "We're not in the war zone yet."

"Some of us aren't even in this war," Matt said. "But others already seem to be conducting military operations."

Kroger laughed, ending in a wise smirk that tweaked his dueling scar. "You criticize me for doing exactly what you yourself do, sneaking after dark."

Matt shrugged. "I'm not the one who's traveling under a false identity."

Kroger affected a hurt look. "You will not believe, then, that I, a poor trader, was just checking on my consignment of furs? You think I would creep below decks and spy in the dead of night, like some others?"

Vane ignored the bad acting. "My spying is for the public, not for one side or the other in an inhuman war. It's my job as a newsman to see and hear all I can and get it into print, if it fits."

Kroger laughed again, reverting at last to the arrogant Prussian. "Try getting what you saw the other night into print in New York, my good friend! Even your socialist scandal sheet will never touch it. As for false identities...this ship itself, a war transport, masquerades as a commercial liner, using you and your lady friends as decoys to hide behind." His laugh softened, seeming cynical and knowing in the arrogant *Junker* way. "Your own home country flies the false flag of a neutral, when all the while they aid the combatants in England and France."

"So what are you going to do, sink the ship and fight the Americans? Send a thousand innocents to the bottom, and add a few million more to the ranks of your enemies?" Vane tried to keep his tone of speech casual so as to avoid drawing attention. "That won't help your cause. If I were you, I'd be talking peace."

Kroger maintained a similar relaxed tone. "I have no desire to sink this ship, though I could do so easily enough. Like you, I'm only interested in finding the truth."

Vane smiled bitterly. "No, I don't suppose you'd want her torpedoed while you're on board yourself. You'd better tell your U-boats to hold off."

Kroger chuckled quite sincerely. "And how do you imagine I'm supposed to communicate with a submarine from shipboard? There's radio silence, you know. I would have to sneak into the Marconi room."

"At night, they're telling us that even a lit cigar is enough to reveal the whereabouts of a ship at sea." Vane nodded at the wrapped stogie sticking out of the Dutchman's vest pocket. "I'm sure you know what to do."

"Yes, but first it would require a rendezvous, even if one wished to use a light or a semaphore. A U-boat would need to know our exact position well in advance. Unless you think we are being stalked by submarines in the open ocean, or watched through a periscope right now, at full speed." He waved a hand dismissively at the vacant waves surging past. 'No, that's nonsense, and there's no need for it. If I wished, I could stop the *Lusitania* in mid-ocean, or even turn her back to New York."

"Well, why don't you, then?" Vane asked, half-hopefully calling the sable-hatted spy's bluff.

Kroger shrugged. "It might be too dangerous. Wait," he said, glancing over his shoulder as a lone deck-stroller ambled past.

"See here," he said once the man was gone. Taking the jumbo-sized cigar out of his vest pocket, he stripped off the band and wrapper, letting the breeze carry them overboard. Holding the cigar in two hands, he twisted the ends first one way, then another, and placed it down sidewise on the deck between them.

"What is it, an exploder?"

"Just wait," the spy said.

After a long, nervous interval the cigar sputtered. From both ends, green flares shot out a foot long, singeing the wooden deck and blistering the varnish. Matt first stepped back in alarm, then kicked out and swept the device overboard with the side of his shoe. It fell to the water and was immediately carried astern in the wake, still flaring and bubbling as it sank out of sight.

Matt looked nervously around, but the idlers far down the rail didn't seem to have noticed anything. He turned back to the spy, composing himself. "A fire could stop us," he admitted.

"In the forward hold, it could sink us," Kroger corrected him. "You were down there. The shells, the fuses—did you see the gun cotton? Tons of it, and not packaged safely." The German spat overboard in disgust.

"I saw enough," Matt said. "Time was short, and it's a hard place to get to, tough getting past the guard. What's inside those two huge crates?"

Kroger laughed bitterly. "What, indeed? When you find out, tell me. I have my suspicions, but we both were interrupted the other night. You and your friend must have taken the difficult way in. Just go down through the crew quarters and the barracks; the whole port-side corridor is unoccupied. In wartime it's, what do you call it?...a skeleton crew, with no hands left to watch the cargo."

"You're not here to sabotage the ship, then? I suppose not, or you would have done it by now. It's easy to start a fire."

"If I were a saboteur, as you say, my mission would be secret," Kroger said. "I would not be chatting with you about it, would I?"

"No," Matt reflected. "We'd be too busy trying to shove each other overboard."

"No need for brutality," the spy said, smiling. "This isn't the battle front. There can still be a gentleman's agreement between us."

"No need even for that," Matt replied. "My mission is to get at the truth, and I'll do my best to see it reported. But I won't report on you, not unless I think you're a danger to this ship or the people on it, or to my country." He reached out, took Kroger's extended hand and shook it. "I'm still a neutral in this war."

Chapter 29

Lace Curtains

Mounting the stoop of the brownstone, Iggy kept his head low. The idlers outside gave him the once-over, gave him the nod. On the corner was Mikey, who knew him from the old block. Studs at the door recognized him, too, and let him in without a word.

Inside was nice...the bay window, with the little chips of colored glass reflecting at the top, letting the spring sunlight in through pretty curtains. In the parlor was all the nice stuff that you saw through the window—Tiffany lamps, crystal jugs, the shiny gas mantelpiece all tiled and mirrored. So it all looked real nice, like a shrine in a church.

"What's it?" Studs asked, reaching for the flat packet in Ig's hand.

"For him, the boss only." Iggy pulled the envelope behind his back. "He here?"

"He is all right, if you're up to it." Bending forward, Studs casually frisked him. "In there," he said, stepping back and pointing to a dark-paneled double door, just opposite the ornate carved rail on the curving stairway. "But go easy. It was a long night."

Going in alone was creepy—a thrill to be sent straight to the man, but who knew how he'd take it? The heavy brown door, the shadows in the room, the broad dark shape against the lacy white window.

There was Big Jim Hogan, the East Side ward boss. His curly red hair was fading to gray, the red mustache drooping over heavy stubbled jowls, eyes all puffy with drink. There on the desk before him stood a crystal carafe of fine Irish whiskey, brown as bog water and half empty. Lots of dead soldiers gleamed out of the elephant's-foot waste basket, bottles emptied the night before. That explained it all.

On seeing it, Iggy felt his stomach pleasantly flip. He could use some of that.

"What is it? Who sent you?" The gruff voice grated hung-over, as the heavy body leaned forward in the swivel chair. The eyes looked bleary and watery.

"Patsy from uptown sends me. I'm Iggy." He pushed the envelope across the desk, his hand almost touching the decanter and the upturned glasses. "This was in the Boston paper on Sunday. Patsy thought you'd want to see it."

"Good ol' Patsy." Hogan's thick paws drew in the envelope and tore it open. "What is it, bad news?"

Iggy said nothing, not wanting to admit he'd seen the picture, but not wanting to lie either. Bunch of women on a boat, so what? He waited while Big Jim smoothed the newsprint and held it up to the light. Then the big fist came crashing down, rattling the glasses on the desk.

"That's her, by damn! The little tart!" Jim peered closer, growing agitated as he read the caption aloud. "'Nurses Departing for Europe on the SS Lusitania.' Nurses, my ass! She'll need nursin' after I catch up with her!"

"What is it, boss?" Studs came in to check on the noise. "Is it Maisie again? You OK?"

"I'm OK," Hogan raged, waving the flimsy newsprint, "but she won't be! It's her, all right, I couldn't miss her."

He heaved himself up from his chair. "That stubborn chin of hers, that little pug nose...I'll puggle-ize her good, if I ever get my hands on her!" He slapped down the picture and thrashed his ham-fists in the air before him, crazy-drunk.

"That's her all right, you bet," Studs said, glancing down at the photo as he moved around the desk. "Take it easy, boss." He shot a look at Iggy. "You, messenger boy, scram outta here."

"The Lusitania, I knew it! That's her style! That's why I sent Knucks down there. Didn't I tell you I knew it?"

He grabbed Studs, mauling the shoulders of his coat. "She was lace-curtain Irish all the way, not shanty Irish like me! Why'd she run out? I tried to make it nice for her."

He waved a ham-hand around the snazzy furnished room. With his violent motions, the smell of his alcoholic sweat mingled with stale cigar smoke in the place.

"Yeah, you did, real nice. Calm down, boss, who knows why they run? Let Knucks worry about it."

Grappling with Hogan, Studs didn't bother with Iggy who still waited, hoping against hope to be offered a drink.

"Knucks'll take care of it," Hogan raved. "He'll settle that thieving dame. Then I won't have to bring her back here and beat her to death myself."

"Yeah, you watch it, boss," Studs said, wrestling the big man back down into his chair. "Just have another drink and keep it quiet." He looked over his shoulder furiously at Iggy. "You, pour him one, and then get lost!"

Iggy reached for the decanter and a glass, poured a stiff one, and slid it across the desk. He thought of pouring a second glassful for himself, but he didn't dare. His hand trembled a little as he set the crystal down.

"Knucks'll finish her." Hogan was raving into the air, held down by Studs. "But first, he'll get me back that muster list, or just toss it overboard, no one the wiser. The money, I don't care. He can use it to weigh down that little tramp's body for all I care!" His drunken babbling stopped momentarily as he sucked down the drink.

"You, wait there!" Studs turned murderously on Iggy, who was already sneaking out of the room. "Come back here." But the bodyguard was still occupied with Hogan, who gripped his sleeve.

"I don't ever want to see her again," Big Jim was moaning. "I don't care, not a bit!"

Meanwhile Iggy was out the door, down the front stoop and up the street. He walked smooth but fast, head down, nodding to Mikey without pausing to chat. Once around the corner he took off running, gaining a block before a whistle went up and shouts of pursuit came from behind him.

He had an earful. The muster list gone, that was some big deal. He knew Patsy would want the information, and wouldn't be too stingy neither to offer him a drink.

That poor dame Maisie, if she was found floating, it could be trouble, he thought as he ran. But this muster list business, that could spell the end of somebody...even somebody as big as Big Jim.

Chapter 30

War Zone

Captain Turner gazed astern at the lifeboats being swung out from the ship's rail. From the starboard wing of the officers' bridge, he looked down on his men toiling in the morning damp. The teams worked their way astern along the Boat Deck, cranking out the curving steel davits and removing the canvas covers from the boats, so that they hung ready for lowering in time of need.

This starboard lot of deck hands, stewards and galley cooks were on their fifth lifeboat since dawn. They'd likely be at it all morning. But they were practiced enough now to do the job with minimal confusion, so the captain turned away.

Looking forward in the flat dawn light, he saw only featureless ocean under the climbing sun. There was nothing visible to tell him this was a danger zone, except lines chalked on the maps in the chart room. He knew his ship's position, too, from the morning sextant reading. But even that wasn't quite knowing.

Only when he finally made landfall would he be able, after thousands of miles of open water, to truly pinpoint his ship's course in relation to the dangers ahead—the shoals and currents and fogs, a rocky lee shore, and the countless lethal hazards of the Great War.

Sightless as he was, with the war zone extending an unknown distance out into the Atlantic, he had to prepare. For now he'd ordered the portholes shut, most of the watertight doors between below-decks compartments sealed, and the lifeboats readied for lowering.

The early morning commotion and the sight of dangling boats would set the passengers murmuring, of course. But he was confident of his ability to quell any panic. Some of them were already in dread, whole families bundling themselves in blankets to sleep on the deck lounges rather than spending the night in their rooms below.

Yet what more could be done? Short of England and their destination, Liverpool, there was only Ireland. In any event, the Admiralty might order him into port there at Queenstown, in County Cork in the south. Had they not done so earlier this year for the Cunard liner *Transylvania*, steaming then under his own command?

His ship's course could also be diverted around the north coast of Ireland, if the danger should appear too great at the south end of St. George's Channel, running between England and Ireland. That too had happened on the former Captain Dow's final voyage in *Lusitania*, back in February.

But Turner would rather not fare north along the ragged western fringe of Ireland. That route was now frequented by U-boats *en route* to and from England's home waters. And there, even if his ship were only immobilized by guns or torpedoes, he might have to watch helplessly as she was driven onto some rocky strand by wind and current, while his passengers and crew struggled to abandon ship in rough, treacherous ocean. Far better, he thought, to risk a straight run eastward through sheltered seas toward England, and then north between the sister isles and across the Mersey River bar into Liverpool harbor.

Such a standard run would require close timing, even if not interrupted by Admiralty orders or his own assessment of danger. The tide tables indicated that the water would be deep enough to cross the Mersey sandbar at four a.m. on Saturday the 8th, the morning after next. With sunrise not until 5:44, that bode fair for a night approach, running without lights to foil any lurking periscopes.

But the crossing should be before five a.m., he decided, to keep his ship from being silhouetted as a target against the false dawn light in the east. Submarines could lurk inside the bar.

Turner would accordingly slow the ship soon, so as not to arrive early and have to linger and wait in dangerous waters for the tide to rise. He should be just enough ahead of schedule to allow for any small detour or evasion. And of course, he would have to keep the boilers warm for a burst of steam needed to escape danger, or to make up any time lost.

Then there was the question of his escort promised by the Royal Navy. If it was on schedule to meet him, it would wait south of Fastnet Rock, the lighthouse off Cape Clear at the southwest tip of Ireland. It would be a battleship or a couple of cruisers, he assumed–probably

Juno, the flagship of the small, almost laughable Queenstown defense fleet. *Juno* was a stately antique, too old and slow for the line of battle in this age of dreadnoughts and battlecruisers, good only for escort duty. If she were the one, his *Lusitania* would have to slow down even more to let her keep pace. Or, worse, the vessel might simply deliver an order, confidentially by semaphore, to redirect his course.

For a rendezvous, the trick would be to find one another without open radio contact. Encoded wireless signals were permitted, but both ships had to be in possession of the right codes and passwords. This had led to a bitter comedy of errors on the Lusitania's recent crossing, a royal cock-up in which the two cruisers designated as escorts had been unable to contact her then-Captain Dow by radio. Instead they had tried, by radio-telephone via the land, to get the passkeys from the captain for an encrypted conversation about where to meet. Dow had quite rightly refused, not knowing whether he was being phoned up from the German Embassy or the deck of a U-boat. Meanwhile, his route had already been diverted north of Ireland without the escorts' knowledge, so they never did make contact. Dow ended up racing into Liverpool under his dubious ruse of an American flag, which he no doubt felt entitled to fly because US President Woodrow Wilson's personal assistant, Colonel House, was aboard on his current peacemaking mission to Europe.

No matter; the international furor caused by the Germans and Yanks meant not the least to Fairweather Dow, since he at once resigned his command of the *Lusitania*.

Did that make old Fairweather a coward, Turner mused? Or had his faith in the Admiralty just been too badly shaken? Or, was he too chummy and cozy with the passengers, a bunch of jibbering landlubbers, to hold such a post in time of war, with everything doubly at risk?

A tough job, ferrying civilians through a war zone, and not every captain had the salt for it. But Turner knew the challenge, and it was one that his career had readied him for. He hadn't fought his way up from the lowly rank of seaman to turn down a posting now, much less an Admiralty command. His past reputation as captain of the *Lusitania* was based on these same factors—planning, reliability and trouble-free journeys, swift Atlantic crossings and swifter turnaround times in port. Those years of experience had brought Cunard a steady stream of income, while making *Lusitania* the safe, reliable, and even carefree

Atlantic shuttle. This element of wartime survival, now...it had only recently been added, but it made his qualifications even more vital: knowledge of this ship and these waters, courage, calm and confidence. He was fit for it. With the backing of the Royal Navy, he did not suppose he could come to grief.

* * *

Winnie stood on the boat deck astern, watching as the lifeboats were swung out over the water. The crews had started at the front of the ship and were just now working their way back past the Verandah Café. They were none too official-looking, in their assortment of uniforms from different parts of the vessel. But their actions, though far from expert under the gruff commands of a deck officer, had a determined, businesslike air. It drove home the fact that this was life-and-death.

Not that she found it overly troubling. Everything seemed life-and-death lately, with the war, Alma's flight from her big-shot New York oppressor, the men's desperate doings below decks, the spies and stowaways...she knew of these things because Flash, in his sweet, intimate hours with her, had confessed more than his boss Matt might want him to. But anyway, finding love in the midst of all this peril, fleeing on shipboard toward a continent at war...it all seemed somehow natural, part of her heightened sensations on coming of age, entering the great world. For wasn't love, too, a matter of life and death?

And yet, she could have no sure expectations. A shipboard dalliance in a war zone was no way to find a husband. Anything could happen, and probably would.

But for now, as far into the future as her mind and heart could see, Flash seemed like the perfect one for her. If his male feelings of devotion could run as deep as hers, if he remembered the vows and confidences they'd exchanged, and if no disasters intervened, then maybe, just maybe....

"Is all of this really necessary?" Winnie suddenly heard Hazel's unmistakable girlish voice piping up behind her. "I bet they're just trying to impress us."

"Maybe it's only a drill," Florence's innocent tones answered. "They haven't sighted any torpedoes yet, have they?"

"It's because we're getting near Europe," Winnie announced as she turned to meet the two younger nurses. "There's probably a rule that says they have to be ready."

"Oh, Winnie, you're looking fine," Hazel cried, running up to embrace her. "In that lovely new coat, too, I barely recognized you. It's been an age since we've seen you!" She stepped aside to let her sister Flo deliver a hug. "How are things going in the stateroom? Has there been any trouble, with anyone snooping after—you-know-who?"

"No trouble at all," Winnie said, making sure no one else was in earshot. "Things have been just heavenly. How about you girls?"

"We did think someone might have been nosing around our cabin," Florence responded. "Some of my personal things were mussed up. But we haven't seen that creeping steward lately. Oh, Winnie, you are looking so nice," she added, keeping hold of her friend's hand.

"Life with bachelors is good for her," Hazel added slyly. "How is Alma doing these days?"

"Alma is just fine," Winnie said, feeling suddenly discreet. "She should be along to speak for herself soon. Where's Miss Hildegard?" she asked with a watchful glance astern. "Has she gotten her sea legs back?"

"Yes, her *mal de mer* was only mid-Atlantic," Florence said. "She's her old self again. She promised to meet us."

"Oh, good," Winnie said—though not entirely sure that it was, in case the head nurse still had her old mind-reading ability.

"So, how's life in Saloon Class, with the men?" Hazel prodded her. "Made any new friends lately?"

"Oh, it's very...civilized," Winnie said in a measured way. This new discretion of hers was an odd feeling, not at all like her younger self. "I told you girls all about the party. I took you to the cabin and the Grand Dining Saloon, so you've seen it all. It all becomes just everyday and boring. The food in Second Class is just as good, really, and ever so much easier to pronounce—Oh, look," she added, finding a distraction. "Here they are!"

They all turned to see Alma approach, svelte in a blue satin dress and feathered wrap, walking arm-in-arm with Matthew Vane on one side and Flash on the other. Matt tipped his hat to the nurses as the three came up, and Flash, detaching himself from Alma, went him one better. He swept up each sister in a hug, with a peck on the cheek for both in turn. He then took his proper place with an arm firmly around Winnie's waist.

"Now, you young ladies, that's enough horseplay," a familiar matronly voice declared from astern as Hildegard came up to join them. "Remember, you're in the uniform of the United Nursing Service League...some of you, at least. Mr. Vane, hello, and hello to you, too, Flash," she said to the men. "I hope that my young pupils haven't been too much of a burden."

"No, not at all," Matt said, replacing the hat he'd lifted to Hildegard. "They're a sheer joy."

"They can be that, I know. But thank you, even so, for taking such good care of them." She surveyed Alma and Winnie in their finery from Alma's trunk, plus their new acquisitions from the First Class *boutiques*. "Ladies, what complete disguises! I never would have known you for hard-working, dedicated nurses. How have things been going for the two you?"

"Going...they're in love, can't you see?" Hazel gaily shrilled out, taking everyone by surprise. "I thought Winnie was acting a little odd at first, trying to hide something. But then the men came up, with Alma in tow, and it's perfectly clear! It's love, the real thing, and there's no denying it. See how they dote on each other!"

"Why my dear, how rude!" Hildegard said at once. "What nonsense are you prattling about?"

"Oh, she's right," Florence chimed in, for once standing up to the head nurse. "I thought so too, but now it's for sure. Look, see them blushing!"

It would indeed have been hard, Winnie guiltily knew, to ignore the interesting range of colors given off by the two couples. Flash, with his red hair and freckled skin, was especially gratifying to watch. Still the two pairs stood together and she clung to Flash, waiting out the jeers and stares. There was nothing any of the four could say.

"See how they coo and cuddle like doves," Florence teased. "They're not afraid of lifeboats, or torpedoes or anything!"

"Well, they're quite right not to be afraid," Hildegard said, ill at ease if not alarmed at the previous subject, and obviously wanting to change it. "Those boats are just a precaution, nothing more. They're being put out to reassure us, not frighten us."

"Someone should tell her that," Winnie said. Having disengaged from Flash and cast about for a new distraction, she pointed aft to a woman standing with two small children, clutching her husband's arm and shrilly questioning him as the next boat in line was swung out. "She doesn't look reassured."

"Really," Hazel gravely added, "a lot of these people have been acting as if there's no danger at all, and now that we're near port they suddenly seem terror-stricken. The women, mostly—a lot of the men won't discuss it at all."

"The Ostrich Club," Winnie agreed, "with their heads stuck in the sand. Flash and I met a young Scots nobleman who was very concerned about needing life jacket drills." She looked to Flash, who nodded his assent. "We even went to see the captain about it, the real Captain Turner, I mean, but I don't think anything was done."

Flash put in matter-of-factly, "I just heard a couple saying they were going to sleep on deck in case of an attack. But I don't think the danger is so great at night, with the entire ship blacked-out as they've been doing."

"Yes, they've even warned the men not to light their cigars on deck after dark," Alma said. "They've designated special indoor smoking areas. It's hard to believe, that even that little bit of light could give you away, or just striking a match."

"I don't suppose we should sleep out on deck," Hazel casually announced. "I'm sure all of us will be much cozier in our beds, don't you think?" she added with a wily glance to Alma and Winnie.

"Now, my dears, don't be naughty," Hildegard scolded. "It's foolish to be worried about a little thing like lifeboats, when there are such great things ahead of us. The old world of Europe, and the war...there is untold suffering right now, but we shall have a wonderful chance to relieve so much of it, and eventually help restore civilization. The things we'll see... well, I'm sure it will be worrisome, but all in a good cause. And Mr. Vane here, and Flash, they can print fine stories and pictures about the war and help to set things right. It's just a short way now to our destination, and then our work, our real lives, can begin."

They talked on in that vein, about their ideas and plans. They didn't talk about love, but it was in the air. No one in the group questioned it, everyone sensed it, and in its glow the future seemed positive and hopeful.

Chapter 31

Kaiser William

If only they had treated me with true respect," the *Kaiser* said to his wife, gazing out over the broad lawns of his ancestor Frederick's New Palace. "That my own people should be divided and skeptical, even of me! Yet so it has been from the start."

William paced restlessly before the tall windows of his drawing room. He preferred this monumental Baroque pile as his family home, because it displayed the power and history of his German dynasty. Built in Potsdam, just two dozen kilometers outside Berlin amid lakes and lesser palaces, the newly refitted mansion gave him ready access to his government, and this without constant, wearying encounters with bureaucrats, politicians and General Staff officers that might appear to diminish his authority.

And yet lately, with his underlings wholly absorbed in the daily conduct of the war, he felt almost an outsider. It was as if his last order that had any force or significance in this struggle had been his very first one: the order to mobilize and send his troops racing according to plan, across uninvolved Belgium toward belligerent France. It was an order he'd given reluctantly under staff pressure, and had later tried to cancel without success. Too late to recall the troops, his Chief of Staff von Moltke had told him. Once set in motion, the necessities of war dictate everything.

And so it went. His Prussian generals controlled the troops and the information he received, and his attempts to direct military affairs were treated merely as rubber-stamping approval, or else dangerous trifling.

But had the generals really needed him as supreme commander to give that first mobilization order, or only as a scapegoat to take the blame if things went wrong...as they were clearly going now, with wartime demands and shortages, and with heavy, unimaginable troop losses in spite of heroic victories in the field?

Der Kaiser addressed his wife at last. "Nothing short of unquestioning loyalty is due a national leader in wartime. They never would have doubted my grandfather, Wilhelm the Great."

"It was the vile English all along," the *Kaiserin* Augusta Viktoria remarked, knitting in an antique chair by his side. "They tried to control you, and when you would not yield, they undermined and slandered you before the world."

The Empress Augusta was well known to dislike the English. That included her own in-laws, William's British mother and his grandmother, the sainted Queen Victoria. William did not mind this, since it was his own bitter disputes with the family that had in part brought on this Great War.

"Oh yes," William told her, "the bastard English press, and those Foreign Office petty aristocrats who dictate to my poor stupid cousin, George V. But, our own good Germans have a part in our troubles, too," he added, recalling other causes for woe. "These whining politicians, you cannot escape them! From fat old Bismarck at the very start of my reign, they all wish to steal away my power. Whenever I try to rally the will of the people, the true soul of Germany, how they howl in outrage! That speech of mine years ago, when I invoked the dreaded spirit of the Huns, out of that they made a circus show! It certainly was never really what I meant, to call our brave soldiers ravaging Huns! It was only against the Chinese, an inferior race. And then later, that press interview where I tried to speak directly to the English people...just because I said that ordinary Germans are not overly fond of England, and tried to point out the various problems..."

"The German people understand you," Augusta assured him, not looking up from her knitting. "They hate England, but they love you."

William heard this with pleasure. His empress, born a Princess of Schleswig-Holstein in the north, could be counted on to support him in all things—though she was seen as dumb and provincial by his mother and the rest of his faithless English kin. A Holstein cow, she had been called, good only for breeding and feeding, so they whispered in their spiteful British way. But she was proud of her role in *Kinder, Küche und*

Kirche. Children, kitchen, and church were, after all, the proper concerns of women in his German empire.

"Yes, my dear," William said to his wife. "But alas that our German people must suffer so—starving and sacrificing for this war, hemmed in by trenches across Europe and by enemy ships at sea. This new British trade embargo is an outrage. Even the Americans protest it. Our troops are denied vital supplies, and the victories they have earned!"

He drew himself up in a military posture, as he would before a crowd of his subjects. The most humiliating thing was that this injustice had been imposed on him by his nearest relatives—Vicky, Bertie, George, and his dear cousin Nicky, the Czar of Russia, who had also perfidiously declared war. And now his British kin talked of denying their German kinship before their own people, by changing names—Saxe-Coburg to Windsor, Battenberg to Mountbatten—the ultimate treachery to their common forebears!

"German superiority will win out, of course," the Kaiser reassured his wife. "With the genius of our General Staff, the best officers in Europe, hard Prussians all, how can we fail?" He turned from the window, primping his handlebar mustaches with his good right hand. "The French are no obstacle to us, just a drunken rabble. But the English have made it so hard...my own cousins, and even Grandmama! How could they treat us so?"

"Your mother too, don't forget," Augusta reminded him. "She tried to raise you as a British pawn, refusing even to call you by your German name, Wilhelm. And that English doctor, who killed your father with the throat cancer!"

"That was likely just their incompetence, not a conspiracy," William told her. "I have suffered my own share of their British doctors' failures." He patted his useless left arm, stunted at birth from a clumsy breech delivery. "But my mother...she never trusted me, and she ruled my poor weak father to the end. Sad to say, but it's a good thing Papa died when he did, after only one hundred days as Kaiser. Germany might never have stood up to England!"

"The English should be beaten already," Augusta observed. "They would be, if not for the help they get from the Americans."

"Alas, the Americans!" William cried out, all but losing his composure. "A fine, young and vigorous nation, like Germany...but just like the English, traitors to their own Nordic Race! Why on earth would the Americans take sides with perfidious Albion, after fighting a war of independence against them?" He paced the room in frustration. "And then later, a hundred years ago, they fought another war against England over, what...? British tyranny on the high seas, stopping and seizing foreign merchant ships! The same thing that Germany struggles against now! What was it the American journalist wrote, about Churchill's new Q-ships that now force our U-boats to attack from hiding?—'Britannia rules the waves, but she also waives the rules!' A joke, you see, my dear..." he explained to his wife, doing his best to translate the pun, since she had no English. "But, alas, the Yankees still welcome British traders and blockaders, while interning our German vessels in port. And their foreign commerce helps to stiffen the backbone of England's war machine."

"Are the Americans going to enter the war? Augusta asked."

"No, they never will join the fight, not on England or Germany's side. The American government is weak, a popular democracy whose rulers are slave to their masses. The Americans love to profit from the war trade, but they lack any real fighting spirit. Bethmann-Hollweg is in dread of world opinion, because of our U-boat successes, but I have explained to him time and again: these neutral nations are not threatened as Germany is, and they will not go to war over mere principle. Tirpitz, on the other hand, says we must increase the submarine blockade and starve England while we can, by being more ruthless on the high seas. I have to mediate between the two of them."

Augusta raised her knitting and inspected it. "Germany must do whatever it can to win," she pronounced.

"Yes, my dear, and we will. We are close to defeating the pathetic Russians in the East, and soon we shall direct our full force against the Western Front. With our brave soldiers and good Krupp arms, we must triumph." The *Kaiser* turned again to survey his green lawns, with his lakes glimmering blue in the distance. "It's a grim business, but the outcome justifies all. We have only this war to win, and Germany can take her rightful place of leadership in a new world."

Chapter 32

Hunter

"Feuer!" The firing order rang out abruptly from *Kapitan-Leutnant* Schwieger atop the submarine's conning tower. The gun on the foredeck below him obeyed with a loud report, blasting out steel and smoke into the pale sea mists surrounding the *U-20*.

From the direction the gun pointed, there rose no column of spray. Instead drifted back a faint crash and a fainter human outcry, proof that the shot had struck home on the ship that they chased through the drifting fog.

Herr Kapitan adjusted his binoculars. After a moment, he judged that the unidentified steamship was not slowing or coming about. To his gun crew, who had already reloaded, he called again *"Feuer!"* and the 3.5-incher barked. No answering crash; a miss this time.

The single-stacked vessel was trying to lose them in the mists of the Irish Channel. At times the ship faded from sight, but by cruising forward and watching, Schwieger could always find her bulky outline. At fifteen knots maximum surface speed, he knew he could keep up with most cargo steamers.

The ship was unknown, flying no flag. And the name on her stern was painted over, which made her more likely British than neutral. No great need for concern about being overtaken and rammed, since his own low-lying vessel was much harder to see in the drifting mist. In this game of cat-and-mouse, his *U-20* was the cat.

"Feuer!" Another hit low astern on the target, but still no white flag or letup in his quarry's speed. And now the ship vanished entirely in a rolling fogbank.

Well, she wouldn't hide for long. Schwieger ordered a reduction to half diesel power. The fog should force the freighter to slow, too, for fear of collision or running aground.

After long moments of chugging through the mist, the electrician Voegele emerged into the cramped well of the conning tower.

"Radio message, *Herr Kapitan*." He handed Schwieger a folded piece of paper. "Pilot Lanz has decoded it for you, since we are in action."

Voegele was the Alsatian...a good electrician, but a conscript, drafted at the outbreak of war. And too, he came from the contested Alsace-Lorraine region bordering France, where German loyalties were diluted, so he required special attention. Schwieger opened the message, read it, and handed it back.

"This is nothing secret," he said casually. "It is public information, that the British liner *Lusitania* is expected to arrive in Liverpool on April 8th. The naval command tells us routinely of her comings and goings."

Not yet dismissing the man, Schwieger waited, plying his binoculars. Voegele spoke again, perhaps deciding that his captain expected an answer. "That puts us on her likely course, does it not, *Herr Kapitan*?"

"Perhaps," Schwieger carelessly replied.

Scanning the misty sea ahead, he decided to test the fellow further. "That is, if the hunting is poor, and we are kept so long in these waters... and if she does not detour north around Ireland. Or else if she does, and we both choose that same route...why then, we might encounter her." Lowering his binoculars, he gave the man a sly wink. "What do you think, Voegele, should I save a torpedo for the *Lusitania*?"

The electrician looked suddenly evasive, with a searching roll of his eyes and a nervous shrug. "I do not know, *Herr Kapitan*, if a single torpedo would be enough for such a giant ship, full of coal and baggage and...passengers."

"And other things too, Voegele," Schwieger solemnly said. "Other things besides passengers and baggage."

He ended their chat with a brusque wave of dismissal, sending the man below. He had no time now, with his quarry on the run, to deal with the faint-hearted draftee. There was danger, as always—at any moment a British warship or armed trawler could appear, drawn by the sound of gunfire so near the English coast.

While scanning for such a peril, he saw the familiar mast appear again above the fog. Lucky he hadn't shot it away as yet! Beside the bare pole, a gray smudge of smoke and steam rose from the funnel, indicating his target's direction. Schwieger raised the speaking tube to his lips.

"Helmsman, two points starboard," he instructed the officer below. "Gunners, alert!"

As the boat turned and the gun crew wound their weapon around to bear, the mists drifted clear of their target, still stern-to, steaming away. A broad space of open water lay ahead. The fog seemed to be lifting for good, enough to expose his position clearly.

"Ready, *Kapitan!*" the chief gunner eagerly called out.

"*Feuer frei!*"

This time, as glass and timbers flew upward from a superstructure hit, the target must have decided that it was hopeless. A white flag ran hastily up the halyard to the mainmast, and the free-fire ended. Crewmen soon appeared at the rail with arms waving in surrender. The ship's engine was reversed, spreading a wake of white sea-foam under the stern as the vessel slowed.

As they drew abreast on the port side, Schwieger could finally make out, using his binoculars, the painted-over raised lettering on the stern. It read "*Candidate*" and in smaller characters below, "Liverpool." A steamer of the British Harrison Line, as he recalled.

He ordered his boarding party to make ready, and raising his megaphone, shouted in English, "Ahoy, *SS Candidate!* Abandon ship!"

The crew needed no command. They were already swinging out the lifeboats, two on a side, and scrambling into them. The sailors, Schwieger saw, were clumsy with fear or inexperience and lowered the falls hastily. The forward portside boat, fully-laden with crew, hit the water before the vessel had even slowed to a halt, and was immediately swamped by the bow wave as the ropes dragged the craft forward.

The occupants of the flooded boat were left to paddle and splash, trying feebly to push away from the big ship as they drifted back along the hull. But the other lifeboat handlers learned from their crewmates' mistake. They paused, hanging onto the ropes until the flooded boat had passed beneath them, and the water barely flowed alongside. Then they dropped the boat into the sea with a splash.

Though obviously afraid, with some calling out "*nicht schiessen*" in bad German, the refugees turned and rowed back to take on some of the crew from the swamped lifeboat. Both boats from the starboard side appeared astern, rowing over to do the same and finally empty the derelict boat. Fortunately the big ship's engines were now at a dead stop, so there was no danger from churning propellers. Meanwhile the U-boat's boarding party rowed across to the prize.

Sometime later they returned, having planted scuttling charges. The explosives went off, sending up small plumes at the waterline, but did no apparent damage. Lowering his binoculars, the captain saw the *Leutnant* of the boarding party salute him from the submarine's deck just astern of his tower.

"*Herr Kapitan*, I must report," the man said urgently. "The steamer is armed. Amidships are two machine guns in sandbag emplacements to port and starboard. Also, one small cannon astern, a 57 millimeter Hotchkiss. The cowards did not use it, but the ammunition was ready."

Schwieger swore below his breath. In a gun battle, his 3.5-incher and machine pistols could have obliterated the ship and its crew. But a single hit could gravely damage or even sink his U-boat. So that is the way Herr Churchill wishes to play.

Aloud, he told his officer, "Very good, *Leutnant*. Dismissed."

While waiting for the crews to get clear, Schwieger ordered an old-style bronze torpedo loaded into one of the forward tubes, and he kept the *U-20's* bow pointed toward the drifting *Candidate*. Now, as the three overloaded lifeboats rowed frantically out of the way, he gave the command through the tube, "*Torpedo los!*"

In a moment he saw the wake streaming behind the "eel," pointing straight to the target. It headed astern toward the engine room. Since the ship wasn't moving forward, it was possible to aim at the vulnerable stern without risking a miss.

When it hit, there came the muffled crack of a submerged TNT explosion. From the sea, a massive column of white rose straight up the ship's side, even as a concentric wave surged out from the underwater impact.

The big vessel lurched slightly and seemed to settle in the sea...but as Schwieger watched, he saw no torrent of inrushing water, or jets of spray from shattered portholes. The ship did not appear to list or sink at the stern. After long moments of waiting, the *Kapitan-Leutnant* shouted, "Gunners, aim at the waterline. *Feuer frei!*" Free-fire should do the job. He would not waste another torpedo on this hulk, not even another one of the old bronze ones, which apparently were useless.

As the gun crew demonstrated their skill at free-fire and swift reloading, Schwieger's mind roved to the recent past. Under the old rules of engagement, it would have been proper to board the ship, inspect it for contraband, and only then, if weapons or munitions were found, order off the crew and plant scuttling charges. For a merchant ship even to flee implied guilt, and was unwise. But now for obvious reasons, the Cruiser Rules had gone by the board. With Churchill's armed merchant Q-ships, radio distress calls and signal flares, and with fast destroyers ever at the ready, it was dangerous for a submarine to show itself, much less stop and board. If *Candidate's* crew had tried any more tricks before surrender, Schwieger would have been tempted, like other U-boat captains he knew, to fire on the lifeboats and inflict casualties as punishment.

At long last, the enemy ship responded to his continued attack, listing steeply to port. Schwieger ordered his gun to cease firing, and his engine crew to turn and run clear.

A few moments later the great hulk capsized. With a sigh of escaping air and a debris-laden convulsion of water, the *Candidate* rolled over to port. No need to stand by and watch her sink.

During the steamer's death throes the fog had cleared considerably. Across a gallery of sunlight and blue sea to the northeast, a fringe of English coast was visible...and before it, the funnels and smoke plumes of another steamship. A double-stacker this time, a richer prize. No flag, but then it scarcely mattered which country. By *Der Kaiser's* latest decree, all merchant ships in these waters were fair game.

"*Alarm! Tauchen!*" Schwieger gave the crash-dive order to avoid being seen by the enemy. He ducked below, following the gun crew, and gave the orders for pursuit. Electric underwater power would be slower to intercept this target, but if they hadn't already been sighted, the steamer might not put on extra speed. Luckily the hulk of the *Candidate* had already sunk out of sight well astern. The crew had been picked up by a trawler that made only a brief appearance.

Without fog, Schwieger couldn't risk hunting on the surface. But no matter; now that he knew the game, it would be quicker and safer to strike from below. He set a course to intercept the steamer and pin her against the English coastline. As the battery engines spun in the underwater silence, he wrote in his battle log, reporting the successful earlier attack and their current course. His shipping expert Lanz went to the periscope and reported back, "Looks like the *Arabic*, British White Star Lines, 16,000 tons. Appears to be making full speed, about twenty knots."

Bad news. At that speed, *U-20* could not hope to intercept. Schwieger went to the periscope and saw how much the ship had dwindled already. A stern torpedo hit would be impossible now, much less a clean bow shot. He watched, hoping that she would change course, and instead saw her disappear into a lingering fogbank.

"Fog above," Schwieger announced. "Increase depth to 72 feet, then go to half speed." As the steering crew ran to adjust the dive planes, Schwieger returned to his log book. If they could not hunt, at least they would be safe from being run over by a big liner with a deep draft, such as the *Lusitania*.

* * *

In the afternoon, *U-20* again rose to periscope depth, and Schwieger found that the fog had lifted. He gave the periscope watch to the faithful Lanz, who almost immediately reported another liner approaching.

"A single-stacker, about six thousand tons. Of the British Harrison Line, though she flies no flag, *Herr Kapitan*."

"What, that sounds like the one we just sunk, their *Candidate*!" As he stood almost upright in his cramped cabin, the *Kapitan-Leutnant* laughed aloud, half-suspecting a joke. "What is it, a ghost ship?"

"Could be the *Centurion*, *Candidate's* sister-ship," Lanz said earnestly.

"Well, then, let's tumble both sisters," Schwieger said, striding toward the periscope. "But this time we'll use one of our good gyro-torpedoes!"

"No surfacing, *Herr Kapitan*?" The question came from Voegele, sitting beside the wireless operator.

An impertinence, this questioning of one's captain, and the other crew in earshot waited to see what would happen. But for morale's sake, Schwieger merely chose to reply. "*Nein*, most certainly not."

To knowingly expose the frail U-boat to another armed merchant would be suicidal. The rest of the crew knew it by now anyway, and would undoubtedly feel relieved at his answer. No further question was raised.

The torpedo shot was easy, straight in amidships from 300 meters. A satisfying explosion was visible in the periscope, with an immediate settling at the bows. As the ship slowed its progress and the crew scrambled for the lifeboats, Schwieger ordered another torpedo loaded, an old bronze one to finish the job. This time he held back until the crew was off.

After the second fish struck home, with *Centurion's* portholes blowing out spray and steam spouting from the hatchways, he didn't surface or stay to witness the ship's final moments. Still four torpedoes left, and more hunting to be done.

Chapter 33

Landfall

The ship's foghorn sounded its baleful note, deep and penetrating in the pre-dawn hour. Captain Turner had been reluctant to order it, since it would further disturb the passengers and, in effect, proclaim their ship's position to all in hearing. But it was necessary to prevent a collision with some unlucky vessel. By night a U-boat or surface raider would have little chance of following them, much less aiming guns or torpedoes in this murk. Sounds were elusive and menacing in the fog, easier to avoid than to follow.

In the night's gloom, so he calculated, they must have passed Fastnet Rock, the southwestern beacon off Ireland, without seeing it...no great concern to one such as himself, who had crossed the Atlantic hundreds of times by dead reckoning. He knew that he must be passing south of any shoal or other fixed hazard by at least twenty miles. The fog merely forced him to slow his ship, as he'd intended to do anyway.

The troubling thing was, he might also have missed his Royal Navy escort in the dark. Should they hear his foghorn, they were to respond with a distinctive note his crew would recognize, and by mutual effort the two could maneuver into blinker-signal range. But failing that, there seemed little chance of a rendezvous. He would just have to push onward and hope.

One thing certain: at some point he would have to get a definite visual fix on a landmark or known beacon light. That might not come until later, probably well after dawn when the fog burned off. Landfall was the key point of any ocean crossing. It served as final confirmation of a ship's position, and the final measure of a captain's skill at navigation.

It had been a long night, and a troubled one. Even during his forced attendance at last evening's dismal charity concert in the main salon, he could tell his ship was freighted with fear.

Immediately after the music he conducted a question-and-answer session in the Men's Smoking Room. He'd had to announce to them the vague warning he'd just received from the Admiralty, worded merely "Submarines active off the south coast of Ireland." Trying to dispel the passengers' murmured dread, he'd assured them that they'd soon be safe in the hands of the Royal Navy. He hoped it was no lie.

Then, going back at the bridge, he'd received a second coded message to all British shipping: "Submarine off Fastnet." That was a serious concern, since he'd expected to arrive there in a matter of hours. Good that he'd be passing the rockbound lighthouse by night, twenty miles out to sea. And better yet if he was going to meet his escort there on schedule.

Then the fog had descended, blotting out the U-boat threat, the light, and any likelihood of a rendezvous. A relief, after all, permitting him to retire to his bunk in good conscience and sleep soundly...only to be awakened six times during the night for the same coded Marconi warning, repeated hourly as the ship steamed onward. "Submarine off Fastnet."

Now it was almost daylight. Once the fog lifted, he expected to see land, the emerald green of Ireland far off their port bow. One more day at moderate speed, and he should make Liverpool by this time tomorrow.

Another successful, uneventful voyage, God willing. Or, perhaps, Gods willing...in this case Neptune and Mars, the less merciful gods of sea and war.

Chapter 34

Fog of War

Knucks pushed open the door to get a breath of morning air, but instead he inhaled damp fog. It reeked of sea stink too, like back home by New York harbor. And the smoke pouring down from the same lousy chimneys. Just like home, without even a breeze to blow away the soot.

A sudden, shuddering blast of the ship's foghorn made him edge back into the stairwell. Nobody in sight, but then the fog shrouded everything. Straight off to the side, he could see the ship's rail and nothing else, just blank grayness. Craning his neck fore and aft, he saw a dozen feet of empty walkway fade away into nothingness. The damp air stuck rank and heavy in his throat, almost as bad as the coal dust and sweat down below decks.

Still, he decided, fog could be an advantage. For the job he had to do, this was better than nighttime. He could find his way in the murk, but if anyone spotted him he could just disappear. With the decks deserted and the few sailorboys on lookout for ships and rocks, he had the run of the place. Fog muffles sound. The long drawn-out noise of that blasting foghorn would cover a lot, like a smothered yelp of somebody being snatched, or a body splashing down over the side–but only if it was timed just right.

Now to find Smyte. The little rat wasn't here up top, where he was supposed to be, and Knucks wasn't gonna waste any time waiting around. The steward must be hiding out in his cabin astern, down in steerage. That meant diving back into the smelly, noisy rabbit warren he'd gotten so sick of on this rotten trip. It was worse than the tenements back at Red Hook in Brooklyn. At least those old shacks didn't bob and dance around and make you throw up all over the place.

The sounds grew louder as he descended—no foghorn down here, just the thrum of the churning propellers a few feet below him, and those jolting engine vibrations you could never get used to. The rooms on this stern deck were tiny and cramped, as Knucks knew from his previous visit. But a lot of them were empty, with most of the doors shut. Smyte, not one to mix in the stewards' bunkroom, had taken over a cabin in this deserted section. Knucks didn't want to knock and draw attention. He just twisted the latch and stepped in.

Smyte, lying on one of the cots, looked surprised. "Knucks, hello! You're early; I was just going up to meet you on deck—"

"Early, hell! I'm sick of waiting around for you." Knucks strode into the middle of the cabin and stood there, his balding skull brushing the low ceiling with each sway of the ship. He stared down at the little Limey's shifty eyes.

"This ferryboat ride is nearly over, and you haven't gotten me what I want. This is when we're going to settle things, right now! You know where that dame is, right, where she sleeps?"

"Yes," the Englishman stalled, "but it's difficult." He twitched nervously on his bunk. "It's forward in First Class, and it's not easy for me to get up there—"

"So you haven't gotten inside, right? And you don't have what I asked for, the book? Do they even have it?"

"Well, they didn't sign anything into the ship's safe, I can tell you that. But I haven't gained access to the room yet, I'm afraid." The white-clad steward shifted uneasily in the big gangster's looming shadow. "I've watched the place for hours, and gotten a passkey, but with the four of them coming and going, there's always someone in there."

"What? Four nurses, you mean?" Knucks felt his temper rising. "Don't they go out together for meals?"

"No, it's two couples, and one of the pairs generally stays in when the other goes out. It makes it hard—"

"Couples, what? Now Maisie is living with two men?"

"Well, yes, it's this Maisie, or Alma Brady as they know her, another nurse, and the two fellows who booked the First Class cabin."

Crum, so that's how it stood with the little tart! Serious business maybe, and not just dame stuff. Knucks felt an icy chill settle over him. "What cabin is it?"

"It's 34, on B deck," Smyte said, sounding nervous.

"These men, who are they?" He bent over and gripped the shoulder of the steward's unbuttoned white jacket, hauling the little man toward him. "What's their names?"

"Well, they seem to be press correspondents. Alma's beau is signed on as Matthew Vane, and the other girl keeps company with a Lars Jansen..."

"What, the reporter and that red-headed pest of his?" Knucks could hardly believe his ears. "It's Matt Vane and his buddy they're palling around with, and sleeping with?"

"Yes, well, he is red-haired, the other one."

Knucks felt his temper going through the roof, a blind rage building. "Why didn't you tell me all of this before now?"

"Well, I only found out yesterday," Smyte said, brushing feebly at the hard fist jammed against his shoulder. "Please, Knucks, let go. You're getting coal dust on the coat."

Knucks ignored him. "You're telling me that this dumb floozy, the one I'm supposed to keep quiet, has been living with a reporter for a New York paper, sharing his crib, spillin' out her heart to him? And his sidekick too, a photographer? Not to mention the other little trick staying with her, and all of their friends? All this time they've had the goods I wanted, for them to read, take pictures of and show to people! And you're only telling me now?"

The steward writhed in the hoodlum's iron grip. "You're right, Knucks, it's a difficult situation, almost impossible. I don't know what we can do—"

"Do?" Knucks threw the steward back down on the creaking cot. "I know what to do. I'll have to kill them all, at least the four of 'em. That's the only way to keep a loudmouth reporter quiet. He saw me on this boat, didn't you know that? If anything happens to his girlfriend, if he or his friend gets to a wire, it'll be all over the New York papers, with my tintype next to it." He swiped both his fists in the air in a fury. "Holy bleeding Jesus, when I get my hands on that little strumpet!"

"Knucks, now let's think about things," Smyte said shakily. "How in God's name are you going to do away with four people on a ship like this?"

216

"How? I'll shoot 'em, that's how!" Reaching behind his back, he whipped the pistol out of his belt. "Bam, bam!" He jabbed the air with his reliable little Colt. "Then I'll throw the bodies overboard."

"All right, but wait," Smyte said, trying to wave Knucks quiet with his palms up before him. "What if there are witnesses? You can't put four bodies over the rail."

"No witnesses," Knucks said, feeling determined. "I'll do it in the cabin when the foghorn blows, so no one hears, and then shove 'em out the porthole. If only two of them are there, I'll wait for the others to get back."

"A human body doesn't fit through these portholes," Smyte said with a nervous glance over his shoulder."

"It doesn't, eh?" Knucks said keeping the pistol in his hand. "So what do you suggest?"

"Can't we just forget it, and go on with our lives?"

"Are you kidding?" Knucks said. His professionalism was insulted by the Englishman's tone. "I was given this job to finish one way or another. If I double-cross who I'm working for—no names—I'll be the one who ends up in the drink!"

The little Limey was thinking fast. "Well then I'd say, we just take what we want and threaten them to silence. Even a press story is no good without proof, once we take the book and their photo plates. If your boss back at home is so all-powerful, he can just have the girl picked up after we get ashore. I'm sure he must have plans for that, in case you fail."

"Fail?" Knucks grunted, outraged. "I didn't spend no week scuttling coal just to fail. Not like you did, you little runt! In my line of work if you fail, you don't get to live to regret it. I've got to shut that blonde up...or black-hair, or whatever she is now. I won't mind putting a few slugs into that smart guy Vane either, him and his little punk."

"Well, I don't know, Knucks," Smyte said, pulling back carefully and swinging his feet off the bunk. "I didn't really sign on for any killings. Once you get your hands on the girl, what you do with her is your business. But I don't want any part of a bunch of bloody murders."

"Then gimme the key." Knucks stretched out his hand, the one not holding the gun. "The pass key for room 34!" he added when Smyte hesitated. "Hand it over."

Reaching into the pocket of his smudged, rumpled coat, the little Brit produced the key and surrendered it into Knucks's big hand. "Don't lose it, and don't get caught with it, if you please. I don't want it traced back to me."

"Don't worry about that," Knucks said, looming over the steward. "There won't be no tracin' nothin' to you, not for long. Remember how you were so worried about witnesses? Well, there's gonna be one less witness, right now." He slipped the key into the pocket of his coal-blackened gray coat.

Smyte froze back against the wall, still seated in the bunk. "You can't shoot me! There are stewards in the cabins around us. They'd hear."

"You're right," Knucks said, reversing the pistol in his hand. "But guns are dangerous. They can kill people lotsa ways. Especially smart little Limey bastards like you."

Whipping the gun down against the side of Smyte's skull, he stopped the cry for help before it was more than a moan. His left mitt emerged from his pocket wearing the shiny brass knuckles, his trademark, and now he worked the little man over, viciously but silently, left, right, left. There was no sound but thuds and the squealing of bunk springs, until the Brit lay limp on the blanket.

"See, you were right," he whispered over the body. "No witnesses."

The crummy little steward turned out to be right about something else, too. A dead body, even one as scrawny as his, couldn't fit out through the porthole...at least, not without some last-minute folds and adjustments.

* * *

The repetitive noise of the foghorn brought Alma slowly to wakefulness. Its patient, relentless blasts vibrated through the cabin, as if the ship itself were the instrument, a giant tuba afloat on a foggy sea. The monotonous noise vexed but also comforted, assuring her the ship was smothered in a soft blanket, and they were under protection. To feel even more secure, she gathered the covers around her and snuggled up against the warm bulk of Matt in their bed.

"Mmm. Looks like morning." He opened his eyes, blinking at the faint gray light coming in through the bedroom's gilt-edged porthole.

"The morning of our last day at sea." Alma said regretfully. "Unless we lie here fog-bound for days, that is."

"We're still making way," Matt observed. "Not anywhere near full steam, but I can feel it."

"Too bad," she said. "Right now I wish the voyage would never end."

"Be careful what you wish for." He said it in his wry comedic way, taking her in his arms as he did so. "But really, I know what you mean."

"Well, what could be better? We're here together, happy and with our friends, cut off from war, politics and crime, all the world's troubles." She sighed and stretched herself in his relaxed embrace. "Why go any farther? What's ahead of us that's better than what we have right here?"

Matt shifted his embrace. "We've plenty to think about, besides the state of the world. Like getting safely ashore at Liverpool, not being spotted, and hanging onto our luggage."

"All the baggage from my old life," Alma sighed. "I'm not sure it's worth keeping."

"It is," Matt assured her. "Mine, too, especially my war journal and Flash's pictures. They could be at risk in port. Not everyone would be pleased with what we've been doing on this trip. That reminds me."

Rolling away from her, he consulted his watch on the bed table. "The best may be yet to come. I have to go soon, right after breakfast."

While he sat up in bed, Alma yawned and stretched. "An early breakfast, you mean? I could second that. I seem to have developed quite an appetite this trip." Rolling after her lover, she twined her arms around his silk-pajamaed middle. "That is, if you don't want to order up room service and lie here all morning."

"I'd love to." He turned to stroke her black-dyed hair and plant a kiss on her upturned face. "But we'd better get a quick bite below. I can't risk missing this appointment."

"Sounds important." She sat up with a sheet draped about her. "Who's it with—or should I say whom, to a writer?"

"Sorry, dear, I can't say," Matt delivered a firm kiss to her already-pouting lips. "I hope you'll understand, my darling,"

Turning to the wardrobe, he added, "You must know, a reporter's sources often insist on remaining confidential. And if today really is our final day at sea, it's definitely my last chance to get the information. It may take me a couple of hours." He took out a dark brown suit and a pair of well-worn shoes.

"I don't know," Alma said, dragging her sheet with her as she rose from the bed. She'd known she would have to deal with this again, and yet when surrendering herself to Matt, she'd resolved to respect his professional privacy. "I might get Winnie up. Will Flash be going with you?"

"No," he said. "If there are pictures to take, I can snap them." As he spoke, he took the discreet-looking satchel with his camera gear out of the closet. "I've already told him to look after you ladies, and to be at your disposal while I'm occupied."

"Sounds pretty serious," She stepped behind the cabin's oriental screen to don a bathrobe. "This must be an important meeting for you."

"Big stuff," Matt affirmed, tying his shoelaces. "It could be the journalistic payoff of this entire voyage—aside from your revelations, of course. That's a windfall I never really expected."

"As your secretary, I should go along," Alma said. "You may need some notes taken, or an extra pair of eyes and ears."

"Well, thank you, my love," Matt said, giving her another peck on the lips, "but I don't think this individual would be too pleased at anyone else knowing his identity. Or hers, yes, of course." He smiled. "But don't worry. It's a he, I'll admit that much."

* * *

With Alma following close behind, Matt slipped out of the cabin through the darkened parlor, where their shipmates lay asleep in a huddle of blankets. He envied them the luxury of a morning together and had no wish to disturb them. Yet here he was, denying the same blessing to Alma, his newly devoted love who, after her recent hardships, was so much more in need of comfort and security. What kind of a man was he to leave her just now? Frowning, he suppressed a sigh. Like so many others in this modern mechanized world, he was a man who believed in his work, a man with a job to do.

The two navigated the ship's electric-lit corridors in silence, not daring to hold hands. A few other passengers had begun to stir, probably roused by the foghorn. For speed and privacy, Matt led Alma straight to the upstairs mezzanine of the Grand Saloon, where breakfast was being served from a long buffet table. Matt requested the eggs shirred over crayfish tails, and Alma the delicate French *crêpes* with fruit and cream.

The white-clad waiter took their order. Matt chose a table hidden behind a pillar, and the food came to them with almost no waiting.

He took time from his breakfast to admire Alma, framed against the ballroom's electric-lit dome. She was no fashion plate this morning, having put on knits and flat shoes, probably in the vain hope of accompanying him.

But with hair hastily pinned up, her face was still radiant—with love for him, it thrilled and pained him to realize. Here they were together, surrounded by the clink of crystal and silver and the pleasant murmur of voices. How much longer, he wondered, could this tranquility last? Not long, at the speed the ship was going. His thoughts turned to the immediate future.

"Getting clear of the port will be our biggest challenge," he told her. "If Liverpool is like New York, it's full of watchers—smugglers, spies, customs agents and cops, some of 'em crooked. Someone with Big Jim's pull might even bribe a petty official to detain you on false pretenses, turn you over to his henchmen, or deport you back to New York."

"I'd rather die than go back," Alma whispered, her romantic glow instantly fading. "I'd rather face a torpedo here and now than one of Jim's...human torpedoes."

"Well, I wouldn't be too concerned about it. If Jim had agents aboard this ship, I'd worry about them keeping you on board and stowing you away below decks for the turnaround trip to New York...drugged, maybe, or locked in one of the empty Third Class cabins. But without having to fret about that, we should be able to get through the port. Getting you off *Lusitania* is only the first hurdle."

"Wherever I go" Alma said glumly over her *crêpes*. "I'll have to worry about being shanghaied like a drunken sailor. White slavery is no joke."

Matt tried to comfort her. "It shouldn't be so bad once the heat is off, as the crooks say. You were right to change your hair. Beautiful as it was, those blonde tresses drew attention."

"They drew yours from the start, I could tell."

"I couldn't take my eyes off you. But now it's not so bad. You're just another lovely girl, and they're a dime a dozen. To really hide, you should grow a mustache." He smiled, ready to duck in case she flung a *crêpe* at him. "But seriously, once we get on the train in England, we can go anywhere. We'll split off together as a couple, if it seems safer—just make sure you know where to join up with your nurse friends. Or else stay with me. I may actually be needing a secretary."

Alma's gaze met his, but her voice sounded dubious. "That would hardly be laying low," she pointed out. "Not with you in the news spotlight. If we have to separate, you and I, it will be difficult, but I can do it." She spoke deliberately, and Matt could tell it was a hard prospect for her to face. "I do have a decent livelihood ahead of me now, thanks to Hildegard and the Nurse's League. Actually," she picked up after a moment's pause, "I'm more worried about Winnie and Flash. These few days have been such a life-changing experience...life-saving really, dear, for me." She reached out and laid her hand on Matt's beside his plate.

"We can work something out." Discreetly he clasped her hand. "Flash and Winnie are mature enough to handle things. If we two have to split off, I've told Flash we'll offer to help you to your destination. Then we can decide. There've been a lot of partings in this war, and there'll be more."

Withdrawing his hand, he took out his pocket watch. "Speaking of which, I have to go right now. Can you make it back to the cabin on your own?"

"I'd rather go with you," she appealed to him. "I have a feeling that you're off on another one of your secret explorations, and I don't like to think of you doing it alone."

"Now, don't be silly," Matt said, rising to avoid further interrogation. "I just have to go meet someone. The worst that could happen is losing the camera for the rest of the voyage, if Inspector Pierpoint turns up."

Taking Alma's arm, he led her through the saloon's mezzanine entry. "We're all better off if I go alone. And I'll stand a chance of really learning something."

"Where is this meeting supposed to be?" she asked, trying not to be petulant. "I promise not to spy on you."

"We're to meet on the Boat Deck forward, portside," he said with a peck on her cheek. "But from there, we'll certainly go somewhere out of sight."

Turning fully to her in the now-vacant corridor, he enfolded her in a brisk embrace. "I plan to be back at the cabin by noon. But give me another hour after that before you start to worry. Promise?"

"I promise." She sealed the vow with a lingering kiss. "All right," she said, letting him go at last. "Good luck."

"Good luck to us all." With mingled regret and relief, he strode off down the passage.

* * *

After watching Matt disappear, Alma turned toward the stairway to their cabin. There must be danger, she told herself, or he would have given her the name, if only in a sealed letter. Assuming that there was some name, and that he wasn't lying...trying, as ever, to protect her.

Well, he could take care of himself, that seemed clear. And a good thing, too, if he planned to survive the war. But of course it troubled her. She had so looked forward to their morning together, and to their whole final day. Was this to be all she would have of their new, joyous love, just a few precious hours?

Matt's offer to take her with him in England had seemed sincere, and a part of her yearned to accept. But did he really understand himself that well? Would he be able to sustain it, or would he lose interest in her? Already he was off on his own, more in love with his job than with her. Or maybe it was a tie, a photo-finish as Flash would say.

Even marriage, in wartime, was uncertain, and she didn't think she dared go from one impossible situation straight into another. She would not risk becoming a burden to the man she loved. Better to prove, first, that she could sustain herself, and to have something to fall back on, even if it meant the risk of losing him.

How dismal. Their talk over breakfast had turned her thoughts to the future, to their parting and the dim, terrible times ahead. Would her pure happiness of this morning ever return, or would she now live in dread, vainly wanting to cling to Matt and hold back time itself? Had the grieving already begun?

Consumed by such thoughts as she drew near their stateroom, she was slow to recognize what stood before her eyes in the corridor. It was a man, large and ungainly, clad all in filthy gray-black, his face and hands hideously smudged with soot. It must be one of the coal stokers, the Black Gang as they called them.

But no, as he came near, that wasn't the gang she knew him from.

It was Knucks, Big Jim's henchman, the one she'd eluded on the pier. No doubt of it...in spite of all the soot, the ugly leer taking shape on his face made him familiar.

"Well, Missy, fancy runnin' into you," the specter said, showing his yellow teeth in a grin. "If it ain't little Maisie, right here to greet me...in your new hair and all. Is that a wig? C'mere, Maisie Thornton, you!"

In a heartbeat Alma turned and ran. She dashed away down the corridor, hearing the hoodlum's heavy steps start up behind her. It was still early, and no one was out in the passage. Nobody to hear, no door standing open. She ran forward a few dozen paces, and then up the stairway...heading toward Matt, who knew this threat and had dealt with it before. Better, in any case, that she led Knucks away from their cabin and the innocent lovers inside. Luckily, her nurse's shoes were fit for running.

But on the stairs, her first burst of panicked speed was already wearing off. Each breath seared her lungs as she climbed, and her legs lost their impulsive strength. Behind her the mobster's clumping footfalls consumed two or three stairs at a time, relentless. She could even hear Knucks's coarse breaths, like the impatient rasping of a lion on the hunt.

Reaching the stairway's end, she burst out the door into fog, thick and swirling, rolling aft against the ship's motion. She lunged forward into its flow, flinging the stair door behind her. But it never slammed, caught instead by her pursuer. She dashed past lifeboats, swung outboard now with ropes and oars ready. She thought of hiding in one, but the fog wasn't thick enough, and her nemesis was too close. Had it been a mistake, she wondered, to come out on deck? She sensed that when Knucks caught up with her, he would fling her straight over the rail, without even time to plead for her life.

"C'mon, little missy," she heard him panting behind her, "Wait up for me, I won't hurt you! I just want the money back, and the other stuff you took. Maybe a little kiss, too, that would be nice!" After his taunts came the grating blast of the foghorn, which startled her, almost making her stumble.

No one was there on the fogbound deck to see or hear, no strollers idling in the damp chill. The officer's bridge was still out of sight, no telling how far ahead. Anyone above on the Marconi Deck might see the chase, but they'd be helpless to interfere. She had no breath left to call for help. Running was all-important.

"Atta girl, Maisie," her pursuer taunted, "slow down and let me nab you! A fast little runner you are, but pretty soon you'll run out of ship."

It was hopeless, she knew. She could actually feel the impact of his steps on the deck underneath her pelting feet, could almost feel his hands on her and his hot breath on her neck. Then she felt it, one big fist scuffing her shoulder.

In a sudden, futile impulse of defense, she spun around and struck him across the face with the back of her hand, even as he collided with her and bowled her backward down the deck. "Get away from me," she heard herself gasping. "Leave me alone!"

"You little hussy, you'll pay for that." Looming tall and barely brushing the side of his face where her blow had struck, Knucks darted out one hand and seized her shoulder. He pinned her painfully by it as she tried to twist free, and clamped his other hand over her mouth. "Now honey, don't you bite!"

Just then from inboard, other footsteps came racing. "That's enough, Knucks! Let her alone!"

It was Matt, and he didn't wait for the hoodlum to obey. Rushing in with fists cocked, he struck Knucks on the face and body. The goon was forced to defend himself, letting Alma pull free.

"Go ahead, run," Matt called to Alma over his shoulder, darting in like a prizefighter to deliver more blows. She staggered back a few steps, but stayed to watch, utterly exhausted and still captive.

"It's you, the lousy scribbler," Knucks growled. "You're no Jack Dempsey!"

Without even bothering to go for a weapon, the big ruffian seized hold of his attacker in both long arms and wrestled him over to the rail. "I got no time to mess with you, Vane," he said, applying his full size and leverage against the flailing reporter. "If anybody's goin' in for a swim, it's gonna be you first!" Snarling his threats, he bent the lesser man back over the water.

Alma, instead of running, used the one thing she'd learned in all her days with the gangsters. Coming up behind Knucks as the two men grappled, she aimed a kick straight up between his legs with the toe of her sturdy nurse's brogan. She felt it connect.

"Why, you rotten floozy!" Knucks yelped. He faltered with the pain, but still pinned his male assailant off-balance against the rail with one arm. The other hand he whipped around his back, pulling a pistol out from under his grimy coat. "I've had enough of fooling with you!" He pointed the gun at Alma, but then said, "Nah, yer boyfriend first."

He pressed the muzzle against Matt's chest, waiting for...what?

The foghorn blast came then, and in the same instant the gunshot hammered out, the report dulled and dislocated by the fog and shuddering noise.

To Alma, in a much deeper fog of horror, it all seemed unreal, impossible...as if the shot had come from nowhere, from somewhere outside. She watched the unfolding tableau as the big figure of Knucks, not Matt, grasped his chest, dropped the gun, and turned paler underneath his soot. Suddenly from behind her, a figure brushed past toward the giant and, with Matt's help, shoved him back against the rail. Then Knucks went over, his big, thrashing shoes the last thing to disappear in the fog. The two men stood looking down as a faint splash sounded, and then turned back to her. Beside Matt stood the well-dressed Mr. Kroger, the German spy, pocketing his own pistol. While brushing off and straightening his fur-trimmed coat, he glanced down and kicked the gangster's fallen weapon overboard after its owner.

"Somebody might have heard that shot," Matt said, even as Alma flew into his arms, sobbing with relief. "And the body will wash all the way astern—someone could see it. We'd better get going."

"Come along," Dirk Kroger said in his gruff accent, leading the way. "I'll take you where no one would ever look."

Chapter 35

Envoy

Palm fronds scraped their jagged edges together as Colonel Edward Mandell House pushed his way through dense jungle foliage. Occasional cool drops fell onto his hatless head from the trees that arched high above in humid stillness.

The profusion of green sprays and bright blooms, orchid and palm, fern and cycad, dazzled him. But Colonel House, raised on dry Texan plains, found the foliage damp and suffocating, until at last his small party broke through into sunlight.

"Quaht a display, Suh Edwuhd, ah must admit," he told his guide, Viscount Sir Edward Grey. He thankfully followed the British Foreign Minister's coat-tails toward the exit of the sweltering greenhouse. He'd seen enough of this Crystal Palace, built for the Great Exposition of 1910.

"All it needs now," House said, "is some of your rayuh birds to flap their braht wings about, and liven it up a bit."

"My ornithology collection, you mean," Grey said with a polite smile to his guest. "Since this war has broken out, I fear it is sadly neglected. You'll find most of my feathered friends at the British Museum—stuffed and mounted, I'm sorry to say."

The Viscount paused as a liveried attendant opened the temperature-sealed door. He then led his American guest out onto the broad walkways of Kew Gardens in the London suburbs.

"An amazing place, Suh," House said, looking back at the mountainous glass domes of the botanical garden. "These exhibits show off the wonders of your British colonies all round the wuhld, and to fine advantage. I wish ouah President Wilson could be here to see it." He felt Grey place a hand on his shoulder, an un-British familiarity that showed his eagerness to please.

"Colonel House, I hope that you, as your President's confidant, will convey to him my personal invitation to come and see what small wonders we have to offer, anytime. I would love to go to America once again and witness your country's latest marvels. But this war will keep me occupied awhile, it seems."

"I understand, Suh. In these dark days, as you so eloquently put it, the lights have gone out all over Europe." Accompanying the impeccably clad Foreign Minister down the walk, House saw fit to further echo Sir Edward's already famous words. "Do you really think those lights will not be lit again in our lifetimes? Won't there be peace?"

"Yes, peace, quite likely," Grey said, "but what kind of peace after such terrible, total war? The losses have already been so great on both sides! But an end to it must come eventually. Perhaps your President Wilson can travel here someday to have a part in making the peace."

"I'll tell him," House said. "I think the President would like that. He very much prefers peace, of course, Suh. And he's managed to keep us out of this war, so far at least."

"Well, we'd best be getting you to the palace," Grey said, stopping at the waiting car. "I daren't make you late to see His Majesty."

At their approach, the chauffeur in gray livery had gone to the front of the Rolls-Royce Silver Ghost and hand-cranked the engine. Now, with the motor briskly chugging, he held open the rear door for his passengers. When they were comfortably in place, the driver seated himself before the steering wheel at the right front.

As the open motorcar rumbled out onto the road across Kew Bridge over the Thames, the two Edwards spoke freely. For House it was a welcome chance to take out a Carolina cigar.

"Your voyage across from New York on *RMS Lusitania* caused quite a stir, Colonel," Grey said. "We in England are flattered, of course, that you chose a British Cunard liner for the crossing, in spite of the U-boat danger. But did you not consider taking passage on a neutral ship, such as one of your own American Lines?"

House was well-prepared to launch into the yarn he'd evolved to handle this diplomatic event, with all its tall-tale embellishments. "Well, Suh, we ended the trip under the Stars and Stripes anyway, didn't we?" With that introductory joke, House passed the cigar to his host and lit up his own. "But really, Suh Edward, you may have heard the story by now that my own deah dad was a blockade runner back in Civil War days, a British migrant himself." He puffed the cheroot to get it going. "That's how our family suhved the Great Lost Cause of the Confederacy, by sending our supply ships through the Union lines off Galveston to unload in our Southuhn ports.

"With that in mah history, it seemed like nothin' much for me to get on board a ship that was doin' basically the same thing. Except for the contraband, of course—we all know Cunahders don't carry any war *materiel*." He elbowed the minister and gave him a broad wink.

"I felt, suh, that I needed to travel on the very best, fastest ship. To do any less would have disgraced ouah family name. At the time, I even thought my presence might make your Lusitania's othuh passengers a little safer, having an American peace envoy on board. And maybe it did."

"So then," Grey asked, "as the child of a blockade runner, was it your idea to raise the American colors when your ship missed its Royal Navy escort and hove into Liverpool?"

"Why Suh, are you callin' me a Son of a Gun-runnah?" The Colonel laughed aloud with his host, smiling broadly to reassure him over the quip. "Come now, Suh Edward, I don't think you British chaps need a Yank to teach you how to bend the rules...or waive them, by waving a neutral flag." He winked again at the point scored. "But nossuh, it wasn't my Stars and Stripes your Captain Dow ran up the mainmast! If I'd raised a banner, it could just as well have been the gray southuhn one, eh?" He gave the Minister another sly nudge. "And if you'll recall, suh, our American government bellowed almost as loudly over it as the Germans did. My boss Woodrow would have been happy to let me go to the bottom, I'm sure, just so long as it kept International Law intact."

Sir Edward responded with an understanding laugh, and the conversation flowed on.

House felt quite at home with these upper-crust British, as no doubt he was meant to feel. But still, neutrality aside, after enjoying all this genteel, homey treatment from the Brits, how was he supposed to look forward to hob-nobbing with a bunch of uniformed, whiskered, goose-stepping and gruff-speaking Prussian generals on his impending visit to Germany?

After a drive through farm estates and the smoky, congested confines of London, the touring car rolled up to St. James Park and the broad gates of Buckingham Palace. Two red-coated and fur-hatted Beefeater guards, alongside British servicemen in drab olive uniforms, admitted the touring car to the broad plaza at the front.

Things appeared duly regal in the courtyard, except for the wartime khaki hues sprinkled among the attendants, and the presence of a pale blue biplane parked before the palace. House recognized it as a De Havilland with the short stubby cockpit, almost invisible tail boom, and Vickers machine gun on the nose. Whether it was there on courier duty, for Zeppelin defense, or just for demonstration purposes, a long strip of the royal plaza had been marked off as a runway.

Colonel House took cordial leave of the Foreign Minister outside the touring car and was ushered by Beefeaters into the palace lobby. A butler led him out again across the vacant inner courtyard to the rear residential part of the great building. He had been told that the audience with His Majesty would be an intimate, informal one. This seemed likely as the single servant led him down empty hallways and through chambers decorated with fine antiques, elegant statuary and imposing royal portraits.

When House was at last conducted into the magnificent library and told to wait, the delay was miniscule. In mere moments, without fanfare, King George the Fifth entered. He was dressed in tweed slacks and a beige sweater over his shirt and foulard.

In spite of the casual attire, England's monarch was instantly recognizable because of his sandy-colored mustache and goatee. The guest noted the close resemblance to His Majesty's Hohenzollern cousin, Czar Nicholas of Russia, whom House had seen only in photographs so far. The King's family resemblance to photos of Germany's Kaiser was also eerily apparent.

"Welcome to our home," George greeted him. "It's large and a bit chilly, but we must keep up appearances, even in wartime."

The monarch glanced around the cavernous library. "It seems rather musty in here. Perhaps we should conduct our meeting on the back terrace. The sun is out, for a time at least. It appears just now to be a delightful day."

House assented, unutterably charmed to be received so graciously by a king. George led him through a salon where a lady was addressing two maids, ordering up tea.

"Here, Edward," George said, "let me just introduce you to my wife, Queen Mary as they call her. Vickie, my dear—as we in the family say," he added with a disarming smile—"this is Colonel Edward House, President Wilson's personal envoy and close friend."

Although her title suggested hoop skirts and a crowned hairdo, the queen was tall and svelte in an informal gown of the latest loose cut, with hair primped in an elegant bun. Turning from the servants, she navigated smoothly across the room to place a slim hand in Edward's.

"Very pleased," she said with a demure smile. Only the mildest trace of a German accent betrayed her Continental origins, and she seemed amused to watch the guest bow in his courtly Southern way.

"Milady, I am the more pleased," House said, as with a polite nod she turned back to her household business.

"Right this way." George touched his guest's elbow and guided him toward the French windows at the back of the salon.

"Because of the confidential nature of your visit we've dispensed with all formalities, as you can see." The regent led the envoy out onto a sunlit terrace. It overlooked the bright gardens and green meadows of St. James Park, under a blue heaven dotted with flotillas of small puffy clouds. "I didn't suppose," the king went on, "that you or your President would desire a great deal of fanfare, press photography and so forth."

"Well, Your Majesty, that's most considerate of you. The President asked me to sound things out over here, test the waters so to speak. He wouldn't want any single government laying public claim to me or to the United States as an ally just yet. I will be going to see your cousin Wilhelm too, you know, and it wouldn't do to provoke the Germans at this point."

"Hmm, yes," King George said, taking a seat at a glass-topped table opposite his guest. "I'd tell you to say hello to my cousin Willie for me, but things have been a bit strained in the family. We've spent several decades trying not, as you put it, to 'provoke the Germans.' But with poor success, I'm sorry to say."

The monarch sighed and fell silent as the tray of steaming tea was brought, laid out before them, and poured out. "Still, Colonel," the king went on in his mild, droll way, "I shouldn't be propagandizing you. We may have an unfair advantage already. I hear that your father was a British subject, a sea captain who emigrated to Texas."

"That's true, Your Majesty," House said after sampling a tea cake. "I spent half of my boyhood on horseback and the other half on a ship's deck." As with the Foreign Minister he lied confidently to the King, knowing that gross exaggeration was expected of all Texans.

"Well, Colonel, did you know that I myself was raised in the Royal Navy? At age twelve I signed on as a midshipman in our old sailing fleet. I made it all the way up to the dreadnoughts before this kingly duty called."

"How very appropriate, Your Majesty, for the ruler of an empire whose strength is based on sea power. It's such an amazing feat, for this small island of yours to spread the boon of Western civilization across all the world's oceans and continents. But now it seems, with the coming of submarines and torpedoes, even your dreadnoughts have something to dread."

"Quite so," the king solemnly said. "Instead of carrying on trade with our colonies and partners, we face being blockaded in our home islands by this undersea menace." George set down his teacup and spoke in earnest. "That is why it's so urgent that our neutral friends, like yourselves, continue to trade with us and not be frightened off by the threat of U-boats. I have every confidence in my Royal Navy to defeat this peril and limit our losses to a manageable level. But if the Germans, in their beastly frightfulness, should succeed in turning away all neutral shipping, it would threaten our defensive efforts in France and the very sovereignty of our kingdom here at home."

House, in view of George's forthright tone, felt emboldened to challenge the king's assertions. "But Your Majesty, what if your neutral friends, as you put it, choose to trade with Germany instead? Has your navy not instituted an illegal long-range blockade of German ports and cut off legal trade with the Central Powers?"

"Indeed," the King said, "I fear so, old chap. With all the advances in sea and air power, mines and submarines, the old three-mile blockade limit is hopelessly obsolete. It would render our ships fatally vulnerable to the enemy."

"Even so, Suh," House ventured, "your blockade is in violation of International Law."

"Technically, perhaps," His Majesty admitted. "But unlike the Germans, we do not sink neutral ships. As to the goods confiscated, we always pay a fair price, so the merchants lose nothing, except any illegal cargoes." George shrugged with his most innocent smile. "In any event, my good fellow, your whole question is moot ever since my dear cousin Willie's declaration of unrestricted submarine warfare. Any neutral shipping that goes near Germany or England, either one, now runs the risk being torpedoed without warning."

"That, of course," House said, "is a key concern of my government and the American people. Rest assured, Suh, that I will raise it with the Kaiser when I go there. Short of ending this war, if we could come to some agreement or strategy to protect neutral shipping, my visit here would be a great success. I came bearing our Freedom of the Seas initiative, as you probably know, Your Majesty. Then when the *Falaba* was torpedoed, as you may recall, the death of just one American passenger caused an international uproar. Now, with this warning that the Germans have printed in our newspapers, the tension is high once again."

"Indeed, my good man. Suppose, just suppose—" the Colonel looked up to find the King's earnest gaze fixed on him—"that they should sink the *Lusitania* with American passengers on board?"

Taken aback by George's directness, House had to gather his wits a moment. "Your Majesty, I'll tell you the same thing I told your Foreign Minister not an hour ago, when he asked much the same question. I told Suh Gray that, if this were done, a flame of indignation would sweep America which would in itself carry us into the war. Ouah people would not stand for it, and my government would have no choice but to pay heed. I think, Suh, that great changes would be set in motion."

"Do you think President Wilson would immediately declare war?"

"Why no Suh, I cannot say that he would. You must know, Your Majesty, that our government is not so centralized as to follow the lead of a single individual. There would be great outcry, great debate in our legislature and the press, and staunch opposition from leaders in our government such as our Secretary of State, Mr. Bryan. And President Wilson himself is above all else a peaceable man."

"Your American government is not, I think, so different from ours," George said with a grave expression. "You do not think, then, that there would be a declaration of war?"

"Not at once, no, Suh," House said after consideration. "Public opinion takes time to shift. Even with urging from our leadership, it could take a year, more likely two, to sway a great nation like ours from peace to war. Strong questions raised by some factions, such as the Socialists, would have to be...settled. But I think the tide would have turned. It would just be a matter of time."

"Time," the king echoed. "Time, you know, is not necessarily a bad thing. I would worry that, if some tragic event such as a sinking were to occur, it might touch off an instant panic in your country, with a trade embargo, say. Or a war frenzy, including a rapid military buildup that might just as seriously interrupt the flow of the American goods our nation and war effort have come so much to depend on. That would be... from our standpoint, you understand...a double tragedy."

"I think not, Your Majesty," House said, nodding. "In a democracy as great as ours, nothing is going to happen overnight."

"Well, thank you, Colonel, for your reassurances. It's good to have a friend on whom one can so confidently rely."

"Your Highness is most welcome, Suh. I understand."

At least, House believed that he did—though he would have many occasions to ponder his royal audience, in the days and years to come.

Chapter 36

Evasion

"You are a good electrician," *Kapitan-Leutnant* Schwieger told his newest crew member. "You know your wires and batteries, but the job leaves you idle during hostile action. Therefore, Voegele, I am reassigning your battle station. From now on it will be right here in the command room."

"*Hier, Herr Kapitan?*"

The Alsatian was, as Schwieger expected, taken by surprise. As a draftee, a near-foreigner from the French-German corridor so recently restored to the Fatherland, Voegele was all but shunned aboard the *U-20*. The captain knew that he must find his assignment lonely. It was time to bring the man into the crew, test his loyalty and, as the *Anglischer* saying went, make or break him.

"*Jawohl, Voegele,*" Schwieger said, clapping a hand on his crewman's shoulder. "During an attack I can use you here. It will give you valuable combat experience."

"Combat, sir?"

The electrician's quavering tone made others in the cramped compartment laugh aloud.

"*Herr Kapitan,*" the pilot Lanz called from his seat astern, "does that mean you will no longer be needing him as ballast?"

The joking term, greeted by more laughter, was in reference to the duty of most crewmen to run forward during a crash dive in order to weigh down the nose of the craft and make it sink faster, out of sight of attackers on the surface. Knowing this, *Herr Kapitan* Schwieger still regarded the question as impertinent. But then, his longtime, reliable pilot was technically a civilian, not subject to the harshest military discipline, so he let it pass.

"Indeed," Schwieger announced, "Herr Voegele's duty will be right here, to listen for my orders from the conning tower—" the captain gestured up to the tiny turret, ladder and hatchway that stood open above them "—and then repeat the commands so that they can clearly be heard here below. In a combat situation, I don't like to rely on the speaking tubes. So you, Voegele, will be my speaking tube...I promote you to *Obersteuermann.*"

The humble steersman rank, only equivalent to quartermaster in the land army, nevertheless had the effect of silencing the crew's snickers.

"If my firing order is made to one of the torpedo rooms," Schwieger pointedly instructed Voegele, "you will run forward or aft to convey it, see that it is carried out, and immediately report back to me."

The electrician looked puzzled and less than enthusiastic—hardly the fitting demeanor for a U-boat officer.

"But sir," the Alsatian said, "once a torpedo is armed and the tube flooded, you also have a Fire button in the conning tower. Wouldn't it be quicker to use that?"

As electrician he would know this, of course. And indeed, failing an instant response to his speaking-tube command, Schwieger fully intended to use the electronic link rather than relying on this weak-livered draftee. By waiting, he would possibly miss the shot. But Voegele didn't need to know all that.

The *Kapitan* responded, "Since you ask, Herr Voegele...yes, indeed it would be quicker, assuming that the electric circuit works. But it is the teamwork that I am interested in, and prompt obedience."

Schwieger also knew it was important, given enough time, to exercise the crew in their appointed duties, the jobs they'd trained so tirelessly for. They valued that and saw it as a privilege. It was good for the boat, good for morale, and there should be no need to tell a raw recruit this.

"And because it is my order," the *Kapitan* finished curtly. "Any more questions? Enough, then, you are dismissed."

As Voegele half-heartedly saluted and turned away, Schwieger listened for more jeers but heard none. Now the Alsatian was put on notice, as was the entire crew...or soon would be, once the word got around. These morale-building duties were tiresome and sometimes embarrassing, but they were a necessary part of his command...at least on a fogbound homeward journey, when there was little to be done, and the men might so easily get into mischief.

Returning to his charts on the map table, Schwieger silently cursed the fog. He cursed England too, and the poor luck that forced him now to turn his course homeward without notable success so far. True, he had sunk the sister ships *Centurion* and *Candidate*—along with one puny Irish sailboat armed only with cheese and chickens. Wartime provisions, and the means of transporting them, had been destroyed—a token revenge, at least, for the British sea blockade that was crippling Germany and threatening to slow the progress of the *Der Kaiser's* armies. He and his crew had done their duty.

Still, this double sinking was hardly the kind of achievement that would advance his career in the *Kaiserliche Marine,* or win admiration from his fellow captains. It was no great feat, such as taking on a warship or some of the troopships setting out from these same ports, carrying new hordes of English invaders to Churchill's Turkish Delight in Gallipoli—or, as was rumored lately, to the very beaches of Northern Germany. It was nothing like sinking one of the great ocean liners that, under a pretense of ferrying passengers and mail, smuggled the munitions used to prosecute this devious war of encirclement against his homeland. The chances of any such accomplishment on this voyage grew slimmer by the hour.

Slim indeed, now that he had abandoned the rich hunting grounds of the Irish Channel and pointed his craft westward, back toward the Atlantic. The fog, at least, allowed them to cruise on the surface and restore their batteries and air, with less risk of being sighted from the south coast of Ireland.

But that ended in mid-morning, when the thinning mist revealed a trawler heading out to sea. Schwieger ordered a dive, since you couldn't tell nowadays whether such a fishing boat might be cruising in service to the Royal Navy, carrying a wireless set or a 2-pounder gun.

He then kept *U-20* on their westward course, but submerged. And wisely so, for within two hours they heard the thudding engines of a large, fast vessel passing overhead, possibly a destroyer or something bigger.

Could it be *Lusitania*? The temptation was delicious. Schwieger ordered the sub to maximum periscope depth, clambered up into the conning tower, and raised the tube. As its lens cleared the bright, calm surface, he saw tall smokestacks and masts bearing two massive crow's nests. Those were gunnery control stations set above the smoke of battle, he knew, not tourist lookouts. It was a warship, a cruiser of respectable size built late in the last century. That kind of vessel would make an easy target, providing she was torpedoed from beneath the surface and unable to bring her gun batteries into play. Otto in *U-9* had sunk three of these white elephants in an hour's work last September. The *Aboukir, Hogue,* and *Cressey* were now names that echoed Germany's naval might.

Elated at the prospect of an easy kill, Schwieger ordered a course change in pursuit, and he called Lanz up to identify the target. The new *Obersteuermann* Voegele was nowhere in sight, but there was no time for that now.

"An old cruiser, *Eclipse* class, top speed 17 knots or so, *Herr Kapitan*," Lanz reported from beside him.

Following around with his periscope to compensate for the *U-20's* turn, the pilot spoke assuredly.

"Must be *Juno* of the south Ireland fleet, likely running back into Queenstown. A poor torpedo shot from this angle." Lanz surrendered the scope back to Schwieger.

"Yes, and they know we're in these waters," the captain said with a sigh. "Maybe that trawler spotted us and got off a wireless message. They certainly have news by now of the two Harrison Liners we sank."

This *Juno* was heading for port at top speed, and after a moment it became clear that she was zigzagging as well. A giddy experience for the warship's crew, Schwieger thought, swerving at high speed. Yet such an evasive tactic made it all but impossible to plot a torpedo track that would intercept the ship's course at the proper angle. He could not waste his last three "eels" taking pot-shots, so he called off the chase and resumed his westward course.

They'll all be running for shelter now, he thought, keeping his disappointment to himself. A dismal voyage ahead. Warships, cruise ships, freighters and dairy boats, all have reason to fear us.

Chapter 37

Deck Watch

Winifred and Flash were delighted to see the fog lifting. After a late breakfast and a leisurely stroll astern, they lingered on the covered promenade to watch the morning vapors scatter.

"The others should be up by now," Winnie said. "I wonder what they're doing?"

"What's the hurry?" Flash placed a sheltering arm around her shoulders. "Let's stay and enjoy our time together."

Before the two lovers' gaze, the Atlantic played a tantalizing game of hide-and-seek. Here through the parting mists shone towering bastions and floating galleons of dazzling white cloud. Meanwhile over there opened out a patch of sunlit sea, a beckoning corridor between islands of fogbound mystery. As the couple stood at the portside rail with arms enwrapped, they saw in that changing seascape a reflection of their own formless hopes and of their mingled tender, indefinable feelings. Even the last remnant of nighttime chill was welcome, providing them an excuse to huddle tightly together.

"Oh, look, I can see the land," Winnie cried. "Right there, it's so green!"

She pointed to a brief ribbon of verdant horizon that unrolled before them, soon again to be swallowed up by drifting mist.

"It's the Emerald Isle, good ol' Ireland," Flash proclaimed with spirit. "That green is solid shamrocks, you can bet. I've heard the four-leaf clovers grow like crazy in the spring."

"And here comes the blarney too, already," Winnie chided him. "Don't try to beguile me with gab, you red-headed leprechaun." She planted a kiss on her companion's lips.

"Mm, *begorrah*," Flash said, dipping his head back in for another peck.

"Oh, and listen, do you hear it?" Winnie burst out suddenly, making her lover look up and attend to the silence. "The foghorn, I mean. It's stopped."

"Why yes, it has," he realized. "It must be clearing up ahead."

The two leaned out over the rail to gaze forward, shading their eyes. Their magical ship seemed to be racing on through the patchy gray into dazzling whiteness.

"The future looks bright," Flash remarked, holding Winnie tight to keep from losing her.

"I love it bright," she said, turning down the floppy brim of her hat to shade her eyes. "I love it dark, too, late at night in our room! I love you," she added, ending with another kiss.

They stayed there in perfect union, hugging the rail and each other. With the ship's steady progress, the rags and fringes of fog seemed to rise up before them like a tattered playhouse curtain, to vanish astern, forgotten. What remained was a broad expanse of twinkling blue, bordered by a low, flat, green coastline.

"How lovely," Winnie said, cuddling close. "A cheerful day."

Other passengers who'd emerged on deck to see the fog burn off were revealed now in the morning light. They warmed themselves in the sudden brightness, but most didn't seem elated. Instead of sighs and laughter, many spoke in hurried murmurs, with an occasional shrill note of anxiety ringing out. One family with bags and blankets appeared to have slept all night in the deck chairs. A bald man wandered past, his shape distorted by the impossible bulk of a life jacket strapped on beneath his loose overcoat.

"Why do they seem so unhappy?" Winnie asked, glancing lazily around. "It's such a beautiful morning."

Flash stayed in their embrace, barely shrugging. "I guess they're afraid it'll be a beautiful day for submarines, too."

"Well then, I hope the submarines are very, very happy," Winnie proclaimed. "Everyone should be happy, I don't care." She hugged him tighter. "Really, Flash, I wouldn't mind if a torpedo hit us right now! It's worth it just to be here, the two of us together. It's like heaven."

"We have this moment, this snapshot in time," Flash affirmed, holding her tight. "What else can matter?"

One cheerful voice did chime out on deck behind them. "Oh look, here they are, the lovebirds!" It was Hazel addressing her sister. "They're not worried about U-boats, mines, or anything. Isn't it adorable?" Coming up behind the couple, the young nurse stood on tiptoe to give them each a peck on the cheek.

"So tell me," Florence appealed, following after. "What do we do if we see a periscope, anyway? Shoot it?"

"Just smile and pose for the picture," Flash answered mildly. "Not much else to do, except pour on a full head of steam and run for port."

"Well, if one comes, I want to be the first to spot it," Florence declared, taking the rail beside Winnie. "I'll go and tell the Captain myself!"

"Where's Alma?" Flash asked, looking around. "Is she with Hildegard?"

"No," Hazel said. "Miss Hildegard should be along any minute now, but we didn't run into Alma."

"Oh, is that so?" Flash said, disengaging from Winnie. "She never came back from breakfast. I thought she'd be with you." He turned to Winnie. "Did you see her at all this morning, my darling?"

"No," Winnie said, undoing her shawl and unbuttoning her coat to let in the day's warmth. "She was already gone out with Matt when I got up. Aren't they together?"

"Well, Matt had an assignment to go to. I'm supposed to look out for Alma while he's gone. I imagined she'd be with the group."

"She probably just went along with Matt to his meeting or...what was the assignment?" Winnie asked.

"No, Win, I doubt it." Ignoring her question in the mixed group, Flash gazed fore and aft along the promenade. "I'll have to check the cabin."

"It's not as if anything could have happened," Hazel reassured them all. "We're far away from New York and all that mess. And Alma is so happy these days, she wouldn't let anything interfere with it." The young nurse sighed in envy. "She's probably walking around on a cloud, just like the two of you."

"As long as she doesn't try walking on water," Flash said. He turned back to see their chaperone approaching. "Miss Hildegard, good morning! Have you seen Alma?"

"Why no, not since yesterday," the chief nurse said. "You men are supposed to be looking after her," she added sternly.

"Well, if you see her, hang onto her," Flash said. "We should all stick together on this last day of the voyage. Winnie, you wait here with the group, and I'll go to the stateroom. She's probably there."

"Shouldn't I come too?" Winnie appealed in a whisper. "It's not more cloak-and-dagger, is it?"

She looked positively distraught at the idea of being separated from Flash, and he turned to embrace her for a long moment.

"Don't worry, darling," he murmured in her ear. "She's right, though, we do have to look after Alma. It's hard to tear myself away, but I've got to go, my love. I'll hurry right back."

As he left, Florence called brightly after him, "Be sure and knock first! You wouldn't want to walk in on anything."

But he was already gone down the companionway.

"It's always a mistake to depend too much on men," Hildegard grimly declared as he left.

To this there was no reply, but when Winnie came wordlessly to her side, the elder nurse wrapped her in a motherly embrace that she found comforting.

Before they'd been alone long, the women were deep in a conversation on what was uppermost in everyone's mind, the threat of U-boats. On the subject of the bloodthirsty Huns, Winnie found she'd had a softening of the heart.

"I don't see why everyone is so upset," she observed. "This morning I heard a gentleman saying in the lounge, very firmly, 'What creature that calls himself a man would send a torpedo into a ship full of women and children?' And I agree with him. I don't think any sea officer, British or German, would do that."

"The Germans wouldn't do it?" Hazel demanded. "Look what they did to little Belgium!"

Nurse Hildegard added, "My dear, one thing you'll learn as a nurse in our modern time is that personal cruelty is slight, almost meaningless, against the impersonal cruelty of shells, bombs, jagged wire, and now poison gas and who knows what! It doesn't take individual cruelty any longer to do terrible things to people."

But Winnie was stubborn. "The *Kaiser* might give the order to torpedo us," she defended stoutly. "The British Lords of the Admiralty might dare him to go ahead and do it. But the sailors wouldn't take the command, the sub-mariners would disobey. There would be a mutiny and a trial. If it became enough of a scandal, it could bring this whole silly war to an end."

"A ship's mutiny on a submarine under the ocean?" Hazel asked. "It would take quite a reporter to sniff that one out. I doubt if even your boyfriend could cover it."

"Well, if Flash was there with his camera, we'd all see it on the front pages soon enough."

Sometime after being mentioned, Flash returned to the group. "Did you find her?" Winnie asked, running to his side.

"No," he said gravely, shaking his head. "No note there for us, either. It doesn't look as if anything has been disturbed since we left. I don't think she's been back to the rooms."

"So, then," Winnie reasoned, "she'll certainly be with Matt. Let's just go and find them both to make sure. Do you know where to look?"

"Well," Flash admitted. "I know his meeting was going to be on the Boat Deck forward, port side. We can go up and see. Do the rest of you mind staying here?"

"No, not at all." Miss Hildegard, who'd taken possession of some deck chairs, spoke up decisively. "The view of the land is so comforting, after all this time at sea, I think we'd love to sit and watch it unfold."

"Yes," Hazel said. "It seems so close you could almost swim to it."

"And look, there's a lighthouse," Florence added, pointing ahead to a black-and-white banded tower on a broad headland. "How pretty, welcoming us across the ocean."

"All right, then, we'll go," Flash answered, steering Winnie away. "You ladies stay here, but be on the lookout."

Chapter 38

Bearings

Captain Turner instantly recognized the lighthouse that the fog unveiled to port. The black-and-white banded tower, rising out of low castle ruins on a broad Irish promontory, was the Old Head of Kinsale, a landfall familiar to countless generations of seafarers.

He now knew their location. Not perfectly, perhaps, but he no longer needed to worry about the submarine reported last night off Fastnet Rock, which lay well astern. It was all but certain that his ship had passed any such danger in the fog. At the speed *Lusi* was traveling, no submarine yet invented could overtake her.

Just now at eleven bells, a new Admiralty message had arrived, this one in a more secure code requiring sign and countersign. Once a mutual cipher was established, the transmission began: "Make certain the *Lusitania* gets this."

This promise of real news, after the vague, general warning that had been broadcast all night, was tantalizing, and Captain Turner hurried into the chartroom to decipher the text. It read, "Submarines active in the southern part of the Irish Channel. Last heard of twenty miles south of Coningbeg lightship."

That definitely seemed promising, although a part of the promise was of future trouble. Coningbeg lightship, at the very mouth of St. George's Channel between England and Ireland, lay at least a hundred miles ahead. If the submarines had just been spotted there, they could hardly be in his immediate vicinity. The message seemed practically to guarantee his ship's safety, for the moment at least.

Of course, there could be even more U-boats than those reported. There was no absolute certainty. To maintain his lookout for periscopes, Turner had already ordered the watch doubled. He now conveyed a message to his crew to report anything suspicious, even a broomstick.

And he kept their course bearing east by northeast, inward toward the coast, to raise the horizon line and obtain a definite landfall.

Then, just after lunch at thirteen bells, a second cipher arrived, stating, "Submarine five miles south of Cape Clear, proceeding west when sighted at ten a.m."

More good news, since Cape Clear lay even farther astern than Fastnet. The U-boat that had been haunting the western sea lanes during the night had given up, its course taking it off around the Atlantic side of Ireland.

Now, with their position known, Turner could dare to feel confident. No Royal Navy escort was yet in sight—but perhaps *Juno* was off somewhere chasing after the marauding subs.

The best indication of there being no imminent danger was that the Admiralty hadn't ordered him into Queenstown harbor, which lay just ahead. The port was well-defended, with forts, patrol craft and a frequently mine-swept channel entrance. They could still send him in, of course, if trouble arose in the next hour or two. Turner and the *RMS Lusitania* were no strangers to the place, having stopped in there many times when Queenstown was a regular port of call for the Irish immigrant passage. He had also been diverted there in January while commanding the passenger liner *Transylvania*. A submarine terror was then underway, with three ships sunk in one day. The Cunarder, transporting four giant 14-inch guns strapped to its foredeck, complete with Bethlehem steel turrets for the Royal Navy, had been considered a vulnerable target. Luckily the ship, passengers, and vital cargo had all been saved.

As the Captain, on whose shoulders the final responsibility for his ship's welfare rested, Turner could even take the *Lusitania* into port by his own order. But the Admiralty certainly knew best and could surely guess his whereabouts. If they saw no need to run for cover, neither did he.

All that remained, then, was to get a precise fix on his ship's location, to navigate the coastlines or possibly that mine-free channel. And here was his chance. After ordering a turn to eastward following the coast, he assigned his new second officer Bisset, or Bestic, whatever his name was, to take a four-point bearing off the Kinsale light. This series of three time-readings, taken as the ship's course reached angles of 45, 90 and

135 degrees to the striped tower, would require the ship to steam in a straight line for some time at a constant speed. But the course data thus obtained would prove essential to avoid the perils ahead—in night and fog, perhaps, and whatever his ship's final destination.

Chapter 39

Flight

Leaving the murder scene, Alma fled inboard with the others. Or was it only an attempted murder, desperately thwarted? It didn't much matter, she decided as they hurried down the dimly lit passage. The hero of the day was a pistol-packing German spy, who now led her forward with Matt bringing up the rear. One way or another it was a crime, something to be concealed.

"This is the deck officers' quarters," Matt said in the narrow corridor, placing a sheltering arm on her shoulder.

"Won't we be seen?" she asked, still shaky from all the exertion and fright. "What will we tell them?"

"Well, it's a lean wartime crew, sleeping in shifts," he murmured back. "Most of the officers are probably out on watch. If they should challenge us, we just got lost in the fog."

His husky voice betrayed some after-effects of the recent struggle—was it from the would-be killer's grip on his throat, or from excess emotion such as Alma now felt? But instead of running away, it seemed to her that they were following a pre-arranged route.

Kroger led them to a doorway on the midships side, secured with a new-looking lock plate. Doing something deft that was screened by his stout overcoated body, the spy clicked the door open onto a staircase leading down. He held it open, followed the two of them through, and closed it softly behind.

Matt took the lead on the stairs, but hearing a door flung open on the level below, he immediately halted. Alma, peering around his shoulder, saw two men headed down, one in khaki shirt and trousers, the other undressed in long-johns and cotton slippers. Their careless voices echoed up the stairs.

"Come down and meet Wesley. You'll like him."

"Is he with the Sixth?"

"Not yet, but his papers are in. He's a capital fellow—"

When the lower door shut, cutting off the dialog, the fugitives waited an anxious moment. Then Kroger urged them along.

Matt said, "Those two looked like enlistees to me."

"The Winnipeg Sixth Rifles is a Canadian regiment," the spy muttered from behind them. "The ammunition for their Enfields is down in the hold, in those cases marked 'Non-Explosive In Bulk.'"

"I guess we're ferrying troops, too, as well as ammo. A shame," Matt added as they slipped past the lower door. "Any other time, I would've liked to interview those boys."

So this was part of the secrecy, Alma saw. Matt had already met this foreign agent on his late-night skullduggery, and now they were headed back for more. It all seemed too much for her to worry about now.

Instead, she counted the flights of stairs taking them deeper—six decks down, lower than she'd known the ship went. At the bottom, instead of cabins, the heavy door opened out on a cargo compartment. The room was vast and cluttered, barely illuminated by sparse electric bulbs.

"This used to be part of Third Class," Matt told her. "Last year it was stripped out for special wartime freight, and the decks above must have been sealed off for troop-carrying."

Alma looked around, nervous. "Are we cargo-creeping again?" she asked, shrinking against her companion. "Is this really the best time for it?"

"It's the only time, our last chance if we dock tomorrow," Matt said. "Anyway, we're probably safest down here, out of sight. Unless you want to go and report what just happened topside," he added.

"No." She shuddered at the idea, her mind racing. Any inquiry about the killing would only get back to Jim in New York. Then he'd have her, with all the more reason to exact vengeance. Far better if dirty old Knucks was just thought to have vanished along the way, jumped-ship so to speak. And she with him...they'd never even be sure she'd been aboard. Or maybe, in Jim's jealous mind, the two of them, Maisie and Knucks, would end up living happily together on some tropical island. She almost laughed at the thought, but shivered instead.

Anyway, this deadly Mr. Kroger would probably murder them both if they tried to report anything to the captain. Though for now, he and Matt seemed like the best of friends.

As if reading her thoughts, Kroger turned and drew something out of his coat pocket—an electric torch, which he flashed on. "Here we are, back in the hold," he told Matt. "I think we are both looking for the same thing."

"Lead on," Matt said, following the torch beam and drawing Alma along by the hand.

Immediately they found themselves climbing and scrambling over uneven-sized crates of cargo. Well, she was dressed for it anyway, and began to recover her strength as she looked around. The unfilled reaches of the hold seemed vast in the dimness, though the space was wedged tight with packing cases, bales and barrels. Alma could hear the faint thud of waves against the ship's hull. They must be just below the waterline, where the ocean swells resounded against the steel plating. She remembered hearing someone say *Lusi* rode low in the water this trip, heavily laden with...what, not just passengers and baggage, but evidently special cargo as well.

The dipping of the bow was giddier here, too; she felt it in the pit of her stomach. To distract herself, she wondered if they were out of the fog. She didn't suppose the sound of the foghorn would penetrate this deep into the ship. The place was dark, damp and gloomy. But then, wasn't dismal gloom the perfect place to hide from a murder rap?

"What are we looking for?" she asked at last.

"You'll see soon enough," Matt said. "Here's where it opens out for the taller pieces."

As he spoke, they entered a broad space with the ceiling cut away to the next level above, heaped higher than ever with goods.

"See, over there are two ambulances headed for the front."

"Well, that's not war contraband," Alma said. "Not any more than I am, anyway."

"No, just medical aid in the name of mercy."

Obviously back in his professional role, Matt still gave her hips a squeeze as they came to a halt.

"Here, Alma, can you set up the photographic gear for me?" Taking the satchel he'd brought along, he opened it up and fished inside. "This is all I need right now," he added, bringing out another battery light and a foot-long pry bar.

"I thought you and Flash had already gotten pictures down here," Alma couldn't help complaining as she took out the camera.

"We did," Matt said, "but we didn't shoot everything. We were interrupted...by Dirk here, as it turned out."

"You and your young friend overlooked the biggest story of them all," Kroger said. "If it is what I think, it will make you a bigger name than Walter Lippmann." The spy gave the American reporter's name a German accent, with the first initial *V* and ending in *monn*.

"Just great, if I don't decide to be anonymous."

Bending over in front of the tallest crate, Matt cupped his interlaced hands for the *ersatz* Dutchman to step into. By aiding each other, the two clambered up to the top.

"We photographed small arms cartridges and artillery bombs, and we dug down to the shell fuses over there," Matt said from his vantage, shining his light toward the starboard side of the hold.

"Did you find the gun cotton?" Kroger asked. "There must be carloads of it scattered about here, don't you see?" He shone his electric beam on a row of crates stenciled "CHEESE–KEEP DRY."

"What on earth is gun cotton?" Alma asked, having to call up to them from below. "I don't suppose it's just padding."

"It's shell propellant," Matt said. "High explosive, in a less dangerous form than TNT."

"That's true," Kroger said, "unless you get it wet. But watch out, it can react with seawater, *poof!* These crates are not the proper containers for such volatile goods."

"What worries me is all the powdered metal down here, especially aluminum," Matt said. "It's highly flammable, all the more so when wet." He flashed his beam down briefly in Alma's direction. "I didn't tell you about all of this, my love. I think you can see why."

Alma merely shrugged and didn't answer. She felt wrapped in an odd sense of unreality. What she'd just lived through made all of these political and packaging details seem remote.

"Powdered aluminum is a key ingredient of our German high explosive, *Perdit*," Kroger casually remarked.

I guess you'd know, Alma thought, still saying nothing.

"My assistant uses aluminum dust for flash powder," Matt said to the spy. "But he's savvy enough to keep his powder dry."

As the men spoke, they were strenuously at work on the twelve-foot-high crate, loosening metal seals and prying up what looked like an access panel at the near corner. The huge box, braced with two-inch thick planks around the middle and edges, was stenciled "TANK" in large letters. But the heavy crating made Alma think it must be a steam boiler or turbine, maybe for another ship like the *Lusitania*. If it was just an empty tank, couldn't they just lower it in and strap it down on top of other, heavier cargo?

Curiosity finally roused her. Climbing around by the lesser crates, including the second-tallest one labeled "HOPPER," she made her way up top alongside the men. The two were straining together, lifting the four-foot square access hatch with a loud creak of twisting metal and timber, and she joined in as best she could. When they had it upright, the men flashed their lights inside the crate.

"*Ach, so,*" Kroger said, shining his lamp down into the open crate. "I was warned there would be some new kind of infernal machine here."

Matt directed his flashlight into the oil-smelling gloom. "It looks like a locomotive."

"But it lays its own tracks, see there," Kroger shone his beam down on grooved metal treads that covered the iron-spoked wheels.

Alma peered in over the men's shoulders. "That's a gun if I ever saw one." She nudged Matt's flash beam toward the short, ugly muzzle at the top of the contraption.

"Quite right," Kroger said. "So much for the *Lusitania* not carrying any weapons."

"It's a land ironclad," Matt said, "a moving fortress armed with four-inch cannons. I read all about it. It's meant to break the deadlock of trench warfare." He turned his light on a second gun barrel at the front of the machine. "It must be our latest American invention, for export."

"Not good, it shouldn't be on a passenger ship," the spy said. "But if this device truly works, your neutral arms merchants should certainly offer it to Germany instead of England. Trench fighting is what's holding up the natural progress of the war, delaying our victory."

"I don't doubt the inventors would sell it to either side, if they could ship it to the Central Powers," Matt said, "But that's not my business." He turned to Alma. "Do you have the camera ready?"

"It's here, if you want to use it." She held up the satchel. "But does finding this make us all spies under British law?" She suddenly worried that, in Flash's absence, Matt might want to use her as a witness if his news reports were questioned.

"We're still neutrals, riding on a passenger ship," Matt said, taking the camera. "I have my press credentials, and you're my secretary. If I can get this story out, it will be open for all to see."

"A fine thing," Kroger said. "The whole world should see this." Meanwhile he propped his own miniature camera on the crate edge, trying a timed exposure by the ghostly light of his battery lamp.

"Here, Alma, hold the flash tray, please," Matt said. "Point it away from your face and don't look at it. That lever is the trigger."

Alma helped, though after several shots she was nearly blinded. Kroger took advantage of their flashes with his mini-camera, cursing and growing agitated in the process. "*Himmel*, the lying British should not have this!" he spat. "Our German factories can easily do better."

"You're not going to start any fires or try to sink this ship, are you, Dirk?" Matt challenged his henchman. "We don't need any of your exploding cigars down here."

"Matt, my good friend, if I wanted, I could have done so before now." The spy tapped his vest pocket where a cigar poked out, but with a gracious smile he went on, "If I can help you get your story out and expose the English cheats, so much the better. But," he added with a glance around the hold, "if this whole floating arsenal blows up *kaputt* sometime, don't blame me."

"Fair enough," Matt said, handing Alma his camera "Now then, if this is what a Tank looks like, let's have a look at a Hopper." With Kroger's help, he shoved the wooden hatch roughly back down in place.

Alma, for her part, still felt strangely unconcerned about the weapons and explosives all around them, even a bit bored by their grim destructiveness. With Knucks gone, this could be the end of Big Jim's pursuit. She was still alive, and for the first time in memory, she had a real chance at freedom. She and Matt were together, involved in a task that had meaning—for him at least, and maybe someday for her.

Rather than blowing up, she was actually more afraid of some crewman bursting in and finding out that she had no First Class ticket.

How odd...it was a strange, terrible time to be alive, in such a dangerous place, with everyone at war. But at least they were alive, the two of them. With her nursing skills, and Matt's notion of informing the public about war and corruption, they had hope.

She watched the men tearing into the second smaller box, and now Matt turned and beckoned. "Alma, come see this, and bring the camera."

She went to his side by the access hatch, which opened across the middle of this crate rather than the corner. She found herself looking down on a bolt-studded tubular thing, shaped more like a water tank than the other. But this was round and tapered, like a fat cigar with a harpoon for a nose. Raised up at the top center was a manhole-sized hatch. Except for the steel spike at the front, the entire object was reddish-gold copper, like a brewer's vat. The resemblance to news pictures of a U-boat was obvious.

"It's a submarine," she said in surprise, "but no bigger than a lifeboat."

"Yes," Matt said, "a small submersible craft, good for short trips. Call it a hopper sub."

"Good for what, exactly?" she asked. "Launching torpedoes?"

"Nope, too small," he answered. "But that barb up front is for ramming. Or it could even carry an explosive."

"So it's a suicide boat," she asked in distaste, "made only for one-way trips?"

The spy Kroger spoke up. "Actually it may be designed for ship defense." He thumped a broken plank-end against the hull, which rang like steel. "This copper electroplating would not last if it were kept in the sea for long periods. Do you see these hooks on top, fore and aft?" He pointed at metal stanchions set along the midline. "This craft can be lowered from davits, in place of a lifeboat, to battle submarines or any attacking vessel."

"Exactly," Matt said. "Just hang it off the deck of a ship to chase away subs, or simply scare them off."

"But is it any match for a U-boat?" Alma asked. "It's so tiny."

"Not so," Kroger said. "In a close fight, maneuver is most important. You will often see, in the air, one or two small birds attack a large bird and drive it off." The spy made swooping motions with his hands.

"Even with torpedoes and a deck gun," Matt put in, "a full-sized sub couldn't touch a mini-sub underwater. But with enough speed, this baby could ram and disable any U-boat. Or plant a timed charge." The idea of a purely defensive weapon seemed to make him boyishly enthusiastic.

While Matt spoke, Kroger knelt down and lifted open the vessel's rubber-sealed hatch, shining his light inside.

"It has an electric motor, can you smell the battery acid? Power enough for short runs, and a ship's dynamo can keep it charged. Two seats," he added, "pilot in front and engineer behind. The only question is," he said with a dismissive shrug, "how is it supposed to find its target in poor visibility underwater, in the dark?"

"I can guess," Matt said. "Hydrophones."

"What?" Kroger turned abruptly. "What do you know about that?"

Matt shrugged, readying his camera and not seeming troubled by the spy's sudden scrutiny. "Just some things I was hearing from the engineers and arms dealers on board. It makes sense to me now. What about you, Dirk, did you know this device was down here?"

Kroger was busy levering up planks astern to expose the hopper's rudder and screws. "No." He stood back to let Matt and Alma snap a photo. "There has been talk from our agents in the shipyards," he added, still panting with exertion. "But I never thought a prototype would be ready so soon."

Alma was surprised by the statement...not so much that there were German spies in American shipyards, but that Kroger would admit it. "Well then, why didn't they just park it out on the Lusitania's deck?" she asked. "It might make us all feel safer."

"I doubt that," Matt said. "More likely it'd scare off their passengers. Anyway, like the so-called tank here, it's probably war contraband, and top secret to boot."

"They will need to do tests, sea trials on this...hopper." Kroger was tearing away the last planking atop the crate. "This model is vital to the project, to prove its capabilities, including the...hydrophones, as you said. Very likely it is the only one in existence. It will have to be destroyed."

"What do you mean?" Alma gasped in sudden fear.

"This device is not going to be offered to my country," the spy said. "At all events, we have no sea commerce left to protect. My duty is to demolish it as a hostile weapon."

"What do you intend to do, Dirk?" Matt carefully set down his camera. "If you try blowing it up, you could sink this ship."

"No need," Kroger said. "Some of that powdered aluminum cargo you found, placed inside and on top, should quickly reduce the metal to slag. A hot flame is enough; there will be no explosion. If they douse it with water, it will only intensify the heat. We are far enough away from the gun cotton—and anyway, without a detonation it will just burn."

"But Mr. Kroger, you can't," Alma pleaded. "That would be utterly crazy, starting a fire with all the people on board, and all these munitions—"

"Don't worry," the spy said, tearing away the last plank. "This ship has fire alarms that alert the bridge directly. We can touch off one as we leave...it will be a useful distraction to help us escape. In minutes they will be down here trying to put it out."

Alma turned to Matt by her side, who was fumbling with his camera bag. "Matt, he's insane," she whispered. "Can't we do anything to stop him?"

"He sounds sane to me, and deadly earnest," Matt murmured back. "He has the gun, remember, in his coat pocket."

"Yes, and how do we know he won't use it on us, just to keep us quiet?"

"You're right," Matt said, slipping the pry bar into his belt. "He saved our lives, but he could just as easily shoot us both down for Kaiser and country. We'll try this: when he comes back, you blind him with the flash and I'll disarm him. Maybe at gunpoint he'll listen to reason."

"All right, but be careful, please!"

As Matt reloaded the flash tray, Alma turned to watch Kroger's progress over the crates lit by his wavering lamp beam.

At that moment, the ship and its cargo jolted beneath them. A clang, vast and deep like the slamming of a great metal door, became a shattering explosion.

Chapter 40

Attack

Kapitan-Leutnant Schwieger stood watch atop his conning tower after *U-20* surfaced. The gradually lifting fog allowed him glimpses of Irish coastline that the periscope might miss, but that were useful for navigation as they headed westward. Schwieger kept his binoculars constantly in use, though they grew heavy in his grip and slippery with spray.

Two other reliable watchers were on duty, Lanz the pilot, and Rikowski. The radioman had come up craving fresh air, with one of the dachshunds peering eagerly out of his half-buttoned coat. There was scarcely room for three officers inside the railings so hastily rigged atop the tower for surface cruising. Even so Schwieger stayed up top, not wanting to entrust this critical part of the chase to anyone else. The *Lusitania* was due in Liverpool tomorrow at the latest. He did not think the great ship had slipped past him in the Irish Channel. When and if she was spotted, he would be there to see it. He craved that joy for himself.

Catching her now might be unlikely. His boat had been so active along this coast—sinking one ship off Kinsale and two off Coningbeg, all in the last two days—that the alarm must still be out. The flight into port of the lone British cruiser this morning had been a clear sign. The Englanders knew of his presence. They would be fools to let their greatest prize, the notorious passenger liner and contraband-carrier, sail heedlessly through these waters...not even with guns mounted on the foredeck, as was rumored, and never again under a false American flag. No use trying that old trick. It wouldn't stop him for a moment.

True, so far it had been a disappointing hunt. Few enemies had been hit, and no real warships or troopships engaged. But it left him with three torpedoes for his homeward voyage. One or two of them might be enough to score him the biggest target of all. That would show up *Herr Kapitans*

Hersing, Wegener, and even the other Otto, Weddigen with three British cruisers to his credit. It could put him at the top of *Fregattenkapitan* Hermann Bauer's list and bring him personal recognition from Tirpitz, or more likely *Der Kaiser* himself.

Perhaps, Schwieger fretted, he should have lain in wait for the luxury liner and attacked nothing else, as Wegener had tried when he hunted *Lusi* in March. But that would have wasted time and fuel, only to risk everything on one toss of the dice. Instead he'd done his honest duty by seeking out targets of opportunity. Now the big ship was due back along this coast, and it might not yet have passed him in the fog or diverted northward around Ireland.

More likely *Lusi* was laid up safe in Queenstown harbor, guarded by *Juno*, waiting him out just a few miles away. But if she had not made it there yet, he had a chance. One never knew about the fortunes of war.

The cry came suddenly from Rikowski, with an echoing yap from the dachsie. "There, *Kapitan*, something off the starboard bow! I cannot tell...it looks like several ships in a line."

Surely enough, they had raised a forest of masts and stacks under a gray smudge of coal smoke, still hull-down beyond the western horizon. A thrilling sight, and frightening too; but indeed, as Schwieger got the binoculars into focus, he could see that it was a single ship. Four stacks in a row, and two tall masts strung with glinting Marconi wires. There could be little doubt.

"Lanz!" he barked.

His intrepid pilot already had his binoculars trained. "Must be the *Lusitania, Herr Kapitan*. Or *Mauretania*, but she's not known to be in these waters. I can tell you for certain once I see the deck ventilators."

"If it's *Maurie*, she's a troopship coming from Canada," Schwieger said. "If it's *Lusitania*, better yet. Good sighting, Rikowski!"

He continued gazing at the ship, trying to determine her course from the spacing of her funnels.

"The sad thing is," he added after a moment, "she seems to be heading inshore. We may not be able to catch her. Those skinny sisters are fast! Oh, well, either way we must dive."

The safety of his vessel came first. He lowered the binoculars to his breast, which had plunged internally now from excitement to despair.

Schwieger helped the others strike the railing and went down last, securing the hatch behind him. *"Alarm!"* he cried, sending the idle crew racing forward. Immediately after the dive, he ordered a starboard turn to cross the big ship's course, and then went to his plotting table to figure the exact bearing. Target speed, what, twenty-five knots? Make it twenty-three, cruising. *U-20's* underwater speed, fourteen knots on battery power. To launch an attack, they must head off the target with time left to angle for a clean bow shot. He must then plot the torpedo's course to strike perpendicular at thirty knots fixed speed.

With the steamer heading in near the coast, Schwieger doubted that he could intercept. No sense trying to pursue a ship that could easily outpace him at his best speed. And no use surfacing to use the *U-20's* diesel power. If he revealed himself, the target could run at high speed, or zigzag to confuse his aim. A glancing torpedo hit would never detonate. The eel had to go straight in.

While calculating, he kept checking his periscope. The big ship was well up on the horizon now, its formerly white superstructure painted over in wartime gray. He gave his place at the periscope to Lanz, who was holding the ship's copy of Brassey's *Naval Annual.*

"Yes, *Herr Kapitan,*" the civilian pilot formally said, "it must be *Lusitania* all right. Both she and *Mauretania* are listed here as Royal Navy reserve merchant cruisers, also in *Jane's Fighting Ships.*"

After a final glance at the black vessel silhouettes laid out on the page, Lanz closed the book. "A pity if we can't catch her." He gazed into the viewer a long moment. "She seems to be turning."

"What's that?"

When Schwieger took the periscope again, he saw the ship's angle changed, the funnels now closer in line, her course converging with his. "Ready one gyro torpedo, three meters running depth!" he called. "Maintain course, same speed," he told the steersman. "We will run up close and wait."

Although he tried, he couldn't keep the excitement out of his voice, not with his prey steaming straight in toward the killing-ground.

"All hands, combat stations!"

* * *

Charles Voegele, electrician of the *U-20,* usually preferred keeping to himself. That was all but impossible in the crowded confines of a submarine. His only refuge from the rest of the crew was his tiny corner astern, formed by a rack where electrical supplies and tools were stored. By standing there over his narrow work-shelf, pretending to study a wiring diagram or test a spare part, he could gain a few moments of illusory solitude. During sleep periods, instead of retiring to private quarters or even a bunk, he slung his hammock along the main corridor with the rest of the lowly seamen.

Yet even his stolen moments of isolation could appear, to some of those aboard, as hostile or suspicious. Voegele felt himself under scrutiny by these solid Germans, men of different types but all partaking to some degree in the current nationalist view that German ideas were best, German efficiency the greatest, and German *kultur* the world's salvation against decadent foreign ways. And now these, what was the term in English, jingo-ists, all found themselves in a frail sardine tin whose survival depended on everyone aboard thinking and feeling the same, with instant obedience.

This captain of his, Schwieger—Walther his first name, same as the automatic pistol—set the best example of all. He was the Blond Beast of Nietzsche's philosophy, with his elegant refinement and love of classical music; the perfect bachelor gentleman, fair and considerate of his crew. But in his chosen profession of piracy on the high seas, with its wanton destruction of property and life, he was pragmatic and ruthless, even passionate. Whatever inner ambition drove him might remain a secret. But it would continue to take them all to the brink of death, Voegele sensed—until someday it crossed the brink.

And now this caring leader had called him, Voegele, to the fore, singling him out to offer him rank and acceptance. Or was it instead to make a public example of him, challenging his loyalty to *Kaiser und Kapitan* before his crewmates?

Already Voegele had much to be insecure about, first of all his status as a draftee. He could hardly pretend to be an eager recruit for this war, which was senseless and sure to bring more suffering and devastation to his own small homeland. His origin in the Alsace-Lorraine district, the former French territory seized during German Unification right after their victory in the Franco-Prussian War, made him suspect.

And yet, what were they afraid of? During a mere forty-four years of German occupation, the Alsatians had been no more moved to embrace

French nationalism than German beliefs. On the contrary, his birthplace, the Free City of Strasbourg, had over many centuries been stubbornly independent, doing its best to resist both French and German control. So it was not, perhaps, French subversion these Germans feared, but independent thought, the ability to question any order or dictate that was passed mindlessly down from above.

And so they had conscripted him, trained and assigned him to this small, tight-knit naval unit—so that, he suspected, he couldn't meet others from his homeland or infect large numbers of troops along the front with his treasonous foreign sentiments. They had their eyes on him and his ilk, with *Kapitan-Leutnant* Schwieger as their agent. Voegele's very birth had marked him. And his name, compounded of the French *Charles* and German *Vogel* for bird, but with a curious foreign spelling, didn't help much.

But even so, there were those on board who gave him kindly looks. Some took time to converse with him, in those moments when he wasn't pretending to be busy. Seaman Ulbricht was a fine sensitive fellow, not yet consumed with the self-righteousness of his countrymen. And Rikowski, the radio officer who saw it as his role to walk around the ship spreading the latest news to all and sundry, treated Voegele with a pleasant, fatherly tolerance. The dachshunds, too, did not dislike him.

"Auf Gefechtsstationen!"

To Voegele, the urgent command to man battle stations seemed to carry an extra sense of excitement. He hesitated, even while knowing that hesitation was treason. In his newly assigned role as *Obersteuermann* and aide to the captain, he was to stand ready in the crew compartment just beneath the conning tower. At such a time he would rather be anywhere else in the world.

Could he pretend not to have heard? But as others jostled past along the corridor, they already eyed him strangely for standing still. On this narrow boat there was no place to hide.

Moving forward into the central chamber, to take his place by the ladder below the open tower hatch, he heard a command given in Schwieger's tense voice. "Ready torpedo tubes!"

A moment later another voice echoed back, relaying "Torpedo tubes flooded and ready, sir!"

"That is not Voegele!" The captain's impatient voice came from above. "Where is *Herr Voegele*, my *Obersteuermann*?"

But as Voegele moved forward to respond, he froze. From the crew standing ready nearby, he heard excited whispers.

"It is the *Lusitania*!"

"*Oh ja*, the big jackpot, eh?"

Now as Voegele went forward to the ladder, the weakness in his belly made him falter and tremble. Taking his place by the speaking tube, he suddenly understood *Kapitan* Schwieger. He was not, after all, Captain Nemo of the *Nautilus*, the Frenchman Jules Verne's romantic undersea-farer. He was Captain Ahab, obsessed with a Great White Whale, a Moby Dick of a ship that just happened to carry innocent passengers.

"Voegele," Schwieger's voice came down, "you are there just in time. Launch torpedo one!"

"*Nein.*"

"*Was ist das?*" the captain demanded. "What do you say?"

"Sir, I cannot relay the order. I urge you not to fire on a ship carrying women and children. Are you not going to rise to the surface and challenge them?"

While he spoke, the torpedo went. Like everyone else aboard, he heard the hissing of the compressed air, and felt the pressure change in his ears as the fish was blown out of the tube. Whether it had been torpedo officer Weisbach responding directly or the captain's firing button, it did not matter. Voegele saw now that Schwieger's act of singling him out had not been a promotion, nor a test of character. It had simply been a way to get rid of the unwanted foreigner.

"Herr Voegele," the captain called down, "you are on report for disobeying a direct order. When we return to base you will face court martial."

But no one else in the crew paid much attention. They were waiting for the eel to strike.

Chapter 41

Looking Ahead

Flash took Winnie arm-in-arm along the familiar deck promenade. By now she was more anxious than on any previous walk during their sleepy mid-Atlantic passage.

"Oh, Flash," she fretted, leaning close to him, "Matt's off on another secret mission, I just know it! But instead of you, he's got Alma along with him. What can we possibly do? Do you think they'll be safe?"

"As safe as any of us, I'd guess," Flash said, trying to downplay the irony. "If Alma is with Matt, she's in capable hands." Seeing her dubious look, he added, "No double-meaning intended this time, my love. For now, I just want to make sure she's not wandering the decks searching by herself."

"Well, she should be easy to spot if she's looking for Matt, or for us. Everyone else on deck is at the rail."

It was true; the port railing of the Promenade Deck was lined with travelers, most of them taking in the view of lush green Irish coastal hills a few miles off. Others leaned out and shaded their eyes forward or astern, scanning the sea for the submarine menace.

"Well," Flash said, "Here's where the deck closes in. We can see perfectly well she's not ahead of us. Let's go up to the Boat Deck."

From that point on, to guard against breasting seas, the promenade was shut in behind steel plating and portholes. Once upon a time Flash would have taken Winnie in there to spoon, but not today. The two turned onto a stairway that took them up one level. There, emerging under open sky, they continued forward. Far ahead where the wide bridge crossed over the deck, blue-coated officers peered out to sea with binoculars. Here too the rail was scattered with sightseers, but none of them looked familiar.

"Everyone's on watch for something," Winnie said.

"That's for sure." Flash didn't want to discuss what it might be.

"Matt was supposed to meet his contact right along here," he added, looking around.

"Who was it?" Winnie asked. "That detective Pierpoint? I wouldn't trust him to play fair."

"No," Flash said, not wanting to reveal anything. But feeling the tug of his sweetheart's impatient gaze, he at last admitted, "Ah, what the heck, it's Kroger, the Dutch trader. Be on the lookout for him, too. Apparently he knows something about other kinds of cargo besides furs." Still feeling a bit guilty, he told her only what she needed to know, not that the man was also a German spy.

"Mr. Kroger, the nice plump Dutchman?" Winnie asked. "Well then, should we check the gentlemen's smoking room? Or the ship's tavern... that's probably where the both of them ended up."

"Somebody was right here," Flash said, dipping discreetly down to pick up an object. The flat metal bar drilled with finger-holes was reddish-yellow, still wet with fog, and well-worn from use—a set of brass knuckles.

"Not what I'd call first-class," he said, slipping it into his pocket. "Not Kroger's style, either...at least I hope not."

"But Flash, oh my," Winnie seemed suddenly in doubt, clinging to his arm. "What does it mean? Do you think the gangsters have taken Alma?"

Keeping Winnie close, Flash moved around the deck and the rail nearby, but saw no blood, broken teeth or other clues. What could it mean, he wondered...nothing, a coincidence? "All we can do is look for her," he said at last. "No telling what's up. Let's go over to starboard. They may have an arrangement like ours, you know, to meet at the opposite side."

Heading forward under the officers' bridge, they went around the very front of the ship's superstructure. The whole foredeck was visible, a slim wedge with the foremast at its center. No one was on it but crewmen standing lookout.

Ahead, beyond the black-banded lighthouse they were just passing, the Irish coastal hills and headlands stretched away into the distance. Off to starboard, under dazzling white sunlight, the sea spread flat and open as ever. The bright, clearing sky brought back the feeling of happier strolls about the deck, and Flash put an arm around Winnie as they hurried along.

"I'll be sticking with you when we're ashore, at least until we get things sorted out," he told her. "If you don't mind, that is."

"Mind?" Winnie said. "Why should I mind? As long as you don't get fresh," she added, giving him a squeeze in an unmentionable place.

"Once we find the others," he responded with a spank to her tidy behind, "be sure to work things out with Alma about contact points and your final destination. She'll probably be separated from us in port. Matt will want to sneak her off the ship and get her past any guards or lookouts."

"How, in a steamer trunk?" Winnie asked, back to being concerned. "What about us, you and me? How will we keep from getting separated?"

"Well, Matt's plan is to escort Alma safely inland so she can rejoin you ladies further on. While they sneak off together, he has assigned me to look after you and the others in England. Assuming Miss Hildegard allows it, that is."

"I think she can be persuaded," Winnie said, squeezing his arm tight against her side.

"Yes, well, I hope so, Winnie. You know I wouldn't want to lose you, not ever." Flash felt the gravity of his words, but in the urgency of it all he saw no point in holding back. "I don't want anything to happen to you, so we'll have to keep in close touch." He punctuated his speech with a hug and a kiss on her cheek, and then tried to be lighthearted again.

"Of course, we'll have to be apart at times. But there'll still be the news reporting to do, the heroic story of young nurses overseas."

"Of course," Winnie replied, clinging close. "But you know, I never planned to be quite this heroic."

Coming to the starboard side, they found fewer passengers along the rail. But Flash soon saw someone he knew, Mary Plamondon. The irrepressible hostess of the first-class dining table was strolling in a loose morning dress with a light wrap. She had met Winnie before and greeted them both, but she told them she hadn't seen Matt or Alma that morning.

"And you haven't happened to run across my husband Charles?" the Chicago brewer's wife nervously asked, blinking behind her *pince-nez* eyeglasses. "I thought he'd be having a cigar out on deck. Last night was our thirty-sixth anniversary, you know. I slept late, what with the champagne and foghorns, and all the noise and stamping feet. And now, when I come outside, I see that the commotion was the lifeboats being swung out." She tilted her small glasses into better focus. "Do you really think it was necessary? Has there been another submarine warning, or a sighting of some kind?"

"I think it's just a precaution because we're near England," Winnie said.

"Well then, shouldn't they have prepared us better? I don't think anyone has been assigned a lifeboat seat yet—have you? If anything happens, it will be first come, first served."

"Women and children first, I would hope," Flash said. "Be sure to have your life jackets handy, you and Charles. We ought to do the same."

"I suppose there shouldn't be any reason to worry," the matron fretted. "Cunard has never lost a passenger yet, so I'm told. Last night after the concert, Captain Turner said we're all safe in the hands of the Royal Navy. But I haven't seen any escort, have you?" She shaded her eyes and looked around the glimmering sea. "Did we miss them in the fog? You didn't see any cruisers over on the other side?"

"No, but I'll bet they're out there," Flash reassured her. "Nowadays they have destroyers specially designed for fighting U-boats. They'll more than match the speed of a ship like ours, and can cut a submarine in two at periscope depth."

"How lovely," Mrs. Plamondon said, obviously chilled by the description. "I'd feel better if two or three of them were in sight now." She stopped searching the sea. "Well, I'd better be off to find Charles. If you should see him, remind him to meet me for lunch."

"All right, Mary. Good luck!"

"Everyone has worries," Winnie lamented to Flash as the woman hurried off. "If Matt and Alma are smart, they're cuddled up in a cargo bin somewhere, resting and enjoying the trip. Just as we ought to be."

"On this run aft we'll check the cabin again," Flash said, giving her a hug and a peck. "Most likely we'll find them down there." He turned to move on.

"Wait." Gripping his arm, Winnie was staring out to sea, diagonally off the starboard bow. Flash followed her gaze, hearing her voice taut and urgent:

"Is that what a periscope looks like?"

Chapter 42

Stricken

Junior Third Officer Albert Bestic, timepiece in hand, stood at the port corner of the glassed-in bridge. He waited for the banded tower of Kinsale Lighthouse to come alongside. In line with the Lusitania's left bridge wing, it should form at a perfect ninety-degree angle to the ship's course.

When it did, he would mark down the time. Then, by comparing it to the time of the first bearing on the tower, taken at precisely forty-five degrees forward—and given the ship's constant speed of eighteen knots—he would know how far they had traveled during the interval. That distance, under the inflexible laws of geometry as applied to the legs of an isosceles right triangle, would be exactly the same distance the ship stood offshore from the lighthouse.

It was an old seaman's trick. It could then be repeated when the tower lay forty-five degrees astern on the same course, to confirm or average out their position with regard to the land. A simple four-point bearing: three points at sea, one ashore, from which Captain Turner would be able to plot their future course with assurance. With it, he could take them safely through shoals, minefields and the mouth of St. George's Channel, which lay ahead on their way to Liverpool.

It was just like Captain Turner to want a precise bearing, so as to be ready for any eventuality—more fog or enemy action, or a possible diversion into Queenstown. The only catch was, given their modest speed and great distance from the land—a dozen miles at least—it would take Bestic the better part of an hour to obtain the time readings. The Captain must be feeling confident to cruise in a straight line, at considerably less than full steam, for such a long stretch inside the War Zone.

Since the fog lifted they had been swerving at intervals, quite likely to avoid targeting by submarines. Bestic had felt the gradual but not-so-gentle turns himself, and had heard the complaint of a passenger tipped from his chair at breakfast. But this latest coded message from the Admiralty may have changed things.

Bisset, so the Old Man had called him again when he ordered up the four-point bearing. He'd been doing it for weeks, since Bestic had first joined the ship in Liverpool. Was it mere absent-mindedness, or was the Captain being witty? It was no insult, since Bestic knew of Leftenant Bisset as a crack Cunard hand and Turner's trusted first officer in his most recent command. Was it his way of saying that Mr. Bestic had the same potential?

The old fellow—Bowler Bill Turner, they called him because of his off-duty hat style—wasn't really a bad chap. He might be partial to his Third Mate because, like Turner, Bestic had come up out of the sailing ships and knew all the old traditions. Two days earlier, for a lark, the Captain had sent down to the officers' mess a freakishly complicated sailor's knot that he himself must have tied, with an order that it be duplicated. Bestic had been the only one to recognize a four-stranded Turk's-head and, with the help of a dog-eared reference manual he kept in his sea chest, he recreated it. The result was sent back to the Captain, who probably also got wind of the knot-tier's identity. So perhaps this continuing name mix-up was a sign of favor.

The change of the watch at fourteen bells was drawing near...a problem, since Bestic was stuck here timing the ship's progress. But then Senior Third Officer Lewis came up promptly to relieve him, and he was free to take leave of the chronometer and attend his other duties. The change actually came slightly before two p.m., because the ship had just switched over to Ireland time, which was twenty-five minutes earlier than Greenwich Mean Time, and the two mates had agreed to split the difference.

On the way astern to do paperwork, Bestic stopped at the Marconi room and spoke to Leith, the telegraphist. From him he heard the scuttlebutt that two radio messages had been received, one placing submarines near the Coningbeg lightship, some eighty miles ahead, the second reporting another lone U-boat some miles behind them at Cape Clear, heading away north. After an initial chill at the news, Bestic decided to feel cheered by it. No subs were reported or likely to be in between—that would explain why the Captain felt safe enough to take stock of things, and get the ship's bearings in a leisurely fashion.

Bestic went to his cabin behind the bridge to compose log entries. But he'd barely started in when a knock came at the door.

It was Crank, the baggage master, a much-dreaded visitor. Every time a passenger wanted something from his bags below, Crank paid a visit here.

It was Cunard's policy that none of the crew, and especially this scratch lot during wartime, should have access to the passengers' baggage without an officer present. And that tiresome duty invariably fell to Bestic as Junior Third. But this time, with the ship nearing port and the sea conditions mild, Crank had been ordered to start the cargo hands moving the luggage up onto the foredeck. That would require an officer below decks in the hold. Just like Turner to be thinking of a quick turnaround in port, even in wartime, and a speedy departure back to the States. Or maybe it meant that the ship had already been diverted into Queenstown, just an hour away.

No matter; since it was the captain's order, Bestic had no choice but to agree.

"But wait," he told Crank, giving him the key. "I'm wearing my dress uniform, and it won't do to get it all smutty. If I change to my drabs first, I'll be able to pitch in and help you shift the bags. Why don't you take the fellows down, and I'll join you shortly?"

"Aye, Sir," Crank said, closing the cabin door behind him.

Bestic proceeded to change uniforms, though he didn't make any particular hurry of it. The baggage handlers would be fine on their own, with Crank there to keep them out of the passengers' valuables.

On leaving the cabin some minutes later, Bestic went by way of the top deck to savor the fine weather. He could then pass by the bridge once again before his plunge into the stifling darkness of the baggage room, which lay just above the main cargo hold.

It was a perfect day at sea, blue and calm, with the Irish coast brilliant in the background. Yet something was amiss.

The first thing Bestic heard was a hail from above, through a megaphone, sounding high and urgent. The shout came from the crow's nest on the foremast, visible aloft over the bridge. As he shaded his eyes to look, the two crewmen up there were already scrambling out and down the ratlines, yelling in alarm and waving to starboard. The one word he made out was enough: "Torpedo!"

Rushing to the starboard rail, he saw it at once: a streak of white bubbles lengthening toward them from a thin, stick-like periscope straight off to starboard.

This is the approach of death...

Even as the thought formed in his mind, reality struck with brutal suddenness and jolted the deck beneath him. A muffled metallic impact deep underfoot staggered Bestic forward against the rail. At once a fountain of seawater shot straight up alongside the bridge, mounting higher than the smokestacks. As Bestic watched it pass astern with the ship's motion, he realized where the torpedo had hit—ahead under the foremast, near the baggage and cargo holds, precisely where he would be right now if he hadn't stopped to change his uniform... and where Crank and his helpers likely were just starting work. The tremors and echoes of the explosion were still making the forward part of the ship shudder to the core. Poor souls, if they were down there, they stood little chance of escaping.

The day around him darkened to night as soot and smoke poured upward from deck ventilators and the giant funnel high overhead. The explosion must have penetrated deep into the hull through the emptied coal bunkers, he realized, maybe even to the forward boiler rooms. To shield himself against falling muck and debris, he raised a blue-coated arm over his head. Clinging to the rail with his other hand, he saw and felt the descending column of seawater smash down on the Marconi and Boat Decks just astern. Fortunately its main force missed him and others forward. But the torrent smashed a lifeboat out of its davits, the third in line on the starboard side, and the downpour spread farther back, sweeping passengers off their feet and washing some few of them overboard through the lifeboat gaps in the rail.

Losses among the passengers already...but nothing to be done about it, with the ship itself at stake. The grim sight reminded him of his duty, to get to the bridge for orders. And if the order was to abandon ship, he must take charge of launching all the forward lifeboats on the port side. He turned to make his way inboard, but it was difficult—slippery and uphill. The wet, sooty deck was tilting steeply over as the ship heeled toward its injured side. He struggled upward nevertheless.

A second great explosion then hurled him back against the rail.

Chapter 43

Crisis

"Winnie, come along. Hurry!" Her lover's voice was sharp and determined as he drew her away from the rail.

When they saw the surge of bubbles before the periscope, and the torpedo's white wake approaching, Flash started off astern with her arm clutched in his. Winnie followed him along the promenade at a run.

Then the explosion jolted underfoot, the blast speeding her along, and she looked back to see a plume of water rising straight up into the air. The deck didn't buckle upward or burst out aflame, so she thought maybe the torpedo hadn't even penetrated.

But then at once a cloud of soot and smoke shot out of the ventilators on the top level inboard, darkening the sky and signaling some deep internal damage to the ship. Winnie ran on, not knowing where and not caring. In the wan faces of people who gazed up at the column of seawater behind them, she saw fear dawning and looked back again. With the ship's forward speed, the waterspout was following them astern.

Then the deluge struck, pouring down along the deck like a tidal wave. She heard screams coming from behind and a great crashing of water and timber. As they reached the Palm Court terrace amidships, the canvas awning above its entry sagged down onto their backs with the drumming weight of water. Meanwhile an inrushing tide surged up to their knees, dragging them almost off their feet.

Once inside the shelter they paused to support one another, drenched and panting from their flight. Winnie could still hear shouts and pleas from those half-drowned outside, crawling or slipping on the promenade, and she fought to control her own rising fear.

"The deck is sinking!" she gasped suddenly to Flash, who only tightened his embrace. Beneath their shoes the wet floor tiles were tilting more and more, as if trying to tip them out overboard, a terrifying sensation.

The passage was astir by now with people darting out to see what happened and clamoring to find loved ones and belongings. The troubled murmur of voices rose to a hubbub, broken by desperate hails and shouted orders, with an occasional stabbing cry of anguish. Some passengers outside clung fast to the rail, the rest staggering in the wetness and the sudden listing of the ship.

"Flash, what can we do?"

Even as she spoke, a fresh explosion more powerful than the first racked the deck underfoot, sending dinner plates shattering down from café tables and sideboards. This must be the end, she thought.

"We've got to look after our own." Flash said amid the turmoil, drawing her inboard toward the central stair. "The best we can do for the others is check the stateroom. There are things in there we need."

"Where's the hold?" she asked, breathless. "Did Alma and Matt go there?"

"No telling. The hold is forward where the torpedo struck," His tone was grim. "Let's hope they didn't."

"They could be back at the room looking for us."

Winnie didn't for a moment believe that their friends were gone, the very first casualties of the attack. She wasn't ready to face such a prospect, not yet.

"You're right, we have to check there. Maybe we'll meet them in the passage, and we can all go and join the others."

They ascended the tilting tile floor inboard, past a steward with his white uniform soaked. He was telling everyone shoving past him, "Never fear, don't panic, the ship won't sink,"

Further along near the concierge room, Winnie recognized the tycoon and playboy, Alfred Vanderbilt. Looking calm and serious, he was telling a woman, "Help me find all the kiddies, and we can put these on them." Dangling from his hands were bundles of child-sized life jackets.

Reaching the stairs, the two headed down resolutely against a stream of emerging passengers. Many clutched life belts, or tried clumsily to pull them on as they climbed. In the tilting stairwell, with the lights dimming and the air tinged with smoke, their faces showed a desperation that was close to frenzy.

Yet some in First Class moved with an air of dignified, almost unnatural calm. Perhaps it was because of all the stories told in recent years about panic aboard the *SS Titanic* after it struck the iceberg, and the undisciplined scramble for the boats that excluded so many poor passengers, women and children. At least, Winnie thought, these voyagers had been reassured that the lifeboats were more than sufficient for all the souls aboard the *Lusitania*.

The stairs became hard to navigate as the list increased. Passengers were forced to jostle together and hug the banisters. Winnie clung to the railing with one arm and to Flash with the other. Once they reached the fore-and-aft corridor, it was easier to maintain footing on the thick carpet without sliding away to starboard.

When they came to their door and unlocked it, they found the rooms empty. There was no sign that Matt or Alma had been there since morning.

"The camera bag is still gone," Flash said as he filled a valise with his precious slides and papers. "What are you taking?" he asked as he saw Winnie stuffing a large purse.

"Just some things Alma will want." She worked speedily, not troubling to conceal from him the fat wads of greenbacks she was shoving in.

"A practical girl, that's what I like." Flash's voice was solemn. "Here's something more practical yet." Climbing up on the bed he grabbed two, four, six life belts from the top of the wardrobe. It was too many to carry, so they left two hanging in the vestibule. "Just in case they come back," he told Winnie.

They left the cabin dark, the unlatched door swinging wide with the list. The passage was empty now, no sign of their friends. Worse, as they started forward they saw that water had already reached their deck, maybe through portholes in the tilting starboard rooms. Winnie heard a distant rushing sound as waves lapped to them across the carpet, and the smell of the sea became rank in the dim corridor. They turned and headed astern toward the main staircase, climbing along with difficulty in the ever-steepening angle of carpet and baseboard. Winnie realized that, besides the list, the front of the ship was tilting downward into the ocean.

On the grand stairway more refugees straggled up ahead of them. Most clung to the balustrades on the high side of the spiral stair. Starting out, the two of them hurried past the electric elevator car as it barely crept up its sloping central track. The worried voices of passengers could be heard inside the mahogany cubicle.

Winnie, burdened with her shoulder bag and two life belts, followed Flash around the crazy circle toward the landing on the upper deck.

Before they reached it, the ship shuddered again and the lights went out, plunging the stairwell into darkness. Only faint daylight shone in through the deck exit above, barely enough to light their way.

But then from below came wails of terror, followed by the urgent, muffled shouts and pleas of those trapped inside the stalled elevator car. They began to thump on the closed door and the walls.

Winnie froze. "We must get them out."

She gripped the railing to hold herself back, and when Flash turned, she gave him a beseeching, wordless look. Pressing close to her, he spoke urgently over the cries and futile thumping that echoed up the stair.

"Dearest, I'll find an officer and tell him. That's all that we can do. Maybe they can restore emergency power." His words did not help the anguish she felt, the shock and utter horror.

"Don't worry, Matt and Alma wouldn't be foolish enough to ride in there."

Unwrapping her fingers gently from the rail, he led her up the stairs and out onto the promenade.

Chapter 44

Abandoned

"A torpedo trail, you say? Off the starboard bow?"

At the first warning shouts over the telephone from the crow's nest, Captain Turner's peaceful afternoon was spoiled. Even as First Officer Hefford acknowledged the sighting and hung up the phone, Turner saw the two lookouts abandon their nest to shinny down the foremast ladder in a panic. The captain, already hurrying to the starboard side of the bridge house, made it only a few steps when the torpedo struck with a clanging, sickening impact.

Before his anxious gaze a column of water shot up over the bridge. It seemed to hang there against blue sky as it passed away astern with the Lusitania's plunging forward motion. Having stumbled from the initial shock, Turner kept going, but he faltered again as he felt the rubber-matted deck sink and tilt from the sudden inrush of water below. With the explosion, his vessel began an unnatural roll that didn't seem as if it would end.

Turner called to Hefford at the controls: "Are the watertight doors all closed? If not, close them!"

Even as he gave the command, he knew it would be of little use. Whatever the electric board showed, the automatic doors between the coal bunkers and the boiler rooms would be jammed partway open by slumping coal and dust piles. No amount of effort could keep them clear while the men worked at firing the boilers. He knew, too, his order might trap some of the coalers below in flooding chambers, or force them to climb straight upward for any hope of escape.

"Lieutenant, what is the degree of list?" he asked, feeling the ship's lopsided tilt growing worse.

Lewis had given up taking his four-point bearing. He went to the commutator device mounted on the tilting rear bulkhead and read the needle. "Seven degrees starboard, Captain. Two degrees forward as well, sir."

"Right. Let me know when it reaches ten starboard." He'd already ordered all portholes to be closed that morning, but had it been done? Too late to check now, and calm was essential in a crisis. Glancing out through the windscreen, Turner could confirm that the ship was well down by the bows, with waves already breaking over the starboard bulwark. Natural enough, with a forward torpedo hit—but how could it be happening so quickly?

To see which compartments had been damaged, he took himself over to the Pearson's Fire and Flood Indicator board. Its alarm bell was ringing monotonously, and should be silenced to let a man think. But as he went, there came another massive concussion underfoot. The bridge shuddered with a second rumbling explosion, louder and more prolonged than the first. Before him, as he grabbed the counter for balance, the lights on the Pearson's board went crazy. The forward compartments, the hold, powder magazine, coal bunkers and boiler rooms, all were compromised. Then the indicator lamps themselves flickered, threatening a power failure.

"Ten degrees list, Captain, and still going," Lewis reported, steadfastly watching the pendulums that showed the average angles.

"All right, then," Turner said. "Notify me if it goes past fifteen. Meanwhile, have the ship's carpenter assess the damage forward and report back to me. Helmsman, rudder hard a-port! If we run her in toward shore, maybe we can beach her."

"Aye aye, sir," the helmsman said, taking in the gravity of the command. As he swung the wheel and the mate rang up on the telephone, Turner headed to the door—a steep downhill shuffle—and out onto the starboard bridge wing.

No submarine in sight now, and no more torpedo tracks. But looking astern, he saw that the ship was in a panic. Under a pall of smoke rising aft from the ventilators, passengers milled along the boat deck. They lurched and slipped on wet tilted planking, with some already lying inert on the deck or staggering with bloodied heads and shirtfronts, likely from falls. White-faced people clustered at the lifeboats, a few even trying to climb in as officers restrained them. One starboard boat was gone, lost in the explosion, and most hung far out from the tilting deck at the limit of their anti-sway chains. At each moment, more humanity crowded out from below.

Surveying the scene, the pitiful passengers clawing and swarming desperately about the decks, the thought came to Turner: *A bunch of bloody monkeys.* He felt a sudden sick remorse for his own callous phrase.

So Captain Dow may have been right after all to resign his *Lusitania* command. Passengers and war explosives don't mix. Just throw a torpedo into the pot, and this is what you get, bloody chaos! So much for the all-knowing protection he'd been promised. Well, he was not beaten, not yet.

Then as he watched, the ship began to right itself. Beneath his soles he felt the deck straightening, the strain on his old ankles easing. But it could never come near an even keel, and the change didn't reassure Turner. He knew it only meant that the flooding had penetrated deeper in, to the transverse coal bunker beneath him or possibly the port-side. A temporary relief at best, when the list that could sink them lay forward. His ship was going down by the bows.

Looking out on the foredeck, where waves washed right in over the dagger-pointed prow, he suddenly realized that they were still making eighteen knots headway. The engines had never stopped, for he hadn't ordered them to do so. The U-boat that had attacked them was left behind by now, and their need to run away was over in any case.

Time to face it, they must abandon ship. This forward motion was lending greater force to the flooding, and worse, making it impossible to launch the lifeboats.

Going to the starboard telephone station, he rang inside to the bridge and commanded, "Engine room, Full Speed Astern." That should stop them soon enough.

"Aye, sir," came the answer. Through the open bridge door, he saw Hefford lay down the phone, ring back and forth on the telegraph repeater to make the alert bells chime, and finally set the lever full astern. If anyone was standing by the engines, as they must be, his order would be obeyed. He turned his gaze aft.

Within seconds new detonations sounded, and ghostly-white gouts of steam shot up topside all the way astern. Amid renewed shouts and panic from the decks, Turner realized his mistake.

Engineering Inspector Laslett had warned him before departure that the low-power steam system was failing, wearing out with age. It wouldn't stand a sudden change, and it was due to be overhauled in port next week. But he had forgotten, and this sudden pressure reversal had been too great.

What an old fool he was! The main steam lines had failed, probably crippling the engines. If he'd merely signaled Full Stop, they might yet have slowed the ship down in time to lower boats.

Well, perhaps they still could. Shuffling up the sloping deck, dragging himself along by the bridge rail, he went back inside to face his officers.

There were no reproaches awaiting him there, but no good news either. He heard first from the steersman: "The helm is not responding, sir. The wheel seems to be jammed at half-port. I cannot make her turn toward land."

"No surprise, man. We're listing to starboard, so your steering engines are fighting the whole weight of the rudder, lifting tons of metal. Just hold her as you can."

"Steam pressure is down, Captain," Lieutenant Hefford reported, "from 190 pounds to 50. The engine room says one steam main is broken. The turbines are still turning, locked in forward motion."

"Try to get them reversed, or stopped at least. We have to lose way."

"Sir, the list is increasing again," was Third Officer Lewis's report. "Seventeen degrees starboard, five forward."

"My God." Turner for once found himself unable to put a good face on things.

As if that weren't enough, the young officer Bisset appeared in the doorway from astern, soaking wet and covered with soot. "Captain, sir, the Marconi room reports their electricity has failed. They're sending out S.O.S. on battery power, giving our position."

He waited in the sharply-angled doorway. "Any orders, sir?"

"Orders, yes."

S.O.S.–Save Our Ship. Turner imagined the plight of those below, now in darkness, his officers and stokers trapped in the coal-black depths. Little enough hope of saving them, much less the ship.

"Lower all lifeboats to the rail," he told Bisset, or Bestic, whomever. "But do not launch them yet, until the ship has stopped. Relay this order to all stations: Prepare to abandon ship."

Chapter 45

Holocaust

Where the torpedo struck below decks, fire was instantly smothered by sea. The explosion flared blazing-yellow along a swath of tearing, buckling steel. Against this bright horizon, the spy Kroger's body was silhouetted as he hurtled back toward the watchers.

Alma, dazed by the blast, came to awareness in the top of a shattered crate. She lay crumpled against its cargo, the mini-submarine. She didn't feel injured as she tried to move, just numb and sore—both at once, and all over. Dirk Kroger's bulky body lay on top of her, pressing her bare skirted legs against the cold metal of the sub. The Dutchman wasn't moving.

Beside them in the dimness, amid a tilting chaos of explosive flares, splintered wood and surging water, Matt appeared, wet and disheveled. He immediately began trying to lift the moaning, semi-conscious spy off her.

"Alma, are you hurt?" he said as he rolled the inert body clear. "Careful, don't try to move too quickly."

"I'm all right," Alma said, struggling to get her bruised legs under her. "He's alive?"

"Yes, but badly injured. He must have absorbed the blast and shielded us from it."

As Matt took Kroger's pistol out of his pocket and flung it away, Alma could see that his hand was smeared with blood.

"Dirk," he asked, shaking the spy, "can you move?"

No reply, just a groan.

"What can we do?" Struggling up to her knees, Alma looked around the deepening chaos. She felt the ship tilting and saw foamy seawater rising, with chemical fires or ammo still flaring and gouting underneath the surface. Suddenly again she felt faint. "It's all over, isn't it?"

* * *

Matt, as he toiled to free Alma, saw the hopelessness of their position. But he couldn't accept it.

Water surged in through the now-invisible hull breach, foaming and fountaining below them in the faint electric light that still burned from the top of the hold. Cold salty droplets sprayed up into their faces from the inflow. Worse, a nearby cavernous roaring told him that the sea must be filling the huge empty coal bunker just astern. Bad luck if the torpedo strike had penetrated both compartments, and God knew wherever else.

As he tried to help Alma to her feet, the ship steeply tilted, bringing the seething maelstrom up toward them all the faster. The lightest crates floated and tumbled in the flood, while other cargo ignited with churning flashes underwater. Likely it was the thousands of rifle cartridges cooking off after the main blast...harmlessly, or so he hoped.

"There has to be a way out," he told Alma as she clung shell-shocked against him. "Come on, darling, let's get going! We need to live to tell this story. It may be too late for Dirk."

Suddenly, sickeningly, the submarine crate and its rounded contents moved beneath them, sliding down into the hungry abyss. As Lusitania's list grew more severe, all the cargo shifted toward her wounded side, the hundreds of tons of metal and ammunition crushing and displacing any lighter goods. Above them the tethered ambulances strained and slid forward in their harnesses, striving to tear free and roll down the unstable slope.

Then just beside them, the largest and heaviest crate started to splinter. It was the bizarre metal monster, the weapon labeled Tank, nuzzling free and rearing up on massive treads. The steel prow, sharply pointed like a steam locomotive, crushed and parted the planking of the beast's flimsy cage. Twin gun barrels broke out through the brittle top, emerging in their heavy casemates as the tracked wheels trundled forth onto the wreckage. The nearest chain of metal treads splintered deep into Matt and Alma's crate. The behemoth threatened to smash it down into the flood, and them along with it.

But even as Matt clung to buckling wood and tried to pull Alma clear, a new menace caught his eye. Lightning flashes from the seething water flared up brighter than ever, blinding enough to paint the entire hold with stark shadows like a flash picture. Cargo cases were igniting underwater, letting off bursts of frothing white smoke.

"It's the aluminum dust," a voice gasped from beside Matt, where the reviving spy Kroger struggled up to a sitting position. "In seawater it can touch off the other explosives. Find cover!"

As he groaned out his warning, the wounded man rolled and dragged himself over to the open hatch of the mini-sub, to dive in through it out of sight. Matt, hardly thinking but alert to the danger, lifted Alma up bodily, led her forward and lowered her down after the spy.

As he turned to grab his camera bag, he glanced again at the underwater detonations. Outlined by their brilliance as they tumbled about in the flood were dozens of light, buoyant boxes—the cheese crates that Kroger had identified as gun cotton, high explosive and more dangerous when wet. Moving fast and shoving the camera bag ahead of him, Matt dove in after Alma through the open hatchway.

Landing on top of her, or Kroger or both in the near-total darkness, he reached up to close the circular hatch—just as its cover was blown shut by the shattering force of the second, larger explosion.

* * *

The rolling, hammering impact of the second blast was muted by the submarine's hull, but the shock of it bruised Alma where her back touched hard metal. The glare lit up the thick glass portholes in the turret above her, fore and aft and to either side. But their light was quickly dimmed to the faintest outlines as seawater surged over them, lifting the tiny craft. As first she thought the frail shell would be crushed, but now it felt as if it was going to roll over.

"Alma, are you OK?" Matt had been reaching up, tightening the latches around the hatch lid. He must have succeeded, because the cold salty drops stopped streaming down into her face.

"I don't know—I guess so. This motion is making me ill."

Now in pitch dark she struggled to sit upright, rolling and bumping with the sub, which must be sliding free amid the wreckage. She felt Matt reach past her to delve into his satchel. When he found and switched on the battery lamp, its waning beam was enough to light the submarine's interior. Matt's haggard face brightened as he saw her—though she must be a fright, with wet hair across her face and seawater smarting in her eyes.

"What can we do?" she appealed to him. "Do we have to stay in here?"

"Well, we've made it so far," he said, touching her damp head. He leaned forward to kiss her cheek in an obvious effort at reassurance. "Out of the frying pan into the...kettle."

His joke fell flat as he shone the lamp beam on riveted metal all around them—a shiny oval prison, or so it seemed to her. She saw batteries beside them, and an electric motor behind, but the levers and gauges meant little to her, even though some were labeled in English: Depth, Ballast, Dive Angle.

"Matt, darling, what's going to become of us?"

She clutched his shoulder, claustrophobic panic and hopelessness battling inside her as the metal capsule's hull slid beneath them and clashed against some obstacle.

"For *Gott's* sake, just get us out of here," a third voice rasped...the wounded Kroger, who lay curled in the engineer's seat behind them.

"Dirk, how are you doing?" Matt turned his beam on the stricken man. The shirtfront inside his open fur coat was bright with blood. "Can you breathe all right?"

"Yes, but it hurts," the spy said, tentatively probing his own chest with bloody fingers. "Some ribs broken, I think. When that torpedo hit, rivets shot out of the hull like Spandau bullets."

"Have you tried to stop the bleeding? Alma, do you know what to do?"

"Let me see." Feeling suddenly useful, she squeezed past Matt in the cramped space. Here her training would help. Kneeling over the half-prone spy in the rear seat, she peeled back his shirt to examine his fleshy, hairy chest by the light of Matt's flash. A wound in Dirk's right breast oozed badly, but it wasn't bubbling as he breathed, and he didn't seem to be choking on blood. Probing gingerly and then applying pressure with her bare palm, she found no bone splinters or embedded metal.

"Turn on a light," Kroger gasped in pain. "There's power in those Galvanic cells, they're a type I've never seen. Use the main switch." He gestured feebly with his left arm.

"Here, you mean?" Matt asked from the front seat. He threw a switch, and immediately blinded them all with electric glare from a bulb set astern in a wire cage. Then he found a way to dim it. "Seems to be no lack of current."

"Good then, use it to steer us out of here." Kroger spoke brokenly as Alma, doubling up his bloody shirtwaist, applied gentle pressure to his chest wound. "Move the tiller forward for speed, left or right for the rudder. Arrgh, woman, enough!" he begged Alma, grasping her shoulder to ease the pressure.

"Here, then, Dirk, can you hold this in place yourself?" Alma guided his hand to the makeshift poultice and pressed it firmly there. "I have to cut a bandage."

"Ach, that feels better! Here, use this." Kroger dragged a pen knife out of his pants pocket with his free hand. Then he called, "Matt, set the gear lever for the dive planes, up or down! But don't get us fouled up in wreckage."

"How will I know where to go?" Glancing over her shoulder, Alma saw Matt peering through the glass apertures around his head in the turret. "I only see bubbles out there."

"Try the outside lights, *dummkopf*," Dirk snarled, irritable with pain, as Alma sawed at his shirt with the tiny knife blade. "The headlamps, dummy!"

"This one?" Trying another switch, Matt caused the forward view slit to light up visibly from outside the sub. "That works—we're drifting free, or nearly so, submerged," he reported to the others. "The ship's hold is filling with water."

Alma caught her breath. "We're going down, then? The *Lusitania* is lost?" The realization felt like a bullet deep in her own chest. "What about our friends, Winnie and Flash, and..." She couldn't hold back a sob as her eyes became suddenly wet. "The children and women aboard, all the men passengers too! What will happen to them?" As she shook away the hot tears, her grief turned to bitterness. "How could the Germans do this?"

"It was the *verdammten* munitions," Kroger growled beneath her faltering hands. "The gun cotton and artillery shells, that's what has blown the bottom out of your fine ship!" While arguing, he shifted in his seat to let her pull his shirtwaist clear. "Even if there was a torpedo—just one—that second blast was no German weapon!"

The cruel folly of it overcame her. "Oh, Dirk, even so," she appealed to him, "how could your U-boats attack us?" Alma found that her bitterness didn't keep her from caring for the patient, as she nicked the cleanest part of his shirt with a penknife and tore off a makeshift bandage. "You were ready to do the same thing," she added, "or risk it at least, to blow up this submarine."

"Enough now, Alma," the spy pleaded. "What's done is done. It's a war, for *Gott's* sake."

Turning his attention forward, he called out, "Matt, what are you doing up there? Have you tried the throttle yet? If we cannot drive this boat out of here soon, we're *tot*, dead!"

Alma worked on in silence, trying to contain her emotions. Mere moments ago she'd gotten over feeling trapped, doomed. Now suddenly she heard that all was lost, everything of value gone. What was the point?

Her patient at least, the German saboteur, looked as if he would survive, without a lung puncture or severe blood loss. But caught in the hold of a sinking ship, could any of them get out, much less help the others? Even the great Houdini would find this an impossible escape.

"Alma, can you tell me what you see? Look outside, here."

Matt had been peering out through the portholes. Now Alma, after knotting the last bandage tight, shifted forward and put her head up beside his in the low turret, sharing the view. Out the narrow front glass slit, by the glare of the headlamps, she saw only the nose of the sub and jumbled crates. But through the right porthole, which Matt tapped with his finger, something else was visible.

It was a pale blue radiance the color of Neptune's deeps—faint and ghostly, but real, as proven by the shapes of boxes and loose wreckage that tumbled toward it. Framed inside a crooked outline, the light dimmed and shaded to darkness as it fell away from its brightest part— the radiance of sun in shallow sea.

"I'm looking out through a hole in the hull," she told Matt, feeling breathless with sudden hope. "The ship's plating is blown open. A huge gap, and I can see daylight through it. It's blue-green, and beautiful! If only we could..."

"That's what I thought, dear. Well, hang onto something. I'll try to get us out there." Matt took hold of the sub's tiller, his arm flexing up tautly against Alma's side.

"Forward and up for power," Kroger called out gruffly behind them. "Or back down, to reverse. Rudder right or left to turn. The propeller is set in a ring, so it shouldn't be jammed."

Alma edged aside to let Matt raise the throttle. Looking past Dirk to the rear of the sub, she could see the dynamo spark to life and the propeller shaft begin to spin. The inside lights dimmed and there was a churning sound, but no forward motion. The vessel barely twitched beneath them.

"I think we're hung up on something," Matt told the others, his low voice denying any hint of despair. "What should I do?"

"Ach, try the rudder," Dirk growled. "If it won't go forward, use reverse."

Swinging the tiller firmly from side to side, Matt seemed to hit resistance on the left—the side from which the giant tank behemoth had been crushing into their crate. "Alma, help me with this," he appealed to her.

When she put both of her hands on the metal pipe and they shoved together, she felt something give—loose planking, perhaps—and she could hear the propeller grinding against wood. Then, with a giddy lift, the small craft surged forward in the water.

"We're free," Matt said to exultant cries from both his shipmates. In joyful relief, Alma gave him a quick hug and kissed his cheek. But with a glance toward the right porthole he warned her, "We don't dare lose sight of the hull breach, or we'll get lost. What do you see?"

"I'm not sure," she said, turning to wipe the fogged glass with her hand.

As Matt dimmed the headlamps to help, she could barely make out the rift. "It's still there, but it's fading and dropping away," Her heart sank with the waning blue patch of light. "We must be going up in the hold."

"The dive planes!" Kroger grunted as he raised himself to see from behind. "You have them set too high."

"Right." Constrained in the tight space, Matt said, "Alma, depress that lever."

Reaching forward to the handgrip, she moved the tubular control down, feeling faint resistance from the water flowing outside. A pointer on a forward gear wheel showed what must be the fin settings.

"That's good," Matt urged her, "all the way down to thirty degrees."

The pointer moved, but to her dismay she felt no change in the sub's angle. "It's not doing anything, is it?" she asked.

"More throttle," Kroger rasped from behind, "to give the fins some bite, yes?"

Alma felt the sub level, but saw the light fading. "It's no good, we're still rising," she said. "At this rate we'll bob up to the top of the hold like a cork."

"By now the hold is flooded," Matt said. "No escaping up there." Looking around, he gripped a valve wheel at one side. "What about Fill Ballast?" he called back to Kroger, reading from the painted placard. "Should I open up the tanks?"

"*Nein*, do not!" the spy yelped at once. "With the three of us in here we don't need more weight. This boat is made for two, and I am no featherweight! If you make us any heavier, we'll never see the surface again! Just do as they do in the U-boats—shift your weight forward and bring down the nose. Alma, go to the front—get along, there's a good *fraulein!*"

In the emergency, Alma ignored the German's brisk pat on her rump as she moved to comply. It wasn't easy in the cramped space, but she ended up perched on one knee, leaning forward against the dive control. Matt huddled close against her, their recent intimacy a help. But his voice in her ear was grim and urgent.

"No good, we're still rising! Not enough weight for'ard. Alma, you take the controls." He shifted behind her, letting her ease into the driver's seat. As he hunched forward, she felt the nose dip slightly more.

"Fine, now give it some throttle," Kroger instructed from behind. "You steer with fins and rudder, not like a motorcar."

"Good thing I never drove a car," Alma said, pressing the tiller forward.

Better than any dial pointer was the surge and dip of the sub's nose, and the brightness outside confirmed—they were diving.

"Excellent," Kroger said as he eased his bandaged bulk astern. "Throttle back gently and keep the keel steady. Back off a little, dive planes to half. Alma, can you see where to go?"

"Yes, down and to starboard. We'll have to dive deep to get out because the *Lusi*'s listing so badly. The light is still below us, but dimmer."

As she steered, the blue patch swung forward in her viewport. The sub's nose was down steeply now, and Alma had to brace herself to keep from sliding forward.

She decided not to worry about whether they had enough battery power to get out. Or enough air, for that matter, even though the tiny metal egg stank of grease and ozone. The dimmed headlamps showed no obstacles between them and the faint daylight. But scrapes and bumps alongside told her they must be striking unseen objects. "I can see the hull breach just ahead of us, further below," she said. "It's dreadful, but lovely."

The rift in the hull, with pale blue sea shining through, was immense. At least two deck levels had been blown open, with cargo crates and wreckage from the explosions still spilling out in a slow-motion avalanche.

"You see those jagged pieces of plate hanging down, don't you?" Matt asked, peering out the side slit.

"Yes—we've got to avoid damage from those." As they sank toward the gap, she felt something shift the sub's nose aside. She shoved the tiller to counteract it.

"There's a current here," she said, suddenly doubtful. "The water's moving, more than just the inflow. It's the ship, still steaming...is that possible?" She played with the tiller, testing the current. "It's going to take all our power to get clear."

Kroger's voice came up gruff in Alma's ear. "If the ship is moving, you must dive forward to avoid a smash. Gravity may help, but let us hope the *Lusi*'s not at full speed!"

Alma understood the danger. The sea rushing astern and inward could drive them up against the jagged rent in the hull, or trap them in the hold. At nearly full throttle now, she was barely holding their place inside the big ship. They were fighting not just *Lusi*'s forward speed but the force of her vast weight sinking. It was drawing volumes of water up through the wound in her hull, the sea bleeding inward.

"I've got to try for it," she told her crewmates. "We can't stay here just wasting power."

"Yes, go!" Kroger barked from behind them. "Matt, all of us, must bear forward like in the U-boats."

"It's now or never." As Alma shoved the control over the sub veered out and down, drawn into the flow. The current caught and spun them, toppling Matt sideways in his awkward crouch. For one wild moment Alma knew how a goldfish feels, darting inside a tiny glass bowl for imaginary safety.

Waiting for the crash, she instead felt the craft slowing, its keel leveling upward in direct light. By the time she regained her view out of the turret, the sea was pale all around them. The Lusitania's dark, scarred bulk slid overhead just outside the right porthole, already leaving them behind.

"We're clear," she breathed, feeling fresh, reborn.

"Yes we are," Matt said, giving her an embrace and a kiss. "Now get us out from underneath, my love, before the poor old ship rolls over and takes us with her."

"Dive planes up," Kroger added. "We head for the surface!"

Chapter 46

Rescue

In Queenstown, Admiral Coke was quick to learn of the attack. Standing vigilant in his Royal Navy office overlooking nearby Cobh Harbor, he had within one-half hour a full picture of the event. Watchers along the seacoast—golfers, fisherfolk and other ordinary subjects of His Majesty's Irish dominions—had seen the approach of the vessel *Lusitania*, by now so familiar and beloved for its frequent stops at Queenstown. They witnessed the plume of the exploding torpedo. They heard the two distinct detonations, and three faint blasts of distress from the ship's whistle. From the tranquil shore they saw her gray-black shape heel over in the noon sunlight and tilt steadily down by the bows, stern rising under a smoky pall.

Those loyal subjects with access to telephones had promptly notified the Royal Navy chief in Queenstown, with his small fleet of vessels there in the harbor. Others with boats in the tiny coastal town of Kinsale, and in even tinier Courtmacsherry, made ready to put to sea and rescue survivors, should the unthinkable happen and the great liner actually sink. All of this had been conveyed to Admiral Coke. Seeing that something must be done, he was quick to respond.

"Signal the cruiser *Juno* using secure naval code," he told his wireless officer. "She has only just arrived, and can get up steam quickly. Order her out to the aid of the distressed ship, say in code, twelve miles south of Kinsale.

"No need for coordinates on a clear day like this," he added as the man began to tap on his Morse key. "Instruct Admiral Hood to proceed carefully. He is to pick up survivors and protect any other rescuers from submarines that may be lurking nearby. With *Juno's* speed, it's no distance at all. I'll expect her to be there inside an hour, tell him. Also alert any smaller vessels that can make it out by nightfall. Then notify the Admiralty."

As he gave his commands, the Admiral gazed through his open office window at the warship herself, anchored there in Queenstown harbor—the venerable cruiser *Juno*, with her knifelike prow canted out for ramming, and her two tall masts with their broad round battletops meant to survey the fight. She might see glory yet.

He soon saw activity soon aboard the flagship, the anchors raised, puffs of steam from the pair of smokestacks at the center. Already there was bustle in the sleepy harbor—sails unfurling, men swarming onto the piers carrying extra oars, and engines snorting to life as the few diesel boats warmed up. This ancient town was always ready to aid any distressed vessel. And most especially old *Lusi*, she that had put into port here so frequently over the years.

Yet this time there was no Admiralty order to divert *Lusitania* to Queenstown, just Coke's own broad invitation in his recall signal to another MFA-class tugboat. Which, in any case, it was now too late for poor Captain Turner to heed.

And there'd been no escort either, once *Juno* was withdrawn. The only protection for *Lusi* had been...no protection at all, really, apart from his own laughable Gilbert-and-Sullivan fleet of nearly unarmed patrol boats, derided in navy circles as a comic opera farce.

Now, when the final crisis came, he had one dubious asset left to throw at it, the old-style steamer vulnerable to torpedoes. There was nothing else, since the Admiralty was so stingy with their new and incredibly fast destroyers, the 35-knot ships based in Milford Haven up-channel.

Well, they'd done it now, with their stubborn indecision, their neglect of duty and their warnings sent twenty hours late. Back there in London, heaven only knew what they were playing at. Here in the War Zone, with innocent lives at stake, there remained little choice. To save the women and children and toffs and neutral Yanks aboard the *Lusitania*, he must do whatever he could.

* * *

Aboard *Juno*, Rear Admiral Horace Hood had read the swiftly decoded message and given orders to get the antique cruiser underway. His tenure as commander of Admiral Coke's flagship, and his only real warship, had been brief, since March when he'd come down from his Dover Straits command in the navy's eastern sector. The transfer had been a demotion for him—a grave injustice, as others would someday come to understand. He had strengthened the wartime defenses of the English Channel with nets, mines and patrols, enough to make it impassable to any German submarine, much less to the surface raiders that had been so feared in the first year of the war.

Yet the Admiralty under Lord Churchill had blamed him for U-boats slipping through to the south of England, and for the sinking of merchant vessels in these very shipping lanes off Ireland.

He'd tried to tell them—and soon enough they'd see the truth of it—that to get this far, or to Liverpool, German subs had no need of creeping through the Channel. The U-boats now had sufficient range and seaworthiness to navigate around the northwest tip of Scotland, and around about Ireland too if they wished. They didn't even need extra fuel for the return trip. No amount of protection east of Dover would keep them away.

But the Admiralty chiefs, landlubbers like young Winston and old fire-breathers like Jackie Fisher, were slow to admit the danger, He was made scapegoat for their ignorance. It was a temporary station, he hoped, far from the main fleet at Scapa Flow, and from any likely big-ship actions. But the irony of it was, to counter the threat to western shipping that they still saw as slight, they'd placed him here at the front line with nothing, as part of a laughable force of patrol boats led by one aging cruiser. And now, in this emergency, this outdated ship, without underwater armor and with side coal bunkers ready to fill up with sea, was just as vulnerable to torpedo attack as the giant *Lusitania*. His mission of mercy, to go out and possibly face one tiny U-boat, could amount to a death sentence for his ship and crew.

Still, he could hardly shirk any order. To rebuild his reputation at the Admiralty, just such a show of courage as this might be needed, with many more to follow.

So be it. As the offspring of a long line of revered admirals, Hood felt confident that this unending war would give him many opportunities to distinguish himself in service to the Crown.

* * *

On the *Juno's* foredeck, Seaman Albright's station was in the bows, there to stand ready with a firehose. He wielded it as the anchor was raised, spraying down the heavy chain links with fresh seawater. That would remove any weed and harbor debris that might foul the mechanical windlass or cause rust.

As they got underway, swerving wide in the sunlit anchorage to turn and making the smaller vessels rock in their wake, Albright kept busy cleaning and tidying the foredeck. They would be picking up passengers from the sinking liner, so he was told. This deck space might be needed to sort out the living from the dead.

"A ter'ble pass, this torpedoin', ain' it?" he remarked to Hollis, the forward watch. "How could the blighty Huns do it? But good ol' *Lusi* won't sink, will she, bein' so big an' all."

"Well, that depends on how many fish the sub put into her," Hollis replied. "An' if they're saving any for us."

"Well, I 'ope they are," Albright said with feeling. "If they're waitin' out there, we can run 'er down, cut that U-boat right in two and send 'er to the bottom. We're fast enough an' we has the ram."

"Yes, well, we were fast enough running away from submarines this mornin' into Queenstown," Hollis said. "Now we'll be runnin' back toward 'em just as fast. I only hope we zigzag."

"We'll 'ave a tough time zigzaggin' while we lower boats pick up survivors," Albright said. "An' the more so after we put old *Lusi* in tow, too, if it comes to that."

"We'll know soon enough," Hollis replied. "There she is."

As the cruiser passed between the forts on the headlands and left the mineswept channel behind, the view out to sea was vivid but not encouraging. Even seen from twenty miles off, the huge ship was obviously in trouble, with her bow-end sloping down into the sea. The hull was angled up astern and also tilted well away from shore. Her dark red under-paint showed above water on the landward port side, with her four leaning stacks trailing out smoke and steam.

"Most of the port lifeboats are still in place," Hollis observed. "Tough job launching 'em with that steep of a list."

"Can we even tow her like that, down so far by the bows?" Albright wondered aloud. "We might 'ave to pull from astern. Not much chance of savin' 'er, if you ask me."

Albright was soon back to work clearing the foredeck, shifting heavy gear up and down the companionway stairs. As he toiled, from time to time he would hear stray shouts coming down from the foretop.

"Survivors and boats are in the water."

"Still underway and trailing out wreckage!"

"She's goin' down fast."

All of a sudden in the bright daylight, he felt the deck sway beneath him as *Juno* heeled in a sharp turn to port. Seaman Albright looked around in surprise. There had been no zigzagging so far, so it seemed strange now.

"What is it, Sir?" he asked a passing deck officer. "Did we sight a U-boat?"

"Not yet, Seaman," the officer answered with a bitter look, as if the words tasted bad. "But no need to worry, you can stand down from your duty. We've received Admiralty orders sending us back to Queenstown at once. The danger is too great."

"Aye, sir!" He saluted, with a glance over his shoulder at the tilting passenger liner poised to sink. Aye-aye sir, though it ain't right, he wanted to add. But he didn't dare speak such a thing aloud.

Moments later they were on a straight course back to harbor, speeding through the gaggle of slow, ill-assorted work and pleasure boats that had set forth from Queenstown to aid the *Lusitania*.

Chapter 47

Mutiny

Through his attack periscope, *Herr Kapitan* Schwieger watched the relentless progress of disaster.

The giant ship plowed onward in a great curve, its prow steadily sinking into the sea and skewing to the right. Behind it spread a long wake—of human bodies, wreckage, and desperate survivors in and out of lifeboats, some of which were also sinking. Control of the steam turbines must have been lost, or the captain would have halted his vessel to lower his boats safely. Instead, many of them now dangled useless from the starboard side. Or worse, they dropped into the waves to crush one another and be swamped by the bow current. And that was along the rail of the ship tilting nearest the water. One could only guess what was happening on the higher port side.

Feeling the press of crew behind him and hearing the murmur of eager voices, Schwieger thrust himself away from the attack periscope, which was now lowered beneath the conning tower into the central crew quarters.

"Here, Pilot Lanz, have a look. Run out the patrol periscope as well. Anyone who wants to may look."

Strangely, he no longer desired to witness the result of his triumphant torpedo strike.

"What chaos, it's a shambles." Lanz narrated what he saw to the others. "The ship is still running away from us, and listing worse than ever. She's sinking fast, but will likely capsize first. Lifeboats full of people are still tied to the ship, being dragged down and crushed as she heels over and sinks. The passengers crowd up to the last high places and drop off over the rails like lemmings."

As Lanz spoke, he had to swivel the periscope to follow the target's motion.

"But yes, it's definitely *Lusitania*. With that list, I can plainly see her deck funnels."

Oddly to Schwieger's ears, the news brought a buzz from the crewmen but no spontaneous cheer of victory. Others had taken turns at the second periscope by now, some with audible gasps of dismay, so likely they found the scene too terrible to applaud. And this unsavory business with Voegele, who now sat under watch in the corner of the room, may have infected their minds with doubt.

Schwieger himself felt sobered, but he knew he'd done his duty. Hopefully it would be recognized by his superiors and duly rewarded on their return home.

Meanwhile Lanz swung the attack periscope in a full circle, edging his way around the crowded command space. "No sign of any rescue ships yet," he reported. "I've seen enough." He turned away and made room for Weisbach, who had been summoned back amidships from his torpedo tubes.

"Well, torpedoman, what do you think of your handiwork?" Schwieger asked after letting him survey the scene a few moments.

"It is amazing that one torpedo could cause such devastation to so huge a target." Weisbach stepped away from the spectacle, relinquishing his place at the scope. "Even one of our new G-type fish."

"It was more than our torpedo." Schwieger let a note of righteous passion creep into his voice for the crew to hear. "There was a secondary explosion. We all heard it and felt it, much more than the first. That ship was stuffed to the gills with ammunition."

"We hit her in the cargo, then?" Weisbach asked. "It wasn't the boilers going up, or the coal bunker?"

"I plotted the strike for the boilers at the center of the ship, to be sure of a hit." With the mood of the crew so uncertain, Schwieger felt obliged to explain things. "But the target was going slower than expected, far less than full speed, and our eel struck ahead of the bridge, just under the foredeck cargo hatch. That tells us what was in the Lusitania's hold."

Among the crew's murmurs in reply to his speech, there were enough *Ja's* to reassure him of their loyalty.

"Now," he continued, "Lanz, take the patrol periscope and keep up a vigil for warships and any others, especially that *Juno* cruiser that ran into Queenstown earlier. Crew to battle stations! Ready to surface if needed, and have ammunition in place for the deck gun."

"Nein!" This time the mutinous word came from Seaman Ulbricht who, as Schwieger turned to face him, held a pistol, a good German Luger, pointed straight at the captain's forehead. "We must not surface or be seen by anyone! We have done a terrible thing here, attacking innocent women and children, and no one must know who's to blame! We should slip away silently and tell nobody. Let them think the *Lusitania* struck a mine!"

"Don't do that."

Rikowski the radio officer reached out and pulled down Ulbricht's arm, taking the pistol out of his hand.

Schwieger blinked, otherwise keeping a straight face. There was no other sign of dissent from the crew, though all of them looked frightened, or at least solemn.

He decided simply to ignore the incident. Young Ulbricht was temperamental; everyone knew that and had accepted it. Keeping too many mutineers under guard might kindle a flame of dissent. Instead, just limit the damage to the foreigner. Already Rikowski had an arm around Ulbricht's shoulder, with the Luger nowhere in sight.

"Very well," he told his crew as they began to disperse. "You heard my orders."

"What about Voegele, the Alsatian mutineer?" his second officer asked. "Should he be in irons?"

"No. I remove him from command, but he may attend to his duties so long as he keeps quiet. Let us get on to business."

Turning back to his periscope, Schwieger added, "Our fight here may not be over."

Chapter 48

Boats Away

Captain Turner stood on the port wing of his bridge, looking aft. The scene along the Boat Deck, to his disciplined eye, was a mad melee—disgraceful, but hardly to be helped given the circumstances. Perhaps if so many of his crew had not been trapped in the baggage room by the explosions forward, or very likely drowned below decks in the sudden flooding, it might have gone better—and if the crew hadn't been shorthanded to begin with, and a green lot at that!

Now a mere handful of officers tried to control the deck, with only one or two crewmen at each lifeboat station. The passengers were running wild, everything was askew, the engines out of control, the electricity dead, the rudder jammed. But at least along the starboard rail, now that the ship had slowed a little, they were getting a few boats away. The starboard side was well down near the water, so the lifeboats could be lowered a short way or merely dropped. If they didn't swamp or land atop one another, or slip down endwise from a single rope, the passengers in them had a decent chance.

It was not a sure thing, not by any means...on that side he'd seen whole boatloads of humanity dragged under by their neglected chains and tackle, or crushed down into the water by the tilting boat davits as the great ship rode under the waves. But with his crew so short, there was little to be done about it.

And here along the port side it was worse. With the *Lusitania* heeled back twenty or more degrees from port and tilting forward, it seemed unlikely that any boat could slide down the canted side of the hull without rolling over or being gouged to pieces by the protruding rivet-heads. Perhaps, as the water eventually rose up along the deck, they could float them off one-by-one—that is, if the bow waves of the still-turning ship didn't drive the boats inboard, trapping them under wires and davits, and if they weren't swamped in the water by an overload of swarming passengers.

For the time being, he decided, loading the portside lifeboats was nothing but a risk. When Turner saw passengers climbing into the forward ones within earshot, he would call down through his speaking trumpet.

"Empty the boats, do not lower them! The ship will not sink, we are all right. Please clear the upper deck."

Even so, the clambering, jabbering monkeys kept milling around and scrambling in, more and more of them as the lower decks submerged and the list increased. For any to go back inside the tilting cabins and wait was too much to ask, he supposed. And now here came that junior mate Bisset, shouldering his way down for'ard through the mob, to shout some gibberish up at him from the boat deck. "Yes, what is it, Bisset? Sing it out, man!"

"Sir, Staff Captain Anderson wants me to request that you flood the port ballast tanks. That might level out the list and make it easier to launch boats."

As if I didn't know that, Turner thought to himself. What to tell him, then, that the tanks were already flooding themselves quite nicely, thank you? That no one could get to the manual controls, or that the pumps wouldn't operate in any case? No; that would give a poor impression to the passengers, and would likely cause a worse panic. Instead he called down. "Quite right, Mr. Bisset. An excellent idea, and I shall handle it. Give Captain Anderson my regards."

But almost before he could finish, something untoward occurred. In spite of all Turner's admonitions, the forward port lifeboat had filled up with women and children, with the male passengers swarming around trying to lower it. There came a sharp metallic sound as someone took a hammer and knocked out the pin to the snubbing chain, the anti-sway link that secured the boat's inside rail to the edge of the deck.

As this was done, the heavy, overloaded timber boat was suddenly released to swing free on its ropes—not outboard, but inboard of the rail. Its immense weight crushed into the crew and passengers on the steeply canted deck, including those waiting ready with the lowering-ropes in hand. Once they let go, either pinned in place or trying to struggle clear, the boat was free to start slowly forward and inward, down the sloping planks, grinding and crushing to death all those passengers who were caught in the V-angle of deck and superstructure.

Amid the shrieks of victims and the sick wails of its occupants the boat, greasing its way with human blood, quickly gathered speed on the incline. Carrying trapped bodies along, it came down and lodged with a sickening crunch under the bridge wing where Turner precariously stood. A lucky escape for young Bisset, who had the seamanlike agility to pull himself up the side of the bridge and avoid being crushed.

Then, amid the horrified cries of the survivors, as the Captain and officer stood helpless, the snubbing chain on the second boat astern was knocked loose, and it too swung inboard and slid free. Amid more screams and a fresh human stampede, it came barreling down the deck in the same bloody path, over the few wounded who had survived the first juggernaut. Sweeping all those before it into the obstacle of the previous lifeboat, it then rode well up over the wreckage. The women and children who cowered inside the first boat were crushed amid a new wailing cacophony of pain and terror.

"Bisset...Bestic...go back! Stop them—" Turner was barely able to choke out the words before his Junior Third Officer began climbing aft along the top rail, hurrying to keep any more boats from being released.

The old captain, unable to offer any help, gripped the rail and watched in vain as injured passengers clawed and struggled to save themselves a few feet below him. Alas, Bisset wasn't in time to keep a third lifeboat, and then a fourth, from breaking free, both careening down the same gory path toward Turner and smashing their pitiful human wreckage into the gruesome tangle of the first two—which now, perhaps mercifully, began to be drowned in rising sea waves as the Lusitania's bow steadily submerged.

Defeated, Captain Turner descended the steep incline back to his bridge house. He had to get the log books and the codes, to safeguard them or sink them to the sea bottom. Calling to the helmsman to save himself, he waded in to do this final duty. The control room was awash now in bright red—not with seawater, but human blood.

Chapter 49

Chaos

Flash left Winnie beside the stairs, after gaining her promise to stay put. Then he went off on the slanted deck to find their nurse friends. The covered promenade was lined with frightened passengers clinging to the high port rail, or bunched together against the inner wall as the list grew worse. Most venturing out across the planking fell or slid, jostling others or seizing hold of them for balance as they struggled along in the noisy turmoil. The ship still rolled and plunged forward, but Flash thought the motion was less now that she was half-sunken under the waves.

He went just far enough to see that Hildegard, Florence, and Hazel weren't where he'd left them before the attack. They would have been easy to miss in this madness.

Fighting his way along the deck, he passed women clinging helpless to one another, calling for lost children or trying to comfort sobbing ones. Men flung themselves urgently along on some mission, or else tried to appear calm while casting about for escape. Others, men and women alike, just shoved blindly in panic. Fallen passengers nursed injuries or struggled to regain their feet in the tilting chaos. Everyone seemed to be crying out for help, or for family members, life jackets, lifeboats.

Flash at last found a blue-coated officer careening down the steep deck. Propping the man up by one shoulder, he told him about the stalled elevator with passengers trapped inside.

"Don't worry," the man replied, "the ship will not sink. We need everyone to stay calm."

Flash leaned close to the man's ear. "But there's water flooding the Main Deck below," he whispered.

"Oh, never fear, that'll be corrected. We're just trying to right this list at the moment."

Another passenger struggled up, clinging to Flash for support. "Sir," asked the officer, "do you know when the lifeboats will be lowered down to us?"

"Just you wait and be patient. All is under control." Touching his cap to them, the uniformed man shoved free and went on his crooked way.

* * *

Winnie kept her place by the door, helping other latecomers drag themselves up out of the dark stairwell. Then she heard a voice—Alma's, it had to be her, shrilling out in such clear tones from the deck above. She threw herself into a swarm of people pushing up the outside stair. No harm, since Flash would be bringing the others back this way in a few moments.

Squeezing through onto the boat deck, she looked around the crowd, listening for the voice to ring out again. The passengers were in a frenzied hurry, but no one seemed certain where to go. She didn't see Alma, just throngs of people milling along the wall and clinging to the rail. As she edged through, an older woman in an unbuttoned coat with no life jacket confronted her.

"Oh, life vests! Thank you very much, my children can use these."

Seizing hold of the two jackets that Winnie still carried, she turned and dragged them away. Winnie trailed after her a step or two but then released her grip on the last one, deciding it would go to a good purpose.

Looking around, she noticed that some passengers in the jackets had put them on backward, just as Ian Holbourn predicted. The realization brought her nurse instincts to the fore.

"Wait, sir," she said to a small, hatless, balding man. "You have your life vest on wrong. Here, let me show you how to fix it so you won't drown."

Looking up in alarm, the man turned and fled. Even though Winnie was already wearing a life jacket, he must have feared that she would steal his. She tried again, but others with backward vests ignored her in their flight for survival.

The focus of the swarming energy, like a row of beehives, was the lifeboats hanging from their davits at regular gaps in the rail. None that she could see were being lowered. But people climbed into them, thrust women and children in, and climbed up to the top deck to unhook the ropes that would lower them. Meanwhile officers appeared and ordered the boats emptied. Willing or not, men and women eventually would climb out while others were busy climbing in. Scuffles and shoving matches broke out, but these class-conscious British eventually gave in to officers' firm commands. Winnie wondered why they weren't lowering the boats, but then she remembered Flash saying that the ship needed to stop moving.

Above her on the Marconi deck she heard singing, but it wasn't Alma. Looking up, she saw two young girls in life jackets gripping the rail, gazing out above the dread and anguish below them, with eyes fixed on the lush coast of Ireland. They had altered the words of a popular hymn to comfort themselves.

"There is a green hill not far away," they chorused, "without a city wall..."

Their sweet notes pierced Winnie's veil of calm. Turning and staggering away from the sight with tears suddenly stinging her eyes, she found herself looking instead at Charles Frohman, the aging impresario. He stood, or rather leaned, against the inner wall, bracing himself with his cane.

Beside him was the actress Rita Jolivet, wearing a life vest that more than filled out her slender form.

"C.F.," she was saying, "if I'd known you were going to give away your life jacket, I would have made you take that seat they offered us in the boat."

"You should have taken the seat," Frohman told her. "Why bother sticking with an old man?"

"Hello, C.F.," Winnie said, blinking aside her tears and entering their little sphere of calm amid the turmoil.

"Hello, my dear," Frohman politely responded, conveying a sense of composure. "I'm glad to see you well."

"And, you, too," she said turning to Rita. "Are they really letting any lifeboats go?"

"Over on the starboard side," Rita answered with a jerk of her head. "Most of them just tip over or sink...it's too dreadful to watch, so we crawled up here. But the boat they offered *him* got away clear," she chided, poking Frohman in the shoulder.

Taking a last puff on his cigar and tossing away the stub, the producer shrugged theatrically.

"Why fear death?" he asked the ladies with a convincing smile. "It is the most beautiful adventure that life gives us."

Winnie recognized the quote from his *Peter Pan* play, so she didn't try to argue the point. But to herself, remembering what she'd heard at the party, she couldn't help thinking that Frohman had ended up here because he preferred the threat of death to an Atlantic crossing with Isadora Duncan.

She then remembered her own purpose. "Good luck to you both! I have to go." She turned away from them, feeling a pang of loss.

Not finding Alma, she'd begun to fear also losing Flash. She felt the sudden frenzy building in her chest and tried to suppress it, but it wasn't easy. Some passengers were lurching about the crooked deck, bowling down others or even treading over them, and their panic was infectious. She strove to ignore the awful sights and sounds around her, watching for friends.

* * *

When Flash found that Winnie was no longer there, he ducked into the stairwell, dreading that she might have gone back down to the stuck elevator. He called her name into the pitch blackness but heard nothing—no cries, no thumping from the coffin below, only the rush of rising water.

Deciding that she could have gone up onto the Boat Deck, he turned to follow. The stairway astern was made steeper by the forward list, and the top opening was jammed with people, but he managed to force his way though.

Out under the blue sky the sights were more extreme. The upper deck was covered with soot from the explosions, and most passengers' hands, faces and life-jackets were black-smudged. Amid the staggering, shoving throng, a huge stoker stood coal-black from head to foot, except for his severely wounded scalp. From what appeared to be his exposed skull a welter of blood dribbled down his dazed, white-eyed face.

Another crewman's face was beet-red and swollen, having been badly scalded by steam. Where he sat blinded in the angle of deck, he was being helped by a kneeling woman in a nurse's cap. It was Hildegard, Flash realized. At her side, getting supplies out of a medical chest and passing them along, were Flo and Hazel, both wearing life jackets.

"Hello, I found you," he exclaimed, grasping a window ledge to steady himself. "Have you seen Winnie? She was with me just a moment ago, downstairs."

Florence looked up at him, wide-eyed and obviously dazed, giving no answer. Was she unhinged, struck dumb by the magnitude and suddenness of disaster? Then her adorable young face lit up with its familiar radiance.

"Oh, look," Flo said all at once, "there she is right behind you!"

Turning, Flash saw Winnie's face smudged with soot and tears. He caught her as she rushed toward him.

"It was your beautiful hair, darling," she said, clinging to him. "I couldn't miss it, even in all this chaos."

He embraced her and kissed away her tears. Then after helping her steady herself against the wall, he turned to the others.

"Miss Hildegard, you need a life jacket," Flash said to the white-caped matron. "Here, just take mine. I'll get another one in no time."

As he reached to undo his ties, Hildegard stood up. "No, young man, you keep it. It would just get in my way. I have to go over and help that poor coal stoker."

Having finished dressing the scalded man's face and hands, she picked up the medical bag that she must have fetched from the cabin astern.

"You haven't seen Alma or Matt since we left?" Flash asked her. "We didn't find them on deck or in the stateroom."

"They'll do just fine on their own," the nurse said confidently. But then she leaned close to him. "Flash, you be sure to get those girls into a boat. Anyone who says this ship will be afloat thirty minutes from now is a liar."

She turned away, but Hazel stopped her.

"Miss Hildegard, wait! We'll come along and help." She glanced around them at the teeming desolation on deck. "It's awful here, but we're learning so much."

"Yes we are," Florence added. "It's just like the Great War, almost."

"No, girls." Hildegard smiled. "You know how to save lives. There will be people in the boats and in the water who need you. Stay with Flash, and he'll get you away safely."

She glanced out to sea, where the green Irish hills fringed the miles of rolling blue. "I've never much cared for the ocean. I'll stay here a little while longer." With a visible shiver she left the group.

Flash, meanwhile, was looking at the boat situation. Those here along the port side had been swung out with the rest, but now because of the list they hung well inboard, canted atop the wood-and-canvas collapsible boats that had been stowed under them on blocks. To shove the dangling hulls out overside would take massive effort, all the more so once they were full of people. Then, as they were lowered, it would be a sliding descent down the sloping steel plating studded with heavy round-edged rivet heads. When and if the boats finally reached the water, they'd be out of sight of the deck due to the curvature of the exposed hull. But hopefully, the ropes would be long enough to let them all the way down.

Then there was the question of space. When Flash first came up on deck, the officers had been keeping people away and driving them out. But now, in spite of the crew's efforts, or because they'd given up, the boats were filling rapidly

Flash led Winnie and her two friends amid the throng to the nearest lifeboat, already almost full. As he helped the women up onto the canvas-covered collapsible and then over the gunwale of the wooden craft, some kind of commotion broke out down the deck forward. Shouts, screams and crashing noises drifted back up to them over the general hubbub.

Flash craned his neck, but he was unable to see past the line of boats and davits. No one else seemed to pay attention. The ladies had found safe seats on the benches, he saw to his relief.

"Flash, come along and get in!" Beneath Winnie's commanding tone he heard her desperate plea.

"Not yet, darling. First I'll help get this thing over the side." He smiled, doing his best to deceive her, but knowing he might need to jump overboard after the boat was launched.

Just then from ahead of them a further tumult sounded, with more shrieks, a rumbling and another distant crash. Flash propped himself up on the rail for a look, bracing against the davit, but he could only see crowds swarming in and readying the nearby boats. No lifeboats were visible on the sea, but it was possible they'd passed out of sight down below.

No sooner had he stepped off his perch than a third outburst of screams and crashes sounded, this time louder. Whatever the menace was, it was getting nearer. Were the smokestacks toppling? No; he looked up and saw them still smoking, though they leaned over to starboard like everything else.

Then at once Flash understood. The lifeboat next to his, full of desperate humanity, slipped suddenly loose from its moorings. Instead of tumbling down into the sea, it swung back inboard onto its handlers, taking them and the canvas-topped collapsible raft with it. Unstoppable it slid down the forward-tilting promenade, a loose juggernaut. Scraping against the deckhouse doors and windows, it scythed into helpless people huddled there as it gathered speed, trailing ropes and writhing bodies behind.

The boat passengers' shrieks of dread had an eerie quality, borne swiftly away like some awful carnival ride. After slewing some two hundred feet it crunched into a pile of boats and bodies below the bridge, sending a culminating wail of agony back up the deck.

As Flash looked on in horror, he saw the still-rising sea wash up into the grisly mass, stirring the wreckage with fresh moans and screams for help.

Tearing his eyes away, he turned back to the boat before him, next in line for an unspeakable fate. He didn't think the women on the benches had seen, but from the yells and wails they must have known something was terribly wrong.

A young officer was trying to control the mob. Flash followed his lead, grabbing an oar to pry against the boat, toiling in his bulky life-jacket.

"Push the boat out, all together," the officer was saying. "We have to shove it over past the rail, and then you men on the ropes let out a couple feet of line, no more. On the count of three we'll push—one, two, three, now heave!"

The boat shifted.

"There, we almost had it! You there, give me the mallet! Don't touch that chain or I'll brain you with this, understand? Now all together, let's push her out again. Put some back into it this time!

"Let's go—one, two, three, push—there! Now slack out the fall ropes, just a meter or so. We've got her, but hold those ropes steady. Room for any more in the boat? We're ready to lower."

Like some others, Flash had been levering the lifeboat desperately outward with his oar. Now it hung safe alongside, but already the rivet heads of the Lusitania's sloping hull were gouging deeply into the wood, raising splinters from the boat's side-wale. As the mate triumphantly knocked loose the snubbing chain, the stout wood hull settled and began to shred against the rivets.

Flash saw at once what was needed. He stepped over into the boat, still prying with his heavy pole and forcing it in lower.

"The oars," he called out to the other men. "Drive them in as rails, so the boat can slide down. Otherwise the bolt-heads dig into the timbers! Shove them down as far as you can! We'll have to do it all the way down, or we'll never make it."

The officer shouted his approval and urged more oarsmen aboard as the rope hands began lowering. The boat skidded down the side, rocking and slipping as the falls were played out unevenly, and the black-painted rivet heads caught and dug at the timber. Yet half a dozen men and women plying four or five oars were able to do some good, prying and cushioning the downward skid with oar blades and hafts.

Working at the bow end, Flash could see the rivets lying in long vertical rows, angling forward with the list. He was able to wedge his oar deep down alongside a triple row of rivets as the boat slid onto it, preventing further damage. Looking over, he found Winnie beside him, bringing up a fresh oar from the middle of the bench rows.

"Wonderful, darling!" he said. "Now grab this one when the boat clears it, won't you? We'll need all of them once we're in the water."

Flash worried whether the next lifeboat in line might break free like the others and run over their rope handlers on deck. But glancing up, he saw it swung out successfully overside and lowered, using the oars to smooth its descent, as his boat had done. Still it faced a problem, for just astern of his own boat's path, the open cutaway of the Shelter Deck began. The other boat dropped down and stuck inside the open railing, where eager passengers on the lower deck caught hold of it and tried to climb aboard. As the falls were lowered farther and the boat began to tilt, the oarsmen had to fight off the new boarders. It became a fierce struggle for survival, but Flash could no longer spare any time to watch.

Thereafter in brief upward glimpses against the noon glare, he saw boat passengers fending off the boarders with oars and fists, distracted from their own toil and unable to get their boat clear. The fighting went on, with bodies falling and tumbling past, down the hull incline into the sea. All for nothing, since the unlucky boat seemed to be jammed tight and didn't descend further.

Meanwhile, Flash blocked off the next vertical row of rivets with his new oar, and then the next row after that with a fresh one as the rounded side of the lifeboat scuffed and grated down the hull. Seeing flaky red bottom-paint on the ship's steel plating, he knew the sea must be near. The descent was smoother now, and glancing aside he could see the water a dozen feet below. But from its flow he realized the big ship was still underway. He worried that the bow current could be enough to swamp them.

Very soon he found out, as first the stern rope slipped free and then the bow. Something must have happened; maybe the ropes ran out, causing the heavy-laden boat to dip and plummet beneath them. The oar twisted out of his grip, toppling him over backward onto others. The heavy craft grated down the ship's side, nearly capsizing. It struck the water bow-first, raising a wave that drenched the passengers, but luckily didn't swamp them.

In the stunned seconds that followed, what shocked Flash most was the color he'd glimpsed in the water-curtain. Having washed back to them from the carnage forward, it rose pinkish-red against the bright blue sea and sky. The *Lusitania*, he dazedly knew, was sinking in a sea of blood.

Well, at least they were afloat and free—except for the ropes that tumbled down onto their heads in the next moment, causing curses and grunts of pain.

"Now I know why they call them fall ropes," Flash heard Hazel feebly say.

"Yes, because they fall on you," Florence added, untangling herself.

At least the two girls had their sense of humor. Maybe they hadn't noticed the blood.

"Let's get clear," Flash said at once, seeing no officer in command. "We've got to push free of the ship. Find an oar and shove away, or row if you can!"

As their craft scraped along the still-moving hull, he was seized by a sudden dread that the boat just astern might land on top of them, or that tumbling passengers would fall in and sink them. Grabbing hold of the oar that had almost clubbed him as it fell, he shoved hard against the steel hull, trying to push off into the blood river. Others joined in, turning the bow of the boat out into the current

And sure enough, things were falling near them. Passengers, with or without life jackets, came skidding and rolling down the hull, taking their chances in the water. Others slid down ropes, leaving bloody strands and clawmarks on the hull as their ropes ran out and they tried in vain to slow themselves.

Then as he gazed upward, the embattled lifeboat that had wedged in the promenade deck began to slip free, bow-first, tumbling most of its six dozen passengers out. They slid down the ship's side screaming and flailing into the sea.

With Lusitania's forward progress, the hanging boat had passed well ahead of them by now, so that when the stern rope came free and the boat plummeted, it landed fifty feet forward, missing their craft but crushing many of the struggling passengers it had just dumped into the water.

"Row!" Flash called out, urging the distracted boat crew to make progress. "We've got to be well away from her when she sinks!"

Fumbling and finally getting his oar into a rowlock with Winnie's help, he tugged on it along with her in the cramped space. As they did so, he could feel cold water sloshing around his ankles, probably seeping in through the boat's seams that had been gouged by rivets or strained from the fall.

But there just behind them, vivid to the rowers facing astern, a greater menace loomed up. As the Lusitania's hull rolled over to starboard its two portside propellers had emerged from the sea. They still turned, sluggishly but with tremendous force behind their twelve-foot-high blades. The inner, sternmost screw next to the rudder was almost completely out of the water, splashing down into the wake and churning up gouts of pinkish spray. And the outboard screw, positioned sixty feet forward along the sinking hull, was half-submerged and spinning like a water wheel, its coppery green blades slicing down every second like giant scythes. They threatened to cut any boat in half and, churning as they did, created a powerful suction.

While the rowers watched and toiled to get away, luckless swimmers were drawn into the hungry vortex to disappear with screams and sprays of red.

The boat's crew pulled desperately at the four oars they had in the sea, men and women straining together, but their boat was filling with water and getting hard to row. Worse, Flash could see the Lusitania's rudder mostly out of the water but tilted far over to starboard. While drifting forward at its crazed angle, the big ship was also turning, its stern swinging out directly toward them. They heard the churning of the screw grow louder and saw it come near. They watched the overturned boat from astern drift into the chaos, with a few pitiful survivors still clinging to it and pushing off too late.

With a terrible crunching sound, timbers, limbs, indescribable things churned upward in the red foam and disappeared. Facing astern as they rowed, they could see their fate before it reached them. It was inevitable.

"One thing I never thought I'd say," Flash panted to Winnie as she rowed beside him.

"What's that, darling?" she gasped in his ear.

"Thank God I don't have my camera along."

Whether it was a good joke or not, he knew it was his last.

At that moment, with a thunderous grinding and a symphony of tortured, groaning metal, the whole huge ship convulsed, sending off a wave that kicked them away from the hull. The giant screw before them still sliced the water, but they soon realized it was no longer propelling the ship forward. The great vessel had stopped.

"She's grounded out," someone in the boat cried. "The bow must have struck bottom."

"Fine, then," Flash said. "Let's pull away quick before she settles."

With the death-ship no longer bearing down on them, their oars began to bite. Although they were half-swamped, passengers went to work with hats and canvas bailing-buckets to lighten the boat. A few survivors in the water got near enough to cling to ropes or gunwales for dear life. The boat's occupants had no heart to drive them off, but even so they made headway straining at the oars.

The rowers faced backward and so by necessity witnessed the last agonies of ship, and her passengers. *Lusi's* hull was now submerged for most of its length, with the stern pointing up at a sharp angle. Desperate survivors climbed to the highest parts, crowding each other off the deck in places. Many jumped or slid into the water, some landing on top of others. One man tried to slide down a cable, but when it carried him over the high stern screw he lost a leg to the still-spinning blade, to plummet screaming into the red wake. Others on the forward decks simply stood and let the rising water sweep them off, with or without life jackets.

Flo and Hazel, tending to a pregnant woman they had fished out of the water, were both in tears.

"Miss Hildegard could still be back there," Hazel said with a glance astern.

"Or maybe she found a boat," Florence told her sister. "Maybe it's even less leaky than this one!"

Their words made Flash remember Matt and Alma...while fighting to survive and save others, he hadn't thought of them in, what, half an hour? Fifteen minutes? Ten? He could only hope they'd been as lucky as he had.

A few other boats were in the water, strung out in the long wake behind the doomed vessel. But most of those in sight appeared to have come from the starboard. That side could not be faring too well now, being so low down in the sea. As they watched, smokestack number three toppled away from them, trailing and lashing out its guy-wires to a faint accompaniment of shrieks.

Along the port side, the rear davits either hung empty or dangled shattered pieces of timber, shredded by the steel hull and rivets. One last lifeboat astern was loaded with people, still snug against the deck, waiting for the rising sea. But as they watched, a gunshot sounded, sharp and imperative over the cries. As if it had been a starter's gun, the boat soon swung inboard like the rest and raced down the forty-degree slope of the deck, amid screams and diving bodies. At the end it of its slide it splashed into the rising waves, to disappear there without a trace.

That done, the great ship seemed to give up. With smoke and steam blasting up out of her ventilators, the sea rushing in and the stern portholes blowing out with loud pops from the pressure, she settled into the deep. A final explosion within sent steam billowing out of the stacks, cloaking the whole vessel in a blinding, scalding mist.

When the fog dissipated, *Lusitania* was gone. Her last great exhalation of foam and debris welled up from below, scattering human bodies on its swell.

Afterwards they found themselves on flat blue sea amid a vast field of wreckage and floating humanity both dead and alive, with life jackets and without. No ships were visible as yet, no blasts of boat whistles, just a few pitiful cries and the flailing arms of those trying to survive. Together they worked, rowing to pick up swimmers and bailing to keep their small craft afloat.

Chapter 50

Survivors

Even at full throttle with dive planes raised, the mini-sub took minutes to surface. Meanwhile Alma worked in the back to control Kroger's bleeding. The spy's strength seemed to be ebbing.

She appealed to Matt, "Can't we go up any faster? Dirk needs fresh air."

"Matt," the spy called out, "try blowing out the ballast tanks, in case there's water in them. Do you see the control there in front?"

"Blow ballast, aye-aye," Matt said, reaching out and twisting a valve. There came a rushing, bubbling sound and Alma felt a slight lift.

"Good, now we'll make it to the surface." Kroger lay gasping weakly as Matt turned off the valve. "You two young ones will, anyway."

"Now Dirk," Alma said, wiping the spy's sweaty brow, "don't talk like that. You'll be fine."

But she couldn't help noticing that, as the sub tilted upward, the bilge water astern near the dynamo pooled red with her patient's blood.

"I see a lifeboat up there," Matt called out. "No oars or swimmers in the water, it's just drifting. I'll steer for it and hope they have room for three."

"Fine," Alma said. "Those boats have medical kits, don't they?" Secretly, she was also desperate to escape this mini-sub before the power ran out, or the air. Good as it had been to them, it still felt like a stifling brass coffin.

As he peered through his portholes, Matt said, "I don't see any other boats, just some floating debris. The ship kept going and may not have stopped."

"They must be having an awful time up there. I hope the others are all right."

"They should be okay. Flash is as smart and able as they come, and I told him to look after them."

"Oh, good! I hope he can." Alma took comfort from Matt's words, even though she knew they meant little in such a catastrophe.

From Alma's supporting arms, Dirk Kroger spoke up faintly. "Just look at the three of us, won't you? We survived against the biggest odds, so far at least. Could your friends have faced anything worse?"

"You said it, Dirk," Matt seconded. "Where there's life, there's hope. Speaking of which, we're getting up near the boat. Still no sign of life there."

"Better slow down, then," Alma said, straining for a look. "We don't want to ram them."

"I'll surface behind and steer up close."

"We may frighten them," Alma said. "They'll think we're the U-boat. I hope they don't have guns to shoot at us."

"Not likely," Matt said. "At worst, they'll throw up their hands and surrender."

They stopped talking as the mini-sub broke the surface, and the light through the portholes dazzled them. Alma tried to leave Dirk in a comfortable position before she turned to help Matt.

By the time she got the hatch open and let in fresh sea air, Matt had brought the sub close alongside the boat. It seemed evident through the portholes that no one was aboard, and when she stuck her head out into daylight she was able to confirm it.

"It's empty," she said, leaning out and grabbing the side of the derelict. "Should I get in?"

"Yes. If you can, get me that rope there," Matt said, looking out through the hatch beside her. "Maybe this one was knocked loose by the explosion," he added as she climbed out into the partly-flooded boat and clambered over benches. "What a waste!"

"Well, we can use it. Maybe we could tow it along to pick up other passengers." Dragging the mooring rope up out of the water, she tossed it over to Matt.

"It's such a beautiful day!" she marveled, shading her eyes against the glare of sun and sea. And then she cried, "Oh, how dreadful!"

Before her, at the end of a mile-long trail of boats, wreckage, and human flotsam, was the *Lusitania*. Amid its haze of smoke and misery, the huge ship tilted downward, poised at a crazy angle for her last voyage into the depths. Even at this distance Alma could see the seething turmoil on deck, bodies plunging overboard, lifeboats caught and dragged under by toppling funnels and wires, with white puffs of explosions blowing up wreckage into the sky. Mercifully, she was too far off to hear the cries of pain and terror. But she could imagine.

"It's terrible," she told Matt as he popped up from the sub's hatch. "What can we possibly do? I don't see any oars in this boat," she added, looking around.

"It looks bad," he agreed, shading his eyes toward the spectacle. "But don't forget about Kroger, here. We should get him up into the air before we lose him."

"All right," she said, moving back toward the sub. "If you can prop him up, I'll pull him over into the boat—"

"Wait, what's that?" From where he stood in the hatch, Matt pointed to a sudden turbulence in the water, something surging forward and rising from the deep.

A few dozen yards ahead, distracting them from the vision of the dying ship, a black wedge broke forth onto the sea's surface. First the bow and conning tower emerged, and then the great length of hull heaved up, streaming off tons of water as it came, making their tethered boat and submarine knock violently together in the swell. On the stubby central tower was painted a red, flaring German Maltese Cross, and on the side of its prow the number 20.

"It's the U-boat," Alma gasped. "The same one that sunk us, it has to be!"

"Maybe they're here to finish the job," Matt said. "Or more likely, attack any rescue ships that show up."

"Have they seen us, do you think? Will they take us captive?"

"A U-boat wouldn't usually take prisoners, or rescue survivors either—unless they knew their spy was on board." Matt bent down to call through the hatchway, "Dirk, your navy is here! Come on now, get up!" But in reply, Alma heard only a faint moan.

"Here they come, the Kaiser's marines," Matt said as he ducked down to get his spy friend.

Once the U-boat fully surfaced, its forward motion halted. Now hatches flew open, with men sprouting up in the conning tower and just astern, to run forward to the muzzled, tethered deck gun. For now, all of them seemed to be craning their necks or standing rapt to stare at the work they had wrought, the ruin of the great British liner.

"This could be bad," Matt said, standing up in the hatch, breathless from his efforts to move the inert spy. "If we can't get Kroger up here to yell at them in German, or give some secret sign, they might just ignore us. Or else open fire," he added, mirroring Alma's unspoken fear.

Even as he spoke, the leather-hatted officer in the tower hatchway began sweeping the horizon with his binoculars, stopping when he came to them. He shouted something, and others aboard turned to look. One of them pointed excitedly down at the lifeboat...or rather, at the floating mini-sub beside it. Responding to another barked command, the three men astern by the deck gun began unlimbering their heavy weapon and swinging it around.

"That does it," Matt said, sinking down in the hatchway. "They've seen the sub, and it's a threat. They think we're armed. I'll have to draw fire away from you and the boat."

"No, Matt, wait," Alma pleaded, grasping desperately at her lover's shoulder as he knelt down in the hatch. "Just get in the boat and raise your hands. We'll surrender, and it'll be all right..."

"No time. They're loading the gun. Get down!"

She turned and saw a crewman shove a shell into the breech as the long barrel swung around. Turning back, she fully intended to jump from the boat and dive in after Matt. But already he was pulling away, too far to leap, the sub's wake quietly frothing and churning. She saw his hand reach up and wave a brief farewell before pulling the hatch cover shut.

In that moment the cannon-shot screamed overhead. Smiting the air, it thudded in her ears and made her drop to the benches in the rocking lifeboat. But the shell missed both her and the mini-sub, splashing in the water and raising a plume fifty yards away.

Meanwhile as she watched, the tiny copper craft surged forward gathering speed—ten, twenty, thirty feet ahead as it sank away out of sight in a froth of bubbles. Before her tears could come, it was gone.

On the deck of the U-boat, the gun crew tried to follow Matt's course with their weapon, but didn't fire again. Instead after a few moments, the crewman unloaded the breech. From the captain in his visor cap, a new order rang out sharply. It sounded like a single word:

"Alarm!"

The alert sent crew members scrambling down the ladders. The deck gun swung back inboard, and the two gunners secured it and closed the hatch behind them. The big vessel was already moving forward, accelerating. Moments later it settled out of view once again, leaving only a distant white eddy on the sea's surface.

So Matt had been right. With the mini-sub loose in the water, the U-boat's crew didn't feel safe sticking around. Had he foreseen this, she wondered, when he risked his life—and very possibly sacrificed Kroger's—to save hers?

If so, and if the little sub could still maneuver, he might come back.

There was nothing more, no bubbles or underwater explosions. Looking toward the Irish coast, she saw that the *Lusitania* was gone too, her long fatal convulsion ended at last. No ships were visible on the vast surface of the sea, just wreckage, and some faint smoke trails near the coastline offering hope of rescue—but no other passengers in sight. The rest of the survivors, if any, must have been strewn farther out along the doomed ship's course.

"Fifteen Hundred Lost At Sea"—the old *Titanic* headline from her youth came back to haunt her. She sat waiting, weeping, thinking of what she'd lost. Her parents, her home and childhood; her name, with half a lifetime of peace and innocence. The old America she'd known would be lost to her after this...and her new friends too, very possibly.

And now Matt, more and more surely as the long minutes dragged on. He had closed the hatch—she'd seen it—and not just sunk outright. But then, he must have flooded the ballast tanks to dive so fast, she was sure. She remembered Kroger's warning. Did he have enough bottled air ever to reach the surface again?

It all was too much! How was she supposed to bear it, without going mad?

And yet she'd gained things, too. Precious things, that had already become permanent parts of her life. And she knew Matt would never want her to give up.

Her damp hair dangled in her face. It was still black; the seawater hadn't taken out the color. Maybe her salt tears wouldn't, either—but they might fill up the boat. Finding a canvas bucket, she began bailing.

Glossary of Characters and Devices

Wholly invented entries are marked with an asterisk*
Lives recorded as lost in the sinking are indicated by the letter L.

Character Names

Albright*–seaman aboard the British cruiser *Juno*.

Anderson, James C.–Staff Captain of the *Lusitania*, an auxiliary officer assigned to handle social duties for the irritable and outspoken Captain Turner. L

Augusta Viktoria–*Kaiserin*, wife of Kaiser William.

Bernard, Oliver (Ollie)–British stage set designer returning from the US to enlist in the British military. After rescue, Ollie drew sketches of the sinking for the press.

Bernhard*–German reservist deployed in the trench lines in Flanders, Belgium, opposite French forces. The action is the Second Battle of Ypres, which lasted nearly a month. The three battles of Ypres together produced almost a million casualties on both sides.

Bestic, Albert–Third Officer of the *Lusitania*. Besides taking the four-point bearing and sighting the torpedo wake, he survived the disaster of the portside lifeboats. At most, one boat was launched. None of the crew would discuss the portside during the court inquiries.

Bethmann-Hollweg, Theobald von–Boyhood friend of Kaiser Wilhelm, who appointed him Chancellor of the German Empire from 1909 until 1917, a year before the Kaiser himself abdicated.

Bissett–A former First Officer of Captain Turner, later a captain himself in Cunard's service. Turner often confused Mate Bestic's name with his, intentionally or carelessly. In a later visit to the retired and reclusive Captain Turner, Bestic was turned away until he mis-identified himself as Bissett; then he was cordially recognized and received.

Bowring, Charles–British merchant shipowner and shipper.

Brady*, Alma–alias of Mairead (Maisie) Thornton.

Brandell, Josephine–British opera singer returning from a US tour.

Bryan, William Jennings–US Secretary of State from 1913 to June, 1915. He ordered his State Dept. to release the German warning. Bryan then resigned in disagreement with a strongly worded US protest to the *Lusitania* attack that he said "would surely lead to war with Germany." His efforts to maintain US neutrality were undermined by Colonel House and by his Undersecretary of State Robert Lansing, who succeeded him as Secretary.

Churchill, Winston Spencer—First Lord of the Admiralty from 1912 to 1915, and much later Prime Minister of Britain. He set strategies in both World Wars. His final Admiralty meeting before the *Lusitania* sinking had no notes kept but is fictionally reconstructed.

Clive*—a steward aboard the *Lusitania*.

Coke, Sir Charles—Admiral of the small British fleet based in Queenstown, Ireland.

Crank, J—Baggage Master aboard the *Lusitania*. L

Depage, Marie—Belgian envoy in service to the Red Cross. L

Dexter*, Winifred (Winnie)—a nurse trainee from Concord, New Hampshire.

Ewing, Sir Alfred—Physicist, British Director of Naval Education, and Chief of Room 40.

Fisher, John Arbuthnot (Jackie)—Sea Lord and Admiral in the Royal Navy of Britain. He resigned from his post shortly after the *Lusitania* sinking. Fisher wrote friendly letters to German Grand Admiral Tirpitz endorsing his policy of unrestricted submarine warfare.

Flash*—see Jansen, Lars.

Florence* (Flo) Hunnicutt—a nurse trainee, sister of Hazel.

Forman, Justus Miles—American playwright and globe-trotter. L

Frohman, Charles (C.F.)—He specialized in bringing English hit productions to the New York stage. L

Gauntlett, Frederick (Fred)—Naval architect for Newport News shipyard, traveling to obtain a license to build British-designed submarines in the US.

Gavin*—seaman, *Earl of Lathom* merchant sailing ship.

George V—King of England and cousin of Kaiser Wilhelm and Czar Nicholas. Under his reign, the German names of British royals were anglicized, the surname Windsor replacing *Saxe-Coburg und Gotha*.

Grey, Sir Edward—British Foreign Secretary who stated, "The lamps are going out all over Europe; we shall not see them lit again in our lifetime." He also asked, "What will America do if the Germans should sink a passenger liner with American passengers on board?" His question to Colonel House was echoed by King George V, with specific mention of the *Lusitania*, later that same day, May 7th, one to two hours before the sinking.

Hall, Sir Reginald (Blinker)–Director of Naval Intelligence, British Admiralty. His father had held the same post. In an island nation ruling a global empire through its fleet, the role was important.

Hardy*–Captain, *Earl of Lathom* merchant sailing ship.

Hazel* Hunnicutt–a nurse trainee, sister of Florence.

Hefford, Percy–second officer of the *Lusitania* (referred to erroneously in later court proceedings as Heppert). L

Hersing, Otto–*Kapitan-Leutnant* of U-21. Hersing, the first German U-boat ace, was awarded the Iron Cross medal for the war's first torpedo sinking of a British light cruiser in September 1914, and for two battleships sunk off Gallipoli in May, 1915.

Hood, Vice-Admiral Sir Horace–Descendant of naval heroes and former commander of English Channel defenses, demoted to captaincy of the antiquated cruiser *Juno*, based at Queenstown. To restore his reputation, he led his battlecruisers into action against German battleships at Jutland in May, 1916. He died when his ship, the *Invincible*, was blown in half with only six survivors.

Hogan*, James (Big Jim)–a New York crime boss and corrupt alderman.

Holbourn, Laird Ian Bernard Stoughton–Oxford professor and Laird of Foula, a tiny isle in the Shetlands, far north of Scotland. Besides petitioning for life belt training, he befriended a young Canadian girl, Avis Dolphin, and saved her life. His wife Marion, at home during the sinking, described having a detailed premonition and vision of it the night before.

Hollis*–British seaman aboard cruiser *Juno*.

House, Edward Mandell (Colonel)–Political kingmaker, friend and envoy of US President Wilson. In April he was dispatched to Europe on the *Lusitania* to propose peace talks and seek "Freedom of the Seas" for neutral shipping. He later indicated that this plan was sunk with the *Lusitania*. (Note: this second visit to England and King George V is reconstructed: House had visited the Kaiser in 1914 to prevent a war.) To Wilson he wrote, "I think we shall find ourselves drifting into war with Germany...."

Hubbard, Elbert—Former advertising executive, novelist, motivational writer and co-founder of the American Craftsman movement and the Roycrofter utopian colony in New York. This fashion influenced American art and design. He told the press that if a torpedo struck, he would "be a regular hero and go right to the bottom." Near the end, he and his wife Mary were seen standing by the rail without life belts, waiting for the ship to sink. A later witness reported him clinging in vain to a barrel and slipping out of sight. L

Iggy*—Messenger boy for New York mobster Patsy*.

Jansen*, Lars (Flash)—Photographer and cub reporter for the Daily Inquisitor*.

Jolivet, Rita—French actress returning from Broadway appearances.

*Heinz—German spy in the Lusitania's brig who is afraid the ship will be sunk.

Kessler, George (Champagne King)—Public relations promoter of French wines.

Klein, Charles—Broadway actor and playwright. His crippled foot may have hurt his chances of survival. L

Knucks*—see Steegle, Elmer.

Krauss*, Hildegard—Teacher and organizer for the United Nursing Service League*.

Kroger*, Dirk—alias of German spy, a Naval Intelligence agent posing as a Dutch fur merchant.

Lane, Sir Hugh—Irish art patron, bringing back Rembrandt and Rubens paintings that were judged unsuitable for display in the US. The paintings were aboard but not known to be recovered from the wreck. L

Lanz—Civilian pilot aboard the *U-20* submarine.

Lehmann, Isaac—American arms manufacturer and dealer. By waving a gun and menacing the crew, he caused the premature release of the last lifeboat on the portside. It swung inboard and careened down the deck, injuring Lehmann and crushing dozens of others.

Leith, Robert (Bob)—Chief Telegraphist, *RMS Lusitania*

Mackworth, Lady Margaret—British noblewoman and suffragette activist, wife of Sir Humphrey Mackworth and daughter of coal magnate D.A. Thomas

Maisie* Thornton—see Brady, Alma

Mary, Victoria–Queen of England, German-born wife of King George V. The passenger liner *Queen Mary* now on display in Los Angeles is named for her.

Matthews, Annie–Wife of Captain Robert Matthews. L

Matthews, Robert–Captain, Canadian 6th Winnipeg Rifles. He appears to have been traveling to the battlefront with his company of enlistees, whom he mustered to help transfer cargo aboard *Lusitania* that may have included their rifle ammunition. L

McCormick, David (Dave)–Second Telegraphist, *RMS Lusitania*.

McCray*, Ruarie (Rory)–Steersman, *Earl of Lathom* merchant sailing ship.

McGonagill*–Mate, *Earl of Lathom* merchant sailing ship.

Meissner*, Gerhardt–Invented name of one of three unidentified spies or stowaways who were imprisoned in the Lusitania's brig. Although not included in most casualty totals, they almost certainly perished with the ship. On her departure from New York, they were found hiding in a pantry and were detained. They had evidently been trying to reveal naval guns or gun emplacements aboard ship, and they may have photographed gun mounting rings concealed under trap doors in the Shelter Deck. Their camera was sent off aboard a British Royal Navy vessel patrolling the New York coast.

Mikey*–Hoodlum for Big Jim Hogan

O'Donnell*, Seamus–Seaman, *Earl of Lathom* merchant sailing ship

Oliver, Henry–Rear Admiral and British Admiralty Intelligence Director under Sir Reginald Hall

Patsy*–New York mob leader and rival of Big Jim Hogan*.

Pearson, Frederick Stark–Millionaire American consulting engineer. L

Pierpoint, William–Liverpool Police Detective-Inspector assigned to protect the *Lusitania*.

Plamondon, Charles–American manufacturer of large-scale brewery equipment, seeking business from the Guinness Company in Ireland. L

Plamondon, Mary–wife of Charles. The day before the sinking was their 36th wedding anniversary. L

Reggie*–British infantryman shipped from Flanders to the Gallipoli marine invasion.

Rikowski–Radio officer aboard the *U-20* submarine

Schwieger, Walther–*Kapitan-Leutnant* in the German *Kaiserliche Marine* and commander of the submarine *Unterseeboot-20*. His success wasn't proclaimed by the Kaiser and he didn't receive the Iron Cross medal until 1917, most likely because his triumph over the *Lusitania* came to be regarded as a foreign policy setback for Germany. In 1916, his *U-20* ran aground in Denmark and was demolished on his orders. He and his crew perished in 1917 when his next command, the *U-88*, was chased into a minefield by Q-ship *HMS Stonecrop*.

Smyte*, Jeremy–A steward in Second Cabin service aboard the *Lusitania*.

Stackhouse, Commander J. Foster–A noted sea captain planning an Antarctic research voyage and rumored to be a British spy. L

Steegle*, Elmer (Knucks)–a lieutenant in Big Jim Hogan's crime organization.

Studs*–Bodyguard for Big Jim Hogan*.

Thornton*, Maisie–see Brady, Alma

Tirpitz, Alfred von–Grand Admiral and Secretary of State for the German Imperial Navy (*Kaiserliche Marine*) from 1897 to 1916. Tirpitz, as naval leader, expressed the view that war against England was hopeless, and later believed that Germany's only chance was a ruthless submarine blockade of Allied shipping. The German public tended to agree, but Kaiser Wilhelm gave equal weight to Chancellor Bethmann-Hollweg's view. In an ongoing furor over merchant sinkings, Tirpitz was finally allowed to resign.

Trevor*–British Expeditionary Force (BEF) rifleman in a foxhole during the Second Battle of Ypres, April 25–May 22, 1915. BEF casualties in this month-long fight were triple the German losses.

Tumulty, Joseph (Joe)–Personal secretary to US President Woodrow Wilson

Turner, Captain William (Bowler Bill)–Commander of the *Lusitania* who, in peacetime, was noted for fast Atlantic crossings and quick turnarounds in port. When his predecessor Captain Dow resigned, unwilling to accept the wartime risk to passengers, Turner was brought back. Targeted after the sinking by Churchill, Fisher, and other British officials as being incompetent or possibly a traitor, he was exonerated by the Board of Inquiry. He later commanded other Cunard vessels in war and peacetime, including the troopship *Ivernia*, which was sunk by a torpedo off Greece. He sought seclusion from reporters, but later maintained that on her last day the *Lusitania* was ordered to run for shelter in Queenstown harbor.

Ulbricht—Seaman on the *U-20* who reacted to the *Lusitania* sinking but was not arrested.

Vanderbilt, Alfred—American tycoon and playboy carriage racer. Rather than seeking his own safety like the rich aboard the *Titanic*, he spent the Lusitania's final minutes securing life belts to child passengers. L

Vane*, Matthew (Matt)—war reporter for the New York Daily Inquisitor*.

Voegele, Charles—A native of Strasbourg in the Alsace-Lorraine corridor, which was ceded to Germany by France after the Franco-Prussian War of 1870–1871. As electrician aboard the *U-20*, his voyage was followed by a court martial and a term in Landsberg Prison. He was released after the armistice, but hardships during his imprisonment ruined his health, and he died in 1926. Some question his existence, but records of his birth, service and death may have been destroyed by the later Nazi occupiers of Strasbourg.

Weisbach, Raimund—*Oberleutnant*, torpedo officer aboard *U-20* who launched the torpedo that sank the *Lusitania*. By 1916, he was commander of the *U-19* which landed patriot Sir Roger Casement in Ireland to lead the Easter Rising against Britain. But due to German radio messages decoded by Room 40, Casement was arrested on the beach.

Wilhelm II—Kaiser of the German Empire, later William Hohenzollern. Before the Armistice, a military mutiny forced him to abdicate and flee to Holland. The Versailles Treaty called for his prosecution, but Dutch Queen Wilhelmina refused to extradite him.

Willie*—Australian ANZAC enlistee deployed to Gallipoli invasion of Turkey.

Wilson, Woodrow—US President 1913–1921. His 1916 re-election campaign used the slogan "He kept us out of war." Even so, the US entry into the Great War in April, 1917, that made it a World War, may already have been inevitable, due largely to the *Lusitania* sinking. Wilson then promised "A war to end all war." He made a valiant personal effort to broker the contentious Versailles Treaty, whose harsh terms likely led to

World War II. The Kaiser called the treaty "a peace to end all peace," and Wilson died unfulfilled.

Winifred* (Winnie) Crocker - A nurse trainee headed for war.

Characters Noted But Not Portrayed

Bauer, Hermann–*Fregattenkapitan*, Commander of the *U-20's* submarine flotilla. After the *Lusitania* sinking, *der Kaiser* urged his dismissal for not transmitting orders to restrain U-boat attacks, but the *Kaiserliche Marine* high command retained him in his post.

Bismarck, Otto von–a Prussian Prince and statesman who unified and militarized the German nation. He was removed as Chancellor in 1890 by Kaiser Wilhelm (William) II.

Casement, Roger–Irish rebel leader who tried to recruit Irish war prisoners to be transported by German ships back to Ireland for an uprising against British rule. Sent in alone by submarine, he was arrested, and a shipload of weapons was intercepted. Discredited by British authorities as being a homosexual, he was executed.

Cavell, Edith–English nurse in occupied Belgium who was tried by Germany for letting Belgian soldiers escape. In spite of international protest, she was executed by firing squad in October 1915.

Duncan, Isadora–The creator of modern dance, a San Francisco-born ballet artist who resided in Europe and later the Soviet Union. She performed barefoot and scandalized Boston audiences when she ripped her bodice during a French Revolutionary tribute.

Nicholas II, Tsar–Emperor and Autocrat of Russia, a cousin of King George V and Kaiser William. After abdicating in 1917, he and his family were slain in the Bolshevik revolution of 1918.

Weddigen, Otto–German U-boat ace and recipient of the Iron Cross medal. As *Kapitan-Leutnant* of *U-9*, he was credited with the "Live Bait" sinking of three British cruisers in October, 1914, the *Cressy* and *Hogue* having been torpedoed as they came to the aid of the already capsized *Aboukir* with 1459 lives lost in the action. The newly appointed First Lord of the Admiralty, Winston Churchill, was blamed by the press for this–unfairly, since he had previously ordered the three antique ships withdrawn. On seeing the *Lusitania* with her vulnerable coal bunkers, he remarked that she looked to him like "another forty-five thousand tons of live bait."

Wegener, Berndt (Bernie)–*Kapitan-Leutnant* of *U-27*. His U-boat was sunk in August, 1915 by the *Baralong*, a Q-ship flying a false American flag. After sinking the sub, the British crew massacred Wegener and other survivors in revenge for the *Lusitania* attack.

Victoria, Queen of England–grandmother to Charles V, Kaiser Wilhelm II, and Czar Nicholas II. Wed to her first cousin, the German Prince Albert, she expanded her empire as Britain's longest-reigning monarch. On her death, her son Edward VII became King.

Devices

Aboukir, Cressy, Hogue–See Weddigen, Otto, above.

Aluminum–Powdered aluminium is listed on *Lusi's* cargo manifest, and this substance is flammable at high temperatures. It was included as an accelerant for the military explosive compounds Perdit and Amerol, and also used as photo flash powder. In a machine shop, this metal dust is not allowed to accumulate. It can spontaneously combust, resulting in a flame hot enough to melt steel tools. Adding water to douse it will only intensify the fire.

Ambulance*–There is no indication that ambulances were aboard the *Lusitania* on her final voyage, although they were sometimes sent overseas by medical charity organizations.

Ammunition–Records show large quantities of shrapnel shells in the Lusitania's cargo hold and rifle cartridges too, which have been found scattered in the trail of the wreck.

Armament–The *Lusitania* and *Mauretania* were designed to serve as armed auxiliary cruisers in the event of war. In May 1913, in readiness for war with Germany, the *Lusitania* was armored along the shelter deck and the forward section closed off. Revolving gun rings were installed to mount twelve six-inch rapid-firing naval rifles, six along each broadside. Although it is still a subject of controversy, the most detailed history indicates that removable guns were placed aboard in August, 1914 at the outbreak of the Great War. The same account indicates that, as the liner continued in passenger service, the guns were taken off again, perhaps for use in other merchant or war vessels. Some question remains whether all of the "defensive" guns were removed.

Battlecruisers–Fast, lightly armored but heavily gunned cruisers, designed to fight battleships and cruisers by outrunning them and staying at extreme range.

Boddy Belt–Cunard's standard life jacket or vest. Many drowned victims were found wearing them incorrectly.

Cigar incendiary device–This item, manufactured by a German scientist, was in use early in the war. It was likely used for port and industrial sabotage in North America.

Destroyer–High-speed turbine steamship, designed to chase and depth-bomb submarines.

Dreadnought–Heavily gunned and armored early-1900s battleships, driven by steam turbines.

Gun cotton–This fibrous, smokeless form of gunpowder, though not listed on the cargo manifests, is believed to have been present in the guise of crated cheeses, to help relieve the severe shortage of artillery ammunition and propellant on the Western Front. The pyroxiline gun cotton manufactured in the US by DuPont was highly combustible and dangerous in seawater. Furthermore, the waterproof containers designed for its transport had been preemptively bought out by a company friendly to the German–Austro-Hungarian Central Powers. It likely was shipped in wooden crates or burlap bundles.

Hopper*–This concept is the author's creation. As with the Tank, it seems possible that such a prototype would be in transport, especially with naval architect Fred Gauntlett aboard. After the sinking, it was rumored that two of these devices were in the cargo hold.

Hydrophones–Methods of underwater sound detection were in use by 1916, both for submarine and surface vessels. This is another technical advance that could theoretically have been delayed by the loss of prototypes and lives aboard the *Lusitania*. This passive listening does not foresee the later development of active, echo-based ASDIC and sonar, leading to radar in the next war.

Juno, HMS (His Majesty's Ship)–An outdated, slow *Eclipse*-class cruiser from 1895, the only capital ship assigned to the Ireland flotilla. With longitudinal coal bunkers, she was vulnerable to torpedoes as the *Aboukir, Hogue,* and *Cressy* "Live Bait Squadron." As flagship of Admiral Coke at Queenstown, *Juno* was assigned as Lusitania's escort but recalled. She later steamed to stricken *Lusi's* rescue, only to be ordered back into port for her own safety.

Lusitania, RMS (Royal Mail Ship)–Ocean liner built by Cunard Co. to Royal Navy design requirements for an auxiliary cruiser. Placed in Atlantic ferry service in 1907, this 790-foot "floating palace" set a new standard in luxury, and for years she and her sister ship *Mauretania* remained the fastest way to travel from the US to England and back. She was the first passenger liner to use steam turbines for enhanced speed, 25 knots (28 mph). Her last, fatal voyage carried 1268 passengers and 694 crew. Loss of life totaled 1201 souls, including the 3 stowaways in the brig and 124 Americans.

Mauretania–The sister ship to *Lusitania*, an almost identical and slightly faster four-stacker launched the same year. She was armed at the outbreak of war and converted to a troopship, then disarmed and used as a hospital ship to evacuate wounded from the ill-fated Gallipoli campaign in 1915. After the war she remained in passenger service until 1937.

Motorcycles–There is no record of these on the *Lusitania*.

Q-ship–These merchant "mystery ships" with hidden armaments were Winston Churchill's answer to the German Kaiser's U-boats and surface commerce raiders. Cannon, machine guns and wireless sets were placed aboard liners, cargo ships and trawlers to threaten submarines. Merchant vessels were also ordered to ignore warnings to stop, and steer to ram the subs.

Tank*–In Britain the armored fighting vehicle (AFV) was developed under the Royal Navy's Landships Committee, formed in February, 1915 by First Lord of the Admiralty Winston Churchill. AFVs were not deployed in combat until September, 1916 at the Battle of the Somme. But it's conceivable that an early US-made prototype could have been shipped to England. This device provides a wholly fictional assertion of the presence of military weapons aboard the *Lusitania*. It's commonly stated that the earliest AFVs were crated for transport as secret weapons and labeled "TANK."

U-20–Unterseeboot-20, one of 12 new diesel-powered U-boats then in service to the German Kaiserliche Marine. The craft was 210 feet long (64 meters) with a crew of 35, armed with 7 torpedoes and a deck gun. Its range was 9,700 nautical miles, at 15.4 knots surface cruising speed, or 9.5 knots submerged on battery power for limited distances.

Notes: Except for the fictional characters, all persons and events are derived from published histories, as are the contents of the cargo hold except for the ambulances, motorcycles, and the two largest crates. The Lusitania's hold was enlarged at the start of the war and gun mountings were installed. The wreck is now under salvage, but due to its deteriorating condition, its full contents, including the Rembrandt paintings, may never be revealed. Survivors of the ship did report seeing the U-boat surface after the torpedoing, and it may have attacked or frightened off rescuing ships. Crucial pages which may address this or the mutiny appear to have been removed and replaced in Captain Schwieger's U-boat log.

Bibliography

Bailey, Thomas A. and Paul B. Ryan, *The Lusitania Disaster; An Episode in Modern Warfare and Diplomacy*. Macmillan Publishing Co. / Free Press, 1975.

Ballard, Robert D. and Spencer Dunmore. *Exploring the Lusitania*. Warner / Madison Press, 1995.

Hickey, Des and Gus Smith. *Seven Days To Disaster; The Sinking of the Lusitania*.

New York: G. P. Putnam and Sons, 1981.

Layton, J. Kent. *Lusitania; An Illustrated Biography of the Ship of Splendor*. Lulu Press, 2007. http://www.atlanticliners.com.

Massie, Robert K. *Dreadnought*. New York: Ballantine Books, 1991.

O'Sullivan, Patrick. *The Lusitania; Unravelling the Mysteries*. New York: Sheridan House, 2000.

Peeke, Mitch, Kevin Walsh-Johnson, and Steven Jones. *The Lusitania Story*. Anapolis, MD: Naval Institute Press, 2004. http://www.lusitania.net.

Preston, Diana. *Lusitania; An Epic Tragedy*. New York: Berkley Books / Penguin Group (USA), 2003.

Simpson, Colin. *The Lusitania; Finally, the Startling Truth about One of the Most Fateful of All Disasters of the Sea*. Boston, Toronto: Little, Brown & Co., 1972.

CPSIA information can be obtained
at www.ICGtesting.com
Printed in the USA
BVOW08s1404110917
494464BV00001B/1/P